Praise for *Butcher's Moon* a

"The Parkers read with the speed of pulp while unfolding with an almost Nabokovian wit and flair. . . . Original editions of these books, and even their later reprints, change hands for scores or hundreds of dollars on the Net, and it's excellent to have them readily available again—not so much masterpieces of the genre, just masterpieces, period."
—Richard Rayner, *Los Angeles Times*

"Richard Stark's Parker novels . . . are among the most poised and polished fictions of their time and, in fact, of any time."
—John Banville, *Bookforum*

"The neo-hero: the ruthless, unrepentant, single-minded operator in a humorless and amoral world. . . . No one depicts this scene with greater clarity than Richard Stark."
—*New York Times*

"Westlake knows precisely how to grab a reader, draw him or her into the story, and then slowly tighten his grip until escape is impossible."
—*Washington Post Book World*

"You can read the entire series and not once have to invest in a bookmark."
—Luc Sante

"[A] book by this guy is cause for happiness."
—Stephen King

"The Parker novels . . . are among the greatest hard-boiled writing of all time." —*Financial Times* (London)

"Along with Elmore Leonard's work, [the Parker novels] taught me almost everything I know about how to express violence on the page. As for Parker himself, he's a watershed character in American noir, nearly incomparable." —Dennis Lehane

"Reading the Parker novels—especially if you are fortunate enough to read several back-to-back—is a little like watching a jazz musician at work." —Charles Ardai

"Moving at a tremendous pace, yet gripping as much by the cold detail of Parker's planning of the heist as by the breathless excitement of its execution. Profit is the motive, efficiency is the touchstone, and Parker doesn't let people or sentiment stand in the way." —*Books & Bookmen*

"To me, Richard Stark is the Prince of Noir." —Martin Cruz Smith

"Westlake is among the smoothest, most engaging writers on the planet." —*San Diego Tribune*

"Brilliant . . . Donald E. Westlake (aka Richard Stark) knows how to freeze the blood." —Terrence Rafferty, *GQ*

Butcher's Moon

Parker Novels By Richard Stark

The Hunter (Payback)
The Man with the Getaway Face
The Outfit
The Mourner
The Score
The Jugger
The Seventh
The Handle
The Rare Coin Score
The Green Eagle Score
The Black Ice Score
The Sour Lemon Score
Deadly Edge
Slayground
Plunder Squad
Butcher's Moon
Comeback
Backflash
Flashfire
Firebreak
Breakout
Nobody Runs Forever
Ask the Parrot
Dirty Money

Information about the complete list of Richard Stark books published by the University of Chicago Press—and electronic editions of them—can be found on our website: http://www.press.uchicago.edu/.

Butcher's Moon

RICHARD STARK

With a New Foreword by Lawrence Block

The University of Chicago Press

The University of Chicago Press, Chicago 60637
Copyright © 1974 by Richard Stark
Foreword © 2011 by Lawrence Block
All rights reserved
University of Chicago Press edition 2011
Printed in the United States of America

20 19 18 17 16 15 14 13 12 11   1 2 3 4 5

ISBN-13: 978-0-226-77095-6 (paper)
ISBN-10: 0-226-77095-8 (paper)

Library of Congress Cataloging-in-Publication Data

Stark, Richard, 1933–2008.
  Butcher's moon / Richard Stark ; with a new foreword by Lawrence Block.
    p. cm.
  Summary: Stark's antihero Parker attempts to retrieve money he had to leave
in an amusement park, but the money is gone. He enlists Alan Grofield to assist,
but when Grofield is taken hostage, Parker assembles a private army to get him
back and rob the mob blind at the same time.
  ISBN-13: 978-0-226-77095-6 (pbk. : alk. paper)
  ISBN-10: 0-226-77095-8 (pbk. : alk. paper) 1. Parker (Fictitious character)—
Fiction. 2. Criminals—Fiction. I. Block, Lawrence. II. Title.
  PS3573.E9B88 2011
  813'.54—dc22
                        2010032164

♾ The paper used in this publication meets the minimum requirements of the
American National Standard for Information Sciences—Permanence of Paper
for Printed Library Materials, ANSI Z39.48-1992.

Hi, Abby

Foreword

One night around the end of 1960 or the beginning of 1961, I was in a second-floor flat in Canarsie, an unglamorous part of Brooklyn, located at the very end of the Canarsie Line, a part of the subway system that ran east across Fourteenth Street from Eighth Avenue, then crossed the river, and wound up running on elevated tracks all the way to Rockaway Parkway. (The train was subsequently designated the LL, until years later they took one of its letters away and it became the L. No one knows why, but I've always figured it was a cost-cutting move. Of such small economies are great savings made.)

I lived in Manhattan at the time, on Central Park West at 104th Street, so I had to take two subway trains and walk several blocks to get to that flat, but I did it often and without complaint because that's where Don Westlake lived. We'd been best friends since we met in our mutual agent's office in July of 1959, where we introduced ourselves before walking a few blocks to his flat in Hell's Kitchen. We sat around there and had a few beers and talked and talked and talked, and that was the pattern that prevailed over the months. I moved home to Buffalo, met somebody, got married. Don and his then-wife moved from an unsafe neighborhood to an inaccessible one. My then-wife and I set up housekeeping in New York, first on West 69th Street, then on Central Park West. And Don and I got together often, and had a few beers, and talked and talked and talked.

And that's what we were doing that night I was telling you about, out in Canarsie. We were young writers together—he was five years my senior, but had spent time in the Air Force—and we talked a lot about what we were doing, and sometimes showed our work to each other. "I started something new," Don said, and handed me ten or fifteen pages of typescript, featuring a fellow named Parker who's walking across the George Washington Bridge, into Manhattan. In the first sentence, a passing motorist offers Parker a lift, and Parker tells him to go to hell.

I thought the chapter was good, and said so, and asked its author if he knew where it was going.

"Sort of," he said. "I'll just keep writing and see where it goes."

Which is how we both worked, more often than not. Don called it the *narrative push* method, and it has a couple of virtues. For one, you can just sit down and start writing, as there's no need to work everything out in your mind ahead of time. And, as Theodore Sturgeon famously observed, if the writer doesn't know what's going to happen next, he needn't worry that the reader will know what's going to happen next.

"I like the character," Don said. "I don't think I'll have trouble finding things for him to do."

Indeed.

* * *

One thing Don found for Parker to do, at the book's end, was die.

And that would have made this the shortest series in the annals of crime fiction, but for an editor at Pocket Books with the splendid name of Bucklin Moon. Moon may or may not have been the first editor to read *The Hunter*, but he was certainly the first who wanted to buy it. But he had a request. Did Parker have to die? Could he get away at the end, and go on to star in a whole series of books? Two more at a minimum, say, because Moon was prepared to offer a three-book contract.

Don had already established that he liked Parker, and that he could find plenty of things for him to do. And he confided that he'd only killed Parker off at the book's end because he thought that's what you were supposed to do with that sort of antihero. So he agreed, and revised the ending, and wrote *The Man with the Getaway Face* and *The Outfit,* and Moon sat down and drew up another three-book contract. Parker, and Richard Stark, were off and running.

* * *

Ah, yes. Richard Stark.

The conventional wisdom these days is that Don created the Richard

Stark pen name to distinguish the uncompromisingly hardboiled Parker novels from the bubbly frothy Westlakean comic mysteries.

Not exactly. The Parker series had six titles in print at Pocket Books by the time Random House published *The Fugitive Pigeon*, Don's first comedic effort. (Don's earlier Random House novels, starting with *The Mercenaries*, owe more to Hammett than to Wodehouse; they're about as light and bubbly as bathtub gin.)

And Richard Stark first saw print two or three years before *The Hunter*. His was no separate persona, no marketing ploy; on several occasions Don had more than one story slotted in a single issue of a magazine, and was asked to use a pen name on one of them. Thus Richard Stark.

I don't know if he originally intended to hang Richard Stark on *The Hunter*. He might have, simply because it was to be a paperback original and he'd been busy establishing his own name at Random House. But if Parker was to start in a multivolume series, then of course he'd need a pen name.

As noted, off and running.

* * *

Let's flash forward a few years, shall we? To 1974, and *Butcher's Moon*, the book to which I am privileged to be writing an introduction, and of which you, Dear Reader, are fortunate to have a copy.

Fortunate, I should say, for a couple of reasons. For one, copies rank somewhere between hen's teeth and the Holy Grail in elusiveness. The book, published in hardcover by Random House, does not seem ever to have been reprinted. When copies come up for sale, the price is high.

More to the point, *Butcher's Moon* would be special even if it were not hard to come by. For over twenty years it looked to be the last book in the series, and while that would have been regrettable, at least Parker's saga would have ended on a high note. Because in addition to being, to my mind, the strongest book in a strong series, *Butcher's Moon* brings Parker's story to completion if not to an end. In its pages, the author manages to tell a gripping and satisfying story while at the same time summing up and resolving the fifteen Parker books that preceded it.

He does so by having Parker confront the book's central problem by bringing in characters from other books, subordinate criminals who've been his partners in other heists dating back to the early days of the series. (I read this book first as an advance reading copy, and as I recall it was annotated; every time there was a reference to an earlier caper, a footnote referred the reader to the book in which the incident was described. I remember thinking that was a nice touch, but evidently someone somewhere along the line thought it was intrusive, and perhaps it was. In any event, the copy I own now is a first edition, and there aren't any footnotes.)

It is strong testimony to the quality of the Parker books that, even decades after encountering them, the supporting cast members remain so sharply etched in memory that one recalls them at once. It is often said in the theater that there are no small parts, only small actors, and one could easily adapt the remark to the field of prose fiction. There are no minor characters, only minor writers, and the extent to which Parker's cast members are always memorable and always wholly human demonstrates that there is nothing minor about them or their creator.

And that, if it's all the same to you, is all I'm going to say about *Butcher's Moon*. You've got the book in your hands, and I can't see why you'd want me to explain it to you. Westlake, in any of his work and under any of his names, is very nearly as accessible as Dr. Seuss. You don't need a study guide, or someone like me to point things out to you.

The one thing I can suggest to improve your experience of reading *Butcher's Moon* is that you set it aside and read the foregoing fifteen books first, in the order they were written. If you've never read them before, or if you missed a few titles along the way, you've got a treat in store for you; if you read them years ago and your memory's a bit tentative, you'll find them a treat a second time around. And it's easy to do this, as all of the earlier titles are back in print in handsome new trade paperback editions uniform with this one.

If you can't wait, well, go ahead and read *Butcher's Moon*. Why not? What the hell, you can always read it again.

Lawrence Block

LAWRENCE BLOCK has written series fiction about Matthew Scudder, Bernie Rhodenbarr, Evan Tanner, Chip Harrison, and a killer named Keller. You can email him at lawbloc@aol.com, check him out at lawrenceblock.com, or look for him on Facebook.

Butcher's Moon

One

Running toward the light, Parker fired twice over his left shoulder, not caring whether he hit anything or not. It was just to slow them down, keep the cops in the front of the store while he and the others got out.

It was a tall rectangle of dim light, a doorway to the basement stairs. Opening this door here when they'd come in must have triggered a silent alarm somewhere, probably with a private alarm systems company. An internal level of protection not mentioned in the plan they'd bought.

Hurley got through the doorway first. There was firing from the front of the store now, and voices yelling "Stop or I'll shoot!" at the same time they were already shooting.

Parker went through the doorway, leaping out into space over the stairs, hearing Michaelson grunt behind him, and a thudding sound as though a sack of flour had been thrown at a wall. Parker's feet hit the fourth step, the ninth step, and the dirt floor. Hurley was already halfway across to the tunnel entrance in the stone wall at the rear, running crouched under the low ceiling crisscrossed by black pipes. Two dim bulbs made black shadows and yellow light, and Briggs stood near the tunnel entrance blinking behind his glasses, clutching his tool kit in his hands. Briggs was a technician, he wasn't used to excitement.

Hurley dove headfirst into the tunnel, disappearing to the knees, and went wriggling away, his shoes twisting and yanking with exertion. Parker stopped beside Briggs, grabbed his arm to get his attention, and pointed back at the stairs. "Knock it out."

Staring, Briggs said, "Michaelson," and bobbed his head toward the stairs.

Parker looked. Michaelson was sprawled across the sill up there, his head and arms hanging down the first few steps. He wasn't moving. "He's finished," Parker said. "We're not. Close it up."

"Oh, damn," Briggs said. He was petulant and pouting, ridiculous mannerisms, but he went down on one knee, opened his tool kit on the floor, took out a metal tube wrapped in black electric tape, twisted the top, stood, and tossed it in a gentle underhand at the stairs. Before it landed, Briggs was on one knee again, shutting the tool kit.

The tube sailed over Michaelson and hit the top step next to his rib cage. The doorway disappeared in a flash of light and sound and smoke and debris. Parker was shoved backward a step, and Briggs, halfway to his feet again, was knocked back to his knees.

Smoke rolled backward at them swiftly across the room. The explosion reverberated back and forth, enclosed in the stone walls. Parker yelled at Briggs, "Come on!" and couldn't hear himself for the ringing in his ears.

But Briggs was moving anyway. Shaking his head in annoyance, he was on his feet again and hurrying to the tunnel. Fussily he pushed the tool kit ahead of himself, and followed it through.

Parker looked over where the stairs and doorway had been, but the smoke obscured everything. And he couldn't hear anything outside his own body, no sounds other than the thud of his own heart and the rush of blood through his veins. Turning in the roaring silence, as the smoke puffed around him, he pushed through the tunnel, twice the length of his body, twelve feet through rock and damp hard earth, and came out in the other basement, where Briggs was fussing over his tool kit and Hurley was across the way at the foot of the stairs.

"Coveralls," Parker said to Briggs, and started to unzip his own.

Hurley called, "Come on, come on, we got no time."

"Get the coveralls off," Parker told him. "We've got time to look like straight citizens."

4

Hurley frowned in urgency up at the door at the top of the stairs, but he unzipped the coveralls in one fast downward motion and shrugged out of the shoulders.

Parker, stepping out of the coveralls, flung them into a corner with a gesture of irritation. Briggs, sounding surprised, said, "Don't we take them?"

"Why? We won't come back here, and they don't trace to us."

"I suppose." Doubtful, shaking his head, Briggs dropped the coveralls he'd been neatly folding and followed Parker across the basement to the stairs.

This was a newer basement in a newer building, with concrete floor and plaster walls and the big green power plant humming to itself away on the right. They'd been coming in here every night for a week, after the old man on guard duty upstairs fell asleep in his chair, the way he always did, and they'd dug the tunnel through to the jewelry store basement in the next block. A wooden crate had hidden the hole by day, and a stack of six cardboard cartons had taken the extra dirt.

Hurley was the first one up the stairs, with Parker behind him and Briggs trailing. At the top, Hurley waited till Parker and Briggs stopped clattering on the metal stairs, then pushed the chrome door open enough to look out at the lobby. "Crap," he said.

"What?"

"The old man's up."

Parker moved up to the top step, to look past Hurley's shoulder. Behind him, Briggs whispered, "The explosion must have woke him."

The guard in his gray uniform was down by the glass doors, peering through them, looking this way and that. Parker looked at him, and saw he was wide awake, and said, "Just cover your faces. Come on."

They pushed through the doorway, Parker in the lead now, and kept one hand up, obscuring their faces. Parker took the two-inch Smith & Wesson revolver from his pocket and held it at his side.

They were almost to the old man before he heard them, and turned around, his eyes startled and blinking. "Who— Who—"

"Stay very tight," Parker said. He showed the gun. "You don't have any part in this," he said. "No reason to get dead."

"Holy Jesus," the old man said. "Holy sweet Jesus."

Hurley had the key. He went down on one knee, because the glass doors had their locks down at the base, and quickly unlocked the nearest door. He pushed it open and rose in the same movement, heading outside and across the sidewalk to Dalesia waiting in the Chrysler.

Briggs followed, holding his tool kit tight to his chest, and Parker said to the guard, "Walk over to your chair. Take your time and don't look back."

"Oh, I won't," the guard said. He carried a gun, but he knew he hadn't been hired to do anything with it. "Now?" he said.

"Now. I'll be watching through the glass."

The guard walked off, staring at the building directory on the rear lobby wall. Parker shoved the pistol back in his pocket, moved quickly across the sidewalk, slid into the back seat beside Briggs. Hurley was up front, next to Dalesia. The engine was running.

"Go," Parker said.

They rolled, and Dalesia said, "Michaelson?"

Hurley said, "He won't be coming."

"He got shot," Briggs said.

Dalesia nodded. He'd been coasting a bit, waiting for the light at the corner to change to green, and now he gunned across the intersection. Moving briskly down the next block—but not fast enough to attract attention—he said, "Wounded? Will he be able to talk?"

Parker said, "He's gone."

"What I want to know," Hurley said, "what went wrong? How come we suddenly got all those cops?"

"There had to be another alarm," Parker said. "An internal alarm on that cellar door."

"We were supposed to buy a clean plan," Hurley said. He was angry, but it was mostly relief. "Morse guaranteed us a clean plan."

"These things happen," Parker said. "That could be a new system, since he knew the place."

"They don't happen to me," Hurley said. "We paid Morse

good money for a good plan, and we got our heads on a plate."

Parker shrugged. They were away, it was over, mistakes happen. They had bought a plan, and a map, and an outline of the alarm protection, and a key to that building in the next block. As to guarantees, nobody could guarantee a thing like this, that was just Hurley spouting off his nervousness through anger.

The fact was, Parker wouldn't have come into this at all if he hadn't been strapped for cash. It was a small score, which somebody unknown to him had set up, and he wasn't in charge of it. This was Hurley's baby. Hurley and his friend Morse.

They rode a couple of blocks in silence, and then Hurley said, "I'm gonna go see Morse. You want to come? Dee?"

Dalesia said, "Sure. I got nothing else to do." He spoke casually, not angry, not caring one way or the other.

Hurley twisted around in the seat to look at the two in back. "What about you? Parker?"

"No, I don't think so," Parker said.

"Briggs?"

"I guess not," Briggs said. "I guess I'll go back to Florida."

"Well, I'm gonna see Morse." Hurley faced front again, and sat nodding his head, apparently thinking about his anger.

Briggs said quietly to Parker, "Do you have any idea what you'll do?"

"I'm not sure."

"I'm running a streak," Briggs said. "A very bad streak. I believe I'll just retire for a while, and wait for it to go away."

"This is my fourth in a row," Parker said. "I've got a streak of my own running."

"Anything else on tap?"

"No." Parker frowned and looked out the side window at the dark storefronts going by. "One thing," he said.

"What's that?"

"Couple years ago I left some money behind after a job. I think I'll go back and get it."

"You want company?"

"I did the job with a guy," Parker said. "I guess I'll get in touch with him again."

Two

Grofield said, "Shouldn't I have income before I pay income tax?"

The man from Internal Revenue rested his forearm on the briefcase he'd put on Grofield's desk. Talking slowly, as though explaining something complex to a child, he said, "You *have* to have income, Mr. Grofield. You *can't* operate a theater at a loss five years in a row, it isn't possible."

Grofield said, "Have you ever seen a show here?"

"No."

"The vast majority of your fellow-men could say the same."

They were having their conversation in Grofield's office in the theater. At one time the office had been part of a lobby kind of thing at the rear of the theater near the box office, but by running the Coke machine and the candy machine out from the rear wall, and adding a door with its own independent stand-up frame, a more or less private area had been divided off, in which Grofield kept a desk and a filing cabinet and two folding chairs. Occasionally the door or the desk was needed in a set onstage, but most of the time Grofield could think of himself as an actual theatrical producer with an actual office. The candy machine made a hell of a noise next to his ear whenever anybody made a purchase from it, but that was a small price to pay for his own private office.

The Internal Revenue man frowned across the desk at Grofield, apparently trying to work out some sort of problem he was having. Finally he said, "If you lose so much money every year, how do you live?"

"God knows," Grofield said.

"How do you go on opening the theater every summer?"

"Stupidity," Grofield said.

The Internal Revenue man made an impatient gesture. "That isn't an answer," he said.

"Of course it is," Grofield said. "Almost always."

"You *must* have a source of income," the Internal Revenue man said.

"I couldn't agree more," Grofield said. "In fact, I'd say it's imperative."

The office had its door at the moment; Grofield's wife, Mary, opened it and said, "Phone, Alan."

Grofield glanced at the phone on his desk. It was an illegal extension from the box-office phone, which he'd put in himself to avoid the monthly charges. "Right," he said.

"At the house," she said.

"Oh."

Since the house phone was also an illegal extension from the box office, meaning that even if Mary had answered at the house he could still pick up this one and have his conversation here, her phrase suggested the caller was somebody he'd want to talk to in private. He stood up, therefore, giving the Internal Revenue man a bright smile and saying, "You will excuse me, won't you?"

"We'll want to see your books again," the Internal Revenue man said, showing bad temper.

"God knows *I* don't," Grofield said, and left the office. Mary walked with him, and as he passed the head of the aisle he looked down toward the stage to where two actors in bathing suits were attacking a set with hammers. Frowning, he stopped and said, "What are they taking it down for?"

"They're putting it up," Mary said.

"Oh."

The two of them walked outside, and Grofield stood for a moment on the wooden platform at the top of the stairs, looking out over the wooded hills of Mead Grove, Indiana. The only sign of human habitation in this direction was the gravel parking lot. The formerly gravel parking lot, lately turning to mud. "We need more gravel," Grofield said.

"We need more everything," Mary said. "That was Parker on the phone."

"Ho ho," Grofield said. "Maybe he has more gravel."

"That would be a blessing," Mary said. She'd played three consecutive landladies in three consecutive rustic comedies recently and hadn't yet gotten rid of the speech habits.

Grofield trotted down the steps and went around the side of the barn toward the farmhouse. The words MEAD GROVE THEATER were stretched in giant white letters along the side of the barn facing the county road. There was no traffic at the moment to see it.

Sometime in the late forties some unremembered genius had first decided to convert this old barn to a summer theater, tucked away here in this remote corner of Indiana. He'd put in a stage at one end, and had arranged seating for an audience on a series of platforms, with the first four rows of seats on the original barn floor, the next four on a platform two steps up, the next four two more steps up, and so on, until he had twenty-four rows of ten seats each, with a center aisle. Two hundred forty seats, and rarely had anybody seen them all full at once.

The problem was, this was not the best place in America for a summer theater. Mead Grove was no big city; in fact, there is no big city in Indiana, with the doubtful exception of Indianapolis, and Mead Grove was in any event too far away from Indianapolis to take advantage of it. There was no college in or near Mead Grove, no well-known tourist attraction nearby, no reason at all for outsiders to come into the area and discover the existence of its local summer theater.

Which left, as potential customers, the citizens of Mead Grove and the other half-dozen towns in the general vicinity, plus the people on the farms in between. Most of them were a little baffled by the need for a live theater anyway, in a world with TV, and doubted it could show them anything they wanted to see. If it weren't for schoolteachers and the wives of doctors, there wouldn't have been any audience at all.

The original converter of the barn to a theater had only lasted a season or two before going broke and leaving the area and his debts behind. For the next twenty years the barn/theater had had a checkered and not very successful career; had been a barn again for a little while, had been a movie house for even less of a while, had been a warehouse full of bicycle parts, and had several times been a financially disastrous summer theater.

It had been nothing at all five years ago, when Alan Grofield had come upon the place. He'd been flush at the moment, from a casino robbery he'd done with Parker, and he'd bought the place outright, full cash, for the barn and twelve acres and two small farmhouses on the other side of the road. His theater was now in its fifth season, was beginning to get a small reputation in the theater world, and had never made a dime.

Well, that was all right. Summer theaters always lose money, particularly when an actor starts them and performs as producer, but Grofield had never expected the Mead Grove Theater to support him. He supported it, and had known from the beginning that he would.

The point was, acting wasn't his living, it was his life. His living was elsewhere, with people like Parker. And it had been a long time since he'd done anything about making a living, not since a supermarket robbery last year outside St. Louis, so he moved across the empty county road at a half-trot, hoping this phone call meant a big easy score that would take the minimum time for the maximum return. Fred Allworth could take over his own parts while he was gone, and Jack . . . His mind full of casting changes, Grofield trotted up the stoop and into the house, full as usual of the racket of resident actors. He went into what had at one time been the dining room but was now his and Mary's bedroom, and sat down on the bed to take the call. "Hello?"

"It's me." Parker's voice, as usual, had the tonal variety of a lead pencil.

"Sorry I took so long," Grofield said. "I was in the theater, with a tax man."

"Mary told me."

"The tax man," Grofield repeated. "What I'm saying is, I'm hoping you're calling with good news."

"You remember that time we were together in Tyler?"

"I remember," Grofield said grimly. He remembered; it had been a thing with an armored car, and it had gone to hell. Money gone, time gone, himself loused up for a while. In fact, as a direct result of that job in the Midwest city of Tyler, he'd wound up with some crazy people for a while in northern Canada. "Oh, I remember," Grofield said.

"We left something behind there," Parker said.

For a second Grofield couldn't figure out what Parker was talking about. Then he thought, *The money!* Parker had hidden it somewhere there. But good Christ, that was two years ago. "You think it's still there?" he said.

"It should be," Parker said. "And if it isn't, we'll find out who's got it."

"That's a very interesting idea," Grofield said.

"A friend of mine," Parker said, "is going to be at the Ohio House there on Wednesday. Maybe you could talk to him about it."

"Ohio House. In Tyler?"

"His name is Ed Latham."

That was a name Parker had used before. Grofield couldn't resist saying, "I think I know him."

Humor was wasted on Parker. "You might want to talk to him about this," he said.

"I probably will," Grofield said. "I probably will."

Three

A copper plate on a stone monument in front of the State Office Building on River Street explains that John Tyler, tenth President of the United States, delivered a speech on that spot during the presidential campaign of 1840, and that the name of the town was subsequently changed from Collinsport to Tyler in honor of the occasion. The copper plate doesn't mention that Tyler was running for Vice-President at the time, on a slate headed by William Henry Harrison, nor that Tyler never did run for President himself but simply inherited the job when Harrison died a month after inauguration; but the omission has been more or less corrected by a historic-minded vandal who has written on the stone, just below the copper plate, in orange spray paint: "Remember Tippecanoe."

By the time Collinsport became Tyler, it was already a prosperous river town on one of the principal waterways connecting the Mississippi with the Great Lakes. Lumber and farm produce were shipped through there, and industry started with a furniture plant and a small company that made farm wagons. At the turn of the century a typewriter factory opened, and a while later the wagon company switched to automobile bodies. The First World War added a paper-box factory, the Second World War added electronics plants, and the boom years of the sixties added computer manufacturing.

Tyler, with a population just under one hundred fifty thousand and a median income comfortably above the national average, was rich and soft and easy in its mind. Encircling the city, there was no wall.

Parker arrived at Tyler National Airport at two in the afternoon. The summer sun was shining, and the flat land all around the airport baked in the dry heat. The cab Parker got into had a sticker on the side window saying it was air-conditioned, but the driver explained the air-conditioning had broken down at the beginning of the summer and the boss was too cheap to get it fixed. "Because we'll turn this one in anyway in September, you know?"

Parker didn't answer. He watched the billboards go by, advertising hotels and airlines and cigarettes, and after giving him one quick look in the rear-view mirror, the driver left him alone.

They came into the city through the used-car lots. There was an election going on locally, with posters slapped up on telephone poles and board fences and leaning in barbershop windows; by the time they reached downtown, Parker knew that the two candidates for mayor were named Farrell and Wain. There were three or four times as many Farrell posters as Wain posters, which meant that Farrell had the most money to spend. Which meant Farrell had the support of the people who ran the town. Which probably meant Farrell would win.

Ohio House was a businessmen's hotel near the railroad station, thirty years past its prime. Sheraton and Howard Johnson and Holiday Inn were all clustered together half a dozen blocks away, in an urban-renewal section by the river. Parker had chosen Ohio House because it was still a salesmen's hotel, seedy but respectable, and for his purposes, the most anonymous possible place in town. Nowhere else would it be more likely for two male guests, both traveling alone, to know one another and want to get together for drinks before going on their separate ways.

Parker's room was on the third floor front, with a good view of London Avenue, the town's main street. Off to the right, Farrell had a banner proclaiming his candidacy spread across the street, hanging from light poles. Oh, yes, that was a winner.

There was a black-and-white television set on the dresser, covered with Scotch-taped handwritten notices from the management. On it, Parker watched reruns and game shows and local news programs until dinnertime. He ate in the hotel dining room with half a dozen other men, each of them alone at a separate table, most reading newspapers, one studying the contents of a display folder. Parker looked less like a salesman than the rest of them, but it wasn't an impossible idea. He might have sold Army surplus equipment, or burglar alarms, or special materials to nightclubs.

After dinner Parker went back to the room again, but didn't turn on the TV set. He sat in the dark in the one armchair and looked toward the windows, watching the reflected light from the traffic down below. It was a week night, so the noise level never got very loud.

At eight-thirty there was a knock at the door. Parker switched on the light and opened the door, and Grofield came in, grinning, saying, "A charming establishment. The chamber pot in my room is autographed *A. Lincoln*. Do you suppose it's authentic?"

"Hello, Grofield," Parker said. "Let's go out to the park."

Four

Grofield fired three times, and three escaping convicts in black-and-white-striped pants and shirts flopped over on their backs. He shifted position, sighted down the short rifle barrel, and plugged five speeding getaway cars in a row. Finishing off with a bomb-toting anarchist and a rolling barrel of bootleg whiskey, he put the rifle back on the counter and nodded in satisfaction at the targets at the rear of the shooting gallery. All around him were the flat reports of other rifles, mixed with the *bings* and *dings* of targets being hit, the constant shuffle of feet going past behind him, the combined noises of several different kinds of music being played in other sections of the park, and hundreds of people talking all at once.

The shooting-gallery operator, a short man in an open black cardigan sweater, with a cigarette dangling from a corner of his mouth, eased over in front of Grofield and gave him a cool and noncommittal look, as between men of the world. "Nice shooting," he said. The cigarette bobbed when he talked, giving the illusion of a Humphrey Bogart twitch.

Grofield fell into the role as naturally as breathing out. "Pays to keep in practice," he said.

"For the perfect score, you get another ten shots free."

Grofield looked around, and a couple of nearby boys about twelve years old were gaping at the targets, watching every shot in fascination. "Hey, kids," he said.

"Huh?"

"You each get five shots here," Grofield told them. "Compliments of the masked man."

The kids moved closer. One of them said, "What masked man?"

"Me," Grofield said.

"You don't have any mask."

In fact, he did: horn-rim glasses, bushy mustache, a bit of makeup to widen the nose and give him bags under the eyes. But he said, "You get five shots each anyway." To the guy behind the counter he said, "Treat these kids good. They're particular friends of mine." Then, having segued somehow from a Humphrey Bogart movie into a western, he sauntered off, visualizing them watching him go, visualizing himself becoming lost in the crowd.

And he pretty well was lost. Fun Island Amusement Park was fairly big as such places go, and it seemed even bigger at night. The idea of the park was that it was an island, remote from civilization, far from the cares of the workaday world. Built in the shape of a large square, it was completely enclosed by a tall board fence, on the inside of which had been painted a continuous mural of ocean scenes, with ships and birds and far-off islands. Just inside the fence, a shallow moat ten feet wide made the park technically a true island, completely surrounded by water.

The space inside the moat was divided into eight pie-shape sections, each with rides and games and displays tied to a different island theme. Grofield had found a certain morbid fascination in hanging around the Alcatraz Island section, but it was now ten-fifteen, time to meet up with Parker again over in the part called Desert Island. So he'd best figure out which direction to drift in, and start drifting.

Down to the left was the fountain at the center of the park, spraying in high arches, lit with amber and red and green. Grofield walked down that way, not hurrying, letting the movement of the crowd take him, and when he reached the fountain he turned right, following an easy semicircle past the entrances to Treasure Island, New York Island, and Voodoo Island before reaching the one he wanted.

MAROONED! said great shivery neon red letters across the sky; inside that building, Grofield knew, was a black-light ride on the general desert-island theme. Half an hour ago he himself had taken the ride, without Parker, to familiarize himself somewhat with the terrain. Parker had been here before, of course, but this was Grofield's introduction to Fun Island.

The Marooned! ride was accomplished in fake rubber rafts made of gray plastic, each holding eight passengers. The raft was pulled on a concealed chain through a shallow waterway that snaked through the dark interior of the building past the lit-up displays. There was a series of the oldest and best-known desert-island jokes; a triggering mechanism in the bottom of the raft caused the displays to light up on either side, with mechanized dolls making small movements in conjunction with the recorded gag lines. Between the displays, in the darkness, fluorescent mock-ups of various kinds of ships swooped down from the ceiling as though to collide with the raft, but always swung back up out of the way again, just in time, usually with a great gnashing noise of ratchets and gears.

All through the ride Grofield had sat brooding over the contrast between the business this tacky thrillorama was doing and the near-emptiness of his own serious theater back in Indiana. Civilization was in a decline right enough, there wasn't any question of that.

It was the last tableau that Parker had told him to take a special interest in. It was bigger than any of the others; almost life-size, it showed a large desert island with a hill in the middle. On first coming around the corner in the raft, one saw another mechanical doll, a male castaway dressed in tattered rags, who was bobbing his head in joy over a chest of gold he'd just accidentally dug up. On floating past him and around to the far side of the island, hidden from the castaway by the hill, one saw a longboat full of pirates that had just landed; armed with picks and shovels, they were obviously here to reclaim their gold.

So were Grofield and Parker. Grofield had studied the desert island and the longboat and all the figures as the raft had slid by, and then had gone on to entertain himself in other sections of the park, and now was back to Marooned! again, drifting along, taking his time. All around, the noise and lights both were fading as the park prepared itself to close for the night. The crowd, which up to now had ebbed and flowed in all directions at once, now tended in two specific currents, one toward the fountain at the center of the park and the other toward the exit, down between the Desert Island and Island Earth.

The rear of the Marooned! building was away from any regular path, a black patch amid the brightness. Grofield turned down that way, walking along next to the featureless green-gray side of the building, and back here he became more aware of the quality of the night itself. The light and noise and movement elsewhere created an artificial daytime, but off in this corner the darkness pressed in, close and pervasive. Grofield looked up at a cloudless sky full of cold tiny stars and a thin crescent of moon, too narrow to give much light. The air was warm, but the sky looked cold and thin and very dark.

Parker was already waiting, by the back door. He was merely a darker shape in the general darkness, and Grofield took his identity on faith, whispering, "How we doing?"

"I've got it open. Come on."

They stepped through into total blackness, and Grofield pulled the door closed behind him without letting it latch. They were now in a narrow corridor formed on one side by the outer shell of the building and on the other by a continuous black drape. From beyond the drape came the echoing noises of the desert-island displays, the recorded gag lines and music and sound effects.

"I deplore this place," Grofield whispered.

Parker didn't answer, but Grofield hadn't really expected him to. They moved away from the door together, traveling to the right between drapery and wall, Parker leading the way and Grofield following, guided by the faint rustling sounds of Parker's sleeve against the drape.

Parker stopped, and Grofield bumped into him. They stood in silence, listening to the tinny recordings. Then Grofield sensed Parker moving again, and a vertical strip of reddish light appeared just to his right; Parker had opened a separation in the drapery, and they could look through to the main floor of the Marooned! ride.

They were just behind that final island tableau, with its lone castaway on the one side and the longboat full of pirates on the other. Looking through the narrow slit in the drapes, reminding himself of himself checking the house before a performance back home in Mead Grove, Grofield could see past the island to a raft full of customers going by. Goggle-eyed and gape-mouthed, the people in the raft looked unhuman and feeble-minded in the red and yellow lights, being drawn along through the darkness as though they too were part of the display. They looked no less waxy and unreal than the pirates in and around the longboat.

The longboat. That was where Parker had left the money, in a suitcase stuffed down in the bottom, with one of the pirate mannequins placed on top of it. And seventy-three thousand dollars from the armored car inside it.

Another raft went by, with its red-faced humanoids. Hard to believe they were actual people, they reminded him so much of the moving targets at the shooting gallery. *Pock pock pock* he went, in his mind, and imagined the heads popping back on hinges, while the torsos remained upright and unmoving. In a little while the same raft would go by again with the same figures in it, their heads back in place.

A space; no raft coming. The island lighting switched off, and they stood in almost total darkness. Music, speeches, sound effects echoing all around them, muffled slightly by the draperies. Bits of isolated light here and there in the black building interior, like Indian campfires on a distant range of hills.

The island lighting snapped back on, triggered by another approaching raft. It went by, and the lights went off. The music and sound effects sounded thinner than before; there were fewer campfires.

Twice more the island appeared in its banks of red and yellow lights, and after the second time there were no more campfires at all, and only one thin wheedle of music. Then that too died, and a more anonymous general sound could be heard; the crowd, outside this building, shuffling away.

"All right," Parker said.

Grofield already had the pencil flashlight in his hand, and now he switched it on. He held it along his palm so that he could adjust how much light he would permit to escape between his first and second fingers: ranging from all the light to none. He laid down a vague ribbon of white aimed toward the longboat, and Parker walked along it, his feet making muffled echoing noises against the platform with its fake sand.

Grofield followed close behind, keeping the light aimed ahead of the two of them. His ears were alert for other human occupancy of the building, but he heard nothing. He remained a pace back when they reached the longboat, aiming the light into the interior of the boat while he looked al! around in the darkness for other lights to appear.

Parker shoved a mannequin out of the way and reached into the boat. He pushed a second mannequin, felt around, and said, "Give me more light."

Grofield stepped closer to the boat, aiming the light directly into it, spreading his fingers more so that the full beam shone out. There was no suitcase in the bottom of the boat.

"All right," Parker said. He turned away, walking back toward the exit, and Grofield followed him. *I knew it wouldn't be that easy,* Grofield thought, but he didn't say anything.

Outside, they walked along with the last stragglers toward the park exit. Grofield said, "What now?"

"When I was in here," Parker said, "some local tough boys knew I was here. They tried to find me, to get the money."

"So they must have searched after you got away."

"Right."

"Do you know how to find any of them?"

"I know the name of their boss," Parker said. "Lozini."

Five

Adolf Lozini, at the electric wok, said, "The trouble with a lot of people is, they don't understand about Chinese cooking."

The three men standing around the patio gave respectful nods. Their wives were sitting over in the pool area with Mr. Lozini's wife, talking about racially integrated high schools. The underwater lights were on, making rippling light streaks all around that part of the yard, and the wives in their pink and blue taffeta looked like dowdy mermaids past their prime.

"The Chinese," Lozini said, "*respect* their food, that's the whole secret. Like it was a person." He poked at the water chestnuts and celery pieces with a fork, and the three men all nodded once more.

The three were executives. The one in the bright blue suit and dark green ascot was Frankie Faran, a sometime union officer and also currently manager of the New York Room, a club downtown with live entertainment: two strippers all week, plus a jazz group on weekends. The one sweating in the white turtleneck was Jack Walters, an attorney and an officer in several holding companies. And the one in the black bow tie and bright madras jacket was a former accountant, Nathan Simms by name, who now ran the local policy game and also took care of a number of personal financial matters for Mr. Lozini.

Although the house in the background was very Northeastern in style, with its steep roof and small double-hung windows and dark shingle siding, the large yard at the rear was completely Southern California, the result of several business trips Lozini had made to Los Angeles a few years ago. Green and amber floodlights glowed on the plane trees and maple trees and the rear wall of the house. The patio was pink slate, the pool was blue and kidney-shaped, the tennis court ran north-south. Stockade fencing enclosed the area, but the ivy that was supposed to have spread over the fencing had mostly died, leaving only straggling remnants climbing upward here and there, like leafy cracks in a rooming-house wall.

The weather was warm tonight, more suitable to the California yard than the New England house. The watery smell of cooking vegetables hung in the air, mixed with the chatter of the women over by the pool. Lozini smiled at his handiwork, then smiled around in a general way at his guests, and they obediently smiled right back.

Lozini considered himself a gourmet cook, and there was no one in his circle to contradict him, either through greater knowledge or greater power. Pleased with his own cooking, and pleased as well with the status of power he had finally reached after many years of struggle, Lozini three or four times each week invited guests from among his subordinates and fed them dishes from Italy or Spain or France or China or almost anywhere; he was a gourmet with catholic tastes. It was considered an honor to be invited to a Lozini dinner, and a disaster to go too long *without* being invited. No one ever refused.

The vegetables were cooking; too slowly, but Lozini didn't know that. He smiled paternally at them, stirred them a bit more, and looked up as Harold approached from the house. Harold's white serving jacket was tailored so carefully that no gun was evident at all; Lozini's wife didn't like the look of guns, especially in the house.

Lozini waited, the wooden spoon in his hand, and his three guests stepped discreetly backward out of the way. Theirs was a world in which it was better not to overhear other people's conversations.

Harold arrived. Leaning over the wok, his face in the upward current of thin steam, he said quietly, "Somebody on the phone for you, Mr. Lozini."

"Who?"

"I don't know, Mr. Lozini. He won't give a name."

Lozini frowned. "Why should I talk to him? What does he want?"

"He said it's about the guy in the amusement park, Mr. Lozini."

Lozini squinted as though it were his own face in the steam, not Harold's. "What guy in the—" But then he remembered.

"I don't know, Mr. Lozini," Harold said. He wouldn't know anything about that, of course. "He just said I should tell you—"

"All right, all right," Lozini said. He nodded briskly to shut Harold up, and stood squinting toward the house. The heist artist in the amusement park, hiding in there with the loot from an armored-car robbery. Lozini had sent some people in to get him, and they'd failed. That was a couple years ago—and who would want to talk to him about it now, on the phone?

Harold waited patiently, his face in the steam. The three guests were in a low meaningless conversation to one side. Lozini came to a decision. "All right," he said, and turned toward the three men. "Nate?"

Simms, the former accountant, came over with his eyebrows politely raised. "Anything I can do?"

Lozini handed him the wooden spoon. "Stir this," he said. "Don't let it burn." To Harold he said, "I'll take it in the cabana."

"Yes, sir, Mr. Lozini."

Harold went back to the house, and Lozini marched over to the cabanas, a row of three dressing rooms, each with its own cot and toilet and sink. The one at the end also held a telephone; Lozini went in there, switched on the light, closed the door, sat on the bed, and picked up the receiver.

"Hello?"

"Lozini?" The voice was somewhat harsh, but neutral.

"Speaking," Lozini said, and heard the click as Harold hung up the kitchen extension.

"Last time you saw me," the voice said, "you thought I was a cop named O'Hara. You thought I hurt my head."

Lozini got it right away; it was the heistman himself, the one he'd helped hunt down in the amusement park. The bastard had gotten out dressed like a cop, palming himself off as one of Lozini's tame cops. "You son of a bitch," Lozini said, squeezing the phone, leaning forward over his knees. He wanted to say that three good men had been killed that time, and that the heister still had to pay for it, but he held himself in check; things like that weren't said on the phone. "I want to see you again," Lozini said. He was breathing hard, as though he'd run up a flight of stairs.

"You owe me some money," the voice said.

That one left Lozini with nothing to say at all. He stared at the sink on the opposite wall, speechless. He couldn't begin to think what the son of a bitch was talking about.

"Lozini?"

"Where—" Lozini cleared his throat. "Where are you?"

"This is a local call. You've got my money, I came back for it."

"What money, you son of a bitch? I don't have any of your money, *that's* not the score we have to settle."

"The money I left behind. You got it and I want it. Do you give it to me easy, or do you give it to me after I make trouble?"

"I won't give you anything," Lozini yelled, "but a one-way ticket!"

The voice was staying calm. It said, "Do you know a guy named Karns?"

"What?"

"He runs things," the voice said. "Your kind of thing."

"No, he doesn't, that's— Oh, I know who you mean." Then Lozini remembered to be mad again, and said, "I don't care who you know. I'm after your head, and I'll get it."

"Call Karns," the voice said.

"I don't have to call any—"

"Call him and ask him," the voice said, "what you should do if you owe some money to a guy named Parker."

"You come over here," Lozini said. "I'll pay you off, all right."

"Ask Karns," the voice said. "I'll call you tomorrow night, tell you where to leave the—"

"I'm not asking anybody anything!"

"You're making a mistake," the voice said.

Lozini slammed the phone down. An instant later he regretted that and picked the receiver up again, but the connection was broken. Maybe he could have figured out some way to get the bastard within arm's reach. Parker, did he say his name was? All right.

Lozini made a quick call. His really good number-two man, Joe Caliato, had been killed in that amusement park, killed by this same son of a bitch coming around now, looking for money. His replacement, Ted Shevelly, was going to be Grade A some day, but that day hadn't quite happened yet. Still, he'd be more than good enough for this.

"Hello?"

"Ted?"

"Yes, sir, Mr. Lozini."

"Ted, you remember that trouble at the amusement park, a couple years ago?"

"Yes, sir."

"The fella that caused it, he says his name is Parker, says he's in town. Just called me on the phone."

"On the level?"

"I think so. I'd like to meet up with him, you know what I mean?"

"Yes, sir, sure do."

"Think you can find him?"

"If he's in town," Ted Shevelly said, "I can find him."

"Good boy."

Lozini hung up, and sat brooding at the phone a minute longer. An itch in his brain wanted him to make a long-distance call to Karns, a man he hardly knew at all, but powerful nationally. But what did it matter what Karns said? If this bastard Parker was really under Karns' protection, he'd come in here openly, with soldiers of his own to back him up. He was a four-flusher, that's all, a cheap heist artist with a gun in his hand.

Besides, even if Karns or anybody else said it would be a good idea to give Parker his money back, it wouldn't do any good. Because Lozini didn't have the bastard's money. He'd had that amusement park tossed from one end to the other two years ago, after Parker had gotten away, and there hadn't been a sign of it. And you can't give it back if you don't have it.

Lozini got to his feet, left the cabana, and walked back over to where his guests were standing around the wok, taking turns stirring the vegetables inside. They were relieved when their host came back to join them.

"Thanks, fellows," Lozini said, and took the wooden spoon back from Nate Simms and looked in the wok. The vegetables had mushed down to a kind of wet green mass, a steaming swamp. The steam smelled like mildew.

Six

"Very nice library you have here," Grofield said.

The girl walking through the stacks ahead of him turned her head to twinkle over her shoulder in his direction. "Well, thank you," she said, as though he'd told her she had good legs, which she had.

They went through a section of reading tables, all unoccupied. "You don't seem to get much of a business," he said.

She gave a dramatic sigh and an elaborate shrug. "I suppose it's all you can *expect* from a town like this," she said.

Oh ho, thought Grofield, one of those. Self-image: a rose growing on a dungheap. A rose worth plucking? "What other attractions are there in a town like this?" he asked.

"Hardly anything. Here we are."

A small alcove held a battered microfilm reader on a table, with a wooden chair in front of it. Smiling at it, Grofield said, "Elegant. Very nice."

She smiled broadly in appreciation, and he knew she knew they were artistic soulmates. "You should see the room with the LPs," she said.

"Should I?"

"It's ghastly."

He looked at her, unsure for just a second, but her expression told him she hadn't after all been suggesting a quiet corner in which they could bump about together. The idea, in fact, hadn't occurred to her; she was really a very simple straightforward girl, appropriate to the town and the library.

Out of habit, and not to offend the child's feelings, he went on with the routine, pitching it slow and simple and without double meanings. "There must be *something* to do around here after the sun goes down."

She pursed her lips to show disgust; all her movements and expressions were a little too heavily done, as though she hadn't figured out the fine tuning of her personality yet. "Everybody just watches *television,*" she said.

He said, "I tell you what. I don't know if I'll be tied up with business tonight or not, but give me your phone number and if I can get free I'll call you. We'll see what good old Tyler has to offer."

"Oh, I can't tonight," she said, and this time came on too heavy with the disappointment.

Just as well, he thought. "Maybe later in the week," he said.

"All right. Fine." Very eager. "You want to write it down?"

He couldn't think what she wanted him to write down. "Eh?"

"My number."

"Oh! Of course." He produced the memo book and ballpoint pen, and stood like a reporter in *Front Page.* "Fire away."

She told him seven numbers and he wrote them down, and she said, "I really am sorry about tonight."

"Well, you're a good-looking girl," he said. "I could hardly expect you to be free at a moment's notice. Especially on a Friday night."

She twinkled again. "What a sweet thing to say."

"I can't tell a lie in a library," he said, to make a transition, and looked around, adding, "About the newspapers . . ."

"Oh, yes!" She became suddenly efficient, but again the effect was too heavy. Pointing with large arm movements, she said, "They're right there, on those shelves. The newest are on the top, and then the older ones are below. And the indexes are those books on the bottom shelves."

"Fine. Thanks a lot."

"Well," she said, and flashed a meaningless smile, and made a couple of awkward hand movements. "I'd better let you get to your work."

"See you later." He gave her a nod and a friendly smile, and waited for her to leave.

She bounced away, more emphatically than necessary, and

Grofield turned his attention to the microfilm files of the Tyler *Times-Chronicle*, the city's only remaining morning newspaper. The most recent bound index gave him three references to Lozini himself, and half a dozen promising-sounding references to organized crime. He took the proper boxes of microfilm from the top shelf, lined them up next to the reader, threaded one in the machine, and sat down to start reading.

Alan Grofield was an actor: always and everywhere, not merely in a play on a stage. Movie background music played in his head as he moved through his life, accenting and heightening everything he did, altering everything to melodrama—even the melodrama. Sometimes he was a bomber pilot, World War Two, bringing the crippled bird home over the Channel, the rest of the crew dead or dying at their posts. Sometimes he was the same pilot, downed in France, being hidden by the beautiful farm girl in the low-ceilinged, dirt-walled basement with the stone archways. Sometimes he was the foreign spy, on his way to the meeting where he would turn over the plans for the new submarine. And always the appropriate music played in his mind, giving him a rhythm to move to, so that he gave an effect of unconscious grace and catlike sinuousness—charged, dynamic and utterly artificial.

The sound track running through his mind right now, though, was not exactly music. He was in a Dennis O'Keefe movie at the moment, made around 1950; a federal agent, he had volunteered to pretend to be a crook and thus to work his way into the inner circle of the counterfeiting ring. So here he was at FBI headquarters in Washington, D.C.—the dome of the Capitol would have been visible in the background in the establishing shot showing him trotting up wide stone steps—studying the files on the known members of the gang, preparing himself for the infiltration. And instead of background music, the sound track was filled with the stern tones of an off-screen narrator. "Agent Kilroy studied the men he would soon—" The rest was fuzzed, the voice without the words but ringing with authority.

For two hours Agent Kilroy studied the men. Adolf Lozini. Frank Faran. Louis "Dutch" Buenadella. Nathan Simms. John W. Walters. Ernest Dulare. Joseph "Cal" Caliato, from whom much had been expected until his mysterious disappearance two years ago. And the names of businesses, linked with the men. Three Brothers Trucking. Entertainment Enterprises, a vending-machine company. The New York Room, a local nightclub. Ace Beverage Distributors. Each name led to the next, back and forth through five years of local newspapers, until at last a pretty good general layout of the local mob was spread out before him. His notebook was full, his eyes were tired, and his back was sore from bending for so long into the opening of the microfilm reader.

He got to his feet, put the final microfilm spool back in its box and the box back on its shelf, rubbed his eyes, rubbed his back, pocketed his memo book and pen, and headed for the exit.

The girl was on the lookout for him, and came tripping out from behind the main desk as he was going by. She gave violent hand signals to attract his attention, and when he stopped she hurried over and whispered, "It turns out I'm free tonight after all."

She'd broken her date; headache, no doubt. Feeling vaguely sorry for the young man, and both irritated and guilty toward the girl, Grofield said, "That's wonderful."

"So if *you're* free—"

"I certainly hope I am," he said, and suddenly realized that although he now had her phone number, he didn't have her name. "I'll call you the second I know," he said. "My name's Alan, by the way. Alan Green."

"Hi, Alan. I'm Dori Neevin."

"I'll call you, Dori."

"I'll be waiting."

He grinned into her big-girl smile, and left the library, and went back to the hotel, where Parker was standing at his room window, looking down at the mayoral banner flapping over the street. He turned when Grofield walked in, and said, "Lozini says no."

Grofield tossed the memo book on the bed. "Pick a number," he said.

Seven

Frankie Faran had indigestion. He figured it was probably that Chinese food at Mr. Lozini's house last night; not that there was anything wrong with Mr. Lozini's cooking, but just that Chinese food never did seem to sit right in Frankie Faran's stomach. But of course when you were invited to Mr. Lozini's house for dinner, you couldn't show up and then not eat, no matter *what* kind of food Mr. Lozini was cooking that night.

But boy, had he paid for it all day today. Lived on nothing but Alka-Seltzer and bread until he came down to the club around eight-thirty in the evening, when he had two bowls of the soup du jour, which happened to be onion tonight. Onion soup was supposed to be good for the digestion.

Angie, the waitress he'd been shtupping lately, came back to the office around ten, but he just couldn't get in the mood tonight. "I'm under the weather, honey," he said.

"Gee, that's too bad." She was tough, but a good girl. Although she was thirty-seven, she was so skinny and bony, it was like being in bed with a teen-ager. She had twin sons, around twelve years of age, both in the custody of their father, an Army man who'd married again and was now stationed in Germany with his family. Sometimes when she'd had too little to drink Angie would get maudlin about those two boys, so far away across the ocean. Faran could live without that kind of crap, but otherwise she was a very, very satisfactory girl, and all in all it was a small price to pay.

"It was something I ate," he said.

"You want anything from the bar?"

"Jesus, no. How's it doing out there?"

She shrugged. "It's a Friday night," she said.

Good, in other words. The New York Room was closed Mondays, did a steady and unspectacular business Tuesdays through Thursdays with live entertainment from two fat strippers, and did great Friday-Saturday business with a live jazz group that also played a lot of rock music. Sunday there was no live entertainment, just family dining and later on recorded schmaltz music for the Geritol crowd to dance to. But Friday and Saturday paid the rent and made the profit.

Angie said, "You want anything else?"

"I guess not," Faran said. "I'll see you later."

"Hope you feel better."

He watched her go out, and felt worse.

Legal closing in Tyler was midnight during the week, one A.M. on Friday and Saturday. At twenty after one, with a few customers still finishing up at the tables outside, Faran sat at his desk with the night's receipts and an adding machine and did a little work. He was totaling the Master Charge slips when the door opened and Angie came in again, looking scared. "These men—" she said, and made a nervous hand gesture at the two guys walking in behind her.

Faran looked at them and knew exactly what they were here for, and couldn't believe it. Knock over one of Mr. Lozini's operations? Nobody could be that crazy.

But Jesus, they had the look. Both tall, mean-faced, dressed in dark clothing, cold eyes scanning the room as they came in. And they had their left hands in their jacket side pockets.

And only Angie was scared. Through the open doorway, before one of the guys closed it, Faran could see the crew working away out there the same as always: putting chairs upside down on tables, closing up the bar. So the two of them had come in like sheepdogs cutting one lamb out of the flock, taking Angie, having her lead them back here to the money without disturbing anybody else. Calm, quiet, fast, and professional.

But didn't they realize what kind of place they'd hit?

Angie, moving to one side and leaving a clear sight line

between Faran and the two heisters, was showing her fright more and more now that she was in private. "These men," she said again, and her voice was skittering all up and down the scale like some kind of crazy opera exercise, "these men wanted me to—they've got—I couldn't—"

"Okay, honey," he said. He felt he shouldn't stand up from behind the desk, but he patted the air toward her with both hands, trying to calm her down. "Don't worry," he said. "They're not gonna hurt anybody."

"That's right," one of them said. "You know what we want."

The other one said to Angie, "Dear, you're perfectly safe. Think of all this as a great story to tell next week."

"Boys," Faran said, "you're making a mistake here."

"Just leave your hands flat on the desk," the first one said.

"I'm not stupid," Faran told him, and pressed his palms down on the desk to prove it. "But maybe you don't realize whose money this is. Maybe you don't know the local situation."

The first one had come over close to the desk, and now he reached out and picked up the thin stack of rubber-banded twenties that Faran had already counted. "We know the local situation, Frank," he said.

Faran frowned at him. Did this guy know him? Both men were wearing hats and mustaches and horn-rim glasses with clear lenses; Faran tried to squint past all that veneer to see the faces. The one nearest him, scooping up the tens and the fives and the ones and putting them away in his jacket pockets, had a broad craggy face with dark wide-set eyes and a thin-lipped mouth. The other one, his back leaning against the door as he kept saying soothing amiable things to Angie, was more slender and easygoing in his looks, with a sort of dark actorish face beneath the disguise, the features sharp and self-confident, but without the first man's stony meanness.

Faran had never seen either of them before in his life, he was sure of it. He said, "Listen, you can take the whole joint, for all of me. But if you really know who owns this place and what the local story is, you're sure as hell going out of your way to find grief."

The big man paid no attention. He finished stuffing the

night's cash receipts into his pockets—less than nine hundred, already totaled on the adding machine by Faran, and surely not worth a house call by professional robbers—and then he reached out for the credit-card slips.

Faran was so startled he actually made a move to grab the slips back, saying, "Hey! What are you—"

The edge of the big man's hand came down hard on the back of Faran's wrist, thudding it against the desk top. "Don't be stupid," he said.

Faran pulled his hand back, astounded at his own actions even more than by the big man's reaching for the credit-card slips. "I'm sorry," he said, bewildered into babbling. "I thought —they're no good to you, what do you—"

Diners Club. The big man picked up the slips, tucked them into his pocket, reached for the Bankamericard stack.

Faran watched him, so baffled he couldn't think. "You can't—you can't use them. You can't turn them into money."

And credit cards were seventy-five percent of the club's business. If there was nine hundred in cash tonight, that meant probably around three thousand in credit-card slips. It would cost the New York Room that much if the big man took the slips away, yet there was no way any robber could convert the slips into cash. The only result, if the slips were stolen, would be that a lot of tonight's customers would have been feeding themselves free food and drink.

American Express. Master Charge. Carte Blanche. Faran watched the slips disappear into the big man's pocket. On the other side of the room, the other guy was still talking to Angie, soothing and friendly things with even a hint of flirtation in them, and Angie was much calmer now, standing there watching it all happen, wide-eyed but no longer in a panic.

But Faran was in a panic, a panic of bewilderment. He said, "That stuff's no use to you. You're costing us, and you're not getting anything for yourself. Jesus Christ, man, what's the point?"

The big man had finished putting everything away in his pockets. Now he took a short mean-looking pistol out of his jacket side pocket, turned it around so he was holding it by the barrel, and leaned forward over the desk. Suddenly *really* scared, suddenly believing these people were crazy after all and not the professionals they looked like, Faran cowered back in his chair and put his trembling forearms up in front of his face.

The big man lifted the gun and smashed it into the desk top three times, making deep gouges in the walnut. Faran blinked at the sound of each stroke, and across the room Angie made a tiny startled sound like a mouse.

Faran lowered his arms. He looked at the gouges and the splinters in his expensive desk top, while the big man stood over him and said, "You call Lozini after we leave here, and you tell him this is interest on what he owes me. We don't subtract this from the principal. You got that, Frank?"

Faran looked up. "Yes," he said.

"Say it back to me."

"What you took is interest on what he owes you. You don't subtract it from the principal."

"That's right, Frank." The big man stepped back a pace, put the pistol away again, and gestured toward Angie without looking at her. "We'll take the young lady with us as far as the sidewalk," he said. "You don't make any moves until she gets back here."

"No," Angie said in a tiny voice, like the squeaking sound she'd made earlier.

The guy by the door said, casually, "Nothing's going to happen, dear. Just another walk through the club together, like before."

The big man was still looking at Faran. He said, "You got that, Frank?"

"I've got it," Faran said. He was thinking that this was some kind of vendetta between these two and Mr. Lozini, or more likely between Mr. Lozini and some big shot who'd hired these two, and he was very glad all they'd wanted was the night's receipts. Sometimes, in Mr. Lozini's world, big shots showed they were mad at each other by killing off each other's people. Faran was suddenly thinking he'd been a lot closer to major trouble than he'd realized.

The big man nodded at him, and turned to Angie. "Let's go," he said.

Angie stared toward Faran, as though needing him to help

her start. He said, "It's okay, Angie. They're not out to hurt any people."

"That's right," said the one by the door. "Absolutely right. We just don't hurt people, and that's all there is to it. Come on, Angie, take a walk down me alley and tell me who do you love." He said the last in a deep Bo Diddley voice, and Angie even managed a shaky grin toward him as the three of them walked out of the office, the big man going last and closing the door behind him.

Faran slapped his hand out immediately onto the phone, but he didn't lift the receiver. He could have, it didn't make any real difference whether he waited for Angie to come back or not, but he didn't. For some reason he just felt better doing it the way the big man wanted.

With his free hand he tapped the gouge marks in the desk top. Ruined, absolutely ruined. And a goddam expensive desk too, solid walnut. Deep bad gouges, rough splinters; no way to patch that up.

Angie came in, running, loud with relief. "Oh, Frank! Oh, my God!"

Faran lifted the receiver, started to dial.

"They had a car," she was saying. She was panting, out of breath as though she'd run a mile. "There was dirt all over the license plate, but it was a dark green Chevrolet."

"Rented," he said. "Under a phony name. Forget it." He finished dialing and listened for the ringing to start.

Angie came around the desk, leaning toward him, putting her hand on his shoulder for support. "God, Frank," she said, "I was so scared."

"Later," he said. For the first time in the last five minutes his stomach growled and rolled. He had to break wind, he couldn't help it; something he hated to do in the presence of a woman. If only it would be quiet; squeezing it out, he heard a horrible long muffled Bronx cheer from behind him. "Jesus," he said, embarrassed and angry and upset and frightened and relieved and hungry and worried and wishing he didn't have this goddam phone call to make. "Jesus Jesus Jesus."

"Frank?"

"*Later*, for Christ's sake!" With a wild arm movement, he

flung her hand away from his shoulder. The phone was ringing at last.

Angie backed away from him, looking at him as though he'd betrayed her. He knew what it was, he knew he was supposed to comfort her, put his arms around her, that whole number, but good Christ, first things first!

A voice came on the line.

"Yeah," Faran said. "This is Frank Faran, down at the New York Room. I have to talk to Mr. Lozini. Yeah, well, you better wake him up, this is important. Yeah, I know, I know, but do it anyway. It's my responsibility. He'll want to hear this."

Eight

Two-thirty A.M. In the watchman's shed by the main gate, Donald Snyder put down his paperback book, got to his feet, and reached for the flashlight and key ring. Time to make his half-hour rounds through the plant. He left the yellow brightness of the watchman's shed for the red-tinged darkness outside and plodded across the blacktop loading area toward the main building. Great red neon letters on the roof of the three-story plant spelled out KEDRICH BEER brightly enough to obscure the splinter of moon above them in the sky, and brightly enough so that Snyder didn't need to use his flashlight at all until he was inside the main building.

Kedrich was a strictly local brand of beer, unknown fifty miles from Tyler but nevertheless a successful brewery for over seventy years. It was an ordinarily good beer, about the same as most others, but its success didn't depend on its excellence. The unstated but generally understood fact was that no bar in Tyler could obtain or keep a liquor license unless it carried Kedrich beer on tap. "We all want to support local business" was the way the Kedrich salesmen described the situation to newcomers.

Unlocking the side door, Snyder stepped into the building, switched on the flashlight, and aimed it down the long empty corridor. No trouble, everything as quiet as ever.

Good. He strolled on down the corridor, flashing his light to both sides, expecting nothing wrong and seeing nothing wrong. Both corridor walls were lined with small-paned windows, and through the glass Snyder's flashlight shone on bottling equipment to the left and brewing equipment to the right. Everything fine on the first floor.

And on the second. The raw materials were stored here, in large cool low-ceilinged rooms lined with rows of fluorescent lights. Snyder opened each door he came to, flicked on the wall switch that turned on all the lights, and saw every time the same proper silent emptiness, the rows of boxes or bins or bales, the clean concrete floors. No smell of smoke, no scampering sounds of rats, no trouble. Unbroken silence and peace.

Third floor. Here were the offices, all the white-collar workers and the bosses. Some of the executives, down at the far end, had really plush suites to themselves, with big picture windows overlooking the river, plus paintings on the walls and thick carpets on the floors and their own private bathrooms and kitchens. Snyder would never touch anything he wasn't supposed to, but he did like sometimes to walk around in those offices, just looking, enjoying the aura of warmth and security that always surrounds well-spent money.

At the near end, though, were all the clerical offices: crowded, busy, brisk, filled with metal desks and filing cabinets, still with their original small-paned windows looking out on the loading area or the parking lot or the secondary buildings. Snyder strolled along, opening doors, flashing his light inside, and at one point as he was walking down the corridor he became aware that there was somebody walking beside him.

He thought his heart would stop. His moving foot fumbled, the flashlight wobbled, he had to touch the wall next to him for balance. Then, blinking repeatedly in fear, he turned his head to look at the man beside him.

He was tall, slender, dressed in dark clothing. Over his head and face he wore one of those wool ski masks, the way terrorists did in photos in the newspaper. He had no weapons in his hands, and he wasn't making any threatening gestures, yet he was terrifying.

Snyder couldn't move, couldn't speak. He was afraid to shine the flashlight directly at the man, but still kept it pointed more or less down the corridor, showing the emptiness down there. Light-spill from the smooth walls was enough to see the man, to watch him nod and make a small strange half-saluting gesture, like the hero of a movie comedy from the thirties.

"I hope I didn't startle you."

It was such an absurd statement, said so quietly and casually, that for a few seconds Snyder could make no sense out of it at all. He just stood there, until the man leaned slightly toward him, obviously concerned, saying, "Are you all right?"

"I—" Snyder moved his hands vaguely, the light beam swinging this way and that. His fright and confusion left him speechless, until he managed to distill it all into one central question; he blurted it out like an actor onstage belatedly remembering his line: "Who are you?"

"Ah." It seemed somehow that the man was smiling, though the mouth-hole in the mask was too small and the light too bad for Snyder to be sure. "I am," he said, "a thief. And you are a night watchman."

"A thief?"

"My partner is breaking into your safe right now."

Snyder looked down the empty corridor. The finance section was ahead on the left, with its big boxlike safe in the corner of the room. The door there was closed, like all the others along the corridor.

The thief was saying, "And you are making your rounds."

Snyder frowned. "There's no money in there," he said.

"Of course there is," the thief said. "All day today the Kedrich beer trucks made their bar deliveries for the weekend. Because there's a blue law in this state prohibiting the sale of liquor on credit, the drivers were paid on delivery. They all turned their payments in at the end of the workday, and the payments were stored in the safe for the weekend, since it was too late either to do the bookkeeping entries or to make a deposit at the bank."

"But that's all checks," Snyder said.

"Mostly," the thief said. "Listen, why don't we walk while we talk? You'd walk this whole corridor now, wouldn't you?"

"What?"

"Your rounds. You go down here to the end. Then what do you do?"

Snyder was having trouble thinking straight. He said, "After what?"

Patiently the thief said, "After you finish your rounds on this floor. Where do you go next? Do you check the trucks, one of the other buildings? What do you do?"

"Oh. I go back to . . . I go back to the shed. I do the rest of it at three o'clock. The main building on the half-hour, everything else on the hour."

"Fine. And do you have to punch a clock anywhere, to show you've really done the rounds?"

"No, I just do them," Snyder said. He was answering questions mechanically, trying to figure out what was happening.

"That's fine," the thief said. "An honest man. There aren't too many left like you."

Two years ago, when he'd been the winter watchman at Fun Island, Snyder had run afoul of some tough guys who'd for some reason broken in; now, remembering them, it suddenly occurred to him this self-declared thief was all wrong. He didn't act or talk like a thief at all; in fact, except for the ski mask he didn't even look like a thief.

A joke? Snyder peered suspiciously at the eyes within the mask, trying to read comedy there. "Just what's going on?" he said.

"We're going for a stroll," the thief said. He touched Snyder's elbow gently, suggesting that he start to walk.

Snyder obeyed, walking slowly forward but continuing to stare at the other man's eyes. There was humor in them, but also a glint of something else. No, this wasn't a joke.

Nevertheless, Snyder was no longer afraid. As they walked he said, "Where are we going?"

"On your rounds," the thief told him. "Right on down to the end of the corridor."

Snyder paused by the finance section's door. "On my rounds," he said, "I open these doors, check inside."

The thief laughed. "Go ahead," he said. "Take a look. My partner won't mind."

The idea of a surprise birthday party flashed idiotically through Snyder's mind. But his birthday was in the spring, and there was no one in any case to do such an elaborate surprise; and besides, this wasn't a joke.

Nevertheless, he was braced for almost any lunatic possibility when he opened the door and shone the flashlight in, and it was almost a relief to see the dark figure hunched over in front of the safe in the far corner. The man turned his head over there, and he too was wearing a ski mask, a black one with green zigzag stripes. He glanced briefly toward Snyder and the light, and then turned back to his work, absorbed and unconcerned. He was doing something obscure in the area of the combination dial.

Behind Snyder, the other man said, gently but firmly, "I think that's long enough."

Snyder stepped back, shutting the door. "Now what?"

"We walk down the hall."

They walked down the hall, approaching the executive offices. Snyder said, "Those checks won't do you any good in there. They'll all be made out to the brewery."

"Absolutely right," said the thief. He didn't seem troubled at all. "But there will be a *little* cash," he said. "A few hundred, anyway."

"You're going through all this for a few hundred dollars?"

Once again the thief laughed; he seemed as easy and untroubled in his mind as if he and Snyder were just strolling along the street somewhere, not involved in grand larceny at all. " 'There are more things in heaven and earth, Horatio,' " he said, " 'than are dreamt of in your philosophy.' " He declaimed the line, just the way an actor would.

"I don't know what's going on," Snyder said, "and I don't want to know."

"Very intelligent." The thief paused and opened a door. "What's back here?"

"That's Mr. Kilpatrick's office. Vice-president in charge of marketing."

"Fine," the thief said. "Let's go look."

Snyder stepped through the doorway, flashing the light ahead of himself, and from back down the corridor came the sound of an explosion: a sudden flat *crump* that sounded low and serious and authoritative.

Snyder looked over his shoulder, startled, but the thief was directly behind him, urging him forward. Moving, walking across the secretary's office toward the inner suite, Snyder said, "Was that the safe?"

"Definitely. Do you ever turn the lights on in here?"

"Sometimes."

They went through another door to the inner suite. The thief patted the wall, found the light switch, and a large rectangular room suddenly blossomed into existence, created by soft indirect lighting. They had entered on one of the short sides, and directly across the way green wall-to-wall draperies covered an expanse of glass giving, by day, a beautiful view of the river. A free-form desk dominated the left side of the room, with a white sofa and several overstuffed chairs forming a conversation area on the right. Down near the green draperies stood a glass-topped dining table flanked by half a dozen chrome-and-black-plastic chairs.

"How mod-dren," the thief said, with what sounded like mockery in his voice. "Do you suppose there's a bathroom?"

Snyder pointed to a flush door just past the desk. "That's it, there. The door beyond it is to the kitchen."

"The bathroom will do," the thief said. "Come along."

They walked across the cream carpeting, and Snyder opened the bathroom door. They stepped in and the thief turned on the lights, and a row of chrome spots gleamed down onto a long chrome counter containing two sinks. The entire wall above the sinks was mirrored.

"Lovely," the thief said, and took a set of handcuffs from his pocket. "Now you put your hands behind your back."

Fright touched Snyder again, and once more his memory of that other time came back. "You don't have to tie me up," he said, his voice rising. He was blinking again, and backing away.

The thief seemed disappointed, as though Snyder had failed to give a useful performance in a simple role. "There's nothing to it," he said. "We just need half an hour or so lead time."

"I don't want to be tied up!"

The thief sighed. "I don't have to show you a gun, do I? I thought we had such a good relationship going."

Snyder watched him mistrustfully. He couldn't seem to stop blinking. "You aren't going to blindfold me," he said.

"I wouldn't think of it. I'll put the cuffs on, leave you in here, pull the desk over in front of the door to slow you down a bit, and that's the end of it. All we want is time enough to get away from here." The thief patted Snyder's arm and gave him a confidential smile, half obscured by the mask. "Come on, now," he said. "Let's not make trouble for one another."

Snyder reluctantly turned around, putting his hands behind his back, and felt the chilly metal bands close around his wrists. His shoulders were hunched and his head ducked down, as though he expected to be struck from behind.

He wasn't. The thief took him by the arms, turned him gently around, and helped him to sit down on the fuzzy-covered toilet seat. "There," he said. "Comfy? That's fine. Now, we have a message for you to give to Lozini."

Snyder frowned up at him. "What?"

"Lozini," the thief repeated. "Adolf Lozini."

Snyder shook his head. "I don't know who you mean," he said.

"You never heard of Adolf Lozini?"

"Never in my life."

The thief pondered that for a few seconds, then shrugged and said, "Doesn't matter, he'll get the idea. Been pleasant talking to you. Good night."

Snyder sat hunched on the toilet seat. A thing like this shouldn't happen to a man, certainly not twice.

The thief paused in the doorway. "I'll leave the light on," he said, and waved, and closed the door.

It took Snyder twenty-five minutes to get out of the bathroom and make the phone call.

Nine

Parker sat at the writing table in his hotel room, counting bills. Nine hundred from the New York Room, three hundred from the brewery. The restaurant credit-card slips and brewery checks had all been ripped up and dumped into the river. The restaurant would never recoup, but the brewery would get new payment checks from at least some of its customers—a long and expensive and irritating operation.

The only light in the room was the table lamp at Parker's elbow. Off to his right the Venetian blinds chittered occasionally in a slight breeze; they were angled upward, to let in air and to show the night-black sky with its thin nail-paring of moon and to block out the street-lit empty expanse of London Avenue. The bed was still made, and two dark-toned zippered jackets were lying on it. Parker counted slowly, separating and smoothing the bills with blunt fingers, organizing them into two equal stacks. His face was expressionless, as though his mind were working on other thoughts behind the mechanical process of counting.

Grofield came out of the bathroom, stretching and yawning and scratching his cheeks. "Wool," he said. "I don't know how skiers stand it."

Parker finished counting the bills. "Four sixty-five each," he said.

"By God," Grofield said. "And to think some people say crime doesn't pay."

"We'll do one more tonight," Parker said.

"We will? What time is it?"

"Quarter to four."

"Lozini must know by now," Grofield said. "He'll have his soldiers out beating the byways."

"They can't watch the whole town," Parker told him. He pulled open the writing-table drawer and took out the notes Grofield had brought back from the library. "Any ideas?"

"Let's see."

Parker got to his feet, and Grofield came over to take his place at the writing table. As he leafed through the notes, Parker went over to the window. He pulled the blind cord, shifting the slats till he could look down through them at the street.

Tyler was a clean town; the breeze gusted through empty gutters. Bright sodium street-lighting glared on the wide empty thoroughfare of London Avenue, showing the storefronts across the way but leaving the upper stories of the buildings in total darkness. There was no sound out there at all, not even when a dark sedan moved slowly past from right to left. The big *Farrell for Mayor* banner flapped in the breeze off to the right. What was the name of Farrell's opponent? Wain. Parker stood unmoving, looking out through the horizontal slits at the sleeping city. It made no connection with him; he'd grown up in different circumstances.

Grofield said, "Got it."

Parker turned.

"Midtown Garage," Grofield said. "It's a parking building, four stories high, open twenty-four hours. On a Friday night they'll do a good business, all of it in cash and all of it still there."

"Where is it?"

Grofield gestured toward the window. "Two blocks from here, on London. We could walk."

"We'll drive," Parker said. "Drive in, drive out. That's what you do in a garage."

"Right." Grofield put the notes away again in the drawer, and hesitated. "The money, too?"

"Why not?"

"Right." Grofield put the two stacks of bills into the drawer on top of the notes, shut the drawer, and got to his feet.

After they put on their jackets Parker looked around the room to be sure nothing had been left out. "Okay," he said.

They took the stairs down to the lobby rather than ring for

the elevator. At the foot of the stairs a left turn would take them into the quiet lobby, but they turned right instead, down a short hall to a small side exit next to the hotel drugstore. They'd used this route a couple of times already tonight, not seeing any hotel employees at all along the way.

The side exit led to a narrow business street lined with appliance stores and record shops. Down to the left was brightly lit London Avenue, but the side streets were still equipped with dimmer and more widely spaced old-fashioned lighting.

Parker and Grofield walked a block and a half away from London Avenue and the hotel, then stopped next to a Buick Riviera, vaguely maroon in the darkness. There were night lights in the interiors of stores, but no illumination showing in any upper-story windows. No headlights anywhere to be seen, nor any pedestrians other than themselves.

Parker took from his pocket a dozen keys on a circular metal ring and began to run them for the Buick's door. The fifth one worked; he opened the door and slid in fast, shutting it behind him to switch off the interior light, and reached across to unlock the other door for Grofield.

They took side streets until they were beyond the garage, so they'd be coming at it from the direction opposite the hotel. There was no other traffic at all until they finally dropped back to London Avenue, but then they saw a prowling police car almost at once, plus a couple of other slow-moving cars with two male occupants in each.

Grofield said, "Your friend Lozini organizes himself pretty fast."

Parker, remembering Lozini in charge of the hoods hunting him down in the amusement park, said, "He isn't stupid, just too impatient. He gets in a hurry and he gets mad."

"*Then* he gets stupid," Grofield suggested.

"Right."

The Midtown Garage was a tan-brick building on a corner, square and functional, with broad glassless window areas on each floor. A vertical red neon sign standing out from the second and third stories spelled out the name of the place, with the word PARKING beneath, like an underline. Under the sign, in the center of the London Avenue face of the building, was the entrance, a broad low concrete driveway bisected by a booth where tickets were picked up on the way in and money was paid on the way out.

A slender sleepy black boy of about nineteen was on duty in the booth, keeping himself awake with bad rock music from an imperfectly tuned station on a white plastic radio. He was sitting on a stool, resting his elbows on a high counter and gazing in a befuddled way out the glass window fronting the booth at the street. He reacted slowly and awkwardly when Parker turned the Buick in at the entrance and stopped next to the booth; it took him a long time to separate one ticket from the pile, and even longer to get it punched by the time clock on the counter. Parker, waiting, kept one eye on the rear-view mirror and saw the police car go by again, in the opposite direction. It seemed to him both the faces in there had been turned this way. Watching the strangers, waiting for something else to happen.

Beside him, Grofield was studying the wall to the right. Parker had only had a glimpse of it while turning in, but it seemed likely to contain the office; in a tile wall, a brown-metal door was flanked on one side by a bulletin board covered with required city and state notices and on the other side by a thick glass window showing a yellow-walled interior.

"Here ya are."

Parker took the ticket, put the Buick in gear, and started slowly up the spiral that formed the interior of the building. There were no separate floors inside, but only a steadily upcurving ramp, leading by gentle gradations from level to level and marked with white lines for parking.

The interior was mostly empty, with only an occasional car parked with its nose to the exterior wall or the central supporting divider. Parker followed the curve of the ramp up and around until they were out of sight of the booth, and then nosed the Buick in against the interior wall and cut the engine. The silence afterward seemed loud and echoing.

Grofield said, "I didn't like all that action on the street."

"You want to call this off?"

"No. But we better make damn sure we give ourselves enough time at the other end."

"We will."

They got out of the car. They both carried handguns in their jacket pockets; Parker a Colt Detective Special in .32 caliber and Grofield an old Beretta Cougar in .380 caliber. They walked down the ramp with their hands in their jacket pockets, and saw the boy nodding in the booth again, facing the other way. The squawk of his radio covered all other sound.

There was no activity out in the street. They reached the brown-metal door to the office, and while Grofield tried the knob Parker watched the boy in the booth; he was more asleep than awake, and completely unaware of their presence.

"Locked," Grofield said.

Parker took two paces forward and looked through the window next to the door. From the car, all he'd been able to see was the yellow far wall, but now he could see the two desks, the filing cabinet, the free-standing wooden closet, and the man in green work shirt and pants sitting at one of the desks, feet up, reading *Playboy*. He was short and heavy-set, Italian-looking, with thick dry black hair and stubby-fingered hands. He had a garage-mechanic look about him, and was about forty years old.

Good. Old enough to be sensible, to neither panic nor be a hero.

To the right, behind the guy at the desk, was a second window, fronting on the street. Parker looked at that, stepped back next to Grofield without having been seen by the man in the office, and said, "Take the sidewalk window. Show him your gun at my signal."

"Right."

"And let me know if anybody's around."

Grofield walked briskly out to the street and around the corner, and Parker stood next to the window again, where he could look through at the man inside and the other window. He glanced over at the boy in the booth, who continued to nod to the echoing blary music, unaware of the world around himself.

Grofield appeared outside that other window. Parker watched him look both ways, then nodded as Grofield gestured to him that they had privacy. He made one last check of the sleeping boy, then took the Colt from his pocket, stepped to the middle of the window, and tapped the gun barrel against the glass.

50

He had to do it twice before the man inside looked up, and then his reaction was so huge it seemed he might be having a heart attack. His ankles had been crossed on the desk top, showing worn work boots; now his feet flew into the air, his arms shot out, the magazine went sailing across the room, and his chair teetered back and forth on the edge of falling over before finally thudding forward to land on all four legs.

The gun was in Parker's right hand. He pointed toward Grofield with his left, both to signal Grofield to make his own move and to attract the attention of the man in the office, who was now leaning forward in his chair, feet flat on the floor and arms out at his sides as he gaped open-mouthed at the gun in Parker's fist.

For a long moment nothing happened. Grofield had taken out the Beretta and was holding it close to his belt buckle, shielding it from the street as he pointed it in the direction of the man in the office. Parker remained where he was, gun aimed and pointing finger indicating Grofield. And the man inside went on being stunned into immobility, sitting like a drugged ape in the zoo, staring at the black circle of gun barrel.

Then Grofield tapped on the glass with his own pistol. The man's head turned, as though some invisible hand had reached down and forced it to swivel on the neck, and when he saw Grofield and the second gun he slowly lifted his arms straight over his head.

Parker tapped again. The man, arms still up, turned and stared at him. He seemed more dazed than frightened, as though the display of guns had robbed him of the power of thought. With his free hand Parker pointed to the locked door. The man continued to sit there, blinking. Parker pointed again and made a move-along gesture with the pistol, and abruptly the man got to his feet and hurried forward on wobbly legs, moving to the door.

Parker waited till he'd reached it, hand on knob; then he moved to the left, so that when the door pushed open outward he was in position to step inside and pull the door instantly closed behind him again. "Take it easy," he said.

"Okay," the man said. It was as though Parker had made some insanely controversial remark, but the man was determined to agree with him anyway. "Okay okay," he said. His arms were still straight up, but he nevertheless patted the air with his palms, as though to pacify an angry opponent.

"Put your arms down," Parker told him. "You don't have heat."

"That's right," the man said, fervently agreeing with everything. His arms stayed up in the air. "I just work here, that's all," he said.

"Put them down."

The man looked startled, then sneaked a look up at his left wrist. It was like a comedy routine, except that the guy was serious. "Oh, yeah," he said, and snapped his arms down to his sides. "I got, uh—I got flustered."

"Today's receipts," Parker said. "Go get them and bring them to me."

"Well, sure," the man said. "Naturally." Backing away, moving at a half-turn, unwilling to look away from Parker and the gun, he kept talking, maniacally cheerful and agreeable. "I fluster easy," he said. "I've always been like that, I get flustered, I— With my wife, like. She's very volatile, you know, and then I get flustered."

He'd reached the filing cabinet. Now he had to turn his attention away from Parker while he searched his pockets for keys, and it was clearly not an easy thing for him to do. He kept reaching in the same pocket, over and over.

"Relax," Parker said. "Nobody's going to get hurt."

"Well, yeah," the man said. "That makes sense. I mean, you're, uh—you're here for money, right?" He finally reached into another pocket and found his keys.

"That's right," Parker said. He glanced over at Grofield, who was looking left and right at the street. Their eyes met, and Grofield nodded; everything still all right.

The garage man was still being flustered. Keys rattled together while he tried to remember which was the right one. Then he got it, couldn't make it work, nearly dropped the whole chain of ten or so keys on the floor, recovered, and unlocked the filing cabinet. Then he stooped to open the bottom drawer and take out two green-metal money boxes, both about the size and shape of small tool kits. Putting them on the floor, he pushed the file drawer closed again, then picked up both boxes and walked toward Parker, waddling slightly from the awkward weight. An apologetic smile on his face, he said, "I don't have the keys for these. When Mr. Joseph comes around, he—"

"That's okay," Parker said. "We're going out of here now."

The man looked stunned. "What? I thought you'd take the . . ." He gestured with both money boxes.

"You'll carry them to the car," Parker told him. "We'll go out of here, you ahead of me, and you'll walk up the ramp. Don't look back at me, don't try to give any sign to the boy in the booth, and don't talk."

"Listen," the man said. He was concentrating himself to explain something very important, as though Parker were an examiner from Internal Revenue. "I'm not sure I can do it," he said.

"You can do it," Parker told him. He put the Colt in his jacket pocket, kept his hand in there with the gun, and reached with his other hand for the doorknob.

"I don't know," the man said. Droplets of perspiration edged his hairline all across his forehead. "My legs give out, I can't always, I don't know if I can—"

"Move," Parker said, and pushed the door open.

Blinking, trembling, stumbling a bit, the man moved forward past Parker and out the door. Parker followed, letting the spring pull the door closed again behind him.

Nothing had changed outside: somnolent boy, raucous music, nobody else around. Parker kept a few paces back, and followed the man with the money up the ramp. They walked past the Buick and on up, and at a Volvo one level higher, Parker said, "Stop right there."

The man stopped.

"Put the boxes down. Go over and open the passenger door."

The man put the metal boxes down; they made sharp little clangs on the concrete. Parker strode quickly up behind him as he moved to the right side of the Volvo. The man reached for the door handle, and Parker took the Colt from his pocket, reversing it. "It's locked," the man said, and Parker clipped him behind the ear.

It wasn't enough. The man sagged forward against the car, air puffing out of his mouth as though he were a balloon, but he didn't fall. Holding him in place with a hand pressed against his back between the shoulder blades, Parker hit him again, and this time he slumped in a boneless way, sliding down the side of the Volvo, Parker easing him to the floor. At this point he didn't want anybody dead; robberies could be kept basically a simple matter between himself and Lozini, but murder would complicate the situation.

Carrying the metal cases, Parker walked back down the curving ramp to the Buick, where he found Grofield waiting for him, looking edgy. "Police car went by again," he said. "I couldn't stand out there, so I came in."

"We're all right," Parker told him.

They got into the Buick, the metal boxes on the floor at Grofield's feet, and Parker drove back down to the booth, where he gave the boy the parking ticket and a dollar. "Keep the change," he said, and drove out, having to wait a second to let a slow-moving dark sedan go by. The two men inside glanced at the garage and kept going.

Ten

When Lozini walked into the office at nine-fifteen in the morning, the other four were already there. They'd damn well better be.

Two of them had been his guests night before last: Jack Walters, Lozini's personal attorney, stout and uncomfortable and phlegmatic, and Frankie Faran. The third man, rusty-haired, well-built, casually dressed, fortyish, wearing squared-off glasses with gold-colored frames, was Ted Shevelly, Lozini's assistant. And the fourth man, slender and dapper in a dark gray linen suit, was Harold Calesian, a plainclothes detective working out of the Organized Crime Squad downtown and Lozini's principal liaison with the Police Department.

They all said hello. Lozini grunted, walked around to sit behind his desk, and stared each man in the face. Wide windows all along the wall to his right let in glaring sunlight and a broad view of richly blue sky. This office was on the seventeenth floor of the Nolan Building, the tallest office structure in the city, in which Lozini and some of his friends had a minority real estate interest. The sign on the corridor door, past the unstaffed receptionist's office, said *City Property Holdings, Inc.*, the corporate entity through which Lozini maintained his holdings in this building and in Fun Island and in several other pieces of real estate around town.

Lozini's stare got to Ted Shevelly last, and held there. He said, "All right, Ted. What the fuck happened?"

"He hit us three times," Shevelly said. "Bing bing bing.

Nobody knew it was coming. He just hit hard, and took off."
Shevelly seemed calm about the whole thing, even a little
admiring of the bastard who'd done it all, but that was good.
That was what made him so right to be Lozini's assistant; he
was strong and tough, but he still kept an evenness of disposi-
tion that put the brakes on Lozini's own impetuousness. He
wasn't as good as Caliato, who'd had more of Lozini's aura of
power about him, but he was good.

Lozini said, "Took off where? You don't know where he is?"

Shevelly shook his head. "Wherever he is," he said, "he's a
loner. He has absolutely no local contacts, I'll guarantee it."

"He has a guy working with him," Faran said. His voice
sounded muffled; his brow was furrowed as though he were
pouting. His skin looked bad, and he kept shifting around in his
chair.

"Not anybody local," Shevelly said. "The two of them came
in together, and nobody in town knows them."

Lozini said, "You're sure."

"We did a lot of leaning the last twelve hours," Shevelly
said. "We shook this town pretty good last night, and nothing
fell out. They're on their own."

Lozini turned to Jack Walters. "What's the damage?"

Walters grunted as he struggled an envelope out of his
suitcoat pocket. He was a fat man who'd never figured out how
to be graceful in the role; his pockets were always too hard to
get at, chairs were always positioned wrong, doorknobs were a
constant problem. It was impossible to imagine him dressing
himself.

Lozini waited, impatient, while Walters fumbled at the
envelope, finally opening it and taking out a sheet of notepaper
that had to be unfolded twice. Then, panting a bit, Walters said,
"At the New York Room they took nine hundred in cash, and
approximately three thousand in credit-card slips. At the brewery, between seven and nine thousand dollars in checks, and
approximately four hundred in cash. And at the parking garage,
three hundred seventy-four dollars in cash."

Lozini added it up as Walters talked. "Almost fourteen
thousand he cost us," he said.

"Not exactly," Walters said. "The cash is gone, obviously,

and so are the credit-card slips. Most of the checks stolen from the brewery can be replaced, though, once previous payments by the customers have been aligned with the current record of deliveries. There'll be some inevitable loss there, but we should make about an eighty-percent recovery."

"Losing about a thousand," Lozini said. "And costing how much to do the paperwork to get the rest back?"

"I haven't attempted to work that out," Walters said.

"Don't," Lozini told him. "What's the situation with employees?"

"The only employees at the nightclub," Walters said, "to become aware of the robbery when it was in progress were Frankie here and a waitress named Angela Dawson. Frankie assures me Miss Dawson will be no trouble."

Lozini looked at Faran. "That right?"

"She's a friend of mine," Faran said. He still looked green and pasty, and when he talked he sounded as though somebody was slowly strangling him. "It's okay, Mr. Lozini, I talked to her and she's taken care of."

Lozini nodded, and turned back to Walters. "What about the rest?"

"At the brewery," Walters said, consulting his sheet of paper again, "the only employee inconvenienced was the night watchman, Donald Snyder. He was locked in a bathroom and—"

Lozini, frowning, said, "What was that name?"

"Donald Snyder."

"Why do I know that?"

Deadpan, phlegmatic, Walters said, "He was also the night watchman at Fun Island when there was that trouble two years ago."

Lozini permitted himself a thin smile. "He's running a streak," he said. "What happened to him?"

"He's the one who reported the robbery," Walters said, "after he got himself out of the bathroom. His description of the general build of the one thief he saw up close suggests it wasn't the one called Parker but the other one. There was apparently, by the way, an attempt made to send a message through Snyder to you."

"A message?"

"As he did with Frankie," Walters said.

Lozini frowned at Faran. "What message?"

Faran licked his lips and adjusted himself again in the chair. "He said to tell you what he was taking was interest on the debt, and didn't count against the principal."

"He did, huh." Grunting, Lozini looked again at Walters. "Same with the night watchman?"

"He didn't get to give the message," Walters said, "since Snyder had apparently never heard of you. He can't remember the name of the thief used, except that he's sure it began L-o."

Ted Shevelly and Harold Calesian both grinned slightly. "Anonymity," Shevelly said. "What do you think of that?"

"It's about time," Lozini said. Anonymity was what he wanted, though he'd had damn little of it the last ten years or so. There was always something or other in the newspapers, all hedged around with words like "alleged" and "putative" so a lawsuit could never be launched to put a stop to it, and it was hell on the family. Newspaper people had no sense of decency. Fortunately, Lozini's six children were all daughters, all now grown and married and with other last names, but there was still his wife, and other relatives scattered around the state.

Walters was saying, "Snyder seems none the worse for his experience. After the last time, when some of our own people roughed him up a bit, he was given the job at the brewery."

There was a comic-opera touch here that Lozini didn't like. He wanted to get past it, get on to other things. "What do we do for him this time?" he said.

Walters shrugged. "A few weeks off with pay. He hasn't the slightest idea what's going on, or even that *anything* is going on. He's your true innocent bystander."

"We oughta put a plaque on him," Lozini said. "Anybody else?"

"One man at the garage," Walters said. "He got hit on the head, apparently by Parker. His name is Anthony Scoppo, and he was released from the hospital this morning."

"He one of ours?"

Walters pursed his lips. "I wouldn't know about that," he said. He kept himself as ignorant as possible of the actual work Lozini's people did.

Lozini looked over at Shevelly. "Anthony Scoppo. Ours?"

"I think I remember the name," Shevelly said. "He drove a car for us a couple of times, but he gets too nervous. We haven't used him for anything for a while."

To Walters again, Lozini said, "Another message to me?"

"No, Parker didn't mention you at all. Apparently he assumed you'd understand without his saying anything, since that was the third operation of the night."

Lozini gave Harold Calesian a glum stare. "Where do you suppose the cops were?" he asked.

Calesian grinned sympathetically, undisturbed by Lozini's implied accusation. He had the easy assurance and humorous arrogance of the long-time cop, combined with the calmness and quietness that comes from being on the inside, one of the masters. He always spoke quietly, with small expressive hand gestures, and nothing ever ruffled him. "The cops were on the street, Al," he said. "By three o'clock this morning we were saturating the streets."

"That goddam garage," Lozini said, "is on London Avenue, the brightest street in the city."

"We had a car in the area," Calesian said. "You had two cars there yourself, Al, there was almost trouble between them and the patrolmen. What happened to your people?"

"They're not trained cops."

"Then why put them on patrol?"

Lozini waved it away like a buzzing fly. "That isn't the point," he said. "The point is this son of a bitch Parker. Where is he, and how do we stop him?"

"I don't know where he is," Calesian said, "any more than Ted does. Remember, Al, we came in this late. If you'd talked to me yesterday, or even the night before when he called you, I might have been able to do something by now."

"Who knew he was going to move like that?"

Calesian shrugged. "We've been on it for six hours," he said.

"Do you have a make on him yet? Who is he, where's he from?"

"We don't have any helpful identification, no fingerprints, just the name Parker. We've queried Washington, and we'll see what happens."

Lozini peered at him. "You don't think much will."

With a small smile, Calesian said, "No, I don't."

Ted Shevelly said, "What do we do about tonight?"

But Lozini was thinking about something else. "There may be a way I can find out who he is. Something about him, anyway."

Shevelly said, "How's that?"

"I'll get in touch with you people later," Lozini said. "I have to make a phone call."

Shevelly said, "What about tonight?"

"I'll call you this afternoon," Lozini told him. To Faran, he said, "Frankie, you keep yourself available. You gonna be at the club or home?"

"Home," Faran said. "I feel crappy, to tell you the truth. I'm gonna try to sleep a little."

"Just stay available."

"Oh, I will."

Walters said, "Anything special for me to do?"

Lozini gave him an irritable look. "About what?"

Walters gestured with the sheet of paper. "These losses."

"Unexplained robberies," Lozini told him. "Deal with them straight. Give that driver from the garage a little something for his trouble."

"Scoppo," Walters said, and nodded.

Getting to his feet, Calesian said, "Let me know, Al, if you want any change in what we're doing. Right now, we're full out looking for them."

"I'll call you," Lozini said.

The four men left the room, saying so long, Lozini giving each of them a short angry nod. When the door closed and he was alone, he sat brooding out the window for a minute, staring at the sunny morning.

He was reluctant to make the call. Doing anything the bastard wanted him to do seemed somehow like a defeat, like knuckling under. Still, it was the only move that made sense right now.

The hell with it. Lozini reached for the phone.

But it wasn't that easy. It took twenty minutes just to find out what city Walter Karns was in right now—Las Vegas—and

another half-hour to track him down on a golf course there. But
finally the heavy authoritative voice did come on the line,
saying, "Lozini?"

"Walter Karns?"

"That's right. You wanted to talk to me."

"I need to ask you about somebody."

A small hesitation, and Karns said, "Somebody I can talk
about, I hope."

"He said I should talk to you," Lozini said. "I should ask you
about him."

"He did? What's his name?"

"Parker. He says."

"Parker?" There was surprise in Karns' voice, but not
displeasure. "You don't mean anybody that works for me," he
said.

"No, I don't."

Karns said, "You don't sound happy about this fellow
Parker."

"I'd like to see him in a pine box," Lozini said.

"What's he done to you?"

"Claims I owe him money."

"Do you?" It sounded as though Karns were smiling.

"No, I don't." This conversation was making Lozini uncomfortable; he had a sense of Karns laughing at him. He said, "But
what difference does it make? Who is this guy?"

"You remember Bronson from Buffalo, a few years ago?"

"You took his place," Lozini said. He was too irritable to be
anything but blunt.

"I did. But I didn't force his—retirement." Bronson had
been shot, Lozini remembered, in his own home. "That was
Parker," Karns said.

"You mean he's the one—" Lozini stopped, trying to figure
out how to phrase the question on the phone. Had Parker killed
Bronson?

"That's what happened," Karns said. "He claimed our outfit
owed him some money. Forty-five thousand, to be exact. The
whole situation was ambivalent, and Bronson decided not to pay
him. So he made various kinds of trouble and—"

"That's what he's doing here," Lozini said.

Karns said, "Well, Bronson finally paid him off, but then he decided Parker shouldn't get away with that, and he sent some people to—annoy him. That was when Parker figured he'd be better off dealing with Bronson's successor."

"You."

"I had nothing to do with it," Karns said. "Though I admit I didn't mind it happening. But I didn't meet Parker myself until a couple years later, when he helped us with some competition we had off the Texas coast. Did you ever hear about that?"

"No. What happened?"

"Ask around," Karns said. "Maybe somebody local could tell you. Ask about Cockaigne."

Lozini frowned. "Cockaigne?" He'd never heard of it.

"An island. But if you're calling to ask me what I think about your problem with Parker, my advice is to pay the man."

"I don't have his money," Lozini said. "He thinks I got it, but I don't. Somebody else did."

"But he holds you responsible?"

"Goddamnit, I'm not!"

"Good luck," Karns said, with cool good humor in his voice, and hung up.

Lozini wanted to go on arguing, but he was holding a dead phone. Feeling angry and foolish, he slammed the receiver down and glared across the empty room. "I won't be pushed," he said aloud.

Eleven

At two-thirty in the afternoon Parker made another call to Lozini. When he'd phoned twenty minutes ago, Lozini hadn't been available. "But I know he wants to talk to you," the male voice had said. "He's between destinations at the moment. Could he reach you anywhere?"

That had been too stupid a question even to answer. "I'll call back in twenty minutes," Parker had said, and had hung up, and now he was in a different phone booth making the second call.

The same male voice as last time said, "Oh, yes. Mr. Lozini just came in. Hold on, please."

"For sixty seconds," Parker said. Two years ago the local hoods and the local law had been in tight with each other enough to work together hunting him down in that amusement park, so maybe they were close enough for Lozini to have friends on the force who wouldn't mind tracing him a phone call.

"Less," the voice said, and went away.

Waiting, Parker looked around at the sunny afternoon. Grofield was at the wheel of the bronze Impala they'd rented this morning, after they'd checked out separately from the hotel. With the amount of fuss they'd made in this town last night, it was a good idea not to stay in any one place too long. The credit card they'd used in renting the car should be good for at least another week, giving them a mobile base of operations; later today, if necessary, they could find another spot to settle down for the night.

This phone booth was on a corner of Western Avenue, nearly out to the city line. The street was wide, lined with used-car lots and discount furniture stores. A supermarket the size and shape of an airplane hangar was a block away. Traffic went by fast, sensing the suburbs, but this was still a local in-town phone call.

"Parker?" .

Parker recognized the rasping voice of Lozini. He said, "I still want my money."

"I called Karns," Lozini said.

"Good," Parker said. "He told you to give me my money."

"Yes, he did. I want a meeting with you, Parker."

"No meeting. Just the cash. Seventy-three thousand."

"I have a problem with that," Lozini said.

"You want a few days to get it together?"

"I need to talk to you. Goddamn it, I'm not trying to ambush you."

"We don't have anything to say to each other."

"We do! And I can't do it on the phone. We've already said too much."

"There's nothing you can say to me," Parker said, "that I need to hear. You going to give me my money or not?"

"If you won't come off the dime, goddamn it, neither will I! I'm not saying no to you, I'm saying we have to have a meeting. There's things to this you don't know about."

Parker frowned, brooding out at the sunlight, the speeding traffic, Grofield waiting in the car. Wasn't this an either-or proposition? Either Lozini would pay off today, or he'd pay off later, after he'd been pushed a little harder. Or whoever took his place would pay off.

"Parker? Goddamn it, man, unbend."

There was something new in Lozini's voice, something older and more tired. It was that different tone, that weaker sound, that changed Parker's mind. Maybe there *was* something more to know.

"I'll think about it," he said. "I'll call you back in half an hour."

Twelve

O'Hara spotted the diner up ahead on the right, and nodded to it. "Time we got some coffee," he said.

His partner, Marty Dean, said, "Good idea. I'm goddam tired."

They both were. It was three o'clock in the afternoon, meaning they'd both been on duty now for a full twelve hours. Driving around in this patrol car, their uniforms getting itchier by the minute, their guns and cartridge belts a dull weight pressing against their stomachs.

And O'Hara, besides being tired, was in a foul mood. This whole business was connected with that amusement-park mess from two years ago, which O'Hara didn't like being reminded of in the first place. And he'd gotten the word that one of the guys involved in last night's robberies was the actual son of a bitch from the amusement park himself, and oh, how O'Hara wanted to be the one to catch up with him. He could taste it, he needed it, he had to even the score or die.

The diner. O'Hara turned the wheel, steered them over into the parking lot, and nosed into a space between a gray pickup and a red Toyota. The two men climbed out of the car, snicking the doors shut in the sunlight, and Dean stretched hugely, arching his back, saying, "Jesus God, it's good to stand up."

"Yeah, it is," O'Hara said. He was trying not to let his bad mood out on the surface, because he had no explanation for it beyond the tiredness and overwork they had in common. He couldn't very well explain to Dean that two years ago a lousy bandit had forced him to strip out of his uniform, had tied him up, and had used the uniform to make a clean getaway. And that instead of the eighteen thousand dollars he'd been anticipating for helping to run the bastard down in that amusement park, how much had he wound up with? Two grand. That money was long since gone, but the humiliation was as fresh as ever.

O'Hara and Dean walked into the diner together and found a couple seats at the counter. Somehow it was less like being off-duty when you sat at the counter; sitting in one of the booths would be more slothful, more as though you weren't ready to leap back into action at any second.

They ordered coffee and pastry, and then O'Hara said, "I'll be right back," and went off to the men's room.

He was standing at the urinal, brooding, when the men's-room door opened, off to his right. He looked over at the new arrival, and his face showed his surprise. "Well, hello," he said.

"Hello, O'Hara." The guy smiled and stuck the barrel of a .25 automatic in O'Hara's eye, and pulled the trigger.

Thirteen

Lozini sat in the back seat of the black Oldsmobile while up front Frankie Faran did the driving as he told the story of the gambling island off the coast of Texas.

It hadn't been a surprise to Lozini when it turned out Faran knew about Cockaigne Island and what had happened to it. Faran was an amiable drinker, a social drinker in a cocktail-lounge sense, and people of his sort were always full of stray anecdotes. Faran had been out in Las Vegas several times the last few years, and on one or another of the trips he'd been told about Cockaigne.

"A fella named Yancy told me this," Faran said, driving along. "He was in on it at the beginning. Just the early stages, you know, when they were setting it up." He sounded and looked better now than he had this morning; probably he'd had a chance to sleep a few hours since the meeting. Or maybe he'd eased himself by drinking lunch. Anyway, his driving was all right, and his voice was clearer and stronger, and he didn't seem to be distracted any more by an overriding physical discomfort.

"According to Yancy," Faran was saying, "there was a small island off the Texas coast, down in the Gulf of Mexico. A fella named Baron made a deal with Cuba where Cuba claimed the island and Baron built himself a casino on it. You know, like a gambling ship outside the three-mile limit."

"Mm." Lozini, listening, watched out the side windows as they drove out Western Avenue. He wondered at what point Parker would contact him.

"The problem was," Faran said, "Baron wouldn't join in with anybody. He wouldn't be part of the structure, you know?"

Lozini knew. Baron, like himself, had been a man with a local fiefdom of his own; but whereas Lozini had connections and obligations within the loose national federation, Baron had stayed independent. Lozini said, "What did they do to him?"

"They tried to deal with him," Faran said. "According to Yancy, they talked with him for six years, but Baron just wouldn't come around."

"Six years!"

"Well, he never went to the mainland. And he had about thirty armed guards out at the island, with only one place you could land a boat, so they could never get their hands on him. He just thumbed his nose at everybody."

"For six years," Lozini said. He couldn't get over it.

"And all that time," Faran said, "he's costing everybody money. All those good high rollers, rich people from Galveston and Corpus Christi, from as far away as New Orleans, some of them with their own yachts, people with money that used to throw it around in organization places, and they're all going out to the island instead."

Lozini nodded. "All right," he said. "Where does Parker come in?"

"He was their outside specialist. One of the higher-ups brought him in. They made him a deal to knock over the casino. So he brought in some friends of his, and looked the place over, and did it. They walked in, gutted the place, burned it down, took the cash, killed Baron, and left."

Lozini hunched his shoulders inside his suit jacket. He didn't like that story. "How many friends? How big a bunch did Parker have with him?"

"Three guys," Faran said.

Lozini had no more questions. Frowning, looking out at the traffic without really seeing it, he tried to remember what Parker looked like, from their one brief face-to-face meeting two years ago. All he seemed to have retained was a memory of very cold eyes in a hard face. Would he even recognize the man now?

"There they are," Faran said suddenly. "One of them, anyway."

Startled, Lozini focused on the car next to them, and saw a bronze Impala with only a driver, no passengers. The driver was dark-haired, in his thirties, handsome in a way Lozini thought of as untrustworthy. He was waving to Faran to follow him.

Lozini said, "That's not Parker."

"No," Faran said, "that's the other one. The one that sweet-talked Angie." He sounded a little sour on the subject.

The Impala surged ahead, and Faran fell in behind it. Lozini, looking around, saw that they were out beyond the city line now, out where the occasional diner or gas station was followed by stretches of empty lot or woods. Western Avenue lost its name at the city line and became State Highway 79: four lanes, no sidewalks, no central divider.

The arrangement Lozini and Parker had worked out for the meeting was that each of them would be accompanied by one other man; Lozini had suggested Faran, whom Parker knew from last night, and Parker had agreed. Lozini and Faran would drive out Western Avenue until Parker decided it was safe to contact him. Then Parker would lead the way to the meeting place, and if Lozini felt it was safe, he and Faran would stop.

There was an intersection up ahead, a country road unmarked except by three suburban developers' billboards. The Impala took the right, and Faran smoothly followed.

The Impala stayed on the country road only a few hundred yards, then turned again onto a smaller blacktop road, barely two lanes wide, meandering off past woods and occasional strips of cleared farmland. Faran said, "I know this road." He waved an arm to the right. "There's a crick over there I used to swim in when I was a kid."

The Impala's brake lights went on. Lozini put his hands on his legs, just above the knee, and held on tight. The Impala stopped, and Faran eased the Oldsmobile to a stop just behind it. There was cleared field on both sides of the road here, good flat visibility for a long way around in crisp afternoon sunlight. A safe place for a meeting—but where was Parker?

The Impala's door opened, and the second man came back, grinning slightly in an amiable way. He opened the right front door and slid in next to Faran. "Hello, again," he said to Faran.

Faran gave him a cold look and a cold nod.

The guy turned to look at Lozini. "Parker's in the other car," he said. "Back seat. You talk to him there, I'll talk to Mr. Faran here."

"I thought you were alone in there," Lozini said.

The guy grinned again, still in a friendly way. "That was the idea," he said. "Parker kept down out of sight until we found out whether you had any other plans or not."

"No other plans," Lozini said. He pushed open the door and got out of the Olds, feeling immediately the heat of the afternoon; the sunlight wasn't so crisp when you were away from air-conditioning.

As he closed the door again, Lozini heard the guy saying to Faran, "My name's Green, Alan Green."

Lozini walked slowly forward to the Impala. Now he could see the silhouette of somebody sitting in the back seat. The Impala's engine was running and the windows shut, for the air-conditioning. The low stutter and growl of the two cars' engines was the only sound. No other traffic on the road at all, not a house in sight. Just cleared fields that hadn't been farmed for a while and were now knee-deep in weeds. No wind blowing, no movement anywhere; the view was like a painting, or a jigsaw puzzle. Lozini paused next to the Impala, his hand on the door handle while he looked around. Nobody and nothing. In the front seat of the Olds, Faran and Green were in cheerful conversation. That was fast; Green's old-buddy style had to connect with Faran, of course, but Lozini was surprised at how quickly they'd become pals.

Lozini opened the door, and cold lifeless air came out of the car. His body was still adjusting to the outer heat, and now he was going to enter air-conditioning again. He stooped and slid into the back seat, and pulled the door shut.

Parker was on the other side, his shoulder against the side window. He was half turned toward Lozini, facing him. Just looking at him; no words, no expression.

"Hello, Parker," Lozini said. He was thinking that Parker didn't look quite as vicious as his memory had made him. He looked like an ordinary man, really; a little tougher, a little colder, a little harder. But not the ice-eyed robot of Lozini's memory.

Parker nodded. "You wanted to talk," he said.

"I got a problem," Lozini said, and spread his hands expressively. "I don't want trouble with you, but I don't know how to get around it. That's why I want to talk."

"Go ahead."

Lozini looked away, out across the front seat and the steering wheel and through the windshield at the empty road curving away behind a stand of trees up ahead. It was colder in here than in the Olds, and Parker was one of those people who almost never blink. Looking out at the road, Lozini said, "I called Karns. He told me about your trouble with Bronson, and he told me about Cockaigne. He said if I owed you money, I ought to pay you."

"That's right."

Lozini turned and looked at Parker full-face. Now he, too, didn't blink; he wanted Parker to know he was hearing the truth, the bottom line. "My trouble is," he said, "I don't have your money."

Parker shrugged, as though it was a minor matter. "You want time?"

"That's not what I mean. I mean I *never* had it. I didn't find it in the amusement park."

"It isn't there," Parker said. "Where I left it."

"I didn't get it," Lozini told him. "I have never had your money."

"Some of your people got it, and kept it for themselves."

"I don't think so." Lozini shrugged and shook his head. "It's possible, but I don't think they'd try it. Not any of the people I had in there with me."

Parker said, "Nobody else would find it. Where I left it, no maintenance man would go near it, nobody else would stumble across it. The only way it's gone is because somebody was looking for it and found it. That's you and your people, nobody else."

"Maybe that's what happened," Lozini said. "I don't say it couldn't have been that way, somebody holding out on me. All I say is, *I'm* not the one who got the money. I never had it and I don't have it now." He leaned closer to the other man, put his hand out as though to touch his knee but didn't quite complete

71

the gesture, and said, "Listen, Parker, I'm on the level. Maybe ten years ago I wouldn't have given you the time of day, I would have just put every one of my people on the street to hunt you down, and not care how long it took or how much noise it made or how many times you scored against me before I got to you. That's ten years ago, when things were different."

Parker waited, watching him, still without expression.

"But right now," Lozini said, "I can't do that. Things have been quiet around here for a long time, I'm not even organized for that kind of war any more. I don't have enough of the right kind of people now; most of my people these days are just clerks. And right now this town is in an election campaign."

"I saw the posters."

"It's a tough campaign," Lozini said. "My man may be in trouble. The election's Tuesday, and the one thing I don't want is blood in the streets the weekend before election. This is the worst possible time for me, things are very shaky anyway and you could make them a lot worse. So that's another reason I don't want a war with you. Besides what Karns told me. All of that, it all adds up to me wanting to get along with you, work something out, figure out some kind of compromise."

"I left seventy-three thousand here," Parker said. "Half of it belongs to my partner." He made a head gesture toward Green back in the other car. "Neither one of us wants ten cents on the dollar, or a handshake, or a compromise, or anything at all except our money. Our full take, everything we took out of that armored car."

"Then you've got to look somewhere else," Lozini said. At that moment a farm pickup truck with an old refrigerator standing up in the back passed them, the first traffic since they'd stopped here. Lozini pointed at it through the windshield as it went bumping away, disappearing around the stand of trees. "If you went to that farmer," he said, "and told him you left seventy-three thousand dollars in Tyler two years ago and you want it back, he'd tell you you're at the wrong door because he doesn't have it and doesn't know where it is. And I'm telling you the same thing."

Parker shook his head, betraying his impatience by a tightening of the lips at the corners of his mouth. "The farmer isn't connected," he said. "You are. Don't waste my time."

Lozini cast around for something else. "All right," he said. "I'll look into it. Maybe it was one of my people—"

"It was."

"All right. I'll check them out, and let you know what I come up with."

Parker nodded. "How long?"

"Give me a week."

The small sign of impatience again. "I'll call you tomorrow evening, seven o'clock."

"Tomorrow! That isn't enough."

"They're your people," Parker said. "If you're in charge, run them. It won't take long. I'll call you at seven."

"I don't promise anything by then."

Parker shrugged and looked away.

Lozini was reluctant for the meeting to be over. He wanted an understanding he could live with, and he didn't feel he had one. He said, "You want to take it a little easy, you know."

Parker faced him again, and waited.

"I go for the easy way," Lozini said. "That's the situation I'm in right now, I go for the easy way. As long as the easy way is to cooperate with you, that's what I'll do. You lean too hard, you make it easier to fight back, then *that's* what I'll do."

Parker seemed to think that over. "I can see that," he said. "I'll call you at seven."

Fourteen

From a street-corner phone booth, Parker put in a call to Claire. Usually she would be at their house on a lake in northern New Jersey, but for privacy they rented the place out to summer people in July and August, spending that time in a Florida resort hotel instead; she was waiting for him now at the hotel.

She was in the room. When she answered, he said, "It's me," knowing she would recognize his voice.

She did. "Hello," she said, the one word filled with all her warmth. Neither of them expressed their feelings much in words.

"I'll be here a few more days," he said.

"All right," she said; meaning not that it was all right, but that she understood he had no choice.

"It might be a week," he told her. "I don't know yet."

"Any chance of my coming there?"

"It could get pretty loud," he said.

There was a small hesitation, and then, in a fainter voice, she said, "All right."

He knew what that was. Three times since they'd known one another his violent world had gone pushing in at her—during the coin convention robbery when they'd first met, and later when some people had kidnapped her to force Parker to help them in a diamond robbery, and finally when two men had broken into the house at the lake looking for him—and she wanted no more of it. Which was fine with him. "Good," he said.

He was about to hang up, but she said, "Wait. Handy McKay called."

Handy McKay was a retired thief, running a diner in Presque Isle, Maine. He was a sort of messenger service between Parker and some other people in Parker's business, and his calling meant somebody wanted to invite Parker in on a score somewhere. He said, "Tell him I was busy?"

"It wasn't like that," she said. "He was calling for himself. He said he wants to talk to you."

"All right."

"He didn't sound good," she said.

"In what way?"

"I don't know. He sounded—unhappy, I think. Or worried about something. I'm not sure."

"I'll talk to him," Parker said.

"Fine."

"I'll get back when I can."

"I know you will," she said.

He broke the connection, and called Handy McKay. Waiting for the call to go through, he remembered old Joe Sheer, another retired safecracker, who used to handle the messages for Parker until he'd got himself killed in some local stupidity, costing Parker an entire legitimate front in the process. Was the same thing going to happen again?

Handy's gravelly voice came on at last, saying, "McKay's Diner."

Without preamble Parker said, "Claire said you wanted to talk to me."

"Hello, there," Handy said. "The fact of the matter is, I need to come out of retirement."

That was a surprise. It had been nine years since Handy had done anything in the way of business; he and Parker had gotten involved in stealing a statuette for a rich man, and in the course of it Handy had been badly shot in the stomach. That's what had led to his retirement in the first place. Hesitating, Parker said, "I thought you were through for good."

"So did I. Little money trouble. The new interstate took all my truck business away, and this just ain't a family joint."

"Uh huh."

"So if you've got anything going," Handy said, "or hear about anything—"

"All right," Parker said. He could understand the situation now. "Nothing right now," he said, "but I'll keep you in mind."

"Thanks," Handy said. "Not as a favor, you know, but because I'm still good."

"I don't do favors," Parker reminded him. "I'll let you know if anything turns up."

"Good. So long."

Parker hung up and went out to where Grofield was waiting in the Impala. He slid in behind the wheel, and Grofield said, "We got the evening off, boss?"

"We just hang loose," Parker said, "till we call Lozini tomorrow at seven."

"Then I do believe," Grofield said, "I'll make a little call of my own." Opening the door, he hesitated halfway out of the car and, grinning, said, "Should I ask her if she has a friend?"

"No," Parker said.

Fifteen

While standing in the phone booth, receiver hunched between shoulder and ear as the phone did a lot of clicking and beeping before going into the ring sound, Grofield breathed on the glass wall, drew a heart in the steam, and inside the heart put AG and a plus sign. Then he paused, suddenly at a loss. What the hell was the girl's name?

It was ringing. What was her name, for the love of God?

Click. "Hello?"

Dori! Dori Neevin; it came to him in a flash at the sound of her voice, bringing him both the look of her as he'd last seen her in the library and the earlier sound of her telling him her name. "Hi, there, Dori," he said, pleased with himself, and then fumbled for a second as he tried to remember his own name. That is, the name he'd given her. Green, that's right. "This is Alan," he said. "Alan Green."

"Oh, hi," she said as he scribbled in a quick DN inside the heart. "How are you?" She sounded very pleased to hear from him; that business of the overreaction again, her trademark.

"I just couldn't get away last night," he said. "Business, you know."

"Well, you told me that might happen," she said. He could hear in her voice her willingness to forgive him anything, anything at all.

"But tonight," he said. "Ah, tonight."

"You're free?"

"Totally." He looked at his watch. "It's just seven now. Why don't I come around for you at eight?"

"That would be just wonderful."

"I don't have your address."

"Oh, ah . . ." He could practically hear the wheels spinning in her head as she worked something out. "I'll, um," she said, "I'll meet you at the corner of Church Street and Fourth Avenue, at eight. Okay?"

Parent trouble. Possibly also a boyfriend to be cooled out. "Fine with me," he said.

"There's an old monastery on the corner there," she said. "Lancaster Abbey. Do you know it?"

"I can find it."

"I'll be waiting right in front."

"Fine. See you then."

He left the phone booth and went back over to the Impala. Parker was sitting at the wheel, listening to the seven o'clock news. Grofield slid in next to him and said, "My love life bubbles."

"You're all set?"

"Just fine."

Parker put the car in gear, and headed out toward the southern end of town, where a number of motels were clustered together. They'd arrange a place for tonight, and then Grofield would take the car for his date. Parker, aside from the fact that he seemed to be monogamous with Claire, never did have anything to do with women while he was working. Grofield understood that in a theoretical sort of way, but it wasn't natural for him not to have something stirring in his own life, and he'd never tried to emulate Parker's monkishness.

Not at home, though. Around the theater he limited his activities strictly to Mary; partly because he liked her enough to be content with no one but her, and partly because he liked her too much to humiliate her. But away, while working, he almost always found some girl to help brighten the laggard hours.

"Listen!"

Grofield looked at Parker, frowning, and saw him pointing at the car radio. The newscaster was talking about a dead policeman, a uniformed cop named O'Hara, shot dead in a diner this afternoon. Possibly, the newscaster said, the work of the same people who had done those robberies last night.

Grofield said, "What's the matter?"

"O'Hara," Parker said. "That's one of the cops from Fun Island. He helped them look for the money."

"Oh ho," Grofield said.

"Watch for a phone booth," Parker said. "We have to call Lozini."

Grofield sighed. "And I'd better call my little Dori back," he said.

Sixteen

Parker got out of the Impala three blocks from the address. "Luck," Grofield said. Parker nodded, acknowledging the meaningless word, and walked away. Behind him, the Impala U-turned as Grofield went off to position himself.

Not quite nine o'clock on a Saturday night in July; two hours since he'd heard the news report about O'Hara. Tyler was a big enough city to have a substantial downtown, and a small enough city to have its office buildings and its weekend entertainment area all in the same place. Dark office blocks loomed over blinking movie marquees, and the traffic on London Avenue and Center Street was thick and slow-moving.

It was another clear night; high above, the sliver of moon was thinner even than last night, giving off no illumination to speak of, shining no more brightly than the white dots of the stars. Tuesday would be the new moon; no moon at all.

The Nolan Building took up a city block, bounded by London Avenue and Center Street and West Street and Houston Avenue. The ground floor was taken up mainly by a bank on the Center Street side and a stock brokerage and a large restaurant called the Riverboat on the London Avenue side. Next to the Riverboat was the entrance to the office building lobby, the elevators and the building directory.

Parker got there a few minutes early, and spent a while studying the copy of the Riverboat menu taped to one of the restaurant windows. In five minutes he saw four men enter the lobby, none of them Lozini. Was he there already, earlier than his assistants? It didn't sound right.

Parker was about to go on in when one more car stopped at the curb in front of the lobby entrance, the same black Oldsmobile Lozini had used this afternoon. Watching, Parker saw Lozini and another man get out of the Olds and walk across the sidewalk as the Olds drove immediately away. The second man was fat and ungainly, walking as though he'd be more comfortable with a cane. Or more comfortable sitting down.

Fine. Parker let another two minutes go by, then followed the rest of them in.

The lobby reminded him of the one they'd been using in that jewelry-store robbery that went bad. It even had the same kind of skinny old man in uniform as the night guard, except that this one seemed awake and alert. He also had an assistant, a grinning young Puerto Rican, in a blue uniform jacket and tattered dungarees, who operated the elevator. Parker signed a name and destination in the night book—"Edward Latham, City Property Holdings, 1712"—and was about to get into the elevator when another man arrived. Parker, looking at him, knew that this was somebody else for the meeting, and waited for him.

The other man gave Parker an ironic smile of acknowledgment, and said to the guard, "Sign me in, will you, Jimmy?"

"Yes, sir, Mr. Calesian." Parker could hear in Jimmy's voice a well-concealed resentment.

To the smiling Puerto Rican boy, Calesian said, "We'll take ourselves up. I'll send it back down."

"Okay," said the boy. Nothing altered in the smile, just as nothing in the external world could explain it.

Parker and Calesian got into the elevator, and Calesian shut the doors and pushed the button for the seventeenth floor. "This thing's self-service anyway," he said. "The building management thinks it's classier to have an operator." He spoke in a quiet, self-assured, humorous manner—a more restrained version of Grofield. A small smile on his face, he said, "So you're Parker."

"You're some sort of cop," Parker said.

Calesian's smile broadened; he was pleased. "How'd you work that out?"

"An employee wouldn't show up later than his boss. A cop on the payroll would, just to show he's still his own man."

Calesian didn't entirely like that, but he kept his good humor. "You're a detective yourself," he said. "You'll be happy to hear we got a negative on you from Washington."

"A negative on what?"

"The name Parker, and a physical description."

That was all right. He was in fact wanted under several different names, and his fingerprints were listed under the name of Ronald Casper, from a time he'd been on a prison farm in California, but the name Parker had never been officially linked up with any felony. As to the description, the face he wore he'd gotten new from a plastic surgeon ten years ago.

The elevator stopped and the doors opened. Calesian pushed the lobby button before they stepped out to the hall, and the elevator went away again. "This way," Calesian said.

1712 was to the right. The door, unlocked, led to a furnished but unpopulated receptionist's office, with an open doorway on the other side through which he could see several men sitting on leather sofas or armchairs. Calesian went first, and Parker followed him through the doorway, to find Lozini seated at a broad mahogany desk, its surface empty except for a telephone, an ashtray, and a pack of Viceroys. Lozini, looking sour and angry, glared at Parker and then at his watch, but said nothing about time. Instead, after a quick snap glance at Calesian, he looked past Parker and said, "You're alone?"

"That's right. I have to make a phone call."

"Why?" Lozini was angry and impatient, ready to forget he didn't really have any weight to throw around in this situation.

"I have to tell my partner," Parker said, "not to blow up your house."

To one side, Calesian laughed. The fat man who had come in with Lozini made a short gasping sound of shock. Lozini just stared, and Parker went to his desk, turned the phone around, and dialed the number of the phone booth where Grofield was waiting. There was, in fact, no bomb at Lozini's house or the time to set one up there, but the threat of it should be enough.

Nobody said anything. There were six men in the room other than Parker, and they all watched him dial and watched his face as he waited for Grofield to answer.

Which happened on the first ring. "Clancy's Steak House."

Parker read the number from the phone in front of him. "Got it?"

Grofield read the number back, and said, "Everything okay?"

"Good," Parker said, and hung up.

Lozini said, "He'll call you."

"That's right."

"If you don't answer and tell him everything's all right, he'll blow up my house."

"That's right."

"I have family in that house."

"I know that."

Lozini didn't seem to know whether to become enraged or reasonable. In a strangled voice he said, "I don't have any plans against you. This is just a meeting, we've got a common problem. Why should I do anything to you?"

"If I'm not around," Parker said, "you don't have a problem any more."

Lozini shook his head. "No. O'Hara didn't pull that on his own, he wouldn't have had the guts for it. I told you this afternoon, I'm in a tough situation in this town, things getting worse all the time. Things that don't connect with you. I may even lose my mayor." Pointing a finger at Parker, he said, "What it comes down to, somebody in this town is up to something. They're coming at me from my blind side, and I wouldn't even know about it until it was all over and I was out on my ass. Except for you. You came in, you stirred things up, you made some trouble, and all of a sudden I'm seeing things I didn't see before."

"All right," Parker said.

"So we're on the same side," Lozini said. "I want them because they're head-hunting after my position in this town, and you want them because they've got your money. But they're the same people."

Parker shrugged.

Lozini said, "So now we know how the money got out of the park. With O'Hara. The next thing is to find out where it went to, who got it."

A man to Parker's right said, "It went to O'Hara. Maybe he

split with somebody else, but probably half of it went to him."

The man named Calesian said, "No, it didn't. I can give you chapter and verse on O'Hara's financial picture. He maybe got three or four thousand out of it at the absolute most, but that's all."

The other man said, "How can you be so sure, Harold?"

Parker said, "Wait a minute. I don't know everybody here." Turning around, he scanned the faces and pointed at Frank Faran. "I know you."

Faran gave a rueful grin, and nodded his head in a kind of salute. "I guess you do," he said.

The man who had said the money went to O'Hara now said, "I'm Ted Shevelly, Mr. Lozini's assistant." Casually dressed in slacks and pullover shirt, Shevelly looked to be about forty, with rust-colored hair and a stocky well-built frame and the general look of a weekend golfer. He wore squared-off glasses with gold-colored frames, and gave the impression he was maybe a little too calm and casual for his own good; something like Faran, but without Faran's chumminess or bent for alcohol.

Parker nodded to Shevelly and turned to the fat man who'd arrived in the Olds with Lozini. He was wearing a black suit and a blue dress shirt with wide collar points but no tie, and he was managing to look just as uncomfortable and awkward sitting down as he had been while on the move. Parker said, "And you're—"

It was Lozini who answered, from behind Parker, saying, "That's Jack Walters, my personal attorney."

"Personal?"

Shifting his bulk around, trying without success to lace his fingers above his belt, Walters said, "Not entirely personal. I do know something about the business side as well."

"More than you want to," Lozini said, "and less than I want you to."

Walters smiled, and nodded at Lozini, and went back to looking uncomfortable. But it was clearly only Walters' body that was awkward; a rock-solid and sharp brain peered out through the man's eyes.

The next man was probably in his late forties, and looked like somebody who had suddenly in middle age decided to stop being dull and start being a swinger. He was slender, but the deep lines in his face and the looseness of the flesh under his chin suggested he'd once weighed quite a bit more and had dieted himself ruthlessly into a spurious youth. He was wearing brown loafers and pale blue slacks and a madras jacket and a yellow turtleneck shirt, as though he'd been dressed by the costume designer of a Broadway show to be a parody of a Miami vacationer.

"Nate Simms," this apparition said, getting to his feet and smiling and extending a manly hand. "I'm Al's accountant. Also, I have a few sidelines."

Accountant; right. Al? That must mean Lozini. Parker took the man's hand briefly, and turned to Harold Calesian. "We met in the elevator."

"That's right." Calesian smiled easily. "And made one another right away."

"What's your job with the cops?"

Calesian's smile became slightly self-mocking. "I'm a Detective First Grade," he said. "I work out of the Organized Crime Squad downtown."

Turning to Lozini, Parker said, "Is he the top cop you've got?"

"They don't come much higher," Lozini said. It was clear he didn't want Calesian rubbed the wrong way.

"But you don't have anybody higher," Parker said.

Calesian, speaking mildly to show he wasn't offended, said, "That's right, I'm their top man."

Lozini said, "What's the point, Parker? So what?"

Parker said to Calesian, "Wouldn't O'Hara go to you?"

There was a little silence while everybody worked out what Parker had just said, and then Calesian's smile drooped like a mustache and he said, "I'd prefer them with a little padding around them."

"I'm just asking the question," Parker said.

"You want to know if I'm the one who wound up with the money? No, I'm not."

Parker shrugged. "O'Hara walked out of that amusement park knowing where the money was," he said. "And knowing he'd need help to get it. Is he going to talk to one of Lozini's people? Not a chance. He'll talk to a cop. Aren't you the cop he'll talk to?"

"Not necessarily," Calesian said. "In fact, not even likely. I never had any direct dealings with O'Hara myself; there are layers and layers, you know."

Ted Shevelly said, "Wait a minute. Let me go back to this question of how much O'Hara got. Harold, you say you looked into the man's finances, and the most spread you'll give him is three or four thousand, is that right?"

Calesian nodded. "He absolutely got no more. Maybe less."

Shevelly said, "I take it what you're doing is checking his bank accounts and charge accounts and looking into his major purchases in the last two years, like a car or whatever."

"That's right."

"What if he didn't do it that way? What if he took three thousand off the top for expenses, put the rest in a plastic bag and buried it in the backyard?"

"Wrong MO," Calesian said. "People have patterns, and O'Hara's pattern was to spend whatever he had. That's how he wound up on the take in the first place, by spending ahead of himself. He was still in debt when he died."

Shevelly said, "He wouldn't change his pattern, if it was important?"

"No. O'Hara didn't have the imagination for that."

Parker said to Calesian, "I thought you never had direct dealings with the guy. You sound like you know him."

Calesian's smile flickered on and off again. "One of the ways I help Al," he said, nodding toward Lozini, "is to check into, uh, defectors from the ranks. If a law officer puts himself on Al's payroll, it can be for one of two reasons: either he's on the take, or he's a plant."

Lozini said, brusquely, "Harold tells me if I'm getting a plant."

"Do you get any?"

"A lot of this town," Calesian said, "is on the square. It isn't all sewed up, by any means."

"God knows," Lozini said.

"There's also the state CID," Calesian said, "and even the Federals every once in a while."

"You can't put your guard down for a minute," Lozini said.

Calesian said, "I can give you a thumbnail on every cop in this city who buys his hamburgers with Al's money. That doesn't mean I have dealings with them. A lot of them I never even met."

"All right," Parker said. "O'Hara wouldn't come to you because he didn't know you."

"He didn't know me well enough," Calesian corrected. "We'd seen each other around."

"Who *did* he know?"

Calesian spread his hands. "A dozen people. You think there's a chain of command? There isn't, not really. O'Hara could have gone to any number of people for help. He might even have done it himself, with just his partner, his squad-car partner."

Parker remembered the squad-car partner—a mouse, afraid of himself. "No," he said. "I don't see the two of them doing it on their own."

"Particularly," the attorney, Walters, said, "if O'Hara wound up with so little of the proceeds."

Shevelly said, "Still, the partner could have been in on it. Any chance he's the one did for O'Hara?"

"Not the same man," Calesian said. "I don't remember who the partner was two years ago, but it was a different man this time." With a little grin toward Lozini, he said, "Not one of ours."

Parker said, "Let's look into that other partner, the one from before. He might know what O'Hara did or who he saw."

"I'll find out about him," Calesian said.

Nate Simms, the accountant in the bright colors, said, "Excuse me. May I make a comment?"

Everybody looked at him. Lozini said, "Naturally, Nate. Go ahead."

"I wonder," Simms said, taking his time, getting his phrases exactly the way he wanted them, "I wonder if we're going about this the right way. I wonder if perhaps we aren't rushing forward, when what we ought to do instead is stop a minute and think."

Lozini said, "Go ahead, Nate. What do you mean?" From

the intense way he was watching Simms, it was clear that Lozini respected the man's opinions and judgments, that whatever Simms said would have an effect on Lozini's actions.

"As you know, Al," Simms said, "we have this election coming up in just three days."

"Don't I know it," Lozini said.

"And we also have other problems." Turning to Parker, he said, "In addition to being Al's personal accountant, I take care of a few other areas, and one of my areas is policy. You know, the numbers."

Parker nodded. "I know."

"Policy has never been a major source of income in this city," Simms said, "because we just don't have enough poor people. We're above the national average in family income, and in employment rate. We don't have the large sections of low-income housing that you need if you're really going to run a large-scale policy operation."

"Go ahead, Nate," Lozini said. "Parker doesn't need all that."

"I wanted him to understand," Simms said, "that I'm not running a huge operation there." Back to Parker again, he said, "An accountant is what I am. If policy were big in Tyler, someone else would be in charge."

"I get the point," Parker said.

"So," Simms said, "I can only talk from one small area of interest. But from my area of interest, this is a bad time to get involved in anything that could cause a great deal of trouble and expense and public involvement. Policy is down, it's been down for the last three years and getting worse every year. We don't have the cash reserves we once had, and we don't have as secure a hold on the legitimate side as we once had."

Lozini said, "I already said all that. Trouble coming in from everywhere, and Parker is what made me see it."

"That was good," Simms said. "I don't deny that, Al, the stirring up was a good thing, it made us all aware of problems that had been creeping up on us with nobody paying any attention. What I'm saying is, we don't want—"

The phone rang. Parker, looking at his watch, said, "That's for me."

Lozini gave an angry-ironic hand gesture, inviting Parker to pick up the receiver himself. He said, "Tell him it's okay now, will you?"

Parker answered, saying, "Yes."

"Everything all right?"

"Yes," Parker said. If things had been wrong—a gun to his head, for instance—he would have said *fine*.

"Good," Grofield said.

"This won't take much longer," Parker said. "I'll see you where and when we talked about."

"Right."

Parker hung up, and turned back to Nate Simms. "You were making a point."

"That we can have too much of a good thing," Simms said, "and then it isn't a good thing any more. A little stirring up, that was good, it made us aware. Too much stirring up and the general public is going to get aware, and that isn't good any way at all."

"That's why we're all being friendly together," Lozini said. "Parker and us, all chums. We'll stay nice and quiet from now on, just dealing inside our own organization. Because that's where the trouble is. O'Hara was one of ours, whoever he went to for help was one of ours, and whoever got the money had to be connected with us, one way or another. Had to be."

"I just want us to wait," Simms said. "Wait till after the election, that's only Tuesday, only three days away."

"No," Lozini said. "After the election I could be in worse shape than I am now. I want to know what's happening, I want to know who has to get weeded out." He gestured at Parker. "And why should he wait?"

"I won't," Parker said.

Simms turned a reasonable face to Parker, saying, "Why not? It's to your advantage, too. If we cause too much disruption, we'll have police authorities in here that we can't deal with or work our way around, and you could wind up in as much trouble as the rest of us."

Parker said, "Pressure is the only thing I've got on you people. Lozini wants to do some housecleaning, fine, but he doesn't need me to help. The only way I get my money is if I keep pressure on. I won't call time-out for three days, it doesn't make any sense."

Simms' face screwed up in a combination of disappointment and hard thinking as he worked that out. "I suppose so," he said reluctantly. "I suppose I can see it from your side."

Harold Calesian, smiling in a patronizing way, said, "You did your best, Nate."

Lozini said, "That's right, Nate. What you're saying is smart from a nice calm accountant's point of view. But that's not where we're at. Where we're at is halfway across the rope with no net. This is no place to stop."

Simms shrugged, displaying resignation. "I guess that's the way it's got to be," he said.

Lozini said, "All right. What we're going to do is, Ted and Frank, you're going to take a look at everybody that was in on the amusement-park thing two years ago. Maybe the cop corrupted one of my people, you never know. I want to be sure they're clean, every last one of them."

"Fine," Faran said, and Shevelly said, "When do you want it by?"

"Do it tomorrow," Lozini told him. "I gave you the list of names, you get together with Frank and work it out."

"Okay."

Calesian said, "I'll check into O'Hara's partner, the old one."

Parker told him, "And any other cop O'Hara might have talked to. Anybody he knew that well."

"That's a tall order," Calesian said. "Particularly without anybody noticing what I'm doing. Running a check on one patrolman is easy, I can slip it into routine business, but when you get to ten or fifteen men, it gets noticeable."

"You'll do your best," Lozini told him.

Calesian spread his hands, easy and assured. "Naturally," he said.

Parker said, "That's tomorrow, too, right?"

"It's tough on Sunday," Calesian said. "I'll do what I can, but some of it may have to wait till Monday."

Lozini said, "Why? The cops work seven days a week."

"Not the clerical staff," Calesian said. "The kind of small-time check we're talking about, no urgency, nothing major,

90

that's always done during the week and during regular business hours. For instance, I can't call a bank tomorrow, check on anybody's balance."

Parker said, "Lozini, the simple answer is, you pay me my money now, and get it back when you find the right people. That way, you can wait till after election and I won't be sitting in a room somewhere getting impatient."

"I don't have the money," Lozini told him. "Nate told you; receipts are down. Not just in policy, everywhere. Receipts down, expenses up. This election cost us an arm and a leg, and my man may not even stay in. Listen, I'm just as impatient as you are."

"No, you're not," Parker told him. He looked around and said, "Is there anything else I have to hear?"

Everybody looked at everybody else.

"All right," Parker said. "Lozini, I'll call you tomorrow afternoon."

"Try me at home," Lozini said, and sourly added, "You know the number."

Calesian, rising, said, "I'm finished, too, for now. I'll ride down with you, Parker."

"By God," Lozini said grimly, "we're going to put this together. I don't like the whole feel of this."

As Parker left, he heard Lozini behind him going on in the same vein, with his three lieutenants silently listening and nodding their heads. Walking across the empty receptionist's office with Calesian, Parker listened to Lozini's voice without the words, and there seemed a slight echo in the sound, a touch of hollowness created both by distance and the tone of the man's voice. Lozini sounded more and more like someone blustering to hide his uncertainty.

Parker and Calesian walked down the hall to the elevator. Calesian pushed the button, then turned to say, "You know, just between us, what Nate said wasn't all that stupid."

Parker shrugged.

"There's such a thing as too much pressure," Calesian said. "You have Al where you want him; now might be a good time to ease off a bit. Let him take care of business first, get this election out of the way."

"No."

Calesian looked puzzled. "Why not? What's the problem?"

"Lozini."

"What's wrong with him?"

Parker said, "He's a man who didn't hear the twig snap."

Calesian frowned a second, then said, "Oh. Somebody's coming up behind him?"

"Somebody *came* up."

"You think somebody's going to try a takeover."

Parker gestured a thumb toward Lozini's office. "Isn't that what that was all about?"

Calesian thought about it. "Maybe," he said. "But who?"

"You know the territory better than I do."

The elevator door slid back, showing an empty interior. Grinning at it, Calesian said, "That's a smart boy."

They stepped into the elevator, and started down. Calesian said, "If you're right, you know, that's even more reason to ease up on Al a little. Don't distract him while he's trying to hold his business together."

"This election you've got coming up," Parker said. "I think maybe that's the key. Come Wednesday, Lozini may not be around any more."

Calesian looked troubled, but had nothing to say.

Parker said, "I wouldn't want to start all over again with somebody new."

Seventeen

The two men sat in the back seat of a darkened car on Brower Road, near the baseball field and the amusement park. It was four o'clock Sunday morning, six hours after the meeting in Lozini's office had broken up, and it was almost pitch-dark. The stars were thin and aloof and far away, the thin crescent of moon was like a tiny rip in a black plastic bag showing the sugar inside. There were no houses out in this part of town, no traffic, nobody moving except the driver of the car, strolling back and forth a hundred feet down the road, kicking at stones he could barely see, while the two men in the car, dark faceless mounds to one another, talked things over.

"So Al knows what's happening, does he?"

"Not yet. He knows *something* is happening, but he doesn't know what."

"The money?"

"You mean from Fun Island?"

"No, the money we've been skimming. Is he onto that?"

"No. He still believes it's just that times are slow."

"So what does he know?"

"That he should take a look around. That something isn't kosher."

"And we have these people from out of town to thank, huh?"

"Mostly."

"What's their names?"

"They call themselves Parker and Green."

"What are they like?"

"Green didn't come to the meeting. Parker looks tough."

"What kind of tough? He talks big?"

"He doesn't talk much at all. He just makes you want to step to one side."

"Scare him, buy him off."

"Not the first. And I doubt you could do the second with less than the full seventy-three thousand he came here for."

"I hate to say it, but I think maybe we need the two of them hit."

"Good God. Like O'Hara?"

"That wasn't my idea. He did it on his own and told me later."

"It was a bad thing to do. We've been clean up to now, no killings, no strong-arm. Sooner or later you're going to have to deal with some people at the national level, Jack Fujon in Baltimore, Walter Karns in Los Angeles. They don't have any complaint against Al, and you don't want them to have complaints against you."

"I've already talked to some of them. Don't worry about it, leave them to me. They'll accept the situation the way it is."

"They won't be happy if we start acting like twenties gangsters."

"What do you mean, gangsters? I'm a businessman."

"I mean O'Hara, for one thing."

"I told you that wasn't me. Besides, I understand he wasn't that strong a personality, it might have been possible to lean on him. This Parker sounds like someone who might have been able to get O'Hara to talk."

"He could have been sent away on vacation for a couple of weeks. The point is, we've already had one killing, now you're talking about two more."

"Drifters. Parker and Green, who are they? We do it right, we don't leave bodies, there's no trouble at all. They drifted into town, they drifted out again. No fuss."

"I don't like to hear about this sort of thing."

"You wanted a piece of it."

"I wanted to be on the winning side. I'm not a fool. But if you want somebody killed, don't talk to me about it, that's not what I'm here for."

"Calm down. I wasn't at the meeting, that's all, I haven't met these two guys. I'm asking your opinion, that's all it is."

"My opinion is, don't talk to me about murder."

"All right, all right. Relax."

"I just don't want to hear about it."

"Fine. Fine."

Eighteen

Grofield awoke to excruciating pain, and a sense that the world had shifted on its axis. Why else was the sun down there in that strange position, why else did he have the feeling of being surrounded by the interior parts of an automobile all turned on their side, and why else did he have the impression he was standing up and lying down at the same time?

And why this excruciating pain? His neck twinged, his right shoulder was killing him, his legs ached abominably. And what was that mounded thing between him and the sun? And what was that awful bonging sound?

He closed one eye and squinted the other, the better to see, and suddenly understood that the mounded thing was a naked buttock. A torso was somehow draped across him so that the buttock was over his waist, with the sun rising over it. And from the roundness and the impression of softness—and from his own past history—he presumed the buttock to be female.

And the automobile parts? An automobile, a true complete automobile, on the back seat of which he was more or less lying.

And the horrible bonging sound? Grofield closed his other eye, tight, the better to muffle the sound (which didn't work), and like an optical illusion that suddenly shifts its perspective and becomes a different picture, the horrible bonging transmogrified itself all at once into church bells.

Church bells? The combination of church bells and a girl's naked ass seemed not only incongruous but downright profane. Taken aback, Grofield opened his eyes again, and the behind was still there, rounded pale flesh cloven into two equal melons, sunlight playing on the soft downy blond hair just above the cleavage where her tail would be, if she had a tail. That was actually pretty; the church bells seemed an appropriate accompaniment, after all.

An ass; an entire body. Pale flesh became tanned flesh at the downy hair; a bikini-wearer, apparently. Good hips narrowing to excellent waist, smooth back extending up in the direction of Grofield's head, shoulder blades like the stubby wings of a demoted angel out of focus just below Grofield's nose. Slow, steady, quiet, foreign breathing in Grofield's right ear. And in the opposite direction, out of sight beyond the hills, incredibly heavy legs lay crisscrossed on Grofield's legs, causing one element of the excruciating pain that had awakened him.

Yes; about that pain. Grofield's right arm was away someplace, out of sight and off in some unimaginable position. He tried to move it, experimentally, to ease the grinding in the shoulder, and felt a nipple rub against his palm. The breathing next to him broke rhythm, became a little purring moan, settled back to breathing again, and a nose burrowed more firmly into the side of his neck. The entire female torso became twenty-five pounds heavier.

Who was this, anyway? Rumps are anonymous, and memory had not as yet awakened in Grofield's head.

But even as he thought that, it did, and he remembered everything. Dori Neevin, madam librarian. Three times he had called her last night; at seven to say yes, at seven-ten to say no, and at nine-thirty to say yes again. Infinitely available, she had prepared to come out, had resigned herself to staying in, and had quickly come out when the green light was given.

And then? Dancing to records at a place called Miss Fotheringay's School for Boys and Girls; a joint, where they watered everything but the bar rag. Then to the New York Room, where the bewildered waitress Angie served them and Frankie Faran came over to sit at the table awhile, chat, have a drink and finally tell them everything was on the house. Dori had been impressed out of her mind by all that, and the drive home had detoured a bit. Neither of them had been sober, Dori had been doing some clutching and unzipping about his person while the vehicle was still in motion, and what with one thing and another, Grofield hadn't paid too much attention to where he parked.

Out the window, above Dori's butt, there was nothing to be seen but sky, with a rising sun in it. The church bells went on and on, like the bore in the next seat on a plane. And Grofield was still in pain.

He grunted. He shifted his entire person somehow, and managed to adjust his head less crookedly. Dori complained into his neck, mumblingly. With his left hand he patted her nearer shoulder blade, saying, "Dori? Hello?"

Mumble mumble.

He patted some more, on the middle of her back, and called her name again, to no greater effect. The sunlight looked so warm on her behind that he rested his palm there, and was surprised to find the flesh cool. She squirmed slightly beneath that touch, pleasurably, and he became aware that underneath her he was just as naked as she was.

They both seemed to be moving. His cupped left hand remained where it was, the nipple hardened suddenly against his right palm, and various complex things were happening in a very simple manner.

"Wake up, sweetheart," Grofield murmured, "we seem to be having intercourse."

Her right arm came up to wrap around his head and close off his windpipe, and her hips began to move more strongly. Clutching with both hands, Grofield gave as good as he got, and the breathing in his right ear became very fast and ragged.

Things went along that way for a while, until suddenly the upper part of the torso reared up, Dori's astonished face appeared directly in front of Grofield's eyes, and she cried, in amazement and delight, "Oh!"

"Hello," he said. His right hand was now free; partly to ease the pain in his shoulder, he moved it down and placed it next to his left hand.

Dori was laughing. She put the heels of her hands against his shoulders, pressing him down into the car seat, and remained with her upper torso straight-armed erect; they were now like Siamese twins, joined from the navel downward.

Laughing and at the same time clenching her face muscles in concentration, she proceeded to bear down, doing things she'd never learned in the library.

Grofield lost track of the church bells, and when he could think about them again, they'd stopped. Dori had collapsed onto his chest, her hair in his nose and her lips against the pulse in his throat. "Good morning," he said, and she murmured something contented, and shot bolt upright, her elbow in his neck as she stared in horror out at the day.

"It's tomorrow!"

"Not any more," Grofield said.

"My folks! I—" Abruptly she was scrambling around on top of him like a puppy on ice, giving him careless shots with knee, heel, elbow, and hip. "We've got to— What time is— Where's my— We can't—"

"Oof," he said. "Ow. Easy! Look out!"

She was putting on coral-colored panties, while sitting on his stomach. "We've got to get *home!*" she cried. "Hurry! Hurry!"

"Get off me, dear. I'll do anything you want, if you'll only get off."

"Hurry hurry hurry." Edging off him, she kept slapping his hip to hurry him, at the same time making it impossible for him to get his legs on the same side of the car as his head.

"Damn it," he said. "Ow, I— Will you move that— I'd like to— Aaahhh!" All in one place, he sat up at last and looked around at a graveyard.

Exactly. The church, red brick, was off behind the car, and this was the congregation's burial ground. Flat land symmetrically lined with weathering tombstones, the symmetry broken by an occasional maple tree or line of hedge. At some distance ahead, woods started, stretching off toward low hills. To the right and left, weedy fields separated the graveyard from tracts of small identical houses.

"In the midst of death," Grofield murmured, "we are in life."

The girl, hurrying into her clothing, gave him a distracted look. "What?"

"Nothing. Just a thought."

"Please," she said. She sounded truly terrified. "You aren't even getting dressed."

"Right," he said, and looking around, found a sock. Putting it on, he said, "I'll drive you home." Then he sneezed.

Nineteen

Mike Abadandi drove slowly past the Princess Motel, looking at the pink-stucco walls and the blue-slate roof and the huge free-form sign out front. The sign's neon was burning, but looked washed-out and anemic in the seven A.M. sunlight. None of the dozen cars parked along the front was the bronze Impala.

This was Motel Row, one sprawling low pastel building after another, the monotony broken here and there by a McDonald's or a Kentucky Fried Chicken outlet. Abadandi pulled in at the next motel along, called the Quality Rest, parked in one of the vacant slots near the office, and strolled back toward the Princess. The sun, still low in the eastern sky away to his right, stood just above the neon signs across the road, pale yellow, very bright, in a pale blue cloudless sky; the sky's color ranging from nearly white in the vicinity of the sun to a rich blue above the horizon to the west. The air was very clear, and not yet too warm; in the seventies, with neither wind nor humidity. A great day, a beautiful day. Walking along, Abadandi's mind turned lazily and pleasurably around thoughts of the big above-ground swimming pool he'd put in the backyard two years ago. Swimming, drinking beer, lying in the sun. Invite Andy Marko over; Abadandi just loved to look at Peg Marko in a bikini.

Separating the blacktop of the Quality Rest parking lot from the blacktop of the Princess parking lot was a six-inch strip of cigarette wrappers and weeds. A knee-high railing stretched along the boundary here, made of a horizontal two-by-four laid on vertical two-by-fours driven into the ground, the whole thing painted white. Abadandi stepped over the railing, walked between two parked Chevrolets, paused while a Plymouth Fury drove slowly by toward the exit with an angry-looking couple inside, and headed around to the back of the motel, where most of the units were located in a large two-story horseshoe.

No bronze Impala. Frowning, Abadandi walked around the horseshoe a second time, studying every car in turn, and the Impala just wasn't there.

So what was the story? Were they being cute, keeping their car someplace else? Or maybe they'd known last night that they were being tailed, and they'd come here just long enough to lose the tail, and then left. Or maybe the tail had loused things up and reported the wrong motel name.

Anyway, there was nothing to do now but find a phone and call for instructions. Abadandi headed for the front of the building again, and as he turned the corner out of the horseshoe the bronze Impala drove in.

He was so startled he almost ducked behind the nearest parked car. He did stop in his tracks for a second, but quickly recovered and walked on, giving the Impala no more than a glance as they passed one another.

Only one guy in it. Abadandi walked on around the corner, stopped, looked back, and saw the Impala pull in at an empty slot across the way. It wasn't Parker who got out—Abadandi remembered him from Fun Island two years ago—so it had to be the one called Green. He was yawning and stretching and scratching his waist at the sides as he walked along to the nearest exterior staircase and went up to the balcony-type walk that fronted all the units on the second floor. Abadandi watched him walk past seven doors and stop at the eighth. He fumbled for keys, found one, let himself in, and the closed door became anonymous again.

But where was the other one? Abadandi, suspicious by nature and by necessity, thought things over for a full minute before moving in any direction at all, and then he turned away and headed at a casual stroll for the front of the motel.

It took four minutes to walk through all the public areas of the motel, and to satisfy himself that the second man wasn't outside anywhere. Then he went back to the horseshoe, took stairs up to the second floor across the way from the marks' room, and walked around the three sides of the balcony to the door he wanted. In his right hand were four keys, one of which would definitely unlock it. His left hand hovered near his waist; his shirttail was out, hiding the snub-nosed .32-caliber Iver Johnson Trailsman tucked inside the band of his trousers.

He looked easygoing and unhurried as he walked along, a slightly stocky man of about forty, in gray Hush Puppies and pale blue slacks and a white-and-blue-striped shirt. He looked as though he wasn't paying much attention to anything, but he was watching the blacktop down below and the doors along the balcony, and he was ready to move in any direction at the first sign of trouble.

In fast; he'd done this work before. Palming three of the keys, he poked the fourth one at the lock in the doorknob. When it failed to work, he dropped it after only one try, inserting a second key in the lock before the first one clinked against the concrete. Number two worked; letting the others also fall from his hand, he turned the knob and pushed, while at the same time slipping out the revolver with his left hand, moving quickly into the room.

A darkened room: drapes closed over the windows front and back. Two light sources: the expanding and contracting trapezoid of sunlight from the doorway, lying across an unslept-in double bed strewn with hurriedly removed clothing, and a ribbon of indirect electric lighting from the slightly open bathroom door midway in the right wall. Abadandi closed the door behind himself, swiftly and silently, while registering the sound of a shower running in the bathroom and a tuneless voice raised in song: " 'If I did-int caaaaaare, more than words can saaaaaaay—' "

Abadandi stood with his back to the door, looking around the room. He was right-handed, but he'd trained himself a long time ago to be left-handed with the gun, partly so he'd be able to use it with either hand and partly because most people expected a gun to come from the other side, and any edge at all was a help.

The room was empty, mostly dark, with only the bathroom

light-spill, and obviously only tenanted by one man. Was that the idea? One of them here, one of them somewhere else.

Maybe he should pull back out again, wait for the guy to move, trail him till he made his next meet with his partner.

No. Separate was better. The partner could be found, that wouldn't be any trouble. A bird in the hand.

Abadandi moved forward, his silent shoes doubly silent on the room's wall-to-wall carpeting. He went around the foot of the bed, looking at the sliding doors of the closet to the left, one side open to show empty hangers on the rod and one small suitcase closed on the floor. The mark didn't intend to stay here long.

The air near the bathroom door was increasingly moist and steamy. Abadandi did some rapid blinking, to moisten his contact lenses, and reached his right hand forward till the palm was resting gently against the beaded wet surface of the door. The door opened inward to the right, and the sounds of shower and singing came from the right, behind the door. Abadandi held the gun out in front of himself with his left hand, took a small step closer to the door to brace himself for the rush, and sensed a sudden breeze of movement behind his back.

He turned, looking over his left shoulder, and the guy coming from the closet was already halfway across the room, moving low and fast. Abadandi had a split second to think, *He's looking at my eyes, not at the gun, and that means he's as professional as I am.*

The singing went on in the shower. Abadandi brought the gun around fast, but he'd started too late and there was no way to catch up. The guy dove, flat and low, his right hand going for Abadandi's left wrist, his head and left shoulder thumping into Abadandi's midsection, bouncing him at an angle into the door and the wall.

Abadandi wasn't a fool; he didn't pull the trigger unless the gun was aiming at something useful, and the hand on his wrist was keeping him from bringing the Trailsman around into play. So he forgot the gun, and concentrated on the weapons he still had available: his right hand, his legs, his head. He was trying to knee the guy even before his back hit the door, and though that first impact knocked the breath out of him, he still managed one good rabbit punch on the back of the guy's neck before the guy dropped down and sideways, pressing his side and back against Abadandi to pin him to the wall while turning under his gun arm, trying to come up with that arm bent around backward, trying to lever Abadandi down into a powerless position on the floor.

And the singing had stopped. Abadandi, with everything else going on, took note of that; the singing had stopped the instant his back hit the door, meaning the one in the shower knew something was going on, meaning there would very soon be two of them in the play.

He hit the guy twice on the back of the head with his fist, but it made no difference. The guy was moving under his left arm, twisting the arm forward and down, pressuring Abadandi's shoulder to follow, his body to follow the shoulder. Then the guy was through his turn, was rising again, was next to Abadandi now instead of in front of him, the two of them both facing out from the wall but turned slightly toward one another, and the guy had both hands on Abadandi's wrist, one above the other, pressing forward and down. Abadandi couldn't turn into that pressure, couldn't get at the guy with anything at all, and he felt himself slowly but steadily bending forward.

There wasn't time for this, not with the other one ready to join at any second. Abadandi had been a wrestler and a tumbler in high school, he still did some of the old tumbling routines out by the pool for the enjoyment of his kids, so now he suddenly dropped to the left knee, dipped the left shoulder, the one getting all the pressure, and rolled, somersaulted in a compact ball out toward the middle of the room, at the same time kicking up and back with his left leg, hoping to hit anything at all.

Nothing. But he did break the hold on his wrist, he did free himself. Spinning around on the middle of his back, still in the tight ball, still rolling away from the doorway, he came up on his knees facing the doorway again, his head coming up out of the ball-shape, his eyes staring up and out, seeing the second man naked and astonished in the doorway, and then seeing a dark shape angling toward him, zooming in at him like a jet plane, and he realized it was the other guy's foot, coming up on a trajectory to meet the flow of his own movement. He hadn't pulled himself free, after all; the guy had let him go, had stayed close to him, had followed the arc of his motion, and was right now aiming a kick at a spot in the air where Abadandi's head was about to be.

He tried to stop, stall, alter, drop, lunge, shift, somehow change the movement, but the momentum was on him and the orders to his muscles were too slow, and he thought, *My contact lenses!* and pain struck the right side of his head like a bucket of fire and blotted him out.

Twenty

Parker kicked the guy in the head, stepped to the right, kicked the gun from the slackening fingers across the room, dropped to one knee as the guy landed heavily on his left side, and chopped down hard on his neck with the edge of his hand.

That was enough; maybe more than enough. Parker shoved his shoulder so that he fell out flat on his back, and patted him quickly for more weapons. A .22-caliber Browning Lightweight automatic in a small clamshell holster attached to the inside of his right shin. Nothing else.

"What the hell is that?"

Parker looked up; it was Grofield, in the bathroom doorway, naked and with a cake of soap in his hand. "Either an angry husband," Parker said, "or somebody from the people who got our money."

Grofield came padding forward, dripping on the rug. Frowning at the unconscious man, he said, "No husbands this trip. He came here to kill me, huh?"

"Both of us," Parker said. "He picked you first because he had a make on the car."

"I'm too trusting," Grofield said. He looked at the cake of soap he was holding. "I'll be right back."

"Sure."

Grofield went back to his shower, and Parker went more carefully through the unconscious man's pockets. Crumpled Viceroys in the shirt. Right side trouser pocket a key chain, containing two house keys, a small anonymous key, and ignition and trunk keys for a Chrysler Corporation car. In the same pocket forty-three cents in change. Left pocket a matchbook advertising the New York Room. Left rear pocket five twenty-dollar bills folded separately into thin flat lengths. Right rear pocket the wallet.

Parker carried the wallet over to one of the room's two chairs, lit the table lamp next to it, sat down, and went through every piece of paper the wallet contained.

The guy on the floor was named Michael A. Abadandi. He lived at 157 Edgeworth Avenue. He was a member of the International Brotherhood of Teamsters and the United Brotherhood of Carpenters & Joiners and the American Alliance of Machinists & Skilled Trades. He had credit cards, driver's license, and a bank courtesy identification card, but nothing indicating his employment. He was carrying fifty-seven dollars in the wallet, in addition to the hundred that had been tucked away in the other hip pocket.

The phone was over by the bed. Parker went over there, carrying the wallet, and put a call through to Lozini, at home. The male voice that answered said, "Mr. Lozini isn't up yet."

"Get him up. Tell him it's Parker."

"He left a call for nine."

"You tell him," Parker said, "that I'll be there in thirty minutes."

"But—"

Parker hung up, got to his feet, and started over to Abadandi as Grofield came back out of the bathroom, one white towel wrapped around his waist as he scrubbed his hair with another. Parker said to him, "We're going to Lozini's."

Grofield stopped drying his hair, but left the towel draped around his head, so that he looked like a sheik's younger son. "Both of us?" Nodding at the man on the floor, he said, "You think Lozini did that?"

"No. This is the other side. But they're using Lozini's people."

"It said so in his wallet?"

"He was in the amusement park two years ago," Parker said. "I recognized him."

Grofield went to the closet to get the suitcase. Putting it on the bed, he said, "Good thing you did. But where was he?"

"Outside." Parker nodded at the room next door, saying, "I was in my place, I looked out the window to see if the car was back, and I saw him doing a circuit down there, looking things over."

"Somebody followed us last night." Grofield was stepping into his clothes.

"He was just giving up when you came in. He watched where you went, and then he faded away for a while. So I let myself in over here, and watched out the window till he came back."

"All the time I was in the shower? Why not tell me something?"

"What point? You're tired and naked and wet, and I can handle it."

Grofield went back to the closet for his shoes. Putting them on, he looked at Abadandi and said, frowning, "He's bleeding."

"Put a towel under him. We don't want marks on the rug."

Getting one of his white towels, Grofield knelt next to Abadandi and lifted the man's head to put the towel underneath. The blood trickling down the side of his face and around his ear into his hair was a slender dark red ribbon. Grofield, leaning close, said, "Jesus, Parker."

"What's the matter?"

"It's his eye."

Parker went over and stood watching while Grofield thumbed back the man's other eyelid. The eye stared upward wetly, without expression, and Grofield gently touched a fingertip to the pupil, then let the lid close again; it did so slowly, like a rusted gate.

"Contact lens," Grofield said. He moved slightly to the side, so Parker could see the blood seeping from Abadandi's other eyelid: thin, unceasing, with a slight pulsing effect in it. "The other one's back in his head someplace," Grofield said.

Parker went down on one knee, and twisted Abadandi's cheek. The flesh was cold, doughlike. There was no reaction to the pinch. "Damn," Parker said.

"He's in shock," Grofield said.

"I wanted him to talk to us," Parker said.

"Not today. Maybe not ever."

"He doesn't die here," Parker said. "You ready?"

"Sure."

"We need tape, some kind of tape."

"Electric tape?"

"Anything."

Grofield went to his suitcase, and came back with a roll of glossy-backed electric tape, half-inch width. Parker ripped two two-inch lengths of it, and taped Abadandi's right eyelid down. The eye felt strange beneath the thin skin. Parker wiped the blood away from the side of the face, and waited. No more blood seeped out from under the tape, which looked like a small neat black eyepatch. "Good," Parker said. He rolled up the towel, bloody side in, and gave it to Grofield. "Stash that."

"Right."

Standing, Parker said, "We'll walk him to the car, leave him somewhere."

Grofield closed his suitcase and put it away again. Then they picked up Abadandi's awkward weight between them, lifting him by the armpits, putting his arms over their shoulders. From a distance, he could be a drunk being helped along by his friends.

They went out to the balcony. Two maids were talking in an open doorway halfway around the horseshoe, but nobody else was visible. They carried Abadandi along the balcony, his feet dragging, and maneuvered him awkwardly down the stairs. Two disapproving middle-aged women in their Sunday finery, purses hanging from their forearms, waited at the bottom of the steps, and glared impartially at all three men as they went by, before clicking huffily up, nattering to one another.

They put him in the back seat of the Impala and drove away from the motel, Parker at the wheel and Grofield occasionally glancing back at Abadandi. After several blocks, Grofield said, in a troubled and unhappy way, "Goddamnit."

"What's the matter?"

"Now he's bleeding from the ear."

"Put some paper in it."

Grofield opened the glove compartment. "Nothing there."

"Turn his head then. We'll unload him in a couple minutes."

Grofield adjusted Abadandi's head. Parker drove away from the city, looking for a turnoff that might lead to privacy. They were going to be late to Lozini's, but there wasn't any help for it. Sunday morning traffic was light and mostly slow-moving; family groups.

"I feel sorry for the bastard," Grofield said.

Parker glanced at him, and looked back at the road. "If I'd slept late this morning," he said, "he could be feeling sorry for you by now."

"An hour ago I was getting laid back there," Grofield said. "Jesus, his skin looks bad."

Parker kept driving.

Twenty-one

Lozini was out by the pool, still on his first cup of coffee. He had dressed in paint-stained work pants and an old white shirt and brown loafers, and he was wearing sunglasses against the morning glare. He felt unwell and uncomfortable, and it was only partly because he'd had too little sleep. The rest was nerves, the accumulating tension and unease and a sense of helplessness that he wasn't used to. He'd lived a life of dealing with his enemies, directly and efficiently, and winning out over them. Now he had a sense of enemies he couldn't find, couldn't deal with, wasn't winning over.

And what had happened now? Parker was late by almost a quarter of an hour, and Lozini wanted to know what the new problem was. His nerves weren't getting any better sitting here.

Movement over by the house. Lozini shifted in his chair, and put the coffee cup back on the glass-topped table. Parker and Green both came out into the sunlight, followed by the houseman, Harold. Lozini waved to Harold to go back inside, and Parker and Green came on alone.

Lozini didn't stand. He gestured to the empty chairs at the table, and as they were seating themselves he said, "Harold ask you if you want coffee?"

Parker said, "Michael Abadandi works for you."

Lozini frowned. "That's right."

"He came to our motel this morning, to make a hit."

"On you?" But that was a stupid question, and Lozini knew Parker wouldn't answer it.

He didn't. "You didn't send him," he said.

"Christ, no."

Parker said, "Lozini, if you've got the digestion for that coffee, you're a tough man."

"I don't," Lozini said.

"You're falling off a cliff," Parker said.

"I know that. Don't talk about it."

"I have a point to make."

"I know the shape I'm in. Make your point."

"In all this city, there are only two people you can trust."

Lozini looked at him. Green, silent, was sitting there next to Parker, with his arms folded, squinting slightly in the sunlight and looking much more serious than when he'd had his little chat with Frankie Faran. Lozini looked from Green back to Parker and said, "You two?"

"How did Abadandi find us? He was told where we were staying. How did anybody know where we were staying? We were followed after I left your meeting last night. How could we be followed? Because somebody who knew about the meeting put somebody outside to follow us. Who knew about the meeting? Only the people you trust."

"All right," Lozini said.

"You've got a palace takeover on your hands," Parker told him. "That means a group, maybe four or five, maybe a dozen. A group of people inside your own organization that want you out and somebody else in. Somebody who's already up close to the top, that they want to take your place."

Lozini took his sunglasses off and massaged his closed eyes with thumb and forefinger. His eyes still closed, he said, "For the first time in my life I know what getting old is. It's wanting to be able to call for a time-out." He put the sunglasses back on and studied them both. Their faces were closed to him, and always would be. "You're right," he said. "You're the only ones I can trust, because I know exactly where you stand and what you want."

Neither of them said anything. Lozini looked around at the California pool and the New England house and the Midwest sunshine and said, "I built this by being fast and smart. All of a sudden I look at myself and I've been coasting, I don't even know for how long. Five years? No; I was still fast and smart when I was after you in that amusement park two years ago."

Parker nodded. "You are different now," he said.

Lozini made a fist, and rested it on the table next to the coffee. "It didn't take them long, did it? I start to coast, and right away somebody's climbing up my back. They can smell it, the bastards. 'Lozini's getting old, time to make my play.' " He thumped the fist softly on the table. "If only I knew which of them it was, if only I had that much satisfaction."

Parker said, "One of them at the meeting?"

"No." Lozini opened the fist and pressed his palm on the table top, splaying the fingers out. Squinting through his sunglasses at the pool, thinking about his people, he said, "Some of them are in it, probably, but not running it. They don't have the strength you need."

"Shevelly? He's your second-in-command, isn't he?"

"Ted's years from being ready to take over. If he ever could at all, and I don't think so. Nobody'd follow Ted, that's the point. It's got to be somebody that the others would follow."

"You know your people," Parker said. "Who's got the strength?"

Lozini had already been thinking about that, despite himself. "There's only three men," he said, "that could organize it, could get enough people to go into it, and could get acceptance from people like your friend Karns."

"Who are they?"

"Ernie Dulare. Dutch Buenadella. Frank—"

Green broke in, saying, "Oh. Is that how you pronounce it? Dew-lah-ree. I thought it was Dew-lair."

Lozini frowned at him. "You met Ernie?"

"No, I just read about him in the paper." To Parker, he said, "Dulare operates the local horserooms. And Louis 'Dutch' Buenadella is our pornography king. The movie houses, the bookstores, and at least one mail-order business."

Startled out of his funk, Lozini said, "You know my operation pretty good."

With a modest smile, Green said, "I'm the research girl."

Parker said, "Who's this Frank? Not Frank Faran."

Lozini nodded to Green. "You know that part, too?"

"I suppose that's Frank Schroder," Green said. "The narcotics man."

"Jesus Christ," Lozini said softly. "You want to tell me which one it is?"

"Well, I've never met them," Green said, "but I doubt it's Schroder."

"Why?"

"He's a little old to take over, to begin with."

"He's five years younger than me."

Green spread his hands, and offered an apologetic smile. "Not old to be running things," he said, "but maybe too old to *start* running things. I don't see him getting enough support. Besides, there's a rumor he's been eating his own candy."

"That isn't true."

"Of course it's true. Even I've heard it."

"That doesn't mean it's true."

"Oh." Green made an erasing gesture with the palm of his hand. "I don't care if the rumor itself is true or not," he said. "My point is, it's true that there is such a rumor, and a rumor like that will keep support away from a man."

Lozini nodded, accepting it. "All right," he said. "Frank's the least likely."

Parker said, "Leaving the other two. Dulare and Buenadella."

"Right." Lozini looked at Green. "Any ideas?"

"Sorry. They're both the right age, they're both strong, they've both got good power bases inside your structure already, they've both got the right sort of connections outside town. You know them; which of them is the most greedy?"

"Both of them," Lozini said.

Parker said, "Give us their addresses."

"You're going to go fight my battle for me?"

"No. Whether you make it or not is up to you. But two years ago, whoever O'Hara talked to about the money in the amusement park was somebody already plugged in with this revolution you've got going on."

"It was set up that long ago?" Bewildered, Lozini tried to remember indications that far back, hints that he should have picked up but had somehow missed.

"They've been waiting for this election," Parker said. "That's what's going to finish you off."

"It is, too," Lozini said.

Green said, "Everybody else in this country has their elections in November. What's with you people, that you have to be different?"

"We made that change on purpose, years ago," Lozini said. "People do things by habit. Run the election in an off-year, or in an off-time, you get a lower turnout, you can control the result easier. Only this time it's working against me."

"And my money," Parker said, "went to either Dulare or Buenadella, whichever one is doing this, to help finance the rebellion. So that's where we go to get it back."

Lozini looked at him with something like awe. "Good Christ but you're single-minded," he said.

"I came here for my money," Parker said. "Not a gang war."

"So you'll go to both Ernie and Dutch? How do you figure out which one it is?"

"We'll find out before we go. We'll ask one of the people that went over to him."

"Abadandi?"

"He can't talk right now," Parker said. "Give me Calesian's address."

"Calesian? Why him?"

"Nobody's going to make a move against you," Parker said, "without having your top cop in their pocket. Calesian's smart enough to know you're on your way out."

"That son of a bitch."

Parker said, "What about Farrell?"

Lozini and Green both looked at him in surprise. Lozini said, "Who?"

"Your mayor," Parker said. "You sure he's on the way out? Maybe he went over, too."

"Farrell isn't my mayor," Lozini said.

Green said, "Wain is the mayor. Farrell's the reform candidate running against him."

Parker frowned at them both, and said to Lozini, "You always kept saying 'my man.' I figured that was Farrell." To Green, he said, "Why the hell didn't you tell me?"

116

"Tell you what?" Green was obviously as bewildered as Lozini.

Lozini said, "What difference does it make? Alfred Wain is my man, and he's on the way out. George Farrell is the reform man, and he's on the way in."

Parker said, "Farrell is the one with the big banner across London Avenue. Posters all over the place."

"That's right," Lozini said. "We haven't been spending that way. Money's been tighter for us the last couple of years, I already told you that. Receipts are down everywhere, you heard that from Nate Simms last night. Besides, we never had to spend that much. Farrell's working in a different league."

"I should have made sure," Parker said. He seemed to be talking mostly to himself. Frowning toward the pool, he said, "It's my mistake, I shouldn't have taken it for granted."

Lozini said, "I still don't get you."

"Your receipts aren't down," Parker told him. "They're skimming off the top. Farrell is *their* man."

Green said, in a small voice, "Oh."

The whole thing opened all at once for Lozini like a sunflower. "Those dirty bastards. They've been financing Farrell with my money."

"And mine," Parker said. To Green, he said, "So we by-pass Calesian, we go to Farrell."

"Right."

Parker got to his feet. "Retire, Lozini," he said. "Go to Florida and play shuffleboard."

Lozini watched the two of them walk through the sunlight and into the darkness of the house. Shuffleboard. Calesian. Abadandi. Ernie Dulare or Dutch Buenadella. Farrell. With *his* money.

Lozini got to his feet. Aloud he said, "I haven't fired a gun in twenty-seven years." His voice was absorbed into the water of the pool: flat, no echo. He walked around the pool and on into the house.

Twenty-two

Paul Dunstan got up at nine, a little earlier than usual for a Sunday. A couple of the guys from the shop were coming around to pick him up at ten to spend the day out at the beach. He got up early enough to have time to spare, padded around his three-room apartment taking care of minor clean-up details, and generally coasted the hour away. It was a relaxed and pleasant interval, spoiled only briefly when he glanced at the table by the front door and saw the retirement check there, still in its envelope. It had come yesterday, and he'd cash it tomorrow.

He hated those checks; they were his only reminder of his years on the police force in Tyler, three hundred miles from here. He'd thrown one away once, but that was even worse; a barrage of letters from the office of the Tyler City Clerk, wanting to know if he'd received the check, what had he done with it, when would he cash it. One reminder a month was bad enough, so now he cashed the check each month when it came in, pocketed the seven dollars and tried to think no more about it.

Dunstan was twenty-nine years old, and seven dollars a month was the pension his four years on the Tyler police force had entitled him to, an entitlement he'd rather have done without. He had a new job now, a new life in a new city, and all he wanted was for the past to stay quietly and permanently in the past.

At one time he had thought he would spend his entire lifetime in police work, even though he'd mostly just drifted into it. The Army had made him an MP during his three-year enlistment, after first training him as a refrigeration engineer, the field of his choice. After the Army he'd had a number of unsatisfying jobs before going with the Tyler force, and had found police work congenial and easy. Most of the time. And profitable, too, in a smallish way.

He and Joe O'Hara had been radio car partners for over two years when the mess happened at the Fun Island Amusement Park. Before then, Dunstan had been in on the take in a minor way, not called upon to actually do anything other than close his eyes from time to time, but the mess at the amusement park had changed all that. He'd been in on attempted murder, he'd seen people killed, he'd wound up with the robber holding him captive at gunpoint, and when it was all over, he'd had it. Not because O'Hara had been so enraged at him, full of yelled charges of cowardice; that had been nothing but O'Hara blustering away his own fear and incompetence. And not because of the cold contempt he had seen in that old man Lozini's eyes; what did he care about the contempt of a creature like Lozini? It was his own attitude toward himself that had made the change. He had suddenly known he couldn't live that way any more, a living contradiction, straddling the fence of the law, a hypocrite in every breath he took.

So he'd quit the force, and moved away from the city of Tyler completely, and had found a job here with a firm that maintained central air-conditioning units in office buildings, the kind of work the Army had originally trained him for. He had a good job, good friends, a good life, a few girl friends in the last couple of years. If it weren't for the absurdity of the seven-dollar-a-month pension check, he wouldn't ever have to think about Tyler again.

What could he do about the checks? Nothing. Move, leaving no forwarding address? Almost impossible in this organized world, not without disrupting his life entirely. It was easier, finally, just to cash the check each month, spend the seven dollars, try not to think about it.

At nine-forty he went and got dressed. He wrapped his bathing suit in a towel, and was just putting the rolled towel on the table by the front door, next to the pension check, when the apartment doorbell rang. He frowned at his watch: ten to ten.

Harry was never early. He pulled open the door, and it wasn't Harry at all. It was a smiling self-assured guy holding a paper bag in front of himself, holding it by the bottom with just one hand. "Paul Dunstan?" he said.

It was a vaguely familiar face. Was he really somebody from Tyler, or was it just that Dunstan had been looking at the pension check that made him think this guy had something to do with that city? He said, "Yes?"

"I'm sorry about this," the guy said, smiling, sounding truly sorry about it, "but I don't know how much O'Hara told you." And he reached into the paper bag.

Dunstan's reactions were slower than when he'd been on the force. He didn't move until the gun with the silencer screwed on the end of it started coming out of the paper bag, and by then it was too late.

Twenty-three

"First-rate sermon, Reverend," George Farrell said.

The minister's noncommittal face suggested he knew he was being used. "I'm glad you liked it, Mr. Farrell," he said.

Farrell kept pumping the man's hand, holding it in both of his so the minister couldn't make a premature withdrawal. Out of the corner of his eye, Farrell watched Jack, standing unobtrusively to one side; Jack would give him the high sign when the photographers and cameramen were finished, and then he would let go of the minister's hand.

Farrell made a lovely all-American picture there in the sunlight, and he knew it. Tall, heavy-set, with a banker's stockiness and an actor's profile and a doctor's professional intimacy, he *belonged* on that church step, shaking hands with that black-garbed white-haired man of God. Four news photographers and the camera crews of two local television stations were fixing the scene indelibly, to be shown to the voters between now and Tuesday. Compare *this* image, voters, with any photograph you choose of Alfred Wain, with his overly large nose and the deep bags under his eyes and his general hangdog air of being the owner of a warehouse full of dubious cargo.

Over to the side, Jack lifted a hand to his medium-long hair, brushing it back. Farrell, smiling a manly smile, said, "Keep up the good work, Reverend," and released the minister's hand.

"You too, Mr. Farrell," the minister said, with no expression at all in face or voice.

And to hell with you, Mac, Farrell thought. Smiling, he turned away, automatically reaching to take Eleanor's elbow. She was there, of course, right where she should be, the perfect complement: tall, ash-blond, competent-looking, attractive without seeming oversexed, with just the slightest touch of apple-pie plumpness about her. Where would a public man be without this wife?

The two of them went down the church steps together, Farrell waving broadly to the curious crowd; mostly churchgoers, attracted by the television equipment, who had stayed because they recognized their mayoral candidate. Sudden spontaneous applause broke out among them, true spontaneous applause, and for just a second Farrell was so startled he almost broke stride. Then he moved on, feeling a great wave of emotion well up within him. They truly liked him, the people really and truly liked him.

The limo was at the curb, and Jack was already there to hold the door open and the citizens at bay. Eleanor got in first, and Farrell after her. Jack shut the door, slid in front next to the driver, and they were off, followed by the unmarked police car with its two plainclothes bodyguards.

"Well," Eleanor said. "So much for that."

Farrell stretched his feet out on the gray carpeting. The limousine had been contributed for the duration of the campaign by a local automobile dealer, and its normal role as a rental vehicle was revealed by the pair of folded bucket seats tucked up against the front-seat back. Farrell opened one of these now and put his feet on it. He felt physically content, and still pleased at that applause. Spending months manipulating emotional reactions, it came as a shock and a delight to be liked without inducement.

Eleanor had taken out her large notebook and was studying it. "Coffee with the volunteers at headquarters," she said.

He nodded; nice kids, the volunteers. Though they bewildered him at times. He'd look at them, see their intense shining eyes staring back at him, and he'd wonder just who in the name of God they thought he was. Well, it didn't matter, did it? You couldn't buy for all the money in the world the work they did for free, out of whatever noble misconception it was that drove them.

Eleanor was closing the notebook, but Farrell said, "What's after that?"

She opened it again. Technically, an old pol named Sorenberg was Farrell's campaign manager, but it was strictly an honorary position, a part of the fence-mending Farrell had had to do early on. Eleanor was his campaign manager, she had the whole structure in her mind and every detail in her notebooks. "Visit the swimming pool at Memorial Park," she said. "Little League game at Veteran's Field. Dinner and speech to the teachers' union. Dinner and speech to the Urban League."

"Enough," Farrell said. "Enough." He had already had breakfast with the Knights of Columbus and listened to a morning concert of the Methodist Youth Federation glee club. Tuesday couldn't get here fast enough.

Eleanor gave him a thin smile—understanding and sympathy, but with some reserve. She had been opposed to his getting involved in all of this in the first place, though she would never be difficult about it. Eleanor was a smart and capable woman, too sure of herself to be difficult. *My best investment,* Farrell said of her at times; it was supposed to be a joke, but it was also more than that.

George Farrell was forty-three, president of the Avondale Furniture Company, tables and chairs, a family-owned business that had been started by Farrell's great-grandfather in 1868; returning Civil War veterans were getting married, furnishing new homes. Farrell had been a part of the family business since he'd graduated from Northwestern University, but he had never taken a great interest in the running of the concern, nor had he ever put himself in a position of real authority or control. He was a figurehead president, the different divisions of the company all being run by competent professionals, and he was content to leave it that way; he had enough to do so he didn't feel like a useless sponge, but not so much that he felt overburdened.

When, a few years ago, he'd been asked by some local pols to run for the City Council, Farrell had accepted at once, only later pausing to wonder why he'd wanted the job. Partly, of course, it had been his pleasure at being asked. But also there was a certain boredom that had been coming over him the last few years, a boredom caused by his general remoteness from his livelihood, by the casual irrelevance of his working day. Would the City Council be a cure for that?

It would. Farrell loved politics, every bit of it. He loved the maneuvering, he loved the deals and the sense of being an insider, the almost frightening feeling of being in a house of cards constructed of winks and nods and handshakes, and he also loved the occasional feeling of accomplishment, the knowledge of a job well done, the people's trust justified, a valuable task competently completed.

He was also a realist. He knew that the workings of Tyler, of any city, required accommodations with men you would never invite into your own home. Men like Adolf Lozini, for instance; a crook, no better than a mobster, with his hand in every unsavory operation in town. But necessary, because crime and vice would go on existing no matter what, and it was important that some sort of control be laid over the cesspool. Lozini, half murderer and half businessman, was that control.

Or had been. But Lozini was getting old, he was losing his competence, and a better man would be taking his place. Better in many ways; not only better at controlling the criminal element, but also better in his attitudes toward the city and toward his fellow-men. Lozini's replacement was a man Farrell could get along with, could understand and even sympathize with—could almost invite to the house.

The removal of Lozini would mean, naturally, the removal of Alfred Wain, who was Lozini's puppet in the mayor's chair. The job had been offered to Farrell, and he knew at once that he would be no puppet, that he could work within the system and still be a much more effective mayor than Wain had ever been. In one sense, his public posture as a reform candidate was a mockery, since he was supported by criminal funds just as much as Wain had ever been. Yet in another way, Farrell told himself that he truly *was* a reformer, in comparison with Wain; under himself, Tyler would be a much better, a much cleaner, a much less corrupt city.

The limo was coming to a stop, at the main entrance of the Carlton-Shepard, Tyler's only first-class hotel. The maroon-uniformed doorman opened the car doors and they all got out, to no reception at all. The few people in the vicinity were all hotel guests, out-of-towners who wouldn't recognize Farrell or care about who he was, well-off people who wouldn't be distracted from their own concerns by the appearance of a chauffeured limousine.

The Carlton-Shepard lobby was cool and spacious. The giant cabbage roses in the carpet design were spaced so that Farrell's stride matched them exactly; he amused himself by stepping from the center of one rose to the center of the next, all the way across the lobby to the elevator that was being held for him. His campaign headquarters was the entire seventh floor, a lavish expenditure in local terms, but necessary as a public display of his big-league aspirations. It had been important at first to demonstrate that he wasn't merely another one of those well-meaning amateurs, those ministers and teachers and other bumblers that the opposition had routinely been mounting against Wain over the years.

Five of them entered the elevator now, with the maroon-uniformed operator: Farrell, Eleanor, Jack, and the two plainclothesmen. They started up, everybody remaining silent in the slightly uncomfortable proximity, and when the elevator stopped, the indicator light over the door read 5.

The operator himself seemed confused. He moved his control bar back and forth twice, then frowned up at that lit number 5. One of the plainclothesmen said, "What are you stopping for?"

"I didn't," the operator said, and at the same time somebody knocked on the door. The operator looked around at the plainclothesmen and said, "Should I open it?"

They didn't seem to know. Farrell found himself suddenly frightened—an assassination? That happened to national figures, not local ones. Who would assassinate him?

Lozini. What if Lozini had found out somehow, if he'd decided to fight back by eliminating Wain's competition before weeding his own garden?

One of the plainclothesmen said, "Yeah, open it." Neither of them had a gun in sight, but they both had their hands back on their rumps, their jackets pushed back out of the way.

There was a gate to open, and then a gold-painted door, and the fifth-floor hall was revealed, with two men standing in it.

One of them nodded to the plainclothesmen, saying, "That's okay, Toomey, Calesian sent us."

The plainclothesmen relaxed, and so did Farrell. So they were police. When he'd first seen them, with their general aura of toughness, he'd thought they were Lozini's men for sure.

One of the plainclothesmen said, "What's up?"

"Trouble on seven," one of the new men said. "A threat against Mr. Farrell's life. We're supposed to take him up a different way. The rest of you people proceed. There's no threat against anybody else. Mr. Farrell?"

The man wanted him to leave the elevator. Farrell hesitated, unsure what to do. The plainclothesman beside him said to the new men, "We'll come with you."

"Calesian wants the rest of you to stay in a body," the new man said. "To cover us when we take Mr. Farrell up the other way."

"We're supposed to stay with him," the plainclothesman said.

"You've got the candidate's wife there."

The other new man said, "Let's not hang around here and be targets."

The plainclothesman said, "I don't think I recognize you."

"Come on, Toomey." The new man took a worn leather wallet from his pocket, flipped it open, held it open with both hands for the plainclothesman to see. "You've seen me around," he said.

The plainclothesman—Toomey—nodded doubtfully, but still seemed reluctant. "Our orders are to stay with Mr. Farrell," he said.

"Fuck," the new man said, sounding disgusted, and took a gun out from under his jacket. Everybody in the elevator tensed, moving involuntarily backward, and the man said, "Hands on heads. Fast."

The plainclothesmen had relaxed sufficiently before this to no longer have their hands anywhere near their own guns. Farrell, who immediately placed his own hands atop his head, saw the plainclothesmen hesitate, saw the second man out there also draw a gun, and saw the plainclothesmen angrily realize there was nothing they could do but obey.

126

"You too," the new man said to the elevator operator, who had been merely staring open-mouthed at everything that was happening. The operator at once put his hands straight up in the air.

The first man gestured with his gun at Farrell. "Come out here," he said.

"D-don't kill me," Farrell said. He was terrified, but he tried to speak calmly, rationally, tried not to blubber. "There's no reason to, I'm not—"

"Shut up, you horse's ass. If I wanted to kill you, you'd be dead now. I want to talk to you." To his friend, he said, "Hold them. I'll make it fast."

"Too bad we couldn't do it the other way."

"It'll work out." He glared at Farrell; he was very angry that his scheme hadn't worked. "Get the hell out here, I said."

Farrell moved jerkily forward. It was true, they weren't going to kill him. Unless something went wrong. But what did they want?

"Put your arms down. Walk easy. Down to the right there."

Farrell obeyed, leaving the elevator behind, walking along the empty hallway, sensing the man coming along behind him. They reached a stairwell door, with its red light glowing above it, and the man said, "In there."

Farrell opened the door, stepped through into the gray-metal stairwell. He stood on the landing, not knowing whether he was supposed to go up or down the stairs, and the man came through the doorway behind him, shut the door, touched his arm to turn him around, and punched him very hard in the stomach, just below the belt.

Farrell bent over, falling backward against the wall, his forearms folding over the sudden flowering pain in his stomach. The pain seemed to rush out like rips in a stocking—lancing up through his chest into his throat, down into his genitals, down his legs to make a tingling weakness in the back of his knees. The breath had whooshed out of him when he was hit, and he opened his mouth wide, trying to replace the lost air, but his throat seemed to be closed, air scraped in slowly and painfully.

The man stood waiting for him, his expression cold and grim, clinical, detached. Farrell struggled to breathe, swallowed down a feeling of nausea, waited out the pain. Gradually his lungs filled with air again, the turmoil in his stomach settled, the pain eased, he could straighten himself. Blinking, mouth open, he stared at the man, wondering what he would do next, why this was happening.

The man said, "I wanted you to know I'm serious. Do you know it now?"

"Yes." Farrell's throat was raspy, it hurt a bit when he talked.

"Good. Who's financing you?"

Farrell couldn't begin to understand the question. "I don't—" He coughed, which also hurt, and pressed a hand to his throat. "What?"

"One of Adolf Lozini's sidemen is financing you," the man said. "Which one is it?"

Scandal: that was the first thought that came to Farrell's mind; this was some sort of insane reporter or scandalmonger, out to verify a rumor he'd heard somewhere. The unlikelihood of a reporter holding people up with a gun or asking his questions with his fists didn't occur to him until later. It was thinking in terms of a reporter, in terms of scandal, that he answered, saying, "No, you're wrong about that."

The gun was in the man's left hand. He lifted it, chopped the barrel down on the top of Farrell's right shoulder. Farrell screamed at the sudden pain, the sound echoing in the stairwell. The man clapped his free hand over Farrell's mouth, bouncing his head back against the wall, holding him there till the echoes died, while Farrell clutched at his burning shoulder. He felt his jaw trembling, knew the man could feel it in the hand pressed against his mouth, and felt angry and ashamed of himself for displaying weakness.

The man released him and stepped back. "I don't want to waste time," he said. "I'm in a hurry. I know where you're getting your financing. I know which of Lozini's people it could be and which ones it couldn't. I've got it narrowed down to just a few. Now you tell me which one it is or I'll break you apart in here and go ask somebody else."

He knows, Farrell thought. He's narrowed it, but he doesn't know which one. Could I lie, give him a false name? Which ones has he narrowed it to? What if I told him it was Frank Faran, from the nightclub?

"If you lie," the man said, "I'll come back and kill you. And I'll get to you just as easy as I did this time."

Farrell trembled all over his body. His mind skittered back and forth, torn by fear and the need to work out too many complexities. How could he dare to tell this man the truth? Of course he could deny it later, but still . . .

The man's hand drew back, closing into a fist.

"Buenadella!" Farrell shouted. "Louis Buenadella!"

Twenty-four

Harold Calesian stepped from the plane at Tyler National Airport just before one o'clock. The sun beat down from a cloudless sky, and not a breath of wind moved anywhere in the flat expanse of land all around the airport. Calesian walked through the heat to his dark green Buick Le Sabre, unlocked the door, and put his attaché case on the back seat. The interior of the car was an oven, from sitting here in this shadeless spot since before eight o'clock this morning, but the air-conditioning cooled the air by the time the car reached the highway.

Calesian was separated but not divorced, his wife and three daughters remaining in the family home in the suburb of Northglen while Calesian had a four-and-a-half-room apartment in an urban renewal section near downtown. The whole down-town section was between the airport and his home, so it was faster to take the Belt Highway around and wind up coming to the apartment from the opposite direction.

The building had tenant parking in the basement. Calesian drove in, took the attaché case from the back seat, locked up the car, and rode the elevator up to his top-floor apartment nine stories up. His terrace had a view toward downtown—dull by day, but interesting with neon by night. He unlocked his front door and entered an apartment that was a lot warmer and stuffier than it should have been. Frowning, he closed the door behind himself, and still carrying the attaché case, went from the foyer into the living room. Was something wrong with the air-conditioning?

No. The double doors to the terrace were standing open, letting in more heat than the air-conditioning could handle. Walking across the large room to close the doors again, he tried to remember the last time he'd gone out there. Not this morning, certainly; he'd left the apartment first thing this morning, in order to catch that eight A.M. plane. Hadn't the doors been closed then? But maybe they hadn't been latched properly, and a breeze had opened them.

What breeze?

Calesian paused midway across the room, and looked around. A professional decorator from Aldenberg's Department Store had done the apartment for him, the living room in blues and grays with chrome accents, low but heavy pieces, modern yet masculine. Nothing looked different, nothing out of place. That feeling of tension in the air was surely no more than the unexpected heat from outside; he was used to this room maintaining a cool dry atmosphere.

There might have been a morning breeze that opened the doors. There was no reason for anything to be wrong, so it followed that there was nothing wrong. Nevertheless, Calesian gripped the attaché case more firmly as he moved the rest of the way across the room and started to close one of the terrace doors.

Al Lozini was outside there, leaning on the rail facing the doorway, eyes squinting slightly in the sunlight. "Hello, Harold," he said.

Startled, Calesian didn't say or do anything for just a second. Lozini's behavior was as strange as the fact of his presence here; he wasn't being tough or hurried or showing any of his normal feistiness. Instead he was just sitting there, one leg swinging slightly while the other supported him on the wrought-iron railing. His manner was calm, emotionless. The harsh sunlight showed his age clearly in his face, but picked out no emotion there.

Lozini said, "Come on out in the sun. Good for you."

Calesian stepped through the doorway, cautious and uncertain. He still held the attaché case. He said, "You surprised me, Al."

"I was a burglar when I was a boy," Lozini said. "That lock

of yours is butter. I could back up a truck and strip every television set out of this building in forty-five minutes."

Calesian had a receding forehead, his black hair thinning badly on top, so that he felt the sun at once. He frowned as much because of that as because of the strangeness of Lozini. "I guess some things we never forget," he said. "Like getting through locks."

"Some things you do forget," Lozini told him. "Like not trusting anybody."

"I don't follow," Calesian said, while thinking, *He's on to us.*

"Sit down, Harold," Lozini said, and nodded at the chaise longue to Calesian's left.

Calesian hesitated. It entered his mind that with one fast step forward, one shove with both hands, he could topple Lozini over the railing. Nine stories straight down to cement sidewalk.

But there'd be no way to answer the questions that would follow such a death, to protect himself against the investigation. And there would definitely be an investigation; not even Calesian swung enough weight in the Police Department to stifle an inquiry into a death like that. Particularly not with the body right in front of his own building.

And even while he was thinking those things, it seemed to him he saw the thoughts echoed in Lozini's eyes; as though Lozini had known it would occur to him he might push, and had further known he would realize it was too dangerous to push.

"Go ahead, Harold. Sit down."

Calesian sat sideways on the chaise longue, keeping both feet on the floor. He put the attaché case on his lap, rested his forearms on the case. He tried to be as casual and unemotional as Lozini. "I guess you want to talk to me about something," he said.

Lozini was silent. He considered Calesian as though trying to decide whether or not to buy him. Calesian waited, keeping a blanket over his tension, and finally Lozini nodded slowly and turned his head to look out toward downtown. "None of those buildings were there when I first moved here," he said. "The tall ones."

"There've been a lot of changes," Calesian agreed.

Lozini nodded some more, still looking out away from the

terrace. Then he turned his head to gaze at Calesian again. "This building right here wasn't here," he said.

"Three years old," Calesian said. He knew because he was one of the original tenants.

"Sitting here," Lozini said, "waiting for you, I spent a lot of time thinking about the past. The way things used to be. The way I used to be."

"Well, everything changes, I guess." Calesian was listening hard, trying to think ahead of the conversation, waiting for Lozini to touch ground, get to the point.

"I'm about finished," Lozini said. "Hard to think about it that way, you know? I look in the mirror, I see an old man, I get surprised. Somebody tells me I forgot a thing I always knew, I can't figure out how it happened. Be like forgetting to put your pants on."

"You're still all right, Al," Calesian said. But he was thinking hard, trying to work it out, and he was wondering if Lozini was maybe saying that he was quitting. Was that it? He'd come here to turn in his resignation, to ask to be allowed to retire with no trouble. Believing that, beginning to feel less tense, Calesian said, "You're still fine, Al, you've got years in you."

"I'm past the bullshit, Harold," Lozini said. "I'm almost ready to quit, walk away from it." His lips curling, he added, "Go play shuffleboard."

Calesian watched him, intent on every word. "Almost?" he said.

"That's right, Harold." Lozini reached inside his jacket so slowly, moving so unemotionally, that Calesian couldn't believe he was actually reaching for a gun until the thing was out and aimed at Calesian's eyes.

Calesian's hands splayed out atop the attaché case. He made no head or shoulder movements. He said, "Take it easy, Al."

"I'll go out," Lozini said, still calm, still casual, "but I'll go out my own way. I won't get shoved. I won't get conned and robbed like an old man."

"Al, I don't know what—"

"It's either Ernie or Dutch," Lozini said. "Can't be anybody else."

Calesian blinked, stunned at the names. But with the gun pointing at him, there was nothing to do but go on playing innocent. "Al, you're miles ahead of me," he said. "I just don't—"

"That's right, you son of a bitch," Lozini said, with even the insult said in a calm and measured way, "I *am* miles ahead of you, though you don't know it. And all I want from you is the name. It's either Ernie Dulare or Dutch Buenadella, and you're going to tell me which one it is."

"Al, if I had the first idea what—"

"I'll shoot your fucking kneecap off," Lozini said, his voice finally beginning to harden, to match the words he was saying. "And you can gimp your way to the discotheque with your teenage twats from now on."

"Al—"

"Don't deny it again," Lozini said. "You know me well enough, Harold. I can shoot pieces off you till sundown and you won't even get to pass out. One more lie and I start chopping."

Calesian's mouth was dry. His scalp was burning in the sunlight, all of his muscles were tense and jumping, and he felt he needed time to go away and relax and work out what was best to do here. But there wasn't any time, he had to do something now.

And he knew Lozini, he knew that cold look in the bastard's eyes, he knew that Lozini actually would start shooting very soon now. Not to kill, just to hurt and maim. He'd seen the remnants two or three times over the years of men who'd been treated that way; the shot-off parts had come to the morgue in a separate plastic bag. There'd been jokes about it, the spare parts in the plastic bag, but Calesian couldn't remember any of the jokes now. All he could remember was the plastic bag, with the bloody bites of flesh inside it.

"All right," he said. He licked his lips, and put his left hand on top of his head to shield it from the sun. "I'll level with you," he said. Then, still thinking hard, he stopped and licked his lips again.

"Go ahead," Lozini said. The gun was still pointing at him, not wavering; the bastard might be old, but he wasn't used up, not yet.

134

"It's, uh—" Calesian felt the hot breath of wrath on him, hotter than the midsummer heat. No matter what he said now, no matter what he did, wrath would come at him from some direction. "It's Ernie," he said. "Ernie Dulare."

Lozini sagged a little. The gun barrel dipped, Lozini's eyes seemed to lose the hard edge of their focus, the skin of his face got grayer, less healthy in the sunshine.

"It was bound to happen, Al," Calesian said. "And I had to go along with it, you can see that."

Lozini had nothing to say.

"In fact," Calesian said, "you know where I just was, I took a plane trip, I went to see a guy from Chicago. Ernie's clearing things with the big people ahead of time, letting them know there isn't going to be any trouble, no bloodshed, a simple quiet changeover."

Lozini, his voice and face duller than before, said, "What guy? What guy from Chicago?"

"Culligan."

Lozini nodded. "That's right," he said. "And he's got no objection?"

"Why should he?"

"Sure," Lozini said. Then he frowned. "Prove it's Ernie," he said.

Calesian tensed again. "What?"

"Call him. Come on, we'll go inside and you'll call him and I'll hear what he's got to say."

"Oh," Calesian said. "Sure, why not? You think maybe it's really Dutch, after all, and I'm covering, putting you off on Ernie? I'll call, you'll hear it for yourself." He started to take the attaché case off his lap, then stopped and said, "Wait a minute, I'll do better than that. I've got a letter in here to Culligan from Ernie, you can read it yourself." He put the attaché case on his lap again, clicked open the snaps, lifted the lid.

Lozini was frowning at him. "A letter—" Then he straightened up suddenly from the railing, pushing the gun out ahead of himself toward Calesian. "Get your hand out of—"

There wasn't any time to fit the silencer on, but up here that shouldn't matter. Calesian fired through the lid of the attaché case, then had to lunge forward and grab a handful of Lozini's jacket to keep the old man from toppling over the railing after all. He lowered Lozini to the slate floor, plucked the gun from his dead fingers, tossed it over onto the chaise longue. His own gun and the attaché case were on the floor where they'd fallen when he'd made his lunge forward, but for the moment he let them stay there.

He went into the apartment, hurrying through the living room and into the hall to the bedroom. The linen closet was next to the bathroom door, and inside it the plastic tablecloth for use on the terrace was right where it was supposed to be, on the top shelf. He carried it back to the terrace, spread it on the floor, rolled Lozini in it. The old man was shot in the chest, left side, heart—half good aiming and half good luck. There wasn't much blood, because he was dead and the heart wasn't pumping any out of the wound.

Calesian dragged the plastic-wrapped body into the living room, shut the terrace doors, and turned the thermostat down to fifty-five, the lowest possible setting. Then he went into the bathroom to rub some A&D ointment on his scalp to guard against sunburn, and while he was in there he got a sudden case of the shakes. He sat down on the toilet and gripped his knees and stared at the rose-colored wall, and trembled all over.

Lozini. Not some two-bit hood, not a dime-store cop, but Lozini himself. *I was always afraid of that bastard,* Calesian or federal people—and call Dutch Buenadella. But the first coming up into his mouth.

After a few minutes he calmed down and took two Alka-Seltzer and left the apartment to find a phone booth—because he couldn't be sure if his own phone was tapped or not, by state or federal people—and call Dutch Buenadella. But the first three times he dialed, the line was busy.

Twenty-five

Buenadella was on the phone with George Farrell, who had just called him, taking him away from lunch with his family. Buenadella was saying, "What the fuck did you give him *my* name for?"

"I didn't know what else to do. He was— He was making it very tough for me. He really wanted to know, do you follow me?"

The phone was a tough way to communicate. They had to tell each other things that they weren't telling the inevitable eavesdroppers. Farrell had begun the conversation by saying, "Do you know who this is?" and Buenadella had said, "Yes, you dipshit, and so does anybody else who's listened to all those fucking radio commercials you did." He'd talked that way because he'd been shocked into rage by the stupidity of Farrell making direct contact with him, two days before the election. They had managed to keep Farrell's skirts clean all the way through up till now, and he just couldn't believe the guy was stupid enough to blow it all at this late date, for any reason.

But since then the conversation had gone on, roundabout and vague but gradually getting the point across, and now Buenadella was shocked in a different way. Because that son of a bitch Parker had gone right through Farrell's security, separated him from his people like a sheepdog cutting out one lamb from the flock, scared the shit out of him somehow, and had gotten from him Buenadella's name as the guy behind the takeover. And that shouldn't have happened. Just as Farrell had kept himself clean and above suspicion on the mayoral side, Buenadella had held himself absolutely out of it when it came to unhorsing Al Lozini. And now this bastard from out of town, this Parker, had come in and opened everything up like an appendicitis case.

And Parker wasn't even supposed to be alive any more. What the hell had happened to Abadandi? Surely he'd had a chance at Parker and the other one by now, so what was holding him back? Once he took Parker out, life would get a lot easier, but if Abadandi waited much longer, Parker would already have opened too many doors, spoiled too many setups, and it wouldn't make a hell of a lot of difference any more if he was alive or dead.

It crossed Buenadella's mind that Abadandi might have made his play and lost; but he didn't believe it. Abadandi was too good, too secure. The answer had to be that Parker and the other one were covering themselves too well and Abadandi hadn't had a good shot yet to take them out.

Well, it better happen soon. And in the meantime, there was this sudden mess to take care of. Buenadella said, "How long ago did you have your conversation?"

Farrell bumbled around, still too shook up to be brisk. "Uh—twenty-five—almost half an hour."

"Half an hour! What the fuck a you been doing?"

"Dutch, I had to, I had to calm everybody here. We had policemen being held at gunpoint here, Dutch, it wasn't something I could just brush off without an explanation. I said they represented some Middle Eastern sect, it was some sort of international political thing, and that I talked them out of holding me."

"You got people to buy that?"

"Reporters, policemen, everybody." A bit of pride touched Farrell's voice, and with it he grew calmer and more confident. "I am good at my profession, Dutch," he said. "I can talk to people."

Which was true. When Buenadella stopped to think about it, the fact that Farrell had made the people around him buy any kind of phony story at all was pretty damn good, and that he'd managed to get away to a telephone by himself within half an hour was even better. Grudgingly he said, "All right. You did what you could."

"Thanks, Dutch. And I wanted you to know as soon as possible."

"Too bad you couldn't have pulled your bullshit number on our friend instead."

"Dutch, you weren't there. Believe me, I didn't have—"

Any choice, he was going to say. Buenadella cut him off, saying, "All right, it's done. And he's got half-an-hour lead to get to me, so get off the phone and let me set things up."

"Right, Dutch. And I'm sorry, I just—"

Couldn't do anything else, he would have said that time. "I know," Buenadella said. "I know. Hang up." And he broke the connection.

Standing there holding the receiver in his left hand and depressing the cradle with his right, counting slowly to five to give the phone company a chance to break the connection so he could make another call, Buenadella frowned thoughtfully at the paintings on the opposite wall of his den. They were French, pastels, crooked streets in Montmartre, in Paris. Not prints, regular originals, he'd bought them in Paris seven years ago when he and Teresa had swung through there on their way back from the trip to Italy. It was funny how everybody in Italy had thought he was German and everybody in France had thought he was Italian, and here he was an American all the time.

Louis Buenadella was fifty-seven years old, a big-boned man who did a lot of eating and who spread two hundred seventy pounds over his six-foot-four-inch frame. His stomach and behind and thighs were pretty thickly padded out with fat, but the rest of him was big and hard, all muscle and sinew. He had fair skin and nearly blond light brown hair, the heritage of a Piedmontese grandmother on his father's side. His hair seemed even paler in the close-cropped crew cut he'd favored for the last thirty years, ever since his Army days in the Second World War, and was mainly responsible for his nickname.

Buenadella was born and raised in Baltimore, and after the Army he went back there for a few years, soldiering in a different way, working for the people who ran the local rackets. He had some lucky breaks, was made a part of the action a few times, and saved his money. He knew he'd never be anything but a dependable minor hood in Baltimore, so in 1953 he'd moved to Tyler, armed with an introduction to Adolf Lozini and helped by the money he'd been saving up. Television had been hurting the movie business badly at that time, so he'd been able to buy up three local theaters on the cheap. He'd brought in sexploitation movies, was the first exhibitor in the Tyler area to switch over to that kind of film, and his three theaters had gone immediately and permanently into the black. He ingratiated himself with Lozini and the other local people who could be important to him, he became a part of their action, and when in 1960 it was decided to get into the paperback sex-novel boom Buenadella was the natural choice to organize the operation; first as a wholesaler, AM Distributors, Inc., distributing books from publishers in New York and Los Angeles, and later as a publisher, Good Knight Books, buying manuscripts for five hundred dollars, doing a print order of twenty thousand, selling fifteen thousand per title in the Tyler area and the rest in towns in a four-hundred-mile radius. AM Distributors handled Good Knight Books, and Buenadella's three sex-movie theaters sold paperbacks in the lobby.

Because Buenadella's entire operation was legal, other money from less legal sections of Lozini's overall structure could be siphoned through Buenadella and thus brought back into legitimate trade. Buenadella had an agreed right to a skim on that money, and all in all was doing very well. But he wanted more.

He thought of himself, in his more solemn moments, as representing the wave of the future. In the old days the rackets had been disorganized, competitive, bloodthirsty. Then, mostly because of the pressures of Prohibition, the boys began to get together, to organize themselves and become more efficient for more profit. After Prohibition, there was a gradual movement out of the traditional rackets and into more and more legitimate enterprises; first as a cover for the real operation, later as a way to explain income to Internal Revenue, and more recently as a simple, sensible business way to deal with the profits through reinvestment.

And the next move, it seemed to Buenadella, was to make

the legitimate parts of the operation dominant, with the rackets simply in support, to provide capital when needed and strong-arm when needed and political clout when needed, but not ever to be the main concern. And if the legitimate operations were to take over as the primary function, then the best leader at any level was a man whose own piece of the pie was completely legit. A man like himself.

Al Lozini was on the way out, he was going anyway, getting old, overstaying his welcome. Buenadella was interested in hurrying him a little, but that was all, and the only reason to do that was to be sure nobody else got the idea to take Lozini's place for himself. Somebody like Ernie Dulare, for instance, or, maybe later on, Ted Shevelly.

And being the new breed, the businessman rather than the racketeer, he had chosen a good traditional business method for replacing the man ahead of him: co-opt his assistants, drain his economic strength, make private arrangements with his associates. He had spent nearly three years on the operation, moving very slowly, like a fox testing the ice across a frozen river; never pushing, never forcing the issue, never succumbing to impatience and old-line strongarm tactics. The final stage was to be the replacement on Tuesday of Lozini's mayor by Buenadella's mayor, to be followed by a meeting with Lozini in which he would be shown that the war was already over, that there was nothing for him to do but retire. Away from Tyler, far away. Florida, maybe. Or maybe he'd like to see Europe; Buenadella could recommend a trip like that. Cultural, healthful, a first-rate investment all the way around.

How smooth it had been, and how simple. And how stupidly it had fallen apart, with one little push from an unexpected quarter.

That goddam money from the amusement park. Seventy-three thousand, and less than half of it had wound up in the Farrell campaign. The rest had greased the ways here and there, minor payoffs, a nice piece to Harold Calesian, smaller pieces to a couple of other cops, a little hush-money piece to a Lozini soldier named Tony Chaka, a handling portion for Buenadella himself. And the fact is, it hadn't even been needed. The goddam money was just a happy surprise, it hadn't been anticipated, they could have gotten along just as well without it.

A happy surprise. With another surprise in its wake, in the two guys named Parker and Green.

Now, all of a sudden, everything was up in the air. That asshole Calesian was out shooting cops, Lozini was getting nervous and suspicious, Farrell was risking his Mr. Clean image, and it had become necessary for Buenadella himself to give up business methods and go back to the blunter systems of simpler days, to put out a hit order.

He still wouldn't do it on local people, on Lozini or Frank Faran or Ernie Dulare. But these strangers, a couple of shirttail heist artists without connections, they were dangerous alive and nobody would miss them if they were dead. But when the hell would Abadandi get around to finishing them off?

Maybe not until after they'd come here, to this actual house, sent by that yellow bastard Farrell. So Buenadella had some phone calls to make, a reception to organize.

He was still holding the receiver in his left hand. He counted to five after finishing the conversation with Farrell, then lifted his right hand from the cradle and poised his finger at the dial, waiting for the hum.

It didn't happen. Silence on the line. Buenadella frowned, clicked the receiver twice, and had a sudden flashing image of Parker and Green cutting the phone line, isolating him in here.

Then a voice said, "Hello?"

"What?" Buenadella felt himself getting red in the face; this last annoyance was the one too many, the straw that broke the camel's back. "What the fuck is going on?" he yelled.

The voice said, "Dutch? Is that you?"

"Who is this? Farrell?" Though it didn't sound like him.

"No. You know who this is."

Then he did finally recognize the voice: Calesian. "For Christ's sake," he said. "Now what?"

"Get to a clean phone," Calesian said. "I have to talk to you."

"There are no clean phones," Buenadella said angrily, "and I don't have time. I got problems of my own."

"I'll have to come over. This is important."

"You do that. Now hang up, I've got calls to make."

"I'll be there in ten minutes."

"Hang up!"

Calesian hung up, and Buenadella depressed the cradle again, once more breaking the connection. As he did so, a voice from the French doors behind him said, "Now you hang up."

"Cock*sucker*," Buenadella said, and threw the phone at the nearest painting of Montmartre.

Twenty-six

As he stepped through the open French doors behind Parker, Grofield thought, *Good God, it's a stage set. And not a very good one.*

The room was a disaster, a combination of so many misunderstandings and misconceptions that it practically became a work of art all in itself, like the Watts Towers. It was a den, or studio, or office-away-from-office; called by the family "Daddy's room," no doubt.

The walnut-veneer paneling, very dark, made the already small square room even smaller and squarer, darkening it to the point where even a white ceiling and a white rug would have had a hard time getting some light into the room. Instead of which, the ceiling was crisscrossed with styrofoam artificial wooden beams, à la restaurants trying for an English-country-inn effect, and the two-foot-by-four-foot rectangles between the beams had been painted in a kind of peach or coral color; Consumptive's Upchuck was the color description that came to Grofield's mind. While the floor was covered with an oriental rug featuring dark red figures on a black background, with a dark red fringe buzzing away all the way around.

Would there be a kerosene lamp with green glass shade, converted to electricity? Yes, there would, on the mahogany table to the right, along with the clock built into the side of a wooden cannon; above these on the wall were the full-color photographs of The Guns That Won the West lying on beds of red or green velvet.

The man in the middle of the room, hurling his telephone at the opposite wall, went with the room so totally that Grofield was almost ready to believe he and Parker had come to the wrong house. This was a businessman, a Kiwanian, a blunt Tuscan pillar of the community, a property holder and a taxpayer, a man with proctological problems. If Grofield hadn't heard Buenadella's conversation on the phone, and if he wasn't watching the man throw the telephone with such force that the wire ripped from the wall and the cradle smashed that sloppy watercolor of Avenue Junot, he'd think they must have made a mistake, this couldn't be a hood named Buenadella, the one wresting control from Lozini.

But then Buenadella turned around to face them, and Grofield revised his opinion. There was a heaviness in the jaw, a coldness in the eyes, a hulking in the shoulders, none of them attributes a legitimate businessman would have permitted himself. This was a man who was used to getting his own way, not through argument or money, but through intimidation. He reminded Grofield of a mobster named Danamato he'd met once in Puerto Rico. There'd been trouble when Danamato had convinced himself that Grofield had killed Mrs. Danamato, and talking sense to him had been like explaining algebra to a brick.

Grofield wondered if Buenadella would be equally thick. He was starting off dumb enough; pointing a thick finger at them, he yelled, "All right, you bastards, you've fucked things up enough around here! You get out of town in the next forty-five minutes and you just may get to live a little longer."

Neither Parker nor Grofield was showing any guns, but they both had them available if necessary. Once inside the room, Parker moved to the left while Grofield pulled the French doors closed and then moved to the right. Parker said, "Sit down, Buenadella. It's time for us to talk."

"I don't talk to punks! Get out of here and keep going!"

Casually, Grofield took from his pocket Abadandi's wallet and tossed it on the desk. "You'll probably want to send that to Abadandi's next of kin," he said.

Buenadella frowned, massively, his whole face shifting downward. "What?"

"With a nice letter," Grofield added. "Proud of your boy,

first-class soldier, died saving his platoon, great loss, will be missed. They can frame it, hang it over the mantelpiece."

Buenadella stepped closer to the desk, picked up the wallet, opened it, and looked at a couple of the documents within. Parker and Grofield waited him out, till at last he lifted his head and glared at Grofield. "Where'd you get this?"

"Off a dead man."

"I don't believe it."

Grofield shrugged.

Buenadella studied him, thinking it over, and then tossed the wallet contemptuously back onto the desk. "There's more men where he came from," he said.

Grofield smiled. "Are they just as good?"

"We'll try them ten at a time," Buenadella said.

Parker took a step closer to him. "You won't try them at all," he said. "We're here with you, all by yourself. We can finish it right now."

Buenadella moved his heavy look from Grofield to Parker. "I don't have anything to finish with you."

"Seventy-three thousand dollars."

"Stolen goods," Buenadella said. "You don't have any claim on the money, and there's no proof I ever saw or touched or spent a dollar of it. You want to take me to court?"

"You're in court right now," Parker said.

Grofield, sincerely trying to be helpful, said, "Mr. Buenadella, a little piece of advice. My friend is a very impatient man. I don't know anybody who handles frustration worse than he does. He's been very calm up till now, he hasn't made any trouble, but I think—"

"No trouble!" Buenadella seemed honestly astounded, surprised right out of his tough-guy role. "Do you realize what you—" He sputtered slightly, moving his hands, finding it impossible to put together the words to express what had been done to him.

"Believe me," Grofield said. "We've been here five days, all we've ever wanted is our money, and all we get is the runaround. There's an election going on, there's a mob war shaping up, there's all this nonsense. We don't care about any of this, all we care about is our seventy-three thousand dol—"

"And you're fucking up everything in sight!" Buenadella shouted. He acted like a man with a true grievance, self-righteous and enraged. "You're doing robberies, you're killing people, you're pulling a gun on the mayoral candidate, you're screwing up a personal business arrangement that I worked *three years to*— You call it a mob war? What mob war? Everything was quiet until you people got here!"

"If we'd been given our money on Thursday," Grofield said, "even on Friday, there wouldn't have been any trouble at all."

"I'm sick of this town," Parker said. "I want my money and I want to get out of here."

"Seventy-three thousand," Grofield said. "That's really not a lot of money. A business expense, that's all."

Buenadella had been about to make another angry statement, but he abruptly closed his mouth on it and gave a speculative frown instead. The term "business expense" had taken root in his head; Grofield could see it growing in there, becoming a lovely green tree.

"Just a minute," Buenadella said. The desk chair was just to his left; he pulled it back from the desk, sat down, rested his forearms on the green blotter, and gazed off toward the French doors.

Grofield shot Parker a look, but Parker was watching Buenadella, his own expression unreadable as usual. Grofield wondered if Parker understood that they'd just won, that Buenadella was going to give them the money.

Yes, he was. He was sitting there now working it all out in his head. Seventy-three thousand dollars to get rid of the troublemakers; a high price, but the alternative was even worse trouble than he'd already had, and in effect he'd be paying the troublemakers with their own money, not his.

And more. Inside that heavy head, Buenadella was working out tax dodges, company dodges. The seventy-three thousand would come from this place and that place, would read one thing and another on the company books and ledgers; and what percent of it would the government wind up paying, in the form of tax deductions for business losses? If Buenadella paid out seventy-three thousand in deductible business expenses, declared it all and lowered his tax bill by one-third of that—say, twenty-four thousand—he would only be paying forty-nine thousand out of his own pocket. And since the seventy-three hadn't been his to begin with, he could look at it that he was making a twenty-four-thousand-dollar profit on the deal.

Buenadella finally broke the silence. He seemed uncertain whether to talk to Parker or Grofield, and looked at Parker first, but then turned to Grofield instead; probably because Grofield seemed friendlier. "I can't pay you all at once," he said.

Grofield grinned; he couldn't help himself. As an actor, and as a summer-theater producer, he had dealings from time to time with the business mentality, and by God, if this wasn't it in full flower. A hood would either pay up or start shooting, it was impossible to think of a hood in terms of time payments. Buenadella, regardless of the business he was in, was more merchant than crook, and that was why it was going to be possible to deal with him.

But not this way. "Sorry," Grofield said. "We couldn't keep coming back for the payments. It has to be all at once."

"Seventy-three thousand," Buenadella pointed out, "that's a big bite."

"You can do it."

"You're going to strap me at a time when I really need the cash."

Parker said, "Stop it, Buenadella. There's only one way to pay us, and you know it."

Grofield saw Buenadella getting his back up again; the very sound of Parker's voice irritated the man. Now, with negotiations finally having been opened, and moving along pretty smoothly considering the circumstances, there was no point going back to the old hostilities. So, to soothe Buenadella, Grofield said, "I'm sure we can work something out, Mr. Buenadella. We don't want to be unreasonable."

"You call yourselves reasonable?" But it was said truculently, not angrily, so no real damage had been done.

"Well," Grofield said, "of course, we're pretty well locked into two conditions here. We have to have a lump-sum payment, and we have to have it in cash. You can see the reasons for that."

Buenadella, the businessman, could see the reasons, but

148

didn't want to. "We could have a paper between us," he grumbled. "We could make a legal thing, that you could take me to court if I missed a payment. If I agree to pay you, I'll pay you."

"It just wouldn't work, Mr. Buenadella," Grofield said, sounding mournful about it. "To have a legal document, you'd have to have my real name, for instance, and I'd rather you didn't have it. Not to mention an address."

"Christ." Buenadella tapped his fingers on the desk blotter; they made small muffled noises, as for a midget's funeral. "Where'm I going to get that much cash right away? I might as well tell you go fuck yourselves, do your worst."

"You haven't seen our worst, Mr. Buenadella," Grofield said gently.

Buenadella cocked his head and squinted at Grofield, and it seemed to Grofield that for the first time Buenadella was taking the threat seriously. Underplay, Grofield thought, always underplay, that's the way to get your effects every time.

Buenadella was still working things out. "It's possible," he said. "But it'll take a couple days."

"Now," Parker said.

Grofield said to Parker, "Wait a minute, let's hear him out. He's got problems too."

"Only you people," Buenadella said. He rubbed the line of his jaw with a knuckle, thinking. "I can't do anything today, right? It's Sunday, everything's closed. Tomorrow first thing I start. But you're talking cash, that's going to take a couple days."

Parker said, "One day."

Buenadella looked back and forth at the two of them, and decided to talk to Grofield again. "You can't collect cash that fast," he said. "You know what I'm talking about, it takes time, liquidating things, converting to cash. I'm in a bad cash flow situation anyway, what with the summer, attendance down, this election—"

"Well," Grofield said, "I sort of think the election is what my partner had in mind. That's Tuesday, right?"

"Sure, Tuesday."

"Day after tomorrow." Grofield shrugged, shaking his head,

as though truly sorry to be the bearer of bad news. "See, that election's important to us. It's part of the pressure we have on you."

"You don't pay up by Tuesday morning," Parker said, "your man loses. One way or another, he loses."

"It can't be done that fast!"

"You can if you really try," Grofield said. "I tell you what; I'll give you a call tomorrow morning, say ten-thirty, see how you're coming along."

Bitterly Buenadella said, "I wish I'd never heard of that money."

"That would have been better," Grofield agreed. "We can find our own way out." He glanced at Parker, who nodded.

Grofield went first. He opened the French doors, stepped through to the cluttered rear lawn with its overcrowded plantings of bushes and hedges and small trees, and he saw the man with the gun just as the gun sparked white and red at the end of the barrel.

There wasn't time to do a thing, not even time to think. He never heard the sound of the shot, but he felt the punch high on the left side of his chest; it felt as though he'd been hit by something as big as a fist, a metal fist.

It spun him around. Everything went out of focus as he turned, like a special effect in a movie. *He killed me!* Grofield thought despairingly, and slid down the invisible glass wall of life.

Twenty-seven

When Grofield jerked back against the doorjamb, Parker didn't need to hear the sound to know he'd been shot. From outside, from people hidden in the shrubbery out there, waiting. Signaled by Buenadella, somehow, since Parker and Grofield had come in here, then setting themselves up outside and waiting for their targets to come out.

But they'd started shooting just a second too soon. Parker moved to his right, crouching, getting away from the open doorway as he clawed out his own pistol. Finish off Buenadella first, retreat through the house. No telling how many of them were out there in the yard.

But when his movement brought him around to face Buenadella, the blank terrified bewilderment of the man made it obvious this wasn't his idea. The people outside were operating on orders from somebody else—Farrell maybe, or Calesian. Buenadella wasn't that good an actor, to have negotiated the way he had with Grofield or to be faking right now that look of stunned horror.

Another shot was fired out there, on the heels of the first, the bullet chunking into the paneling somewhere on the far side of the room. Grofield wasn't moving. He was body hit, probably dead. This room would fill up with them in a minute; Parker turned some more, showing Buenadella the gun in his hand, and headed for the interior door.

It had all gone so fast there hadn't been time for words, but Buenadella croaked out something as Parker pulled the door open and ran through. He couldn't make out the words or the meaning, and didn't slow down to worry about it. Slamming the door behind himself, he trotted down a corridor, went through a doorway on the right that should lead toward the front of the house, and strode across an empty family room with a ping-pong table at one end, a bar at the other, and a television set in the middle. He carried the pistol in his right hand, but kept the hand close in against his leg in case he should run into members of Buenadella's family.

Then he almost walked into a dining room full of them, but just in time heard the clinking of silverware and the sounds of voices in idle conversation. The shots from the yard had not been very loud, and had apparently not been heard at this end of the house.

Parker veered away from the doorway, found another hall, and walked quickly along it. There was no sound of pursuit from behind him, probably meaning that Buenadella wouldn't permit a shoot-out in his own house, but Parker moved fast anyway, wanting to be long gone by the time they'd decided what to do next.

He came to a living room, also empty, and then finally the front door. Opening it slightly, he looked out at a semicircle of blacktop driveway, a meticulously neat lawn dotted with small shrubs, and a genteel residential street. A dark blue Lincoln went by, purring. A television-repair truck was parked across the way.

There was no one in sight. The shrubs were too small for a man to hide behind, nor was there any place else out there to hide, except in the television-repair truck, and that was surely some sort of police stakeout; more likely to be state or federal than local.

And the truck would give Parker his safe passage. There just might be men with guns in the upstairs windows who would see Parker leaving, but they wouldn't fire, not with that truck out there. Any cop hidden in there would just love to watch somebody shot down on Buenadella's front lawn; it would give them all the excuse they needed to enter the house and give it a complete toss, end to end.

So there wouldn't be any shooting in front of the house,

though they'd have to try following him, hope to catch up with him someplace safer. He'd deal with that when it happened.

He opened the front door, went out into the sunlight and the overly warm air, walked briskly but casually out the driveway to the street. He turned right, headed down the block with no change in the regular pace of his movements.

Back to Lozini, now. Time to mobilize him, use him to break this town open.

It was too bad about Grofield.

Twenty-eight

Calesian fired a second time, over the falling man's head at the guy coming out behind him. But it was a harder shot, the second target still being in the semi-darkness inside the room, and with a few seconds' warning to start moving out of the way. He knew without looking that he'd missed, so he ran forward toward the open doors, crouching and weaving, making himself as difficult as possible to aim at.

He had come here directly after the phone conversation with Buenadella. Knowing that at least two police agencies kept routine watch on Buenadella's house, just to have a general idea who his visitors were, Calesian had come around the back way, across several well-tended spacious rear yards, having to deal with one Great Dane along the way, and when he'd arrived here he'd gone directly to the French doors leading to Buenadella's office. He'd almost opened the doors, but with his hands on the fancy handles he had heard voices from inside, and he'd wanted to know who it was talking to Buenadella before he showed himself.

There were spaces between the orange drapes covering the French doors on the inside; Calesian had stooped to peer through, and when he'd seen Parker he'd immediately backed away from the house, taking shelter amid the hedges so he could think things over.

So; Parker too had figured things out, but unlike Lozini, he had chosen to go directly to the top. Was he here because he wanted to find out if Buenadella was the man organizing the takeover, or was it because he already knew?

154

Whichever it was, they were obviously just talking in there. Parker wanted his money, not a lot of corpses, so he wouldn't shoot Buenadella. On the other hand, it wouldn't be good for Calesian to jump him inside Buenadella's house. Better to wait for him to come out.

Which was what he'd done. Except that it hadn't been Parker all by himself in there; the other one, Green, had also been present, though Calesian hadn't been able to see him in looking through the space between the drapes. And that was why Calesian had made his mistake.

If he'd known Parker and Green were both in there, he would have stayed out of sight until both men had emerged completely from the house into the outer daylight. He was fast and he was accurate, well-trained on the pistol range in the basement at headquarters, and he had no doubt he could step out from concealment and drop any two men on earth before they could reach for their own weapons. Even fast-draw artists from rodeos or movies; anybody.

But he hadn't known about Green. So the French doors had opened, a man had come out, and Calesian had stepped out from behind the hedge to kill him, to finish him off once and for all. And it was as he was coming out, raising his arm in the formal shooter's posture, elbow locked, entire arm and hand and gun pointing at that man's heart, that he saw the second one coming out behind the first and realized his mistake.

And by God, they were fast. Both men were moving when he squeezed off that first shot. There wasn't a chance in hell for the first man to get away, but the second one was still inside the house, and he moved fast, and the second shot missed.

So Calesian ran forward, crouching, weaving, and burst through the French doors to see the interior door slamming on the other side of the den. And Dutch Buenadella was on his feet behind his desk, yelling something Calesian didn't hear and didn't pay attention to.

Goddammit. In the house, actually inside the house, with Buenadella's family present. The situation couldn't be worse, but the guy couldn't be allowed to get out of here alive. Calesian crossed the room on the dead run, yanked open the door, and something grabbed his arm, spun him backward around off balance, and shoved him away toward the side wall.

Buenadella. Calesian, flinging his arms out to get his balance back, saw Buenadella slamming the door again, and he couldn't believe it. "Dutch!" he yelled, and surged once more at the door. "He's getting away!"

Buenadella stiff-armed him. "God damn you son of a bitch bastard asshole, stop where you are or I swear to God I'll rip your head off your shoulders and kick it into the street!"

The tone of voice got to Calesian more than the words. He stopped, panting, adrenalin pumping, and finally saw that Buenadella's face was purple with rage, and that the rage was directed at him, at Calesian. "Jesus Christ, Dutch," he said, still panting, "I could have had them both."

"I just made a deal with them!"

Calesian blinked. He lowered the pistol in his right hand and looked dazedly around the room. "You did what?"

"A deal. You know what a deal is, you half-assed Armenian hot shot? You know what anything is except shoot people?"

"How a deal? What kind of a deal?"

"I give them their money back."

Calesian stared at him. "I don't believe it," he said.

"For peace and quiet?" Buenadella was leaning forward, not exactly shouting but nevertheless pushing the words very hard into Calesian's face. "To get my man safely into the mayor's office? To take over from Lozini with no problems, no questions, nobody gunning for me? When I can write the whole fucking thing off to begin with, and pay out of skim money in the second place, and wind up with the Feds and Al Lozini paying the whole thing between them?"

"Goddammit, Dutch," Calesian said, reasonably, apologetically, "how was I supposed to know that? This morning you had a contract out on them."

"Never mind this morning. They came here, we talked sense, we made a deal." Buenadella's hand swept toward the body lying on the grass just outside the French doors. "And now look."

"All I knew was, you wanted them dead." Calesian self-consciously put his pistol away, trying not to draw attention to it in the course of the movement.

"You think everybody's supposed to be dead," Buenadella

said in disgust. "That cop O'Hara, that was a bright stunt. And now this guy. Who else you been killing, hot shot?"

Calesian became horribly embarrassed; in fact, he felt himself blushing. "Look, Dutch," he said, and then couldn't go on.

Buenadella peered at him in wonder. "By God," he said, "there *is* somebody else. Who?"

"Al Lozini came to see me," Calesian said unhappily. "At my home. He—"

"You killed *Al?*"

"He had a gun on me, Dutch, I couldn't—"

"You killed Al Lozini? Do you realize how many friends Al has around the country? Do you realize how many—" Buenadella stopped, spread his arms out wide, appealed to heaven. "Give me strength."

"There wasn't any choice, Dutch. I didn't *want* to, for Christ's—"

"Didn't want to? You've killed us all, you blood-drinking bastard! Karns, Culligan, a dozen of them. They'd let us retire Al, everybody gets old, everybody has to move over, we were making that play out, everything fine. But *kill* him? I know three guys off the top of my head that know Al Lozini thirty years; they'll send an *army* in here when they find out Al's dead."

"They won't," Calesian said. "Nobody goes that far for a dead man, there's no point."

"They won't deal with me," Buenadella said. "Never again. I'm through, I'm finished. Nobody will deal with me. Even if I give them your head on a plate, say it was your idea and I punished you, they won't believe me and they won't deal with me."

That much was right, and Calesian knew it. Casting around, feeling helpless, feeling as though he was being unfairly blamed for a series of bad happenings for which he shouldn't really have to carry the weight, he looked around the room again and his eye lit on the body outside on the grass. "Then," he said, "we palm it off on them."

Buenadella frowned. "What?"

"Those two guys. Your deal with them is blown anyway. So we claim they killed Lozini while trying to get their money."

"Why would they kill Al?"

"To deal with you. They weren't getting anywhere with Lozini, and they knew you were next in line, so they killed him and came to you. To threaten they'd do the same to you and deal with the next man down the line." Leaning forward, speaking softly and earnestly, Calesian said, "It'll play, Dutch. It'll read just like the truth."

"Christ," Buenadella said, looking around, thinking it over. "What a goddam mess."

"It'll play, Dutch."

Buenadella said, "But Parker's supposed to know Walter Karns. What if it comes down to our word against his?"

"We have to kill him," Calesian said. Hastily, seeing the expression on Buenadella's face, he added, "I'm not being trigger-happy, Dutch, it's the simple truth. If they're both dead, there's no more problem."

Buenadella looked over at the one out on the lawn. "Is he dead?"

"Naturally."

"Take a look."

Calesian shrugged and went over to the body and rolled it over onto its back. Blood gouted from the chest, high on the left side. Too much blood, and too high on the chest. Frowning, Calesian touched the guy on the side of the neck, and damn if there wasn't a faint pulse there. The pulse was keeping the blood flowing out of the wound.

It was seeing the second one in the doorway that had distracted Calesian, thrown his aim slightly off. Two inches from where he'd wanted the bullet to hit.

Buenadella was standing next to Calesian, looking down with distaste. "He really is dead, huh?"

Reluctantly, not looking up, Calesian said, "No."

Fear in Buenadella found release in anger. "Goddammit! You can't even do *that* right! Killing's all you know how to do, and you don't even know how to do that."

A dull anger moved in Calesian, but he didn't have the will to follow through. He could defend himself, he could yell back, he could get up and punch Buenadella in the face. All he did was stay on one knee next to the dying man and watch the blood pulse out, while Buenadella's words ranted above him.

Twenty-nine

Parker couldn't stay in one place. Rage drove him, and frustration. He waited in Lozini's house for twenty minutes, then had the houseman call Shevelly and Faran and the fat lawyer Walters and the swinging accountant Simms, but nobody knew where Lozini had gone. Parker couldn't wait any longer. He was prowling the living room, pacing back and forth, aware of Lozini's family huddled away upstairs, and after the last useless call he grabbed the phone book and looked up Harold Calesian.

He was listed, with an address on something called Elm Way. Parker tossed the phone book at a chair and told the houseman, "When your boss comes back, tell him to stay here. I'll keep in touch."

"Yes, sir." The houseman had the pale face and out-thrust cheekbones of someone who's terrified without knowing what to be afraid of. He hurried ahead of Parker to hold the front door open, then seemed reluctant to close it again after Parker had gone on through, as though afraid Parker might think it an insult.

Parker drove to the nearest gas station and got directions to Elm Way. It was on the other side of the city, past downtown, so the attendant recommended he go the other way to the Belt Highway and take it around.

Elm Way sounded suburban, ranch-style houses on green plots penetrated by slowly winding blacktop streets, but when Parker reached it the street was straight, concrete, and flanked by big-shouldered apartment buildings, upper middle income, urban renewal, less than ten years old.

Calesian's building was the biggest of them, taking up a full block width on the right side of the street. The shrubbery at the base of the building looked too green, as though it were artificial, as though in winter it would still be there, arsenic-green, thrusting out of the snow.

There was tenant parking in the basement. Parker drove down the ramp from sunlight to fluorescent light, and found most of the spaces empty; it was Sunday, and the Sunday drivers were out. He backed the Impala into a space near the exit, and took the elevator up to the first floor, where the mailboxes told him Calesian's apartment was 9-C, at the top of the building. He rode up there, rang the bell twice, and popped the lock with a credit card.

The apartment was cold, the air chilly and flat. Parker moved silently across the foyer, looked across the living room at the view of Tyler through the closed terrace doors on the far side, saw the thing wrapped in plastic on the floor near those doors, and went on to check out the rest of the apartment.

It was empty. None of the drawers or closets contained anything that he wanted to know or study; but Calesian wasn't the type to leave evidence against himself lying around.

Finally he went back to the living room. He thought he knew what that thing was, wrapped in plastic in there on the floor. Kneeling, he folded the translucent plastic back.

Yes. Lozini.

Thirty

Driving across town, Ted Shevelly felt very nervous. He didn't like going to Dutch Buenadella's house in the first place, and he doubly didn't like it that Harold Calesian was the one who'd summoned him. And to make matters worse, he couldn't find Al Lozini, couldn't talk the situation over with him to find out what the hell was going on.

Turning in at the curving blacktop driveway to Dutch's house, he noticed the TV repair truck across the street, knew it meant either the Feds or the state CID were taking movies of his arrival, and didn't much care. The cops already knew who he was, it hardly mattered whether he visited Dutch Buenadella or not. Besides, his main trouble wasn't cops. At least, not the cops outside. His main trouble was Buenadella and his tame cop on the inside, Calesian.

It was one of Buenadella's rougher-looking goons who led him through to the den, where Buenadella was sitting at his desk, looking uncomfortable and unhappy and even a little sick, while Calesian paced back and forth, a slow and measured tread, frowning at the floor, obviously thinking very hard. He looked up when Shevelly entered, and stopped in the middle of the room to say, "Hello, Ted."

Shevelly felt it important to maintain the hierarchy. He didn't know why he had that feeling, but he followed it. "Hello, Dutch," he said to Buenadella, then turned to nod at Calesian. "Harold."

But it was too late to maintain a chain of command.

Calesian had taken over here, and Shevelly saw that right away. While Buenadella sat at his desk looking worried, his eyes never leaving Calesian, it was Calesian who did the talking, his voice hard and authoritative as again he paced back and forth. "We've got a problem, Ted," he said. "It seems Parker and Green killed Al Lozini."

"*What?*"

"I'm sorry, Ted." Calesian paused to touch Shevelly's arm, then moved on. "I know you liked Al, I hate to have you hear it this way."

"What the hell did—" Shevelly couldn't encompass it. "What *for?*"

"I think they got impatient," Calesian said. "I think that just comes down to it, they got impatient. They looked around, and decided Dutch here would probably be the number-one boy if Al checked out, so they dropped Al and got in touch with Dutch and told him he had twenty-four hours to cough up their seventy-three thousand or they'd kill *him* and deal with Ernie Dulare."

"Holy Christ," Shevelly said.

"It all happened this morning," Calesian said. "Dutch called me, and between us we set up an ambush for them, Dutch told them to come here and collect the money. When they got here we shot one of them, but the other one got away."

"Which one?"

"Parker."

"You shot the wrong one," Shevelly said.

Calesian shrugged. "They're both hard cases," he said. "Parker's the more obvious, that's all. The point is, he's still out there. We need to finish him off before he makes more trouble. We're in trouble enough with Tuesday's election as it is."

Shevelly rubbed a palm across his forehead. "Every goddam thing at once," he said. "And Al— I can't get over it."

Buenadella finally spoke up. "I loved Al Lozini," he said. His voice was trembling as he said it; Shevelly, looking at him, suspected the tremble was caused more by fear than by love, but he didn't make any comment.

Calesian said, "The point is, we've got to get Parker. We need to bring him in again, and finish him off."

Shevelly frowned at him. "Bring him in? How?"

"I know how to get in touch with him," Calesian said. "I can make an arrangement with him, a meeting. You go to the meeting, you tell him the story, and he comes in."

"You're out of your mind," Shevelly said. "Why's he going to meet with me? He'll think it's another trap."

"He'll pick the spot," Calesian said. "It *won't* be a trap, so what do we care where you meet? The point is to tell him the story, *that* brings him in."

"What kind of a story," Shevelly said, "is going to make somebody like Parker come back in again where you can get your hands on him?"

"A story with evidence," Calesian said. He strode to Buenadella's desk and picked up a small white box, the sort of box that inexpensive earrings or cuff links come in, nestling on a bit of cotton gauze. Shevelly noticed Buenadella looking at the box with repugnance, his lips drawing back from his teeth as though he might suddenly throw up.

Calesian brought the box over to Shevelly. "This evidence," he said, and opened the box, and inside, on the inevitable bit of cotton gauze, was a finger, severed just below the second knuckle.

Thirty-one

When Parker got back to Lozini's place, the houseman told him, "There was a telephone message for you. Not from Mr. Lozini."

No, not from Lozini. Parker said, "Who from?"

"Detective Calesian. He left a number for you to call him back."

Parker looked at the piece of paper: a name, seven digits. "This number mean anything to you?"

"Yes, sir," the houseman said. Sometime in the last hour he had either lost his fear or grown used to it; in any case, he was all right now, operating without that buzzing sense of tension. "That's one of Mr. Buenadella's home lines," he said.

"All right," Parker said. "Get me Dulare, Shevelly, Faran, Walters, and Simms. I want them to meet me here, all five of them, right now. I'll use the hall phone here, you use a different one."

The houseman looked doubtful. "Is this okay with Mr. Lozini? I don't have any instructions about you."

"You know those five names," Parker told him. "Your boss wants them here."

That made sense to the houseman. "Okay," he said. "I just wanted to check, you know?"

Parker turned away to the hall phone, and after a second the houseman left. Parker dialed the number from the piece of paper, and on the first ring it was answered in Buenadella's voice, sounding wary. "Yeah? Hello?"

"This is Parker."

"Oh." Buenadella sounded almost relieved, as though some other caller might have been even worse news. "Listen, Parker," he said, "that wasn't my idea. That was a mistake."

Calesian's mistake; Parker had already figured that out. And Calesian was in the room with Buenadella, which was why Buenadella had identified the caller by name.

"Parker?"

"I'm here."

"You didn't say anything."

"I didn't know you were finished," Parker said.

"I'm not—I'm not exactly finished." Nervousness was coming into Buenadella's voice, meaning some sort of lie or con or trap was about to be brought out. Buenadella's problem was that he wasn't mobster enough; he could run circles around somebody like Lozini when it came to politics and business, but a job like Lozini's wasn't the right slot for a politician or a businessman. Buenadella would have found that out sooner or later; he could consider himself lucky he found out before he tried on the crown.

"Parker?"

"If you have something to say, Buenadella, go ahead and say it."

"About your partner—"

"That isn't the subject."

"All right. The money."

Another goddam pause. What did Buenadella want, fill-in about the weather, how's the wife and kids, what do you think of the Miami Dolphins? A fucking businessmen's lunch, on the phone. "I'm in a hurry, Buenadella," Parker said.

"I want to set up a meeting." Which was said all in a rush; leaping into the lie, meaning the lie was in the form of an ambush.

"What for?"

"To—to explain things. To make another deal."

"Where and when?"

"You say. And it won't be with me, or Calesian, or any of my other people. You know Ted Shevelly, don't you?"

"Yes."

"He's not my man, absolutely not. He's Al Lozini's man all the way."

Parker believed that. It made sense to tether a goat out as bait. "All right."

"He'll carry the message," Buenadella said. "You meet with him, talk it over, make your decision. Okay?"

"Where is Shevelly now?"

"Right here with me. You can talk to him yourself, set up the meeting any way you want it. I swear to God, Parker, that last time was a mistake. I was negotiating in good faith."

Parker believed that one, too. What he didn't believe was that Buenadella was *still* negotiating in good faith. "Put Shevelly on," he said.

"Just a minute."

Shevelly, when he came on, sounded scared and mistrustful, as though he, too, had the whole thing figured for an ambush, but didn't know yet whether he was supposed to come out of it standing up or lying down. He said, "Parker?"

"What's your car look like?"

"A maroon Buick Riviera. License number five-two-five, J-X-J."

"Get up on the Belt Highway going clockwise," Parker told him. "I'll get in touch with you."

"What car do I look for?"

"You'll recognize it," Parker told him, and hung up, and went looking for the houseman, who was still on the phone. "Forget Shevelly," he said, "I'm going to go meet him now."

"Yes, sir."

"You get the others?"

"Mr. Faran and Mr. Dulare, yes, sir. I'm trying to reach Mr. Simms and Mr. Walters now."

"When they get here," Parker said, "tell them to wait, until either Lozini or I get back."

"Yes, sir."

Parker went outside and around to the rear of the house, where a four-car garage stood next to the tennis court. Only two spaces inside it were occupied, one by a tan Mercedes-Benz sedan and the other by a red Corvette. The keys were in both cars, and Parker chose the Mercedes because it was likelier to be associated with Lozini in Shevelly's mind. He drove it out to the Belt Highway, went up the ramp, and stayed at forty in the right lane until he saw the maroon Buick Riviera go by. He hung well back, watching the other traffic, and could see no sign that Shevelly was being followed, so finally he accelerated until he was less than a car length behind the tight-clenched rear end of the Riviera, and then tapped the horn until he saw Shevelly's head move as the man checked his rear-view mirror.

All right; Shevelly would recognize the car and would now know that he had been met. Since they were both in the left lane, Parker eased over into the middle and accelerated past Shevelly, glancing at him on the way by, seeing the strain in the man's face and posture.

The Mercedes was a strong and graceful animal, more bull than horse. It was powerful and responsive, but there was no softness or leniency anywhere in the controls. It would be a good car if you wanted to leave a place fast.

Sunday afternoon traffic on the highway was moderate, mostly slower drivers with no sense of urgency, and leaving enough gaps so that it was possible to get through them at any speed you might want. Parker pushed it for a while, to see how good Shevelly was, but when the Buick began to lag far back, he slowed again and took an off-ramp at random, turning right on the local street, toward the center of town.

This was a lower-middle-income section, small houses set three or four feet apart, mostly with enclosed front porches, many with false-brick sheeting over the original clapboard. Parker made half a dozen turns in a maze of narrow side streets before being convinced that Shevelly wasn't being followed, and then went looking for the right place to stop.

He found it right away, a business block lined with small stores, all of them closed on Sunday: a dry cleaner's, a meat market, a record store, shops like that. Traffic here was almost nonexistent, and only three cars were parked at the curbs along the whole block.

Parker stopped in front of a children's clothing store, and Shevelly pulled in behind him. Parker waited where he was, and after half a minute Shevelly got out of the Riviera, came hesitantly forward, and slid into the front seat of the Mercedes next to Parker. "You've got Al's car," he said.

"So you'd recognize it."

167

"Al was a friend of mine," Shevelly said. He seemed very intense about it.

So they'd told him Lozini was dead. It was a surprise he'd carry messages for them after that, but maybe he figured the only thing to do was line up with the winners. Parker himself had nothing to say about Lozini, so he said, "You have some sort of message for me."

"Right." Shevelly reached into his jacket pocket, and Parker showed him a pistol. Shevelly froze, then said, "It's all right. I'm taking a package out."

"Slow."

"Very slow."

Being very slow, Shevelly withdrew his hand from his pocket, bringing with it a small white box. "This is it," he said, and extended it toward Parker.

Parker still had the pistol in his hand. "You open it," he said.

Shevelly considered, then nodded. He took the top off the box, and showed Parker what was inside it.

Parker looked at the finger. The first knuckle was bent slightly, so that the finger seemed to be calm, at ease, resting. But at the other end were small clots of dark blood, and lighter smears of blood on the cotton gauze.

Shevelly said, "Your friend is alive. This is the proof."

Parker looked at him and waited.

Shevelly seemed uncomfortable now, but to be pushing himself through the scene out of some inner conviction or determination. Almost as though he had a personal grudge against Parker. "The deal is," he said, "that you come to Buenadella's. That's where Green is. They've got him in bed there, and they called a doctor. You come there by noon tomorrow, you can have your money, and you can take Green away with you. Buenadella will supply the ambulance to take him wherever you want out of town. Even two or three hundred miles from here."

Parker glanced at the finger. "That's no proof of anything," he said.

"If you don't get to Buenadella's by noon tomorrow," Shevelly said, "they'll send you another finger. And another finger every day after that, and then toes. To prove he's still alive, and not a decomposing body."

"And if I go there by tomorrow I get him and the money both, and an ambulance to take him away in."

"That's right."

Parker said, "Do *you* believe that, Shevelly?"

"He's alive," Shevelly said. "I saw him, he doesn't look good, but he's alive."

"The deal is Buenadella's way of doing things," Parker said, "but Buenadella isn't in charge any more." He gestured with the pistol at the finger in the white box. "Calesian's running things now."

"It was a stupid thing to kill Al Lozini," Shevelly said.

Parker frowned at him, looking at the coldly angry face. "Oh. They told you I did that, huh?"

Shevelly had nothing to say. Parker, studying him, saw there was no point arguing with him, and no longer possible to either trust him or make use of him. He gestured with the pistol toward Shevelly, saying, "Get out of the car."

"What?"

"Just get out. Leave the door open, back away to the sidewalk, keep facing me."

Shevelly frowned. "What for?"

"I take precautions. Do it."

Puzzled, Shevelly opened the door and climbed out onto the thin grass next to the curb. He took a step to the sidewalk and turned around to face the car again.

Parker leaned far to the right, aiming the pistol out at arm's length in front of him, the line of the barrel sighted on Shevelly's head. Shevelly read his intention and suddenly thrust his hands out protectively in front of himself, shouting, "I'm only the messenger!"

"Now you're the message," Parker told him, and shot him.

Thirty-two

Nathan Simms did dogged laps in the pool out behind his house. At his age it was hard to keep in shape, to trim away those fat rolls at the sides of the waist, to keep the belly from hanging out as though he had swallowed a soft basketball, to keep from panting like a walrus after making love to Donna. Swimming was supposed to be good for all that, wind and belly and spare tire, so whenever the weather was at all good enough Simms was in the pool, exhausting himself, plodding earnestly from end to end, keeping track in his head of the number of laps he had done, and from time to time lying like a discarded doll on the hot concrete beside the pool, listening to his heart drum while he waited for strength to go on.

Elaine came out, shielding her eyes from the sun like an Indian looking for cavalry. It had been ten years or more since she'd made any effort to keep herself in shape, and now she was a dumpy woman with bad digestion and a perpetual manner of ill-treatment. "Phone, Nate," she called, managing to imply by her tone of voice that the phone call was frivolous and that it had interrupted something very important that she had been doing.

Simms was grateful for any excuse to stop the endless back-and-forth swimming. He churned laboriously to the steps, and by the time he got out of the pool Elaine had already disappeared back into the house. He was grateful for that too; Elaine's presence, the last few years, grated on him like an old bedsore.

Dripping, he padded into the house and used the wall phone in the kitchen. "Hello?"

It was Harold, Al Lozini's houseman. "Mr. Lozini wants you to come over right away."

Now what? A wooden ball of apprehension formed high on Simms' stomach. "I'll leave right now," he said, and hung up, and went upstairs to his bedroom to dress. Putting on plum-colored slacks, brown suede high-top shoes, a white turtleneck shirt and a madras jacket, he thought about last night's meeting with Dutch. Had a contract really been put out on Parker and Green, were they dead now? Had something gone wrong, did Al know the whole truth all of a sudden?

These last few days were grinding him down. He wished it was all over, that the dust was settled and he was already comfortable and safe at the new plateau, with more money and more power and more to offer Donna.

He drove across town to Lozini's house and was met by the houseman. Simms said, "Mr. Lozini in his office?"

"He isn't here yet, Mr. Simms. Would you wait in the living room?"

"Not here? Where is he?"

"He went out this morning. He's supposed to be back pretty soon."

That wasn't satisfactory, but Simms could see it was the only answer he was going to get, so he gave an irritated shrug and went on into the living room, where he found Frank Faran standing by the window, swirling a colorless drink in a tall glass. A bit of lime in the drink suggested it was probably a vodka-tonic.

Faran turned and gave Simms his professional smile and a salute with the glass. "How de do, Nate. Your hair's wet."

"I was in the pool."

"Harold!" Faran shouted. When the houseman appeared in the doorway, Faran gestured to him, saying to Simms, "Have a drink."

"No, thanks," Simms said. He was worrying about the meeting, the reason for it, and he wanted to ask Faran as soon as they were alone. But then he suddenly thought that a drink might calm him, and he said, "Wait. All right. I'll have one of those."

Holding the glass up, Faran said doubtfully, "It's made with rum."

"All right. No, vodka. No, wait, I'll try the rum."

The houseman left, and Faran grinned at Simms, saying, "You seem nervous, Nate. Trouble at home?"

"I'm fine," Simms said. "What's this meeting all about, anyway?"

Faran shrugged. "Beats me. Probably something with that Parker and Green."

"I wish to Christ those two had never showed up."

"Amen," Faran said, and Jack Walters waddled in, looking absurd in a short-sleeved white shirt open at the collar and a pair of trousers left over from some suit. A balled-up handkerchief was in his right hand, and when he lifted it to pat his damp forehead, he made it look as though he'd never attempted that particular movement before in his life and was finding it very unnatural to his body. "Good afternoon," he said.

"You look hot," Faran told him. "When Harold gets back, get yourself a drink."

"No, thank you. Where's Al?"

"Out somewhere. We're supposed to wait."

Simms said to Walters, "Jack, do you know what this is all about?"

"No idea."

The houseman brought the drink and Simms took it, while Faran made cheerful small talk with Walters. They were all standing, like an underattended cocktail party. Simms tried the rum and tonic and found it sweeter than he would have guessed, but not cloying. He lowered the glass, and discovered with astonishment that he'd downed half the drink.

"I'll be right back," he said, and put the glass on an end table. But as he was about to leave the room Ernie Dulare walked in, and he changed his mind again.

Dulare ran the important gambling concessions in town, everything except Simms' own stepchild, policy. A tall, smooth, self-contained man in his fifties, he usually dressed in casual jackets and no tie, and his frequent trips to Las Vegas and the Caribbean had given him a deeper and glossier tan than was possible for people limited to the summer sun of Tyler. He had what Simms thought of as a radio-announcer's voice, smooth but with a kind of mellifluous gravel in it. His presence always made Simms very nervous, for no rational reason.

There were hellos back and forth, through which Simms waited impatiently, until he could say, as though casually, "Ernie, what's this meeting all about, do you know?"

"No idea," Dulare said. His ignorance didn't seem to bother him. "I got a call, and I came. I haven't seen Al for quite some time. Where is he?"

"Due back pretty soon," Faran said.

"Excuse me," Simms said, and went out to use the phone in the front hall, but Dulare's bodyguards were there, two burly men in pastel jackets, talking pro football with one another.

The bodyguards were, so far as Simms knew, Ernie Dulare's only affectation. Nobody traveled like that any more, nobody had to. Even Al Lozini didn't cart bodyguards around with him wherever he went. But Dulare, who did a lot of traveling and hosted a lot of parties and spent a lot of time in public, never made a move without his two sluggers. There was no need for them, but Dulare apparently liked the idea of them; like a professional gunslinger in the Old West having pearl-handled revolvers even though a normal grip was safer and less likely to draw the wrong kind of attention.

Well. With the bodyguards in the hall, Simms went in search of another phone. He heard faint movement sounds from upstairs; probably Mrs. Lozini, and her resident married daughter, whose husband was in prison on check-kiting charges. It had been a first offense and he would have gotten off with probation if he hadn't been an in-law of Al Lozini; the judge had gone out of his way to demonstrate that he hadn't been bought.

There was a phone in the library, a room full of magazines and religious books. Simms called Donna, and when she answered, her voice clear and happy, he found himself smiling at the phone. "Hi, honey," he said. "It's me."

"Well, hi." He could visualize her in her yellow and red kitchen, leaning against the wall by the phone, one ankle crossed over the other. "Long time no see, stranger."

"You know how things are sometimes," he said. "Listen, I'm in a meeting now, but why don't I come over as soon as it breaks?"

"Sure, honey. How long?"

"I don't know. We're waiting for Mr. Lozini now. It shouldn't be too long, and I'll call you the second it's over."

"Just come on when you can," she said. "I'll be here."

She likes me, Simms thought, and felt warmth spreading through his chest. "You're a sweet girl," he said.

She laughed. She really did like him. "Don't be too long," she said.

"I won't."

He hung up and went back through the hall to the living room. On the way by, the bodyguards gave him flat incurious glances. In the living room, Dulare and Walters and Faran were standing in a group near the window, talking. Dulare was just finishing Simms' drink.

Thirty-three

When Parker got back to Lozini's house, two burly men in the front hall stopped their conversation to look at him. One said, "You looking for somebody, friend?"

Parker glanced at them. "Which one brought the army? Not Faran, not Simms, not Walters. You're with Dulare."

"You want to see somebody?"

"Not you," Parker said, and headed for the living room. When they made a move at him he showed a gun. "Go in ahead of me," he said.

They glared at the gun and frowned at one another. Slowly they started to raise their hands.

"I didn't tell you to put your hands up," Parker said. "I told you to go into the living room."

They were reluctant to do it, to walk into their employer's presence at the end of somebody else's gun, but there just wasn't any choice. Looking twice as tough as usual, hunching their shoulders so they looked as though they were wearing football equipment, they turned and went through the archway into the living room.

The four men in conversation over by the far window glanced casually, and then with curiosity and surprise, toward the new arrivals. Only one of them had a face Parker didn't know, so that one must be Dulare. Talking to Dulare, Parker said, "Are these yours?"

Dulare, a tall tanned man with an autocratic manner, frowned deeply, saying, "What's the problem?"

175

Frank Faran was suddenly grinning. "Mr. Dulare," he said, "meet Mr. Parker. Mr. Parker, Mr. Dulare."

"I know who it is," Dulare said. "I want to know what he thinks he's doing."

One of the tough boys said, "We didn't know who he was, Mr. Dulare."

Faran, still grinning, said, "They braced him, Ernie, that's what happened."

It was clear that Dulare didn't like any of this. He was mad at his bodyguards and mad at Parker, but he obviously realized he couldn't say anything to either of them without somehow making a fool of himself, so he turned on Faran, saying, "I don't need your help, Frank."

Faran, offended, stopped grinning. After a second he shrugged and turned away and ostentatiously sipped from his drink.

Parker said to Dulare, "Send these two home."

"They stay with me," Dulare said. "And put that gun away, nobody's showing guns around here."

A pair of imitation Victorian chairs flanked an imitation Sheraton drop-leaf table on the opposite side of the room. Parker pointed the pistol toward them, saying, "Tell them to sit over there. I'm here to talk, not waste time."

Frowning again, Dulare said, "Who called this meeting, you or Lozini?"

"I'm doing Lozini's talking for him."

Walters said to Dulare, "When I got here, Harold told me we were supposed to wait for either Al or Parker."

Dulare hesitated, then made an angry sweeping gesture with his arm, telling his two men, "Go on over there, take a seat."

They hulked away, aggravated and upset, and Parker put his pistol back out of sight. He said to Dulare, "How much do you know about what's going on?"

"I know about you," Dulare said. "You're causing trouble. Where's Al Lozini?"

Parker said, "Have you heard from Buenadella?"

"Dutch? What about?"

Parker looked at Faran, then Simms, then Walters. He said to Walters, "Doesn't anybody tell this man anything?"

Walters spread pudgy hands. "We didn't know, of course, if he, uh . . ." He gestured helplessly; it was intended to be a delicate motion, a subtle one, but with Walters' ungainliness it came out as a kind of lumpish dance movement.

Still, Parker got the idea; Lozini hadn't known whether he was being attacked by Buenadella or Dulare, so he'd kept them both in the dark.

Dulare had turned on Walters. "What's going on, Jack?"

"Dutch is trying to take over," Walters said.

"From Al?" Dulare sounded unconvinced.

"It's true, Ernie," Faran said. He seemed to take a vindictive pleasure in giving Dulare bad news. "Dutch has been setting it up for a couple years."

Dulare frowned around at everybody, then said to Walters, "Tell me about it."

"Let Parker tell you," Walters said. "I think he knows more about it than I do."

Dulare gave Parker a suspicious look. "All right," he said. "What is it?"

Parker said, "The reform candidate, Farrell, is Buenadella's man. The finish of the scheme is Farrell taking over as mayor from Wain. Buenadella already talked to some of the other people around the country that he needs okays from. I figured maybe he talked to you, too."

Dulare's attention had been caught; he was no longer irritable because of the defusing of his bodyguards. He said, "Who says Farrell belongs to Buenadella?"

"He does. I asked him."

"And he just told you?"

"I had a gun in my hand."

"Christ Almighty." Dulare looked around at the other three. "What the hell is going on around here?"

Walters said, "We wouldn't have known anything about it until it was too late, except for Parker and his friend stirring things up."

Parker said to Dulare, "You're sure Buenadella didn't talk to you?"

"No," Dulare said. Then he said, "I see what you're driving at. No, he wouldn't come to me in front. Dutch and I aren't that close, and he knows I'm a good friend with Al. He'd come around afterwards, when Al was out and he was in and everything was set. Then I'd go along with him, because it would be stupid to start a war after the game's over."

"All right." Parker turned to Simms. "How much has Buenadella got?"

Simms blinked at him, terror hiding behind confusion. "What?"

"He's been skimming from Lozini's take," Parker said. "Plus my seventy-three thousand. He's had expenses, with Farrell's campaign and some of Lozini's people he's bought, so how much does he have left?"

"How should I know?" Simms jittered inside his dudish clothing like a dressed-up turkey.

"Because you went over to him," Parker said. "He couldn't have skimmed from Lozini without you."

"That's a lie!"

The others all looked at Simms, and Parker said, "Don't waste time, Simms. How much does he have left?"

Faran suddenly said, wonderingly, "It's that honey blonde of yours."

Simms, as though grateful at the chance to concentrate on anyone but Parker, turned his head toward Faran, saying, "What? What, Frank?"

"What's her name? Donna. You brought her around to the club a few times, Nate, you were happy as a nun with a new habit."

"Frank, I didn't—"

Dulare said, "Nate, if you tell another lie, I'll have my two boys over there redeem themselves by walking on your head."

"Ernie, you don't think I'd—"

Simms stopped talking when Dulare pointedly turned toward the two burly men over on the Victorian chairs. There was a little silence while Simms worked it out in his head. Parker was impatient and angry, but this was a moment when it was better to hang back, let the group find its own pace, work things out for itself.

Simms said, in a small voice, "Ernie, I never would have—"

"For God's sake," Dulare said, "don't give me excuses."

"Reasons, Ernie. Not excuses, reasons."

Parker said, "How much is left, Simms? What does Dutch have in the war fund?"

"Ernie," Simms said, pleadingly, "just let me ex—"

"Answer the man," Dulare said.

Simms hung fire, driven by the need to explain himself yet held by the requirement to obey. Finally, his voice barely above a whisper, he looked away from Dulare and said, "About forty-five thousand."

"Not enough," Parker said. "I came here for seventy-three thousand."

"That's not the problem," Dulare said. His attention was still on Simms.

"Yes, it is," Parker told him. "And it's your problem, because Lozini's dead, and now it's a tug of war between you and Buenadella."

They all stared at him. Dulare said, "Al's dead? Since when?"

"He wasn't sure," Parker said, "if the guy climbing up his back was Buenadella or you. He went to Harold Calesian to find out, and Calesian killed him."

"That *cop?*"

"The body is in Calesian's living room," Parker said. "Calesian and Buenadella are going to say that I did it."

Dulare watched him carefully. "Where are you headed?" he said. "What's on your mind?"

"My partner and I," Parker said, "went to make a deal with Buenadella. When we were coming out, my partner got shot. I was sent a message that he was still alive and I could come get him. They'll send me a finger a day to prove he isn't dead."

"Buenadella?" Dulare shook his head. "Dutch wouldn't do anything like that. He wouldn't even think of it."

"Calesian," Parker said. "Once things got rough, Buenadella folded. Calesian is running things."

"Calesian can't run anything except hookers," Dulare said.

Faran said, "But by God, that sounds like his style, Ernie. A finger a day, that does sound like our Harold."

"All right," Dulare said. Back to Parker, he said, "So what do you want?"

"Seventy-three thousand dollars and my partner. You people have the manpower. I want you to send people with me to Buenadella's. I'll get my partner out, I'll get my money, I'll leave."

Dulare shook his head. "No way."

"Why not? You and Buenadella are in a war now anyway."

"No, we're not. I'll call Dutch right now and tell him we'll stay equal, him in his area, me in mine." Dulare gave a thin smile, saying, "He won't try anything with me. I'm not as old as Al, or as trusting."

Parker said, "You're not going to leave my partner there, and you're not going to hold back my seventy-three thousand."

"I'm not going to move a muscle," Dulare said. "If Al's dead, there's no problem any more. I don't give a damn about Wain, I'm just glad as hell to hear that Farrell's already been bought. All you bring me is good news."

"You're making a mistake," Parker said.

Faran, looking worried, said, "Ernie, maybe we ought to—"

"We do nothing," Dulare said. Looking at Parker, his expression flat, he said, "Your problems are your own. And if you'll take my advice, you'll leave Tyler on the next plane. No matter where it's going."

"You've just lost a home," Parker said, and left.

Thirty-four

Calesian was up. He couldn't remember when he'd felt so alive, so self-confident, so expectant, so in control of things—not with women, not with the job, not anywhere. It wouldn't have surprised him if little bolts of lightning were to shoot from his fingers and eyes.

Standing in the main front hallway of Dutch Buenadella's house, watching Dr. Beiny come slowly down the stairs, Calesian smiled to himself as he comtemplated his own suddenly expanded future. Dutch was up on the second floor, hustling his family to greater speed in their packing; acting like an old woman, he was sending his family out of town for fear of some nameless horror he felt descending on them all. "We're going to the mattresses, Hal," he'd said a little while ago, and it had taken Calesian a minute to figure out what he was talking about. Then it came back to him: a phrase from the movie *The Godfather*, meaning a gang war. Tyler had never in its history had a gang war.

And it wouldn't now. Who was going to dispute? Al Lozini was dead. Frank Schroder was too old, and anyway, content with his piece of the action in the narcotics trade. Ernie Dulare was also content with what he had, and in any event was too smart to go to war on a problem that could very easily be worked out through negotiations; Dutch didn't intend to take anything away from Ernie, so why should Ernie care one way or the other? And who else was there to go to these famous mattresses? Nobody.

181

Dr. Beiny reached the bottom of the stairs and gave Calesian a sour nod. "I'll look in again this evening," he said. A tall stoop-shouldered saturnine man in his late forties, Dr. Beiny had made just about every mistake a respectable middle-class doctor could make. He had performed illegal abortions and had a girl die in his office. He had vacationed in Las Vegas and lost far more than he could pay. He had involved himself with women who were guaranteed to bleed him as much as they could. Although not a drunk, he had been drinking the night he'd been involved in an automobile accident, during which he could have been found guilty of criminal negligence both as a driver *and* as a doctor, had either case ever gone to court. He had mishandled controlled narcotics, misdiagnosed fatal illnesses, and even managed to get caught out by the Internal Revenue Service for nondeclaration of patients' fees that he'd received in cash. The Lozini organization maintained him as a kind of house doctor, and he managed just barely not to be more trouble than he was worth. He was apparently willing to do absolutely anything that was asked of him, and to find pleasure in nothing on earth.

Calesian, nodding toward the second floor, said, "Is our patient sleeping comfortably?"

"He's alive," Dr. Beiny said. "I don't say he'll stay that way for very long."

"Nobody wants him to live forever," Calesian said, grinning. "Just long enough to kill his partner."

"Taking fingers off him won't help," the doctor said. "No matter how careful I am, it shocks the heart."

"Just one a day," Calesian said cheerfully. "We'll give him plenty of chance to rest up in between."

"But what if it kills him?"

Calesian gave him a suggestive smile. "Then we'll just have to take fingers off somebody else, won't we?"

The doctor's sour expression turned even more sour. "I'll stop back this evening," he said.

"You do that."

Calesian watched the doctor leave the house, then glanced up the stairs, thinking about Dutch Buenadella again. He wasn't in sight up there, so Calesian strolled away through the house to the den and sat down at Dutch's desk, swiveling the chair so he could see the rear lawn.

With all those bushes and trees out there, it wasn't possible to see very far, but Calesian knew there wasn't any chance of Parker's sneaking up to this doorway as Calesian himself had done earlier today. The second-floor windows were now occupied by armed men, watching every approach to the house. After dark the floodlights would be turned on. Parker could come here any time, but his arrival would be announced.

It was pleasant to sit here by the open French doors, looking out at greenery in the light of the late afternoon sun. Things were organized, things were under control. Two of Dutch's men were dealing with Al Lozini's body right now, Parker had been contained, his partner Green was being kept alive long enough to be useful, and Calesian himself was on the threshold of a life for himself that he had never dreamed possible. Dutch Buenadella, a businessman as smart and as cold and as nerveless as they come, had collapsed completely when the guns came out. He had made himself dependent on Calesian now, and he would stay dependent from here on. Dutch Buenadella would be the figurehead running Tyler after the death of Al Lozini, but Harold Calesian would be the power behind the throne. The true power.

Until just today Calesian had been content with the power he already possessed, the power implicit in his job with the police force and the power that came as a side effect of his association with Adolf Lozini. But when this new door had opened, this sudden unexpected chance to leap up to a completely different level of life, he hadn't hesitated for a second.

The repaired phone rang, on the desk. Calesian swiveled away from the lawn view to look at it, surprised, and almost reached out to answer it. Then it occurred to him that it wouldn't be for him and that there were other extensions in the house also ringing. Let someone else answer it.

Someone else did, in the middle of the second ring. It was almost as though that, too, was part of Calesian's new range of power; he had reached out with his thoughts in a command to someone to answer the phone, and it had been answered. Which wasn't what had happened, of course, but it *felt* that way, and the feeling of power he was relishing operated at the same level.

Smiling to himself, he turned back and gazed out at the lawn again.

Two minutes later Dutch Buenadella came into the den, and Calesian was taken aback by just how bad the man looked. His flesh seemed too big for his skeleton all at once, as though he'd shriveled somehow inside there. Calesian stared at him, not wanting to ask what was wrong, and Buenadella said, "Ted Shevelly was just found shot to death in the street. Over on Baxter Street. Shot dead."

Thirty-five

Parker drove a dozen blocks before he was certain Dulare hadn't sent anybody to follow him and see what he did next. Good; a man who underestimates you is already half beaten.

There were still three hours or so of daylight left. Parker needed a new base of operations, and he wanted to be set before nightfall. He needed someplace he could use for the next few days without drawing any attention to himself, and where he could arrange for other people to meet him.

Usually the simplest way to make that sort of arrangement was to rent a local whore for a few days, pay her for her body and use her apartment. But this time he couldn't take a chance on that, not when the people he was going up against were the ones who ran the local whores. If he rented one's apartment and let her go out, she might talk too much to the wrong person. If he made the rental and didn't let her out, she might be missed by the wrong person, who might come looking for her.

So the simplest way was out. And any hotel or motel was also out, partly because a determined effort to find him would get him caught at any hotel, and partly because of the phone calls he intended to make.

This was July, midsummer, and a lot of people would be away on vacation, so a possible alternative was to find an empty house or apartment and move in there. But there were problems with that; it would have to be a location where nosy neighbors wouldn't be a likely annoyance, for one thing. For another, this was Sunday, which meant that late tonight some vacationers would be coming home, due to go back to their jobs tomorrow morning. He would have to make sure any place he holed up was occupied by people who had just left, and not people who were just about to come back.

To deal with nosy neighbors, he'd be better off in an apartment than in a private house. The clear spaces around houses made secrecy difficult, and people who lived in houses tended to know their neighbors better than people in apartment buildings.

The one section in Tyler that Parker knew of with large anonymous apartment buildings was Calesian's neighborhood, so that was where he headed. He was still driving the Mercedes, having left the Impala behind at Lozini's house; he knew he'd have to change soon to a less-identifiable car, but the pressure to have a home base was more urgent and at the moment nobody was actively looking for him, so he could wait until dark to make another switch of automobile.

There shouldn't be any danger in using Calesian's neighborhood, but it would be too risky to use the actual building he lived in. Parker drove by it, nine stories of windows winking orange at him from the setting sun, and kept on, looking for another building approximately the same size—big and anonymous.

He found it two blocks farther on, seven stories high, wider than Calesian's building, red brick, with its identical rows of windows and with tenant parking in the basement. This time Parker drove around the block, to the rear of the building where it hulked over a row of small two-family houses across the street. The small houses looked diminished by their huge neighbor, like plants that have shriveled for lack of sun.

Parker walked back around to the front of the building. As with Calesian's place, this one had a locked front door but an open basement-garage entrance. He went in that way, took the elevator up to the lobby, and strolled over to look at the mailboxes: two facing brass ranks in a tile alcove. The building was laid out with four apartments on the first floor and twelve on each of the higher floors, which meant seventy-six mailboxes. Eleven of these had mail inside, showing through the narrow slits in the doors.

In a building like this, tenants going away for a week or so would arrange with the superintendent to pick up their mail for them, to keep it from accumulating too much in the small boxes. But the super wouldn't be working on Sunday, so these particular eleven tenants had apparently not been around since at least yesterday. Parker made notes of the apartment numbers.

The closer to ground level the better. None of the eleven apartments were on either the first or second floors, so he took the elevator up to three to check out the four potentials there.

3C. The doors were standardized, with a normal double-action lock. The third key that Parker tried opened this door, and would probably open every other door in the building. He stepped inside to darkness and a musty smell. When he shut the door behind himself, the only light came through narrow slits in the closed Venetian blinds at the far end of the living room. Patting the wall to his left, he found the light switch, turned it on, and saw at least a week's accumulation of mail piled up on the coffee table in the middle of the room. More than a week; two copies of *Time* were there, one near the top of the pile and one near the bottom. Parker switched off the light again, left the apartment, and used the key to double-lock the door.

3F. The key worked with a little more difficulty. Parker entered a room lit with a weird blue-purple glow. The light came from a fluorescent fixture over a large potted plant; the plant was nearly six feet high, with long bladelike green leaves. A glass-topped table near the front door contained a pile of mail plus a long chatty typewritten note of instructions to the superintendent. In with the directions to Herman concerning plants, birds and mail, there was included the date that Caroline would return: today.

3K. Parker, pausing at the door, heard a television set going inside. He turned away and took the stairs to the fourth floor.

4A. The key worked smoothly, but Parker entered a cool room dominated by the hum of an air-conditioner. This was someone who had gone away only for the weekend.

4J. Again no trouble with the key. The apartment smelled somewhat of rotting garbage. Parker switched on the light and saw disorder and dirt in a living room furnished in odd pieces probably bought secondhand. No pile of mail. A door on the left led to a small sour bedroom in which a fat man wearing only a gray T-shirt slept moistly. His legs were pocked with scabs from hard things he had walked into, and several empty bottles were on the floor around the bed. Parker withdrew, making a note of the place; if nothing else worked out, the fat man could be kept in a closet for a couple of days.

5B. The key didn't work. A different key finally worked, reluctantly. Parker entered a living room with one lamp burning in the far corner, giving a low yellow light. The room was neat, furnished in the style of a decorating magazine, and it contained no pile of mail. There were two bedrooms, one for adults and one for two male children who used bunk beds. The closets seemed full and there were pieces of luggage on the shelves, but that didn't necessarily mean anything one way or the other. But the refrigerator in the small neat kitchen contained an open bottle of milk, half a homemade chocolate cake, and leftover casserole in an orange oval pot with lid. The people in this apartment were too neat to leave things like that in the refrigerator if they planned to be gone for a week or so; they would be back tonight.

5D. The first key worked. The living room was dark, dry, and hot. Parker switched the light on, looked around, and saw no pile of mail. Green drapes were drawn across the window at the far end of the room. The furnishings were ordinary: a sofa and two chairs all arranged so that they faced the television set, and with the appropriate tables and lamps. One bedroom, dominated by a king-size bed and apparently occupied by a couple. No luggage on the closet shelves, and visible spaces amid the clothing, particularly on the woman's side. No razor or toothbrushes in the bathroom. An almost completely cleaned-out refrigerator.

This one looked good. Parker went back to the living room, where a secretary stood against the wall near the front door. Opening the desk part of the secretary, he found papers in pigeonholes, and went through them looking for an indication of this couple's travel plans.

Brochures describing the Caribbean. A pencil-written list of woman's clothing and accessories, each item checked off. And a telephone bill inside its opened envelope; the cancellation date on the envelope was three days ago, Thursday. Since the payment card and return envelope were both gone, the bill had been paid, no earlier than Friday.

All right. Parker had left his and Grofield's luggage—one small bag each—in a locker down at the railroad station, and hc'd go down there tonight to get them back. At the same time he would switch cars. Before then, though, he had other things to do.

The phone was in the living room, next to the sofa. Parker switched on the air-conditioner mounted in the wall under the windows, sat on the sofa, and called Handy McKay collect, using a name that Handy would know: Tom Lynch. Handy, sounding surprised and confused, accepted the charges, and when Parker came on, Handy said, "How come collect?"

"I don't want your number to show up on this phone bill."

"Ah."

"You still looking for something to do?"

"I still eat."

"I have something. It's a little different from regular."

"Will it pay?"

"Yes."

"Where and when?"

"Tyler. The address is 220 Elm Way, apartment 5D. Get here between noon and sundown tomorrow. Arrive quiet."

"On tiptoe," Handy said, meaning that he understood he shouldn't merely take a cab direct from the airport or railroad station to 220 Elm Way.

"See you," Parker said, and broke the connection and made another collect call.

He phoned a total of twenty-five men. Some of them took two or three calls to locate. By the time he was finished, full night had descended on Tyler and eleven of the twenty-five had said they were in.

Thirty-six

Sunday was early closing; local ordinances prohibited liquor sales after midnight. Not that Faran or any of the other local saloonkeepers really minded, since Sunday was a dead night anyway. They were mostly glad of the excuse to close up, throw the few regulars out, and go home.

Angie came into Faran's office a few minutes after midnight, bringing him a final drink. "Everybody's set outside," she said.

He was totaling the figures. "Fine."

"I'm taking off now."

He kept his eyes and his mind on his paperwork. "Okay."

She hesitated. "Will I see you later?"

He looked up. "I'm not sure, Angie. I'm feeling a little shaky."

"Is it me, Frank? Did I do something?"

"Hey, no," he said. Getting to his feet, surprising himself with the sudden rush of tenderness he felt toward the girl, he went around the desk and took her upper arms in his hands. "Nothing wrong with you at all, Angie. It's just all this trouble we've been having. Give me a couple days, let things calm down, then everything will be just fine again."

"Okay," she said, and gave him a tentative smile. "You had me a little worried."

"Don't worry, Angie. Don't worry about a thing." He kissed her briefly and released her. "I'm just nervous these days, that's all."

"Okay, Frank. Good night."

He watched her walk toward the door, skinny and tight, and felt the old ripples in his loins. "Maybe—" he said.

She turned to look back at him.

He grinned and bobbed his head. "Maybe I'll stop over later on."

"Any time, Frank."

"I'm not sure. Just maybe."

"If I'm asleep," she said, "just wake me." She gave him a lazy grin and said, "You know how."

"Yes, I do."

He watched her leave, but the instant she was out of sight his mind veered away again. Al Lozini's death, the replacement of Farrell for Wain, Dutch Buenadella taking over, Hal Calesian suddenly some kind of major power, that guy Parker still prowling around—it was enough to give a man nightmares. Even if he could get to sleep in the first place.

Faran had another ten minutes' work. The numbers distracted him, soothed his mind, and the drink Angie had brought also helped. He was feeling a little better when he left the office, made his way through the empty club, turned the lights off at the main box by the front door, and went outside.

He was locking the door when he felt the gun in his back. His knees weakened, and he leaned against the door. "Jesus God," he whispered.

It was Parker; Parker's voice, saying, "Come on, Frank. Let's take a walk."

Thirty-seven

When the doctor left he switched off the light, leaving the room in total darkness. A window was open to let in the warm night air, but no illumination entered with it. The sky was black, dotted with high thin stars that showed nothing but themselves. The room remained black and silent, undefined except by the vaguely lighter rectangle of the window and the hair-thin line of yellow light under the door.

After two hours the sliver of moon appeared in the left edge of the window. Tomorrow night it would finish its monthly wink, closing down completely, but tonight it was still visible, though heavy-lidded. It gave very little more light than the stars, an almost unnoticeable pallor that wouldn't be able to make its presence known if there was any other light source at all.

But in the bedroom there wasn't. The gray light crept at an angle across the room, picking up a dresser against the wall and a corner of the foot of the bed. As the moon eased across the sky, more of the bed came into existence, until the light touched on a bandaged hand. Dr. Beiny, being as considerate as possible, had taken the last finger of the left hand.

The moon's angle reached Grofield's face, the skin as pale and bloodless as the light that defined it. His breathing was very slow and very shallow, and his eyes did no moving at all behind the closed lids. At times his brain fluttered weakly with incoherent dreams that he wouldn't remember if he ever woke up, but mostly he was quiescent.

The bullet had gone through his body, entering between two

ribs and taking a small chip from one of them, passing near the heart, tearing tissue and lung, and exiting through a much larger hole in the back. Dr. Beiny had filled this body with medicines meant to promote healing and guard against infection, had closed and bandaged both holes, had added blood to the depleted store, and was feeding Grofield intravenously with a liquid composed mostly of protein and sugar. The apparatus in the room, chrome and glass, glinting dimly in the moonlight, gave the place the air of a hospital or a medical station near a battlefield: inverted bottle suspended from a chrome armature, syringes, beakers, full and empty squat medicine bottles with cork stoppers through which the hypodermic needle would be thrust.

By midnight the moon was halfway across the window space. A small sound occurred in Grofield's throat, his eyes twitched inside the lids, the remaining fingers of his left hand contracted slightly. His heart beat slowly but erratically, and then it stopped. The fingers opened out a bit again, losing their tension. The eyes became still. The heart thudded again, blundered forward like a blind man in a dense woods. A long, slow, almost silent sigh emerged through Grofield's slightly parted lips; not quite the soul leaving the body.

The shred of moon moved on, showing other parts of the room, gradually leaving the bed in darkness. Toward morning Grofield died again, this time for three seconds, in silence and total darkness; then lived again, tenuous, clutching.

Thirty-eight

There are three planes a day from La Guardia Airport in New York City to Tyler National Airport in Tyler, the second one leaving just before noon. Stan Devers, having spent the night before with a girl he knew in Manhattan, took a cab at eleven in the morning and reached the airport with plenty of time to spare.

Stan Devers was in his late twenties, muscular and smiling and self-confident, with a clean strong jawline and curly blond hair. He had an easy long-strided walk and a manner of open honesty that was maybe just a little too good to be true. For as long as he could remember he'd been a swimmer upstream, a rebel for the sake of rebellion, opposed to everything that plain stolid ordinary society stood for. He'd been thrown out of two high schools and one college—having already, in the college, been thrown out of ROTC—he'd been fired from most of the jobs he'd ever held, but he'd survived nearly three and a half years of enlisted service in the Air Force before making the move that had thrust him out of square society forever.

He had been a finance clerk in the Air Force, on a base where the payroll had still been in cash, a thing that didn't happen anywhere at all now. He'd worked out a way to take a month's payroll and had involved himself with some professional thieves to pull the job, including Parker. They'd succeeded in getting the money, but then things had gone wrong and Devers' connection with the robbery had become known by the authorities. He'd had to take off, and Parker had sent him to

Handy McKay in Presque Isle, who had finished the job of turning him into a professional thief. He'd worked six robberies in the last five years, with varying success, including one with Parker last year, a hijacking of paintings that had gone very badly, with no profit for anybody. He'd had a minor score since then with some other people, but not enough to make him really easy in his mind about his money cushion. Which was why he'd been happy to hear from Parker again, even with Parker's cryptic warning that this wasn't an ordinary job.

The girl at the airline counter seemed mildly surprised that Devers was buying a one-way ticket. He hadn't bought one round-trip ticket in the last five years, and doubted that he ever would again. In a way, it symbolized the kind of life he lived, the theme of it that he enjoyed: never go back to anything, never move anywhere but forward.

A noon plane on a summer Monday to a third-level city in the hinterlands; there weren't many passengers. The tourists had done their traveling on the weekend, the businessmen had taken the earlier morning plane, and all that was left was oddities like Stan Devers. Checking in at the gate, he saw no more than a dozen other passengers in the plastic seats there, all gazing moodily out the big windows at the white plane waiting to take them aboard. Of course, it was still fifteen minutes before takeoff time, but he doubted the plane would be very full when it left.

He carried a black attaché case and a black raincoat. Between them, they contained everything he needed to travel with. Getting his ticket back from the check-in clerk, he walked over to the side wall of the waiting area and sat in a chair that gave him equal views of the windows and the check-in desk. Five minutes later he saw a huge bald man arrive and hand over his ticket, and he grinned to himself. Now why would a man mountain like that be going to Tyler this fine morning, unless he was another member of Parker's team?

Dan Wycza accepted his ticket back, muttered a thank you, and moved into the waiting area, looking around for a seat away from the other passengers. He saw a kid sort of grinning at him from over by the side wall, ignored him, and sat down in the front row, right near the plate-glass view of the airplane. Putting his old brown-leather bag on the floor at his feet, he took out the health magazine he'd been reading and went on with the article about the skin-drying effects and other disadvantages of sunlight.

Wycza hadn't seen Parker in almost ten years, not since the time a bunch of them had knocked over a whole town together —banks and jewelry stores and everything. Copper Canyon, North Dakota. What a mess they'd made of that place, even more than they'd intended. Since then Wycza had done a number of jobs, none of them as big or as gaudy as that Copper Canyon business, but they'd kept him in wheat germ and yogurt. Whenever things had gotten slow he'd gone back to his other trade, wrestling, but given his choice, he preferred armed robbery. It was always better to be paid in thousands than in hundreds.

He felt eyes on him. He was sensitive to that kind of thing, being a big man and completely bald, sensitive to being stared at, and he didn't like it. He glanced around, irritated, and it was the young guy over by the wall. Grinning at him, as though he knew something about something. And not shifting his eyes away when Wycza glowered at him. In the end, it was Wycza himself who looked away, facing front again and trying unsuccessfully to go on reading the article in the magazine.

That was the only thing wrong with this life, the fear of arrest. Could that possibly be a cop over there, could some old score have suddenly blown up, could he be on a wanted list without knowing it? This wouldn't be the first time a guy squealed on everybody else he knew in order to keep from doing a little time himself, and an airport was a natural place to look for a wanted man.

Guardedly, Wycza looked around the waiting area, but he couldn't see any more of them. Just the one grinning clown over by the wall, who was still looking at him.

Waiting for the boarding to start? Waiting to collar him when he started toward the plane?

Wycza found himself wishing he had a gun in his luggage, despite the danger of air marshal searches.

He had never taken a fall, had never spent even one night in jail, and he wanted it to stay that way. Because he knew what would happen to him in jail, he would die there. A year, two years at the most, and Dan Wycza would be dead.

There were things he needed in order to stay alive, things beyond the simple food and shelter and clothing the prison would supply. Exercise, for instance. He needed to be able to run, to run for miles and to do it every day. He needed to work out in gyms whenever he wanted. He had to keep using his body, or it would dry up and die, he knew that with utter certainty.

And women. He needed women almost as much as he needed exercise. And special foods: steak, and milk, and green vegetables, all properly cooked and not steam-tabled till all the nutrition was out of them. And food supplements, vitamin pills and mineral pills and protein pills.

Not in jail. In jail he wouldn't be able to exercise, not properly. And there'd be no women, and none of the food or pills he needed. In jail he would shrivel up, his teeth would rot, his muscles would sag, his body would shrink in on itself and start even before he was dead to decay.

He wasn't going to jail. If it came down to it, if it was down to it right here and now, he wasn't going to jail. There are two ways to die, fast and slow, and he'd rather go out the fast way. He wouldn't go to jail because in order to put him in jail they'd have to lay hands on him, and before they could lay hands on him they'd have to kill him.

Movement. Wycza lifted his head, and faintly reflected in the plate glass in front of him he could see the young guy coming this way. Wycza carefully folded his magazine and put it away in his jacket pocket. Every muscle in his big body was tensed.

The young guy passed between groupings of plastic seats and stopped in front of the glass, just to Wycza's right, looking out at the plane. Wycza kept his head down, watching the guy from under his brows, and after a minute the guy turned and gave him a cheerful smile and said, "Hello, there."

Wycza lifted his head. He felt dangerous, and he looked dangerous. He said, "Something?"

The young guy didn't seem troubled. Still smiling, he said, "I wonder if you know a friend of mine in Tyler."

What's this? Wycza, frowning massively, said, "No. I don't know anybody in Tyler."

"This friend is named Parker," the young guy said.

A cop. A definite cop. "Never heard of him," Wycza said.

"He lives on Elm Way," the young guy said.

"Don't ring a bell," Wycza said.

The young guy's expression began to change; doubt was creeping in. "Are you sure? I could have sworn you were somebody on your way to see my friend."

"Not me, friend," Wycza said. "You got the wrong guy."

The guy shook his head, obviously all at sea. "Well, I'm sorry," he said. "I'm sorry I troubled you."

"Yeah, sure."

The guy started away, and Wycza reached in his pocket for a magazine. Then the guy suddenly laughed aloud, and turned back, and gave Wycza a huge happy grin. "Well, of course!" he said.

Now what? Wycza waited, saying nothing.

The guy came over closer, bent down so no one else in the waiting area would be able to hear what he had to say, and whispered, "You thought I was a cop!"

Wycza still did. "I don't know what the hell you're talking about," he said.

The guy dropped down into the seat on Wycza's right, and said, quietly but excitedly, "My name's Devers, Stan Devers. Parker never told you anything about me?"

"I told you before, you—"

"Wait a minute now," Devers said; if that was his name. "Didn't Parker tell you there were other people coming? Doesn't it make sense there'd be one or two on this plane? I'll tell you, I worked with Parker twice before this. I'm the one set up the air-base payroll job upstate here about five years ago. You ever hear of that?"

"You're still making a mistake," Wycza said, but he was no longer entirely sure that was true. He didn't know anything about an air-base payroll job, but Devers' line had a ring of reality to it.

"The other one," Devers said, still talking low and fast, "was hijacking some paintings last year. We worked with, uh, Ed Mackey. You know him?"

"No."

"Handy McKay."

That was a name Wycza knew. He also knew that McKay had retired a few years ago. Meaning to be clever, he said, "You worked with Handy McKay last year?"

"Don't be silly," Devers said. "He's up there in his diner in Presque Isle, Maine. I hid out with him when I first went on the bent. You want me to describe him to you? He lips his cigarettes something fierce."

That was true. Wycza found himself grinning, then immediately sobered up again. "You got a good line of talk," he said.

"You're a tough man to convince," Devers said. "What does it take?"

Wycza wanted to believe the kid, but caution was strong in him. It had to be. "Why brace me?" he said. "What's the point?"

Devers shrugged. "Why not? We're both going the same place for the same reason. Why not talk, have a pleasant trip?"

Wycza studied him a minute longer. "You're a strange guy, Devers," he said.

Devers' smile broadened. "Stan," he said, and held out his hand.

One more hesitation, a brief one. Then Wycza shook his head and said, "Yeah, I guess I believe you." Taking Devers' hand, he said, "I'm Dan Wycza."

"Dan and Stan." They shook on it, and Devers said, "Glad to know you, Dan."

Fred Ducasse barely made the plane on time. The passengers were already boarding when he got to the gate. He submitted his small canvas bag to a luggage search, and was the last person to board the plane.

It was a fairly small plane, one class, with three seats to the left of the aisle and two to the right. Less than half the seats were occupied, so even though he was last, Ducasse could just about pick his spot. He preferred the rear, so he moved that way down the narrow aisle, holding his bag ahead of himself.

On the left, two men were in casual low-voiced conversation. One of them was a young good-looking guy with curly blond hair, and the other was a bald giant of about forty. They made a strange-looking pair, and Ducasse glanced at them curiously on the way by. The young one looked up at the same time, and for just a second their eyes met. It seemed to Ducasse, as he looked quickly away, that the guy had had a questioning look in his eyes, as though wondering if he maybe knew Ducasse from somewhere. Ducasse looked back at him again, but he wasn't looking up any more. He was deep in his conversation with the bald one, and Ducasse was sure he'd never seen either of those two before.

He was just settling himself into a window seat well back of the wing when the plane started taxiing, and a minute later the stewardess started broadcasting safety announcements. Ducasse settled in, watched out the window as the plane took off, and then drifted away into his own thoughts.

He hoped this one was really it. He'd been living on his case money for over a year now, he definitely needed something good, and he needed something soon.

He was a little worried about this being Parker again. Not that he had anything against Parker, or Parker's ability; it was just that Parker, too, seemed to be running a bad streak, and Ducasse was just superstitious enough to wish he was teaming up with somebody who'd been riding winners lately.

Two things with Parker last year, and both of them had gone to hell. A department-store robbery set up by a guy named Kirwan, and then an art-treasure robbery in California set up by a fool named Beaghler. Ducasse and Parker had been in on both of them, and neither one had happened. Then Ducasse had gone in on an armored-car job that hadn't worked out, but while it was still on he'd tipped Parker to something involving hijacking paintings, and he'd heard that one, too, had fallen apart. So it had been a bad year all the way around, and all Ducasse hoped was that he and Parker wouldn't between them jinx this new score, whatever it turned out to be. Something simple, that's what he wanted, simple and clean and profitable and fast.

Gazing at that bald head up toward the middle of the plane, idly thinking his thoughts, Ducasse dropped off to sleep and didn't wake up again till the plane set down at Tyler.

Thirty-nine

Hurley and Dalesia drove west toward Tyler, Dalesia behind the wheel of the stolen three-year-old gray Mustang and Hurley beside him bitching about Morse.

In the two weeks since the busted jewelry-store robbery, Hurley had spent most of his waking hours looking for Morse, the guy who had sold them the plan, but Morse had absolutely dropped out of sight. Dalesia had traveled with Hurley, not because he himself felt any rage about the busted plan—that extra alarm could have been put in at any time, it wasn't necessarily Morse's fault that he hadn't known about it—but simply because there hadn't been anything else to do.

Now there was something else to do. Parker had called and said he had something kind of unusual in Tyler and would they like to be counted in. Was there money in it? Yes, there was. Yes, they wanted to be counted in.

But still Hurley couldn't get over bitching about Morse. "After this business," he said, as they made the transition from the Pennsylvania Turnpike to the Ohio Turnpike, "I'm really gonna take my time and find that son of a bitch. I'm one guy he doesn't hide from."

"I'm going to take my time, too," Dalesia said. "I'm going to take my time up in the Laurentians, up above Quebec."

Hurley gave him a quick look. "You think Morse is up there?"

"No, I think there's a lot of trout up there," Dalesia said. "You can go hunting, Tom, after this is over, but I'm going fishing."

Ed Mackey and his girl Brenda drove north from New Orleans in a yellow Jaguar Mackey owned under his Illinois name of Edwin Mills. Hairy, stocky, just under average height, Mackey was about forty years of age and had an aggressive, pushing, cocky manner like a good club fighter. Though his chest and shoulders and back were covered with curly black hair, he was beginning to thin on top, a fact he usually hid, like now, with a cloth cap at a jaunty angle down over his eyes. He drove with his head back a bit, looking out from under the bill of his cap and through the narrow windshield of the Jaguar at the road unwinding toward Tyler.

Brenda said, "This fellow in Tyler. Isn't he one of the people in that hijacking last year? Those paintings?"

"Parker, yeah," Mackey said. "You remember him, the mean-looking one."

"We went to that party with him."

Mackey grinned at her. He really liked Brenda, she was okay. "That's the one," he said.

"He didn't exactly turn me on," Brenda said. A slender girl in her mid-twenties, Brenda was good-looking in a no-nonsense way, and had a lot of leg. She was the best woman Mackey had ever gone with, because she was easy in her mind; she knew who she was, and she liked who she was, and she was very easy to get along with. Most people, men and women, weren't like that; most people didn't know who they were, didn't like who they thought they were, and weren't at all easy to get along with.

"You're okay, Brenda," Mackey said.

She nodded, agreeing with him without making an issue of it, because she was thinking of other things. She said, "Do you think this one will work out?"

"It better," Mackey said. "You know how nervous I get when I start wallpapering."

"I don't see why," she said. "I never have any trouble at all."

"Well, you always go to some guy behind the counter," he told her. "He's so busy looking at you, it don't matter what you write on the check. You could put Fuck You down for your signature, they'd still cash it."

"Don't talk dirty," Brenda said.

"In the car," Mackey amended.

She smiled at him, with a sidelong look. "In the car," she said.

It had been six years since Mike Carlow had worked with Parker; he was looking forward to seeing him again. Parker had been square the last time, when they'd knocked over that coin convention in Indianapolis, and it wasn't too often you worked with somebody you could trust.

What had happened, Carlow had wound up in custody after the robbery, but Parker had gotten away with the coins. Another guy in on it, a Nazi named Otto Mainzer, had also been picked up by the law, and the only thing that had saved Carlow's skin was Mainzer's obnoxious personality. Mainzer had made the cops hate him so much that they offered Carlow a free ride out of town if he would put Mainzer on ice for them. Hating Mainzer himself, Carlow had sung like the Andrews Sisters and had come out of it all clean and clear and safe, and when he'd gotten home to San Diego, damned if Parker hadn't sent him his quarter of the profits: fifty thousand dollars.

That had turned into the JJ-2. Three wins, two third places, and one spectacular crash at Ontario Speedway. A good car, the old JJ-2.

A car, to Mike Carlow, was something that took you from Point A to Point B in one second flat, regardless of the distance in between. That was the ideal, anyway, striven for but not as yet reached in either Detroit or Europe; or in the workshop of Mike Carlow. He was a racing driver, in his early forties now, who'd been at it since high school, when he'd started by pushing one clunker after another around the stock-car tracks. While still a teenager he'd designed a racing car with a center of gravity guaranteed to be unaffected by the amount of fuel left in the tank, because there wasn't any tank; the car was built around a frame of hollow aluminum tubing, which would hold the fuel supply. When someone he showed the idea to objected that it might be a little dangerous to surround the driver with gasoline, he'd said, "So what?"

Racing cars would probably be his death, but until then they were his life. And if they didn't cost so damn much to design and build and care for, he never would get involved in jobs with people like Parker, taking them safely and quickly away from the scene of a score. But they did cost, and he did refuse to simply become a hired hand for one of the major companies, so here he was again, back on the road, pushing his modified Datsun 240Z toward Tyler. And considering the different guys he'd driven for over the years in jobs like this, he was pleased that this time it was a score set up by Parker.

Frank Elkins and Ralph Wiss took turns driving their Pontiac down from Chicago. They'd worked together for fifteen years, they owned homes in the same Chicago suburb, their families visited back and forth, and it was beginning to seem that in a few years Elkins' daughter Pam and Wiss' son Jason would be getting married. Both wives knew what Elkins and Wiss did for a living, but the children and the cousins and the nieces and all the rest were kept in the dark. "We do specialty promotions," Frank Elkins would say, if asked, and Ralph Wiss would nod. Specialty promotions.

Wiss was a safe man, a jugger, a man whose specialty was opening safes by whatever means was most appropriate. He was comfortable with liquid nitro and with plastic explosive, he was expert at peeling, he could drill out a combination lock or cut a circular hole in the top of a solid steel safe. He had helped to tunnel into vaults, to by-pass time locks and to remove wall safes entirely, so they could be worked on at leisure somewhere else. A small narrow man with a concentrated look, Wiss was a skilled craftsman, as devoted to his work as any fine jeweler.

Elkins was a general purpose man, a utility infielder. He would hold the gun, or carry the duffel bag full of cash, or keep an eye out the front window. He was the eyes and the muscles, complementing Wiss' brain. They knew one another completely by now, trusted one another, and worked together with no waste motion.

The last time these two had seen Parker was in Copper Canyon, the time the whole town had been cleaned out. Before that, they'd worked with him in St. Louis, hitting a syndicate operation, a place where the local bookies' comeback money was collected. Normally, people like Wiss and Elkins left syndicate places alone, but at the time Parker had had some sort of feud on with a boss named Bronson, and since it was bound to be a safe and profitable score, Wiss and Elkins had been happy to work it with him.

They didn't talk much on the drive, being too comfortable with one another to need to force conversation. They did both wonder aloud about the score they were coming down to, but they didn't worry about it. Elkins said, "If it's Parker, it's all right."

"He gets gaudy sometimes," Wiss said. He was a man with no taste for melodrama at all.

"But safe," Elkins said.

Wiss shrugged. He was always guarded, always kept a little in reserve. "It's worth the drive," he said.

Philly Webb drove the Buick west from Baltimore. The new blue paint job sparkled at him from the hood, the new license plates were a complementary blue from Delaware, and the new identification in the glove compartment and his hip pocket said that the Buick was registered to one Justin Baxter of Wilmington and that he himself was the same Justin Baxter.

Webb was a driver, like Mike Carlow, but he never had anything to do with racing. Robbery was his only profession, partying and gambling was where the money went, and the Buick was his single hobby.

This was his fifth Buick. He bought one every few years, buying it new and legit, straight out of a dealer's window. But within a week a new car in his possession had completely lost its original identity and would never find it again. He switched engines so as to switch motor numbers, he altered serial numbers, he changed the paint job, he bought false registration and fake license plates. And after he'd had the car for a few months he would do the same thing all over again, changing things around, re-establishing yet another new identity. By the time he'd owned a car for three years, it would probably have operated under ten or twelve registrations, colors, and sets of license plates.

In addition to the periodic face lifts done mainly for the hell of it, Webb also completely redid his current Buick immediately after working a score. The blue paint on this car was less than three weeks old, but the car would be some other color within twenty-four hours of his returning to Baltimore. He prided himself on having attained the absolutely untraceable car, but in truth most of the changes he put his cars through were unnecessary, done more as a hobby than for any real reason.

Short and chunky and olive-complexioned, Webb had the chest and arms of a weight lifter, giving him a vaguely apelike look. He fit behind the wheel of a car with the naturalness of a cabdriver, and always seemed a little awkward when forced to walk. He had last worked with Parker in the air-base robbery with Stan Devers in Upstate New York. He'd come away with forty-two thousand out of that, every dollar of it long since spent, and he was looking forward to working with Parker again.

Forty

A murmur of voices woke Faran. He was very uncomfortable and he had a lousy cottony headache, and at first he couldn't remember where he was or what was going on. Then he tried to shift on the bed, and realized his wrists were tied behind him, and it all came back.

Parker. The son of a bitch had kidnapped him last night, just as he was closing the club. Standing there in the street, cool and calm and taking his time, he'd tied Faran's wrists and put some sort of bag over his head and then walked him to a car and drove him here—wherever here was.

In an apartment building, he knew that much. They had driven for a while, not long enough to be out of the city, and just before the car stopped, it had dipped down some sort of short incline. An apartment building with a basement garage. And an elevator, in which they rode up together, his head still inside the bag, silent Parker's hand on his elbow. Then along a corridor until Parker stopped him and withdrew his hand for a few seconds. The grate of a key in a lock. He was led into the apartment, the door was closed, and the bag was taken away.

The apartment was a surprise. He'd expected a grubby room somewhere, but it wasn't like that at all. It was a pleasant middle-class apartment, sofa and chairs and TV and lamps and tables. Green drapes covering windows in the far wall. Carpeting, with a bit of dark-stained wood flooring showing around the edges of the room.

Near the entrance door was a dining area: an oval table and

four chairs, tucked into the corner. Parker sat Faran down there, produced pen and paper, and started asking questions. At first Faran wouldn't answer, and he expected to be threatened and maybe punched around, but Parker didn't do anything like that at all. He just took a small white box out of his pocket and put it on the table where Faran could see the severed finger lying inside it. Then he asked the questions again, and after a short hesitation Faran started answering.

The questions went on till long after sunup, till Faran was so exhausted he could barely keep his head vertical and his eyes open. But Parker kept pushing, wanting to know more, demanding details, writing it all down on sheet after sheet of paper. Doing sketches and blueprints and insisting that Faran study them, tell him where the details were wrong. What kind of window is this? How many people work in that office? What time does this place open?

Till at last it was finished. Faran fell asleep at the table while Parker read through his notes once more, to be sure there wasn't anything else he needed to know. Then Parker had to thump him and shout at him and yank him by the hair to wake him up enough so he could stand and be marched into a bedroom and locked away in a closet. It was wide enough so he could lean his back against one side wall and stretch his feet out to the other, and that was the way he slept, until midafternoon. At any rate, he thought it was probably midafternoon, since there hadn't been any direct sunlight on the closed drapes in the morning but there was when Parker unlocked the closet door and let him out.

Parker had obviously slept in the bed, and looked rested and hard. Faran felt cramped, stiff, and logy, and his stomach was acting up again. He couldn't keep from breaking wind all over the place, even after Parker untied his wrists and let him use the john. For the next hour or so Faran remained untied, but the way Parker looked at him, he knew better than to try anything. The two of them had a silent meal together, made out of cans from the kitchen closet, and then Parker let him sit in the living room for an hour or so. They watched television, and it seemed to Faran that Parker didn't care what program he watched. It was as though he wasn't really watching television at all, but was concentrating on things inside his own head and found it restful to fill the time with the flittering shadows and piping voices from the TV set.

Then the doorbell rang, and at once Parker turned off the TV, tied Faran's wrists again, and marched him to the bedroom. In the bedroom he pointed at Faran's face and said, "Those teeth in the front. They caps?"

"On the top, yeah."

Parker nodded toward the window. "If I come back in and that shade is up," he said, "I'll take those caps out of your head."

Faran just nodded. He didn't want to open his mouth to say anything.

Then Parker left him, and he sat on the bed, and gradually the light against the window shade dimmed. From time to time he heard the doorbell ring again, and after a while he could make out several male voices. He was having trouble believing it, but it had to be true: Parker was going to start a war. He was supposed to be a loner, an orphan without true connections, but he was bringing in people from somewhere, and he was honest to God going to start a war against Dutch and Calesian and Ernie Dulare. Especially Ernie Dulare, who was the most vulnerable to the kind of war Parker apparently intended to wage.

If they found out, if Ernie and Dutch and Calesian ever found out where Parker had gotten his information, Faran knew they would kill him. No question, no bullshit about this being the bloodless new order, they would flat kill him.

Unless Parker killed them first.

And after a while he was no longer entirely sure which side he wanted to root for.

Somewhere in through that space of time, his mind full of muddled thoughts, he had fallen asleep again, curled up awkwardly on the bed with his wrists tied behind him, and now he was awake once more, listening to the sound of voices in the living room, wondering what was going to happen next and what Parker would be doing with him when it was all over.

Then the bedroom door opened, letting in yellow light that made him squint, and he suddenly realized that the scraping metallic noise of the key in the lock was what had brought him up from a fuzzy, shallow, unsatisfying sleep to a fuzzy, headachy, unsatisfying wakefulness. Sitting up, blinking fast, trying to accustom his eyes quickly to the light, he made out the black silhouette of somebody entering the room, and he thought, *He kills me now. I'm not useful to him any more.*

Then the overhead light switched on, and Parker crossed the room to lift him up with a hand clutching his upper arm, saying, "Come on, Faran. Some people for you to see."

"What? What?"

"Walk."

"I was asleep, I—" He cleared his throat, coughed, cleared his throat again. He was waking up now, at least a little. He put one foot in front of the other, urged on by Parker's hand holding his arm, and walked shakily out of the bedroom and around the short hall to the living room.

The people there woke him up for good. There must have been a dozen of them, ranging in age from mid-twenties to late forties and in size from small and narrow to huge and heavily muscled, but every one of them had the same tough cold self-sufficient look as Parker. They gave him those flat emotionless stares, classifying him, deciding about him, and he stood there blinking and licking his lips, terrified beyond the call of rational argument, as frightened as a bird in a den of snakes.

And the pile of pistols on the big table by the front door didn't help either.

Parker stayed beside him, and he had to give his order twice before Faran heard it: "Tell them your name."

"My n— What? My name." He hurried to obey. "Frank Faran."

"What do you do for a living, Frank?"

The use of his first name might have been meant to reassure him, but the cold impersonality in the sound of it had just the opposite effect. Striving to be calm, trying to be capable of instant accurate response to any question that might be put him, he said, "I manage the New York Room. It's a—it's a local nightspot." The word "nightspot" echoed in his ears, sounding foolish and limp, and he was horrified to feel himself blushing.

Parker had more questions. "What else do you do, Frank?"

"Well, I've still got— I used to be heavily in union management, I've still got a few posts, minor, uh—"

"Local union executive?"

"Yeah, uh— Yeah, that's right."

"Sweetheart unions?"

"Well, we, uh, mostly have, uh, good understandings with the employers."

"What else are you connected with, Frank?"

Faran tried to think of anything else, but there wasn't any more. "Nothing," he said. "That's all."

"You're not thinking, Frank." There was a small threat shimmering in the words. The dozen men sitting on sofa and chairs, standing leaning against walls, continued to watch him. Parker said, "Who do you work for, Frank?"

"Oh, Mr. Lozini. I mean, I did, but he's dead. So I guess now it's, uh, Dutch Buenadella or Ernie Dulare. Or both, maybe."

Parker pointed, and Faran saw that on the coffee table in the middle of the living room papers were spread: the blueprints and notes Parker had taken last night during the question-and-answer session. Parker said, "You told me all that, didn't you, Frank?"

"Yes," Faran said. "Right, yes."

"And it's all straight goods, isn't it, Frank?"

Faran tried for a joke, a laugh, a bit of human contact. "I'm not going to lie," he said.

No change in the faces in front of him, except that one of them said, "How can we be sure of him?"

"Because," Parker said, "he knows we don't let him go until after we've checked out everything he told me. And he knows that if he lied to us we'll kill him. Don't you, Frank?"

Faran nodded. He didn't trust himself to speak.

There was a little silence. He looked no one directly in the eye, looked only at the spaces between them, but felt them all staring unblinking at him. Trying to decide about him. His throat ached, felt raspy, as though he'd been shouting at the top of his lungs for half an hour.

Parker said, quietly, "You want to change anything you told me, Frank?"

Faran shook his head, but at the same time he was trying to

think, trying to remember everything he'd said. Could he have made any mistakes? No, it wasn't possible, Parker had made him go over every detail again and again. "I told you the truth," he said. "I swear I did."

Faran turned to look at Parker, and saw Parker looking at the dozen men, waiting for them to say whether they were satisfied or not. Faran couldn't face front again, he had to keep blinking at Parker. His left cheek, the one toward the men, prickled, felt pins and needles.

One of them said, "Okay. You made your point."

Parker nodded. "Anybody want to ask Frank anything?"

None of them did. Faran was grateful for that, and grateful, too, when Parker said, "All right, Frank, let's go back."

The two of them walked back to the bedroom. Faran entered it, and Parker remained in the doorway. Faran turned around and said, "You can trust me, Parker. I won't cause any trouble."

"That's right, Frank," Parker said. He switched off the light and shut the bedroom door.

Forty-one

Parker put Faran on ice and went back to the living room, where the eleven men had formed themselves into small groups and were talking things over. He let them talk, waiting it out, knowing sooner or later they'd all decide to come in with him.

One of the groups was Devers and Wycza and Ducasse; they'd never met before, but they'd all flown in on the same plane from New York, Devers and Wycza connecting in New York, the two of them realizing that Ducasse was also a part of this once they'd landed in Tyler. Clustered around the sofa to talk were Wiss and Elkins, who always worked together as a team, plus Nick Dalesia, who'd done the driving on the busted jewelry-store job, and Tom Hurley. Handy McKay was listening to an opinion from Philly Webb, and both Ed Mackey and Mike Carlow were sitting off by themselves, thinking about it.

Parker had moved one of the chairs from the dining table to the end of the room nearest the door so he could face the entire group. He sat down now, saw by his watch that it wasn't yet ten P.M., and waited for things to quiet down.

But they didn't quiet, not exactly. Instead, Tom Hurley, who finally seemed to have forgotten his grudge against Morse, at least for a while, got to his feet and pointed at the papers scattered on the coffee table and called across the room, "Parker, where are you going to be while we're running all this other stuff?"

The others all stopped talking and looked at Parker, who said, "Right here. I hold Faran, I keep this place for everybody to get back to, and I'm the phone drop you're gonna need."

Hurley pointed at the papers again. "So you've got these capers here," he said. "We go do them, we hit all at once, that's sensible, I like that. Keeps us clean of cops. You're back here, you keep the coffee and the doughnuts."

Quietly, Handy McKay said, "And he set them up. Every score is worked out there."

Parker, jabbing a thumb back at the pistols piled on the dining table, said, "And I got you hardware from a gun store last night. All new pieces, with ammunition. I couldn't test-fire them, but you shouldn't need to shoot them."

"That's okay," Hurley said. "That's all very nice. My question is, what's your piece?"

"No cash," Parker said.

They all looked at him. Ed Mackey said, "Parker? You don't want any cut?"

"There's eleven of you," Parker said. "You go out, you pull the action, you come back, you put all the take in one pile and split it eleven ways. So everybody gets the same piece."

Hurley, frowning as though looking for the butcher's thumb, said, "Except you?"

"That's right."

Fred Ducasse said, "What's in it for you?"

"I want you to do a piece of work for me," Parker said. "Tomorrow, after all this other stuff is done and you've all made your money."

Hurley, looking satisfied, as though he thought maybe he finally did see that thumb resting on the scale after all, said, "What kind of a piece of work, Parker?"

Parker got to his feet, took the small white box from his pocket, took the top off it, and put the box on the coffee table amid the papers. Then he stood back and let them study it.

That wasn't the butcher's thumb; Hurley's lips curled back in distaste and he said, "Who is it, Parker?"

"A guy named Grofield."

Dan Wycza said, "Alan Grofield?"

"That's right."

Frank Elkins said, "Yeah, I remember him. He worked with us in Copper Canyon."

"That's right," Wycza said. "He's the clown brought the girl out with him. Telephone girl."

214

Nick Dalesia said, "I worked with a guy named Grofield once. An actor."

"That's the one," Wycza said.

Ralph Wiss said, "A very humorous type of fella."

"Right," Dalesia said.

"I don't know him," Hurley said. He made it sound belligerent, and his manner was aggressive as he looked around the room at the others. "Do I know this guy?"

Nobody answered him. Ed Mackey said, "I know him. We got together once on something that didn't work out. Seemed like a good guy."

Wycza said, "Wha'd he ever do with the telephone girl?"

"Married her," Parker said. "They run a summer theater together in Indiana."

"A love story," Wycza said, and grinned.

Handy McKay said, "I know Alan. What happened to him? How'd he lose that finger?"

"He and I did a job here a couple years ago," Parker said, and told them the story in a few quick highlights: the money in Fun Island, Lozini, Buenadella, Dulare. When he finished, Tom Hurley said, "I get it. These are mob places we're hitting."

"That's right."

Fred Ducasse said, "We put pressure on them, then you tell them to turn over Grofield and the cash or they'll get hit again."

Ralph Wiss had been sitting there paying no apparent attention to the conversation, seeming to be sunk in his own thoughts. Now he said, "That won't work."

"I know it," Parker said. "That's not what I have in mind."

Ducasse, turning to Wiss, asked, "Why won't it work? They'll want their places left alone, won't they?"

"I know this kind of people," Wiss said. "They're not used to losing a fight, they don't know how to go about it. They'll spend double the money to bring in more talent, guard everything they own, and start hunting for Parker."

Stan Devers said, "While they send him a finger a day. That's sweet."

Hurley said, "So what do you want, Parker?"

"I want Grofield back," Parker said, "and I want my money. And I want those people dead."

Hurley gestured, wanting more. He said, "So?"

"So I set you people up with scores, you go do them, you've got good money you wouldn't have had. You'll all be finished, back here, by when? Three, four in the morning?"

Most of them shrugged in agreement. Hurley bobbed his head, saying, "Probably. Then what?"

"Then you come with me," Parker said. "The twelve of us hit Buenadella's house and get Grofield out of there. And if they moved him somewhere, we find out where and go hit that place." He checked off names on his fingers, saying, "And we make them dead. Buenadella. Calesian. Dulare."

His intensity had startled them a little. Nobody said anything until Handy McKay, speaking very quietly, said, "That's not like you."

What kind of shit was this? Parker had expected a back-up from Handy, not questions. He said, "What's not like me?"

"A couple things," Handy said. "For one, to go to all this trouble for somebody else. Grofield, me, anybody. We all of us here know we got to take care of ourselves, we're not the Travelers Aid Society. You, too. And the same with Grofield. What happens to him is up to him."

"Not when they send him to me piece by piece," Parker said. "If they kill him, that's one thing. If they turn him over to the law, get him sent up, that's his lookout. But these bastards rang *me* in on it."

Handy spread his hands, letting that point go. "The other thing," he said, "is revenge. I've never seen you do anything but play the hand you were dealt. Now all of a sudden you want a bunch of people dead."

Parker got to his feet. He'd been patient a long time, he'd explained things over and over, and now he was getting itchy. Enough was enough. "I don't care," he said. "I don't care if it's like me or not. These people nailed my foot to the floor, I'm going around in circles, I'm not getting anywhere. When was it like me to take lumps and just walk away? I'd like to burn this city to the ground, I'd like to empty it right down to the basements. And I don't want to talk about it any more, I want to *do* it. You're in, Handy, or you're out. I told you the setup, I told you what I want, I told you what you'll get for it. Give me a yes or a no."

Tom Hurley said, "What's the goddam rush? We got over an hour before we can hit *any* of these things."

Stan Devers, getting to his feet, said, "Just time enough for a nap. I'm in, Parker." He turned to Wycza, beside him. "Dan?"

Wycza wasn't quite ready to be pushed. He frowned up at Devers, frowned across the room at Parker, seemed on the verge of telling everybody to go drop dead, and then abruptly shrugged and said, "Sure, what the hell. I like a little boom-boom sometimes."

Handy said, "Parker, I was never anything but in, you know that."

Ed Mackey said, "Shit, we're all in. I know Grofield, he's a pleasant guy, we don't want anybody out there dismantling him."

Mike Carlow, the driver who hadn't had anything at all to say up till now, said, "I don't know this guy Grofield from a dune buggy. In fact, I don't even know any of you people. But I know Parker, and I'm in."

They were all in. Parker, looking from face to face, saw that none of them was even thinking of bowing out. Some of the tension eased out of Parker's shoulders and back. "All right," he said. "All right."

Forty-two

In the den, Calesian paced the floor, prowling back and forth while Buenadella sat at the desk with furrowed forehead and watched him as though he were a one-man tennis match. The French doors were closed against the night's mugginess but the curtains were drawn back, and through the glass panes the floodlit lawn could be seen, the grass and shrubbery and trees all an artificial unhealthy shade of green in the glaring light.

Calesian was sure he was on top of things. He'd nailed down the relationship between himself and Buenadella, he'd had a good productive meeting this afternoon with George Farrell, he'd been present and listened to during the first exploratory meeting this afternoon between Dutch and Ernie Dulare, and he had Parker on the run. And still he was keyed up, tensed and poised and ready as though a starting pistol were about to be fired somewhere and he had to be ready to leap.

It was waiting for the election, that's all. Nine o'clock tomorrow morning the polls would open, eight o'clock tomorrow night they'd close again, and then it would all be over. Everything would be in place, all the relationships assured, the reins securely in the right hands, and no more possibility of anything lousing up, or of anybody making trouble.

Parker, for instance. If he came back after tomorrow, if he really was stupid enough to come back to this town, it wouldn't matter how much noise and fuss and trouble he made. The entire local organization could shut down for a day or two and go find the bastard like a thousand cats looking for one rat in a barn, and that would be the end of him. If he ever came back. Which wasn't in any case going to happen.

There was a tap at the door. Calesian glanced over at Dutch, and saw him sitting there with his eyebrows lifted, waiting to find out whether he should let the person in or not. His own den in his own house, and he was letting Calesian tell him whether or not to say *Come in*; that was how far Calesian had come into control, and he resisted the impulse to smile as he nodded: Yes, you can let the person enter.

"Come in," called Buenadella, and Dr. Beiny walked in, looking disgruntled and sleepy. But that was the way he always looked—except for those moments when he'd got himself in deep water again, when he would look wide awake and terrified.

Calesian said, "How is he?"

"Breathing," the doctor said. "That's about all."

"What about the finger?"

Dr. Beiny looked puzzled. "What finger?"

"You're supposed to take one off."

The doctor looked to Buenadella, and Buenadella said, "I told him not to, Hal."

Mutiny? Calesian said, "What the hell for?"

"He said it was too dangerous, the guy could die of shock maybe. And we don't know where Parker is, how to even send the thing to him."

The pleading note in Buenadella's voice reassured Calesian; not quite a mutiny. And it was true they didn't know where Parker was, or how to get in touch with him. Messages had been left at Al Lozini's house, and with Jack Walters and Nate Simms, but so far the guy hadn't popped to the surface anywhere. Maybe he wouldn't, maybe he'd had enough and just ran away. Calesian tried to suit that action to his memory of Parker, and as time went on, it seemed to him more and more likely that a run-out was just what Parker had done. So, magnanimously, he told Dutch and the doctor both, "That's okay, then. We'll leave the guy alone for now. But, Doctor, if we hear from Parker I want you on tap. I want you to get over here with your little saw double fast."

"Whatever you say."

Buenadella said, "But what if it kills him?"

"After tomorrow," Calesian said, "we don't need him alive anyway."

"I don't want to hear that," Dr. Beiny said. He was suddenly in a nervous hurry. "I'm going home," he said. "If you need me, call me and I'll come right back."

Calesian gave him a mocking smile. "Good of you to make house calls, Doctor," he said.

Beiny bowed himself out, closing the door behind him, and Dutch said, "You figure to kill him, don't you?"

Thinking the doctor was meant, Calesian frowned at Dutch and said, "What? What for?"

"You keep saying we don't need him alive after tomorrow."

"Oh, *Green*. Well, what the hell, he's dead already, isn't he? If it wasn't for our doctor, he'd be dead a long time ago."

"He's alive, Hal."

"Not if nobody takes care of him," Calesian said. "Besides, we don't have to kill him. All we have to do is pick him up out of that bed, put him in a car, and drive him out of town. Leave him beside the road, the way he and Parker left poor Mike Abadandi. Mike died, didn't he?"

"A lot of people are dying," Buenadella said gloomily. "And where the hell is Frankie Faran?"

"Under a rock," Calesian said. "He's deep in hiding, a bottle and some broad. Don't you worry about Frank Faran, that's one guy that *runs* when he sees the whites of their eyes."

"He should have said something." Buenadella fidgeted with papers and pencils on his desk. "He shouldn't just run away like that."

"Relax," Calesian told him. "We're on top of it. Tomorrow's the election, and then it's all over."

"I wish it was Wednesday," Buenadella said.

Calesian laughed. He wished the same thing, but he couldn't admit that to Dutch. So he laughed, and condescendingly said, "Poor old Dutch," and walked over to gaze in easy unconcern out the French doors at the floodlit lawn. He looked up toward the sky, but the bright lights kept him from seeing anything but blackness. He kept looking up anyway, his stance deliberately carefree as he gazed upward as though watching a milk-white full moon ride across the sky.

Forty-three

It was the night of the new moon: no moon. Earlier in the evening a pencil-line arc of white had defined the lightless moon's location in the sky, but by eleven-thirty that line had narrowed to nothing. Stars shimmered in the heat haze, surrounded by black sky.

State Highway 219, angling northwest out of the city, was as dark and unseeable as the pine woods through which it cut. A man walking along the road would have had to guide himself by what was under his feet—the hardness of concrete, the rattle of gravel, the yielding texture of dirt—rather than what was in front of his eyes; except when an automobile would come along, following its own headlights through the dark.

At quarter past eleven a recently stolen Mercury Montego drove by, northbound, driven by Mike Carlow, with Stan Devers beside him and Wycza spread out on the back seat. Ten minutes later Nick Dalesia followed, with Hurley and Mackey both next to him in the front seat of their just-stolen Plymouth Fury. Occasional cars passed them southbound, but they overtook no one else going north.

Seven miles north of the Tyler city line, in a blaze of red and yellow neon that kept the night slightly at bay, was a rambling two-story white clapboard farmhouse now operating under different management. The sign out by the road that said

TONY FLORIO'S
R
I
V
I
E
R
A
Dining — Dancing
Appearing Nitely
Paul Patrick
and
The Heat Exchange

might have been airlifted by helicopter directly from the Strip in Las Vegas. The pine trees visible across the road in the sign's glow looked unreal, a clumsy stage setting, as though the sign had a greater vitality and truth than they, and had overwhelmed them.

Monday was a good night at Tony Florio's Riviera; in fact, every night was a good night there. The blacktop parking lot out behind the main building was over half full when, at twenty past eleven, the Plymouth drove in and joined the Mercury already parked there.

Inside, Tony Florio himself was on hand to greet his regular guests and to give a smile and a friendly word to any passing transient who recognized him. A one-time light-heavyweight contender, Florio's body had grown rounder and bulkier since the days when he'd made his living in the ring, but the pockmarked square-jawed face hadn't changed much at all, and with the steady secret use of hair dye, the mass of tight curly black hair cascading over his forehead was just the same as it had been in the days when it was the trademark used to identify Tony Florio by all the sports-page cartoonists. Florio's eyes were clear, his handshake strong, his manner expansive and confident, and so far as most of his customers knew, this was Tony Florio's own place, set up and paid for out of the money he'd earned during his years as a professional boxer. Very few people knew that Florio, like most professional boxers, had been in his heyday nothing but a commodity, pieces of him owned by individuals and groups from all over, every fight purse being sliced up a hundred different ways, and with the federal government the first in line. Whatever had been left in those days Florio had spent himself, at once, in places very like this Riviera.

But what difference did it make who owned the place, so long as it was fun to go? And for the older male patrons, Tony Florio was still a recognizable name, and to shake his hand was a pleasure of a kind not often available in a backwater like Tyler.

When Dalesia and Hurley and Mackey walked in, Florio looked them over from his casual spot near the headwaiter and did a saloonkeeper's rapid fix on them: They were strangers, new to this place. They didn't give the impression of being local citizens, so they were more likely to be traveling men, passing through town and wanting an evening's entertainment. They would have a few hundred on them, but they would neither make nor break the bank. It was possible that a cabdriver in town had steered them out here for a late dinner in the main dining room—called, obscurely, The Spa—but not likely. They were definitely not the type for The Corral, where younger local couples danced to the rock music of The Heat Exchange. Were they for upstairs? If so, they would have a card with them, from one of the six desk clerks, nine bartenders, and seven cabdrivers in town whose judgment Florio trusted.

And when Florio stepped forward to give them a glad hello, it turned out they did have a card, but the source of it was a surprise. Looking at the familiar name in the familiar handwriting on the familiar business card, Florio said, "Ah hah." He looked up, reassessing these three, saying, "So you know Frankie Faran, do you?"

"From good old union days," Ed Mackey said, and gave Florio a tight hard grin.

Florio recognized that grin, and that kind of man. It was the sort of expression you found sometimes with professional sparring partners, guys whose goal in life was to prove they could take more without flinching than anybody else in the world. Men like that were dangerous because they almost always wanted to test themselves against somebody or other, but once you knew how to handle them, they were babes in the woods. This one would throw away his last dime upstairs, given the opportunity.

So let's give him the opportunity. "Well, any friend of Frank's," Florio said. "Would you boys care for a drink before dinner?" Then, when he saw them glancing off to their left at the entrance to the bar—called The Salon—he gave them a big smile and said, "Not in there. Private." He turned and gestured to a waiter who wasn't a waiter, but whose job it was to escort customers who weren't going to The Salon or The Spa or The Corral, and when the waiter came briskly over, Florio said, "Show these gents to my office, will you, Angy?" And to the three men he said, "I'll be along in just a minute."

"That's very nice of you, Mr. Florio," Nick Dalesia said, and the other two nodded, with slightly belligerent smiles on their faces.

In the dining room, Mike Carlow and Stan Devers and Dan Wycza were eating a late supper of omelette or steak tartare. Carlow was seated so he could see the main entrance, where the exchange between Florio and the other three had taken place, and now he said, "Well, they're in." Neither of the others said anything or looked around from their food, and after the one comment Carlow, too, went back to eating.

Wiss and Elkins left the Pontiac—their own car—on a side street, and walked down London Avenue past the darkened windows of the closed shops toward the Mature Art Theater, a block and a half away. It was twenty to twelve; London Avenue was deserted. The last show at the Mature Art had let out fifteen minutes ago, a couple of dozen hunch-shouldered men who had wandered off in separate directions, none of them looking as though they'd had much of a good time. Now the sidewalks were empty of pedestrians, the street empty of traffic. Night lights shone in the interiors of stores, the sodium arc streetlights spread their bright pink glow on silence and inactivity, and the sky was as black as the velvet in a jeweler's window display.

Wiss carried a small black leather bag with a brass catch, like the bags doctors carried in the days when they made house calls. Elkins strolled with his hands in his pockets, looking constantly left and right, far ahead, back over his shoulder. They moved along like a pair of workers off a night shift somewhere, and when they reached the Mature Art Theater they stopped and looked at the posters.

A double feature was playing currently at the Mature Art: *Man Hungry* and *Passion Doll*. The posters featured black-and-white photos of slightly overweight girls in their underwear kneeling on beds or pulling one another's hair or kissing one another or cowering with arms raised self-protectively in overlit corners of bare rooms.

There were four glass doors leading to the theater lobby, but three of them featured red arrows pointing toward the fourth. Just inside that fourth door a chrome railing led the customer past the cashier's window, where money was paid but no ticket was given. By eliminating tickets, the management—Dutch Buenadella—found it possible to lie to everyone about the number of paying customers who had seen the show.

There were strong advantages in being able to lie about the size of the audience. Tonight, for instance, a typical Monday night—a slow night generally for dirty movies—one hundred eighteen people had paid five dollars apiece to see the show. Of each five dollars, not quite one dollar was due the city and the state in sales and other taxes, a dollar-sixty was to be turned over to the distributor of the movies for their rental, and another fraction was to be paid the projectionists' and ushers' unions for their pension funds; leaving about two-forty out of each five dollars for the owner of the theater, before overhead. But the books for tonight would show that eighty-seven people had paid to see the double feature, meaning that thirty-one people, paying one hundred fifty-five dollars, had not been counted. Which meant that eighty dollars and sixty cents would not be paid the city, the state, the distributor, and the pension funds, and that next March the remaining seventy-seven dollars and fifty cents would not be declared as part of the corporation's income for tax purposes.

For Dutch Buenadella, this potentiality of lying had an additional advantage. He wasn't alone in this operation, he had partners. The entire local organization was an interlocking board of directors, so that a piece of Buenadella's skim eventually wound up in Al Lozini's pocket, and another piece in

Ernie Dulare's pocket, and another piece in Frank Schroder's pocket. These partners of his knew he was lying to the tax people and the union people and the distributor, so he couldn't very well tell *them* he'd only had eighty-seven customers tonight. But he could say he'd had one hundred eleven. He could keep not two but three sets of books, and on top of the normal skim, take an extra thirty-five dollars directly for himself. Every night of the year. Which meant something like thirteen thousand tax-free dollars a year for himself, personally.

Frank Faran hadn't known about the extra skim, which Buenadella took home in his pocket every night and put away in a wall safe in his den, but he did know about the regular skim and what happened to it, so now Wiss and Elkins knew about it too. And Wiss, looking to his left toward the nearest glass door while continuing to face the movie posters, murmured, "All we got to do is breathe on that door."

"Not before twelve o'clock," Elkins said. Glancing at his watch, he said, "Two minutes from now."

The cables, sheathed in heavy iron pipe, ran through the sewer system, crisscrossing beneath the downtown area, London Avenue, and all the business side streets. Feeder cables branched out from the main lines, burrowing through dirt under sidewalks and into basements, culminating at metal boxes that looked as though they might contain fuses, and from which wires led up to all the doors and windows of the participating business establishments. Every evening at closing time the proprietor would turn on a switch discreetly tucked away on the rear wall, and from then until the following morning the opening of any door or window would cause an electric impulse to travel through the wires to the box in the basement, through the feeder cable to the main cable in the sewer, and along the main cable to the offices of Vigilant Protective Service, Inc., where it would cause a buzzer to sound and a light to flash on a large complex wall display in the ready room. And whenever that happened, one of the men on duty would immediately phone the police station nearest the business establishment, and would also dispatch a car of Vigilant's own, containing four armed uniformed men.

Vigilant's offices were in a small two-story brick building on a corner a block from London Avenue. The ready room was upstairs in the back, the billing office, executive offices, and files were upstairs in the front, the downstairs front was the visitors' waiting room and the salesmen's cubicles, and the downstairs back was divided into rooms for the on-duty men—a dayroom with tables and easy chairs and a television set, plus two smaller rooms containing cots—and an interior garage holding two radio cars.

Monday was usually a very slow night at Vigilant, but for some reason this Monday was a night of minor annoyances. At six-fifteen, some kid—apparently it was a kid, there wasn't anybody there when the cops and the Vigilant guards showed up—tried to get in through a back window into a local toy store. Then at ten-thirty somebody who also got away jimmied open the front door of an appliance repair shop, and not five minutes later in another part of town it was a gas station that was broken into, and yet again the perpetrator got away before anybody showed up. It wasn't bad the way Halloween is bad, but it was a lot worse than the usual Monday night.

Particularly considering the size of the crew on duty. There were two men in the ready room, and only one crew of four men on duty downstairs. When the gas station was broken into, the ready-room man had had to radio the car at the repair shop to go on over there. Only on weekends were there two groups of on-duty men, because usually only on weekends were they needed. Besides, the police were supposed to be the first line of defense; Vigilant's primary job was to inform the police that a felony was in progress, and what they were doing. Three break-ins so far tonight, and not a single loss to a subscriber. Damages to doors would be paid for by insurance, and in no case had there been damage to the stock or interior of the store, nor any removal of items.

Then at eleven-fifteen the fourth alarm of the night went off in the ready room, this one indicating that something had just happened at Best's Jewelry Store, quite a ways out River Street. One of the ready-room men immediately phoned the River Street police station while the other one called downstairs to where the guards were playing a long-standing game of double-deck pinochle. They were told the name and address of the store, and they at once dropped their cards, climbed into their Dodge Polara, and the driver pressed the button on the dashboard that electronically raised the overhead garage door. They drove out onto the dark side street, their headlights flaring as they bounced down the steep driveway and then up toward the middle of the street. They turned right, the driver pushed the button to shut the garage door behind them again, and they headed at high speed for River Street, unaware of the two men dressed in black who had been crouched to either side of the garage entrance and who had rolled into the building under the descending door.

Handy McKay and Fred Ducasse got to their feet, took their pistols from their pockets, and moved cautiously toward the open door to the dayroom. There hadn't been much time or opportunity to case this outfit, so they weren't sure exactly where things were inside the building, or just how many men were in here. Parker had come in the front way this morning to apply for a job, but hadn't managed to see much. He'd also done the toy-store break-in at six-fifteen, just before meeting with everybody at the apartment, had seen the Vigilant car arrive with its Minute Man decal on the doors, had followed it back here, and had seen the electrically controlled garage door in the side of the building.

Philly Webb and Fred Ducasse had done the appliance-shop and gas-station break-ins, while Handy had watched the Vigilant headquarters. Now it seemed there was only one car's worth of guards on duty, but how many more might be working inside the building it was impossible to say, so Handy and Ducasse moved silently and cautiously forward until they had assured themselves that the dayroom and the two rooms with cots and the salesmen's cubicles and everything else on the first floor was empty. Then they headed for the stairs.

The Polara with the four guards in it raced out River Street, a blue light flashing on the roof. They passed a blue Buick traveling sedately in the other direction, and paid it no attention. Philly Webb glanced at the receding blue light in his rear-view mirror, grinned to himself, and stepped it up a little.

The two men in the ready room were talking about which

actresses on their favorite television shows they would like to go
to bed with when the door from the stairs opened and two men
dressed in black, with black hoods over their faces, came in
pointing pistols, moving fast, slamming the door back against
the wall, one of them thumping his pistol butt on a desk top
while the other one shouted, "Freeze! Freeze, dammit, one move
and I blow your ass off!"

The ready-room men were both in the gray Vigilant uniform
with sidearms, but the holster flaps were snapped shut, there
hadn't been any warning, and the two intruders were making a
lot of distracting noise. The one who had shouted was trotting
around behind them, along the wall, while the other one kept
banging things: hitting the pistol butt against this and that,
kicking a metal wastebasket, knocking over a chair.

The one running around behind them kept shouting too:
"Goddamnit, one move out of you, one sound out of you, you
dirty bastards, just give me a chance to drill you down, give me
a chance, goddamnit, just make one fatal fucking move and I'll
smear you around this room like strawberry jam!"

They weren't moving. Startled, stunned, terrified, they sat
open-mouthed, paralyzed by the sudden barrage out of nowhere.

"Up!" shouted the runner. He was behind them now, and
the other one in front, and they couldn't watch both at once.
"Up, you bastards, hands on your heads, get your dead asses out
of those chairs, get up on your goddam feet, *move*—or you're
fucking dead men!"

They did it. They did everything they were told, surrounded
by threats and racket, the other one still making a noisy mess of
things, throwing phone books and ashtrays around and still
always keeping his pistol pointed in the general direction of the
two men standing there with their hands atop their heads.

The other one, mouthing threats, sounding enraged with
some sort of insane personal grievance, came moving in behind
them, took their automatics away, got handcuffs out of a desk
drawer and cuffed their wrists behind them, forced them with
shouts and prodding and threats to stumble over into a corner of
the room and sit on the floor there, back to back, trembling,
expecting the rage and craziness to spill over any second into

bloodshed, half convinced there was no way out of this, they were dead already.

Then all at once things quieted down, and the one who had been doing all the throwing of things, all the pounding and kicking and thumping, stood in the middle of the room with his pistol held casually down at his side and started to laugh. Not crazy laughter or mean laughter, but casual amused laughter. The two ready-room men stared up at him, bewildered, and heard him say through his laughter, "Fred, that's just beautiful."

Now the other one chuckled too. All his rage was gone as though it had never been. "It is kind of nice, isn't it?" he said.

"I've never tried anything that way," the first one said. "I always do it gentle, you know? Reassure everybody they're not gonna get hurt, take it easy, don't worry about anything, we're professionals, we're not out to spill any blood, all that stuff. Get their first names, talk to them easy and calm."

"Sure," the second one said. "I've done it that way too. But sometimes this is nice. Come in mean and loud and half-crazy. Then all *they* want to do is reassure *you*."

The two men laughed, and the men sitting with their backs together on the floor looked over their shoulders at one another in anger and humiliation and rue.

Out at Best's Jewelry, it turned out someone had thrown a brick through the plate-glass window, but didn't seem to have taken anything. Two police radio cars had arrived by the time the Vigilant car got there. The store's owner had been informed and was on his way over. The Vigilant guards, according to company policy, waited for his arrival, to demonstrate to him that they were on the job.

Philly Webb parked the anonymous Buick a block from the Vigilant building, walked the block, and knocked on the garage door in the side wall. It slid upward, and Handy McKay, hood off, grinned at him and motioned him to come in. "Only two guys," he said. "Fred's upstairs with them."

"I do kind of like this," Webb said. "Parker does come up with them, doesn't he?" He and Handy had worked together in the past, ten or more years ago, but this was the first time they'd both been together on the same score with Parker.

"I was saving my comeback for him," Handy said. "There's some cards in the next room."

Out at Best's Jewelry, the Vigilant guards touched their visors in salute to the customer, got back into the Polara, and headed home. The driver took it slow and easy now, with the blue light turned off, and chose to head down London Avenue even though it was a block or so out of the way.

It was a quiet night, moonless and dark. London Avenue was deserted except for two guys drooling over the pictures outside one of the dirty-movie houses. "They're on line kind of early, ain't they?" one of the guards said, and they all laughed.

"Twelve o'clock," Elkins said. "But wait for that car to go by."

At Vigilant headquarters, Philly Webb and Handy McKay were playing draw poker with a pinochle deck. "Royal flush," Handy said.

Webb, with a little smirk, spread out his hand. "Five aces."

"Damn it." Handy tossed his hand in with true annoyance. "The cards are dead," he said.

From upstairs came a buzzing sound. Looking up, Webb said, "There goes the movie house."

Upstairs, Ducasse stood frowning at the wall display with its flashing light and droning buzzer. He called to one of the guards in the corner, "How do I turn that off?"

"Fuck you," said the guard. They were both upset at learning that Ducasse and Handy weren't crazy men, after all.

Ducasse went over and kicked the guard on the shin. "Don't talk dirty," he said. "How do I turn that thing off?"

The guard, wincing with pain, tried to outstare a man with a hood over his face, but when Ducasse drew his foot back again he said, "There's a switch on that desk. Turn it off and then back on again."

"Good," said Ducasse.

Downstairs, Webb and Handy played cards until they heard the garage door lifting. Then they pulled their hoods down over their faces and stood to either side of the dayroom door, their pistols held down at their sides.

The guards came in talking together, taking it easy, and all four were in the room before they saw the strangers. It suddenly got very quiet, and Handy, doing it his way, said, "Okay, gents, just take it easy. We don't want any guns going off."

There were no slot machines. The image they tried for at Tony Florio's Riviera was discreet class, but not so discreet that the mugs wouldn't recognize it. James Bond elegance, that was the approach. The mugs, seeing maroon-velvet draperies, assumed it was elegant. The mugs, seeing slot machines and equating slot machines with pinball machines in truck-stop diners, assumed it was cheap. So there were no slot machines.

But there was a lot of maroon velvet. Dalesia and Hurley and Mackey followed the waiter upstairs and through maroon-velvet drapes into the main gaming room, a long low-ceilinged room lined with heavy draperies. All that cloth, plus the thick green carpeting, muffled noises in the room until the place sounded like a stereo system with the bass control up full.

"The cashier to your right, gentlemen," the waiter said, bowing slightly, smiling and gesturing. "And good luck to you."

"Good luck to you, too," Hurley said.

The waiter went away, and the three men took a minute to look over the room. There were six crap tables, only three of them in action. Two roulette wheels, both operating. On the far side of the room, card games at several green-baize tables. The players were about two-thirds men, and most of the women seemed to be married to the men they were with. It looked to be a professional-class crowd, lawyers, doctors, businessmen, managers, with most of the men in jacket and tie. Very few of the customers appeared to be under thirty-five, and those few mostly emulated their elders in dress, deportment, and hair length. The room wasn't crowded, but it wasn't empty either; it was probably operating at half capacity.

Dalesia said, "Good mob for a Monday night."

"Maybe we ought to invest," Mackey said.

Dalesia grinned. "No, I don't think so. I think they're a bad risk."

The three of them walked over to the cashier's window. It was an oval hole in the wall, flanked by the ever-present maroon drapes. In the center of the grayish bullet-proof glass, at mouth level, was a microphone, and just above the window a speaker brought out the cashier's voice. It was like a drive-in window at a bank; they put money in a metal drawer, which the cashier drew back to her side, then pushed out again with the chips in it.

They each took a hundred dollars in five-dollar blues, and the cashier's metallic voice said over their heads, "Good luck to you."

"And good luck to you, too," Hurley said.

They wandered the room for a few minutes, looking at the action. The crap tables and roulette wheels were run by men, but all the card games were operated by women, showing a lot of breast and a lot of plastic smile. "That's what I call poker tits," Dalesia said. "Harder to read than a poker face."

Mackey said, "Well, if I'm going to throw it away fast, I can't do better than roulette. See you."

Mackey wandered off, and Hurley and Dalesia kibitzed a blackjack game for a few hands. The girl dealing flashed them a couple of smiles while waiting for players to decide whether to hit or stay, and after a minute or two Hurley said, "Think I'll settle in here till spring," and took one of the empty chairs at the table.

Dalesia roamed some more, considered the lone chemin de fer table with its slender black-haired girl dealer, and went on to one of the crap tables. They used the full Las Vegas layout, and most of the female customers were here, betting the field and the hard way. Dalesia, whose one superstition was that he had a mystical relationship with the number nine, made a sensible bet on the Don't Pass Line and a dumb bet on the nine to come. He glanced at his watch while the shooter breathed on the red transparent dice, and saw he had twenty minutes in which to lose the hundred dollars.

Over at one of the roulette wheels, Mackey was frowning like a steam engine and writing numbers in a notebook. He was betting on every other spin, and these were alternating between a square bet somewhere in the second twelve and the line bet at the top, the 1, 2, 3, 0 and 00. He was losing practically every time, but his frown of concentration never changed. He looked exactly like yet another chump with a system, and all the employees in the area became aware of him within five minutes. So did several customers, a couple of whom began to follow his betting even though he was losing.

At the blackjack table, while the other players looked at their cards or the dealer's breasts, Hurley watched her hands.

She was good and smooth, but she didn't seem to be doing anything mechanical. Not that she had to; most of the players here didn't know how to stand on anything less than a twenty. Hurley hung back with his low teens whenever the dealer's up card was low, never hit on sixteen or higher no matter what she had showing, and slowly inched ahead of the odds. But it was a slow way to make money.

Mackey went through his hundred dollars in eight minutes. Still frowning, still checking things off in his notebook, he went back to the cashier's window, absent-mindedly fumbled his wallet out of his pocket, and said, "Better let me have——" He paused, fingered the bills in the wallet, and regretfully drew five twenties. "Just a hundred," he said.

"Thank you, sir."

He seemed to come slowly back to a full awareness of his surroundings. As the girl was sending the drawer back out to him with his twenty chips inside, he said, "Uh, miss."

"Yes, sir?"

"Is there a manager around?"

"Is something wrong, sir?"

"I want to establish a line of credit." He seemed on the verge of dropping his wallet into the drawer, and hadn't yet taken his chips out. "I have identification, I'm fully, uh——" He hesitated, then scooped the chips out and stuffed them distractedly into his jacket pocket.

"Yes, sir," the girl said. "You'll want to talk to Mr. Flynn."

"Thank you," Mackey said, and a second later did a double-take, when he remembered that Flynn was the name *he* was using. Thomas Flynn; he and Parker and a couple of other people all had ID in that name. "Flynn, you said?"

"Yes, sir." Leaning forward so her hair was touching the glass, she looked and pointed down to Mackey's left, saying, "You'll find his door along this wall, sir."

"*My* name's Flynn," Mackey said.

The girl gave him a blank smile. "Well, isn't that a coincidence," she said.

"It's an omen," Mackey told her. "I have a feeling I'm going to make some money tonight."

"Well, I hope you do, sir. Should I tell Mr. Flynn you're coming to see him?"

He seemed to think about it, then to make a solid decision. "Yes," he said. "I might as well be prepared."

"Thank you, sir." She reached for a phone beside her, and Mackey moved away from her window.

Dalesia, winning most of the time on Don't Pass and losing all of the time on nine, was slowly turning his hundred dollars over to the house. When the dice came around to him, he elected not to shoot but to pass them on to the next player, and while doing so, noticed Mackey walking along the wall toward a brown wooden door.

There was a man in a black suit, black tie, and white shirt standing near the door, watching the action the way a cop on a beat watches cars go by. When Mackey approached he turned and gave him a flat look and said, "Can I help you, sir?"

"I'm supposed to see Mr. Flynn," Mackey said.

"Yes, sir. And your name was?"

Mackey gave a half-apologetic smile. "Flynn," he said.

The man's face wasn't meant for smiling, but he tried. "Well, that's a coincidence," he said.

"I guess it is."

The man reached for a black wall phone next to the door. "Related, by any chance?"

"You never know, do you? I'll have to ask."

"Yes, sir." Into the phone, he said, "There's a Mr. Flynn out here to see you. Fine." Hanging up, he said, "Go right on in."

"Thanks," Mackey said as the door began to buzz. He pushed it open, the buzzing stopped, and he entered an ordinary receptionist's office, ordinary in every way except that it was windowless. Several framed photographs of Tony Florio in his boxing days were on the walls. At a green-metal desk sat an ordinary receptionist, who smiled brightly and said, "Mr. Flynn?"

"That's right. I guess it's some coincidence, huh?"

"I guess so," she said. "Mr. Flynn's on the phone long-distance just now, but he'll be with you in a very few minutes."

"Thank you."

She extended a large document toward him. "While you're waiting, would you mind terribly filling this out? It could save you some time."

The document was a four-page credit questionnaire. "Of course," he said. "Of course."

She pointed to a library table on the side wall. "I think you'd be comfortable there, Mr. Flynn."

"I'm sure I would."

The questionnaire wanted to know everything but his attitude about fucking sheep. He filled it out in a tiny crabbed hand, keeping the lies generally realistic, avoiding old gags like having a checking account in the Left Bank of the Mississippi, and when he was finished he gave the questionnaire back to the receptionist, who smiled her gracious thanks and carried it at once inside to her long-distance-telephoning boss.

The magazines available to read were *Forbes* and *Business Week*. Mackey read about businessmen for five minutes or so, until a buzzer sounded on the receptionist's desk. "Mr. Flynn will see you now, Mr. Flynn," the receptionist said, and got to her feet to open the door for him to the inner office.

Mr. Flynn was a short balding man who had put on some weight but who moved as though he were short and skinny. He wore a tan jacket and a blue-and-red bow tie, and he had come around his desk to give Mackey a firm but friendly handshake. The questionnaire was open on the desk, and Mackey could tell by Flynn's outgoing manner that he had called the local phone number Mackey had given—as being his company's "local leased personal premises," as he had put it on the form—and had been told the story by Parker at the other end. Parker, playing butler-caretaker, would have said that yes, this was General Texachron's local leased apartment, where company executives could stay when business brought them to Tyler, and that yes, Mr. Thomas Flynn was currently in residence although not at the moment present in the apartment.

But before they got to General Texachron or the other invented particulars of the questionnaire, they had to get past the coincidence of the last name. Mackey was getting heartily sick of the coincidence by now, and was wishing he'd chosen one of his other available identities instead, but eventually the casino's Mr. Flynn had satisfied himself that the two of them weren't blood relatives in any directly traceable way, and they could get themselves around to the matter at hand.

Downstairs, Mike Carlow and Dan Wycza and Stan Devers had all skipped dessert and were having a cup of coffee. Carlow, glancing at his watch, said, "Time for us to make our move."

Wycza put down his cup. "Right," he said, touched his napkin to his lips, and got to his feet. While Devers and Carlow stayed at the table, Carlow with his hands out of sight on his lap, Wycza crossed the room to where Tony Florio was standing in his usual spot near the headwaiter. "Mr. Florio?"

Florio turned around, his greeter's smile on his face, his hand ready to come out for a brisk shake. "Yes, pal? What can I do for you?"

Wycza moved in close to him, turning his shoulder so as to exclude the nearby headwaiter from the conversation. Pointing into the dining room, he said, "You see those two gents there at my table?"

Florio was expecting to be asked for an autograph, which he would give, or to join these out-of-towners in a drink, which he wouldn't do. "Yes," he said. "I see them."

Wycza said, "Well, the fella with his hands under the table is holding a target pistol down there, aimed at your balls."

Florio stiffened. Wycza's hand was on his elbow in a confidential way, and quietly Wycza said, "Now, don't make a fuss, Mr. Florio, because I've got to tell you something. That guy is with me, and I know about him, and I know he gets very nervous in moments of stress. You follow me?"

Florio said nothing. It never even occurred to him this might be a gag; he believed it was the truth from the instant he heard it.

Wycza said, "For instance, if you were to make any sudden motions, or if you were to shout, anything like that, that nervous son of a bitch over there is just likely to shoot. I hate to use him, he makes me a nervous wreck myself, but the thing is he's a marksman. He can shoot a pimple off a fly's ass at sixty feet, he's just amazing. If only he was calm like you and me, but he doesn't have our size, you know? A big man like us can be calm, but a little guy like him gets nervous."

Florio, in looking now at this soft-spoken baldheaded giant, was invited to notice that although Wycza had spoken of them both as being big men, Wycza was clearly much the bigger and much the stronger of the two of them. Florio, who was used to being the biggest and toughest-looking man in any gathering, wilted a bit more. Half whispering as drops of perspiration appeared on his upper lip, he said, "What do you want?"

"Just come on over to the table," Wycza said. "We'll talk a little." He nudged Florio's arm, and Florio began to walk.

The two of them moved through the mostly empty tables to the one where Devers and Carlow were waiting. Carlow kept his hands under the table, and Devers kept watching the employees behind Wycza's back, none of whom were behaving in any way out of the ordinary.

Crossing the room, Wycza staying next to him, Florio said, "I don't really own this place, you know. I just front it for some people in town."

"Ernie Dulare," Wycza said. Pleased by the startled look he got for that name, he added another: "Adolf Lozini."

"You *know* those people?"

"Does a baby know its mother's breast?"

They'd reached the table. Wycza sat Florio across from Carlow, and took the remaining seat to Florio's right. Florio said, "If you know them, then what the hell is going on?"

"A little heist," Wycza said. "Nothing to worry about."

Devers kept looking around the room. Carlow said, to Wycza, "There won't be any trouble, will there?" He didn't exactly act nervous, he seemed more tense, keyed up, as though at any second the rigid control might let go and he would explode.

Wycza, reassuring him, patted his upper arm and said, "No trouble. Tony's going to cooperate. What the hell's a few bucks? This place manufactures money, he'll make it all back by the end of the week." He turned to Florio. "Isn't that right, Tony?"

"There's no money down here," Florio said. "I'm not out to cross you people, but it's God's own truth, there just isn't any money down here."

"I want to talk to you about that, Tony," Wycza said. "But while we talk, let's get a phone to this table. Will you do that, Tony?"

"A phone?"

Devers was raising one arm, signaling a waiter. When the

man came over, being deferential because the boss was sitting at this table, Devers gestured to him to listen to Florio.

Florio hesitated, not out of a spirit of rebellion but simply out of bewilderment. Then, feeling the silence, he turned abruptly to the waiter and said, "Paul, get us a phone here, will you?"

"Sure, Mr. Florio."

The waiter went away, and Wycza said, "Now, about the situation upstairs, Tony. We've got a man in with your manager up there right now."

Florio looked at him in open shock. "You what?"

"The manager doesn't know what's going on yet," Wycza said. "When you get the phone now, see, I want you to call his office up there and explain to him how he should do what our man tells him to do."

"Jesus Christ," Florio said. This was the first time in the nine years' existence of Tony Florio's Riviera that the place had been knocked over, and the reality of it was just beginning to hit him. This was a full-blown, big-scale, professional robbery. "How many of you guys are there?"

Wycza gave him a tight grin. "Enough," he said, and the waiter came with the phone. They waited silently at the table as he put the phone down and walked off with the long cord to the nearest wall-jack. He plugged it in, came back to the table, picked up the phone and listened to it, replaced the receiver in the cradle, and said, "There you are, Mr. Florio."

"Thanks, Paul."

The waiter went away, and Stan Devers said, "It occurs to me the waiter's name might not be Paul."

Wycza frowned slightly and said to Florio, "You wouldn't do anything cute like that, would you?"

"Am I crazy?" Florio spread his hands. "How heavy can you hit me for? A Monday night's receipts isn't worth dying for."

Devers, watching the waiter, said, "He seems okay."

Speaking softly, Wycza said to Florio, "How about the forty thousand in the safe? Is that worth dying for?"

Florio stared. "Wha—what forty thousand?"

"You keep forty thousand cash in the safe," Wycza said. "Back-up money, in case anybody hits a streak on you. That's the money we want, Tony."

"You can't walk in off the street and know about that," Florio said. Pale circles of anger showed on his cheekbones. "Some son of a bitch in my shop is in it with you."

Grinning, Wycza said, "I got it from Ernie Dulare." Then, wiping the smile from his face as though it had never existed, he said, "Now, you call your manager upstairs. Our man is in there with him, and he's calling himself Flynn."

"Flynn? My manager's name is Flynn."

"That's some coincidence," Wycza said. "Except your manager's *real* name is Flynn. Call him."

Florio picked up the phone, and hesitated with his finger over the dial. "What do I tell him?"

"Tell him God's simple truth," Wycza said. "You're down here with a gun stuck in your crotch, and your Mr. Flynn should do what *our* Mr. Flynn tells him to do or you'll start singing soprano."

"What if he doesn't believe me?"

"It's up to you to be convincing," Wycza said. "Dial."

Upstairs, Mackey and Mr. Flynn had gone through the extra support Mackey had in that he'd been recommended to the place by Frank Faran, Mackey telling a couple of stories about himself partying with Frank Faran in Las Vegas, stories that were absolutely true except for the names of the participants. Now they were working their way through the questionnaire Mackey had filled out, and Mackey was beginning to wish he'd kept a carbon copy for himself; it was one thing to fill four pages of stupid questions with on-the-spot lies, and another thing to remember all those lies ten minutes later.

Then the phone rang, at long last, and Mackey relaxed a little. The call was late, and he'd been beginning to wonder if maybe something had gone wrong somewhere, if maybe the casino was onto the whole ploy somehow and maybe this chummy Mr. Flynn here was just stalling him with a lot of credit questions while waiting for the cops to show up. But then the phone did finally ring, and Mackey relaxed and put his hand inside his jacket, closing his fingers around the butt of the pistol there.

"Yes, Mr. Florio." Flynn nodded and smiled at Mackey, asking him to wait just a second. "Yes, he's here right now." A surprised smile toward Mackey: Why, Mr. Florio himself knows about you. Then, a look of bewilderment: "What? What's that?" Mackey smiled and took the pistol out. He showed it to Flynn and calmly put it away again. Flynn was sitting straighter in his chair. "I don't understand, Mr. Florio." Listening, blinking, he seemed like a man who didn't *want* to understand. "Do you realize what you're asking me to—"

Mackey couldn't make out the words, but he could hear the angry buzz of Florio's voice in Flynn's ear. Flynn blinked, swallowed, began to nod his head. "Yes, sir," he said. "Yes, sir, of course, I just wasn't think— Yes, sir." His face pale as bread dough, he extended the receiver across the desk to Mackey, saying, "He wants to talk to you."

"Thanks, cousin." Mackey took the phone, said into it, "Yeah, I'm here."

It was Florio's voice, recognizable and bitter, that said, "One of your friends wants to talk to you."

Mackey waited, and Dan Wycza came on a few seconds later, saying, "Everything fine?"

"Couldn't be better," Mackey said.

"Then we might as well get started," Wycza said.

"Right. Hold on." Mackey kept the mouthpiece near his face so Wycza would be able to hear him, and said to Flynn, "I have two friends outside. I want you to bring them in here."

"You want me to go out and—"

"No no no, Mr. Flynn," Mackey said. "You call your man on the door out there. Tell him two gents are coming over and he should let them in. And then tell your receptionist to buzz for them."

"All right," Flynn said, but there was something in his voice and in his eye that Mackey didn't like. "Hold it," he said.

Flynn gave him an attentive look.

Mackey said into the phone, "I think this fella here needs a pep talk from Florio. He looks like he's nerving himself up to something."

Flynn, all wounded innocence, said, "I wouldn't—" but Mackey shushed him with a wave of his hand.

Wycza said, "Hold on," and turned to Florio. He said, "My

man Flynn says your man Flynn doesn't understand the situation. He might have something cute in mind."

Angrily, Florio said, "Over my—" and stopped.

"That's right," Wycza said. Extending the phone toward Florio, he said, "Maybe you ought to tell him that yourself."

Mackey, hearing Wycza, held his phone out toward Flynn. "Your master's voice," he said.

Flynn took the phone doubtfully, held it to his ear as though it might bite him, and said, "Mr. Florio?"

The phone bit him. Looking pained, Flynn tried to break in three or four times with no success, and finally managed to say, "Of course, Mr. Florio. You're the boss, Mr. Florio, I wouldn't— No, sir, I won't."

Mackey waited, looking around the room. According to Faran's sketch, that door on the right should lead to the vault room where the money was kept, and the door on the left should lead to the employees' parlor where the dealers and stickmen took their smoke breaks and where the three armed guards hung out when they weren't out patrolling the floor. Coming at the joint this way, through Florio and Flynn, they were by-passing all the security devices, the armed guards and the timelocks and the buzzer alarms and all the other protective arrangements that had been set up around here.

It was Parker's plan, to Faran's inside information, done without any casing at all, and it was working just beautifully.

Flynn, chastened, finally handed the phone back to Mackey. He was still a trifle mulish, but Mackey didn't doubt he meant it this time when he said, "I'll do whatever you want."

"That's fine." Mackey said into the phone, "You there?"

Wycza said, "Right here."

"Everything's fine now."

Flynn said, "I'll need to use the phone. I can put that call on hold if you want."

"Good idea." Into the phone, Mackey said, "You're going on hold for a minute."

Flynn took the phone, called his receptionist, and told her, "Call George and tell him there are two men about to come over to the door. He's to let them in, and then you should let them directly through in here. That's right. Thank you." He pressed a button that took Dan Wycza off hold and returned the phone to Mackey. "There," he said.

Outside, Hurley had quit the blackjack game twenty dollars ahead and was now kibitzing the crap table where Dalesia had so far lost thirty-five dollars. Hurley saw the man on duty at the brown wooden door reach for the wall phone, and tapped Dalesia, saying, "Time to go."

"Right." Dalesia left a five-dollar chip riding on the nine, and the two men walked across the room to where the doorman was just hanging up the phone. He said, "You the two gentlemen Mr. Flynn's expecting?"

They thought he meant Mackey. "That's right," Dalesia said, "we're the ones."

The door buzzed, and the doorman pushed it open. "Go right on in," he said.

"Thanks," Dalesia said.

Dutch Buenadella owned two more dirty-movie palaces in Tyler besides the Mature Art. One was called the Cine, and the other was the Pussycat. But the Mature Art was the only one of the three with a good burglar-alarm system and a solid reliable safe, so the skim cash from all three theaters was kept there, piling up until once a month it was split into so many pie slices and distributed to the partners.

It had been three weeks since the last distribution, and the safe upstairs in the manager's office at the Mature Art held nine thousand two hundred dollars in skim cash from the three theaters. In addition, there was eight hundred fifty dollars cash maintained as a sort of floating fund to help grease the ways should any unexpected problems come up, or to bribe a fire inspector, or pay a fine if it should come to that. And there was also an envelope, sealed and wrapped with two rubber bands, marked *Personal* in Dutch Buenadella's handwriting and underlined, containing four hundred dollars; one of Buenadella's private caches in case it ever turned out to be necessary to leave town in a hurry when the banks were closed, such as at four o'clock in the morning.

Ralph Wiss had breathed on the lobby door and it had opened. Elkins had looked in the cashier's drawer and found it empty, and then the two of them had gone on upstairs, following Elkins' pencil flashlight. The manager's office was next to the men's room, from which came a muted but rancid odor that it seemed impossible to get used to.

Because the manager's office had a window that overlooked the street, they couldn't switch the overhead fluorescent light on, but with the Venetian blinds closed over the window, they could operate by the light of Elkins' flash. The office was a small cluttered room with a sloppy desk piled high with papers, an incredible number of notes and messages taped to the walls, a bulking water cooler next to a scratched metal filing cabinet, and a stack of metal film-carrying cans piled messily in one corner.

In another corner stood the safe, a dark green metal cube twenty inches on a side, with an L-shaped chrome handle and a large combination dial. Elkins gave Wiss the flashlight, and Wiss studied the front and top and sides of the safe, running his fingers over the metal, squinting at the line where the door joined the edge. He made a kind of whistling *S* sound between his tongue and his upper teeth as he studied the safe, a noise that Elkins had at one time found annoying—it sounded like a tire going flat—but over the years had grown used to, so that he no longer really heard it.

"Drill," Wiss decided.

Elkins nodded. "Sure."

Wiss brought an empty film can over, set the flashlight on it so that it shone on the face of the safe, and sat on the floor directly in front of the safe with his black-leather bag at his side. As he opened the bag, Elkins said, "I'll go on downstairs."

Wiss was involved in his own head. "Uh huh," he said, taking things out of the bag, and didn't look around when Elkins left the room.

Elkins made his way downstairs in the dark, entered the cashier's booth, and sat on the stool there with his elbows on the counter. He could look out diagonally through the cashier's window and the glass doors at the street, where absolutely nothing at all was happening.

After a minute he heard the faint whirring of an electric drill from upstairs.

At Vigilant, the four guards and one of the ready-room men were tied and gagged and locked in one of the smaller rooms downstairs. Handy McKay and Fred Ducasse and Philly Webb were upstairs, playing pinochle. The other ready-room man was tied to a chair and blindfolded, so that the three men wouldn't have to wear their hoods. They needed the ready man present in case the phone should ring. As Handy had told him, "If it rings, you'll do the talking. If you say the right things, there won't be any problem. But if you say something that brings trouble here—guess who'll be the first one in the line of fire?"

"I'm not crazy," the man said. He had gotten over being annoyed that Handy and Ducasse weren't crazy either.

"That's fine," Handy told him, and then made a phone call himself to Parker. "Everything's fine here," he said.

"Good."

Handy gave him the phone number at Vigilant and said, "See you later."

"So long," said Parker.

Flynn stood in the vault doorway, lips pursed in disapproval, watching Dalesia and Hurley stuff wads of bills into two flat black dispatch cases they had been carrying beneath their shirts. When both soft leather cases were bulging with bills, the two men brought out money belts from around their waists and began packing the compartments of those as well.

Next door, Mackey sat at Flynn's desk, the phone to his ear, occasionally exchanging a word with Wycza. Mackey had his feet up on the desk and was smoking a cigar from Flynn's humidor. He had considered putting Wycza on hold long enough to call Brenda, waiting for him at the Holiday Inn, but decided he shouldn't fool around like that. Besides, she was probably asleep by now.

Downstairs, Wycza and Florio talked health food. Wycza, like most professionals, believed in keeping the civilians as calm as possible, since nervous people tend to insist on getting themselves shot, so he had tried several conversational openings with Florio, talking about the boxing world and the nightclub world and the gambling world, until he got around to physical exercise, care of the body, and health food. That turned out to be Florio's subject; the floodgates opened, and out it came. "Now, Adelle Davis—"

"Carlton Fredericks—"

"Natural sea salt," Wycza insisted, "is a fake. That's one case where it doesn't matter, salt is salt."

"The processing plants." Florio, forgetting Mike Carlow's gun, forgetting the robbery going on upstairs, leaned over the table, gesturing, talking emphatically and learnedly.

Wycza, too, was a health nut, and had almost himself forgotten the reason they were all here. He rode his hobby-horse just as hard as Florio did, the two men finding broad areas of agreement and occasional bumps of deep disagreement of a depth that was almost religious.

Carlow stayed out of the conversation completely. His own hobby-horse was racing cars, which had nothing to do with health or with proper care of the human body. He simply sat where he was, right hand under the table, watched the action around the room, and let the words wash unheeded over him.

Stan Devers did get into it from time to time. He himself was in good physical shape and always had been, but had never worried about it or adjusted his eating habits or life style to suit some physical ideal, and his belief was that Florio and Wycza were both crazy. He kept this opinion to himself most of the time, but every once in a while he would hear them agree on some piece of raving lunacy and he would just have to jump in and tell them he thought they were wrong. Then they'd team up on him, Wycza reeling off statistics, Florio telling horror stories about boxers and wrestlers and other great physical specimens who had ruined themselves with smoking or carbohydrates or improper sleeping habits, and Devers would retire again, overwhelmed but unconvinced.

It was turning into a grand social evening for everybody.

At twenty minutes to one Ralph Wiss drilled his sixth hole in the front of the safe, heard the snap of the mechanism inside, turned the handle down, and the safe door slowly opened. "Good," he said to himself, packed his tools away in his leather bag, and got to his feet. He was stiff all over, but particularly in the knees and the back, and his mouth was incredibly dry. His mouth always became dry when he was working on a safe, but it was the result of his unconscious S whistling and not of any nervousness.

There were paper cups with the water cooler. He drank two cups of water, crumpled the cup and threw it away, and went out by the men's room to call down the stairs, "Frank."

"Coming."

Wiss held the flashlight so Elkins could see to come up the stairs. Elkins had been half dozing in the cashier's booth, and he came up yawning and stretching and scratching the back of his neck. At the top of the stairs, he said, "You got it?"

"Sure."

They went back into the office and took the money out of the safe, and it totaled ten thousand, four hundred fifty dollars. About half of it went in their pockets and the rest into Wiss' leather bag with his tools. Then they took out handkerchiefs and gave a brisk rubdown to the few surfaces they'd touched, and went downstairs and out of the theater and walked to the car.

The phone said to Wycza, "We're all set, now. Coming down."

"Huh? Oh, right."

He and Florio had been talking about polyunsaturates. Wycza, feeling a slight embarrassment, as though he were an insurance salesman pretending to be on a social call, hung up the telephone and said, "I'm sorry, Mr. Florio, but it's back to business."

Florio looked startled for just a second. Then he glanced at Devers and Carlow, looked back at Wycza, and gave a sour grin. "You had me going there for a while," he said.

"I wasn't conning you, Mr. Florio," Wycza said. "I wish we could keep talking."

Florio studied him skeptically, then grinned again, not quite as sourly. "Yeah, I guess you do," he said. "Well, I'll tell you one thing, pal. You didn't pick yourself a job that's too good for your health."

"I hope you're wrong," Wycza said. "But anyway, you'll have to walk us outside now."

Florio nodded. "I figured that much. Do I get hit on the head later? I'm worried about concussions."

"We'll work something out," Wycza promised.

"Thanks."

"Now," Wycza said, and got to his feet.

Upstairs, Mackey was having a little more trouble with Flynn. "If I go out with you people," Flynn was saying, "how do I know I won't get shot down in the parking lot?"

"Because we're not crazy people," Mackey told him.

Dalesia said, "Why should we get ourselves wanted for murder?"

But it was Hurley who put in the clincher. "If we were going to shoot you, you asshole," he said, "we'd do it right here, in the privacy of your office. So shut up and walk."

Flynn shut up and walked. He and Mackey and Hurley and Dalesia walked out to the main gaming area, Mackey and Flynn side by side in front, Hurley and Dalesia carrying the dispatch cases behind them. George, the man on duty at the door, looked startled when they came out, but Flynn did his job well, talking to the man just the way Mackey had explained it. "Keep an eye on things, George," Flynn said. "We have to go downstairs for a few minutes."

George, plainly surprised and curious, said, "Okay, Mr. Flynn."

"If anything comes up before we get back, I'll be with Mr. Florio."

"Yes, sir."

They went downstairs, and found Florio and the other three standing in a tight conversational grouping near the front door. The two groups combined, and all eight men went outside and walked around to the parking lot, which now had about half the cars that had been there an hour earlier; Monday was an early night.

The parking lot was illuminated by floodlights mounted on high poles. As they all walked along, Wycza said to the others, half apologetically, "I promised Mr. Florio nobody'd get hit on the head. Why don't we just take them a mile down the road or something? That'll still give us the time we need."

There was no objection. Shrugging, Mackey said, "Fine with me. Okay with you, Mr. Flynn?"

Flynn had nothing to say. Florio said to Wycza, quietly, "Thanks. I appreciate that."

"It's the least I can do," Wycza said.

Forty-four

There wasn't anything on local television after one o'clock, so Parker put Faran away again in the closet, found a deck of cards, and spent the time with some solitaire.

When he'd first taken over this apartment he'd gone through all the drawers in the place and found a spare set of keys for both the front door downstairs and the apartment door in a night table in the bedroom. He'd had four more sets made up, and had given them out to Elkins and Mackey and Devers and McKay, so the different groups could move in and out without ringing apartment bells in the middle of the night. Elkins used his key now as he and Wiss came in, Wiss carrying his black-leather bag and both of them looking moderately pleased with themselves.

Parker had been playing cards at the dining table by the front door. He stood up, leaving the incomplete hand spread out, and said, "Any problems?"

"Simplicity," Wiss said. Walking deeper into the room, he put his bag on the sofa, and then he and Elkins emptied money from the bag and their pockets onto the coffee table. "All very nice," Wiss said.

Parker looked at the stacks of bills. "Did you count it?"

Elkins said, "Ten thousand, four hundred and fifty dollars."

"A little more than we figured."

Elkins grinned. "I thought maybe I'd palm a couple hundred, who'd know? But it isn't worth it."

"You'll all do good tonight," Parker told him. "You won't need to nickel-dime."

Wiss said, "You hear from anybody else?"

"Everything's okay at the burglary-alarm place. The manager out at the Riviera called a while ago, checking on Mr. Flynn's credit."

"Lovely," Wiss said. He poked around in his bag for stray bills, found none, and closed the bag. "So we'll be off," he said.

"I'll call Webb."

They walked to the door. Elkins said, "See you later."

Parker nodded. They left, and he called Philly Webb, the driver at Vigilant. "Wiss and Elkins are on the way," he said, and went back to finish the game.

Ten minutes later Mackey and Hurley and Dalesia came in, carrying the full dispatch cases. Mackey was grinning his hard aggressive grin, and he said, "Parker, you should of been there."

Parker left the cards again. "No trouble?"

"Piece of cake," Mackey said. "Goddam piece of cake."

Hurley said, "That big baldheaded monster, what's his name?"

"Wycza," Parker said.

"Yeah, Wycza. Him and Florio got to be buddies. You never saw anything like it."

Dalesia said, "What do we do with the money?"

Parker swept the solitaire hand off to a corner of the table. "Put it here. You count it yet?"

"We'll do that now," Mackey said. Rubbing his hands together, grinning his hard grin at everybody, he said, "I just love to count money. Other people's money."

"Our money now," Hurley said.

The dispatch cases were zipped open, the money belts were taken off, and the cash was piled up like a green mountain on the table. The four men began counting, each of them making stacks, and when they were finished they added their four totals together. Dalesia did it, with pencil and paper. "Forty-seven thousand, six hundred," he said.

Mackey said, "That's really nice."

Looking over at the smaller stack of money on the coffee table, Hurley said, "That's from the movie house?"

Parker nodded. "Ten thousand, four hundred and fifty."

Dalesia said, "So far, that's fifty-nine thousand and fifty dollars."

Mackey, laughing, said, "And fifty dollars?"

Hurley gestured at the living room. "We'll leave it for the householders," he said. "As a tip."

Parker said, "Wycza and the others already off on their next one?"

"Right," Dalesia said. Looking at his watch, he said, "We better, too. See you later, Parker."

The three of them trooped out of the apartment. Parker went into the bedroom, glanced at the locked closet door, and went over to check dresser drawers. The top one was nearly empty; he put the remaining few clothes on top of the dresser, carried the drawer into the living room, and lined it with the cash from the two robberies. He brought the full drawer back to the bedroom, put it away in the dresser, and returned to the living room to deal out a fresh hand of solitaire.

It wasn't yet two o'clock in the morning.

Forty-five

Calesian dreamed of white skis on a black mountainside. He couldn't see the skier, only the black-clad legs, the white skis, the glistening black slope, the featureless gray-white sky. The skier raced at a downward angle, moving very fast, the wind whistling with his passage, rushing on and on and yet never seeming to get anywhere, sailing across a slope like some gigantic pool ball, empty and alone.

The sound of the phone confused his mind, which tried to interpolate it into the dream as church bells. But there was no church, the image broke down, and he awoke, dry-mouthed and disoriented, to hear the phone ring a second time. He didn't need to switch the light on to find the receiver on the bedside table. Lying on his side, hearing the beating of his heart in the ear pressed into the pillow, he held the phone to his other ear and said, "Hello?"

"Calesian?" It was an angry voice, and a voice he recognized, though he couldn't immediately put a name to it. But he knew it was someone of power; the tone of voice alone was enough to tell him that much.

He said, "Yes? Who is it?"

"This is Dulare, you simple bastard. Wake up."

Dulare. "I'm awake," Calesian said, feeling a sudden flutter of nerves in his chest. Lifting his head from the pillow, hiking himself up onto an elbow, he repeated, "I'm awake. What's the problem?" And blinked in the darkness; though the curtains were open at his bedroom window, no moonlight shone in. It seemed black as a closet out there.

"I'll tell you the problem," Dulare said. "Six guys just knocked over the Riviera."

"Did what?"

"You heard me, goddammit."

"Robbed—"

"It had to be your friend Parker," Dulare said. "There's no way it's anything else."

"Good Christ."

"Christ doesn't come into this." Dulare was raging; his words were made out of sharp pieces of metal, shaped and flung. "No two-bit heist artist is going to take me for fifty thousand dollars, Calesian."

"I don't—" Calesian rubbed his face with his free hand, trying to think. He was now sitting up completely on the bed, the dream forgotten. "Six of them, you said?"

"He's brought in friends," Dulare said. "The son of a bitch is starting a war, Calesian. You've mishandled this thing every way you knew how, you and that goddam moron Buenadella."

"They got away clean?" It was a stupid question to ask and Calesian knew it, but he couldn't find anything sensible to say and silence would have been even worse.

"I'm going over to Buenadella's," Dulare said. It was a bad sign that he was calling Dutch by his last name. "I don't want any of you damn fools here at my place, not with Parker after your asses. I'll be there in fifteen minutes, and you be there, too."

"Of course," Calesian said, but Dulare had already hung up on him.

Calesian cradled the phone, then got out of bed and stood there for a second in the darkness, reluctant to turn the light on, face the reality, start moving.

He should have known. He should have guessed that Parker would pull something like this; it's why the bastard dropped out of sight. The way he'd applied pressure to Lozini last week, hitting the New York Room and the brewery and that downtown parking garage. Only this time, instead of three small annoying stings, taking useless credit-card papers and checks, he'd done one big punch, hitting for fifty thousand dollars.

One big punch? All at once, with the conviction of a revelation, he knew there were going to be more punches than one. Looking toward the window, Calesian thought, *He's out there somewhere, right now, hitting again. Where in hell are you, Parker?*

Still in darkness, he turned his head toward the phone he couldn't see. Call someone, warn somebody? Who? He had no idea where the hit would come, or even if it would be something his own people, the police, would be able to do anything about. A robbery out at the Riviera would be outside local law jurisdiction anyway, even if they reported it. And if there hadn't been any injuries or too many civilians upset, they probably wouldn't report it at all.

Fifty thousand. And it was only the first.

Calesian moved over to the window, looked out at the dark city under the moonless sky. The spotted streetlights, aping the stars, emphasized the darkness rather than cutting it. Calesian sensed Parker out there somewhere, scurrying in the dark with his army.

He looked up at the sky. Why the hell wasn't there a moon, for Christ's sake? The air would be hot just the other side of the window glass, but the air-conditioning was on in here, and he shivered slightly from the coolness of it. And the unrelieved darkness. *A hell of a night to die,* he thought.

Forty-six

Two stretches inside, before he'd smartened up, had bred in Ben Pelzer a taste for orderliness, neatness in everything he did. The third-floor walk-up apartment on East Tenth Street where he was known as Barry Pearlman was always as neat as a pin, and so was his house out in Northglen, where he lived under his own name with his wife and his three-year-old twin daughters, Joanne and Joette.

Pelzer's life was as neatly organized as his homes, and the beginning of his week was Friday, when he would get up in the house in Northglen, pack his bag, and take a plane; sometimes to Baltimore, or Savannah, or New Orleans, or more rarely New York. He never knew ahead of time where it would be, and he didn't concern himself. He would simply stop at Frank Schroder's real estate office, pick up the tickets and his instructions and the bag with the money in it, and be on his way.

In that port city, whichever one it turned out to be, he would usually have a phone number to call, though every once in a while there would be an actual physical meet at the airport; New York was mostly done that way. He would turn over the money, receive his stock, and take the next plane back to Tyler. Then he would drive to the house on East Tenth Street, go up to his apartment, and wait for the first knock on the door.

It was never long in coming. Ben Pelzer was the Man's Man, the wholesaler for all the street dealers in Tyler. Frank Schroder had other wholesalers for other territories, but the nickel-dime action on the street, for the pillbox or paper twist you bought downtown in a doorway or on a park bench, was where Ben Pelzer's merchandise changed hands.

And the weekend was the rush season. On Friday night and Saturday morning the retailers would come by Barry Pearlman's place to stock up, and by Saturday night they'd be coming back again to replenish. They couldn't buy it all at once because this was strictly a cash business, and none of the retailers ever had enough cash on a Friday to buy a full weekend's supply.

On an average week, Pelzer's goods brought in about one hundred thousand dollars on the street. Twenty percent of that stayed with the retailers, the rest coming to the Pearlman apartment. Pelzer's cut was two percent of the weekly cash in hand, averaging about sixteen hundred dollars, which was a very healthy weekly wage indeed. The remaining seventy-five or eighty thousand, Frank Schroder's share from which additional stock was purchased and the law was paid off and the main partnership received their dividends, was amassed all weekend in a suitcase under Pelzer's bed.

That was a lot of cash money to have in one place, particularly when people like Ben Pelzer's customers knew about it, but there'd never been any attempt to steal it. In the first place, everyone who knew about the money also knew whose it was. And in the second place, Pelzer and the cash were never alone in the apartment; two of Frank Schroder's men always sat in, arriving on Friday no more than half an hour after Ben himself took occupancy, and staying with him and the money all through the weekend. The two regular men, Jerry Trask and Frank Slade, were big and tough-looking, a strong contrast with slender, neat Ben Pelzer, and over the last few years the three of them had filled in the idle hours on the long weekends with an endless game of Monopoly. They loaned one another money, forgave one another rents, invented easy new rules, and did everything possible to keep the game going. They were all paper millionaires by now, using the cash from three Monopoly sets for their liquid assets, with hotels on every property, and wholesale swaps of entire complexes. None of them ever got tired of the game, which was permanently set up on a card table in the middle of the apartment living room.

Pelzer's work-week—and his time as Barry Pearlman—

ended late Monday night. Following the weekend trade, there was always one last spurt of buying on Monday, as the retailers stocked up for their daily business, the serious customers as opposed to the weekend joy-poppers. By midnight on Monday that final rush of business would be completed, but Pelzer always kept the shop open until one A.M., just to be on the safe side. Finally, at one o'clock on the dot, he would leave the Monopoly game and lock himself in the bedroom while Trask and Slade washed the dishes and generally tidied up. If anybody rang the doorbell after one o'clock, they were out of luck—nobody would answer.

In the bedroom, Pelzer would put the suitcase on the bed, take the money out, and slowly count it. This week the total was eighty-two thousand, nine hundred twelve dollars. His two percent of that would be sixteen hundred fifty-eight dollars and twenty-four cents, but he was supposed to even that off down to the nearest hundred, so this week he was exactly making his average: sixteen hundred dollars. He took that money in the cleanest bills, mostly in twenties and fifties, and stuffed it away in a money belt he took from the closet, then put on under his shirt. He took another five hundred dollars, in tens and twenties, set it to one side on the bed, and closed the suitcase. Then he unlocked the bedroom door and carried the suitcase and the extra five hundred dollars out to the living room.

The five hundred was his associates' pay: two-fifty apiece. He had never discussed his own salary with them, so they were unaware of the disparity between his sixteen hundred and their two and a half; being unaware of it, they were not made troubled by it.

From here on, the routine was that they would leave the apartment and drive in Pelzer's car over to the parking lot behind Frank Schroder's real estate office, where another car would be waiting for them. Trask and Slade and the suitcase would transfer to the other car, and Pelzer would go home, where his wife would be waiting up for him with a midnight snack. They'd eat together, do the dishes, and go to bed, Pelzer then remaining at home, puttering around his garden and his workbench, until Friday morning and the beginning of another week.

It was an easy schedule, clear-cut and relaxed. It gave him four nights and three full days with his family every week, it offered him interesting travel and introduced him to a wide variety of human types, it paid him handsomely, and there had never been a bit of trouble.

Until tonight.

Carlow said, "Here they come."

The routine was, they had Pelzer's Oldsmobile Cutlass spotted, nearly a block from the apartment, and they were parked behind it—in a different car now, Carlow having traded the Mercury in on an American Motors Ambassador. The air-conditioner worked better on this car, but there still wasn't room for all three in front, not with one of them Dan Wycza. He sat in back, leaning forward with his forearms on the seat back, and he and Devers and Carlow watched the three men come out of the small tenement-style apartment house a block away and turn in this direction. The smaller man in the middle carried an apparently heavy suitcase, while the bigger men flanking him kept looking left and right as they walked.

"I look at them," Wycza said, "I look at those people, and I know they aren't sensible."

Devers said, "You think they'll give us a hard time?"

"I think we ought to start right off by shooting them in the head."

Devers looked troubled. "I don't know," he said.

"I do," Carlow said. Nodding his head toward Wycza, he told Devers, "He's right. The two big ones are hired to mother the money. They lose the money, they're dead anyway."

"I'm a pretty good shot," Devers said. "Let me just plink one, and then we'll give them a chance to work it out for themselves."

Carlow twisted around to look at Wycza, get his opinion. These three men didn't know one another, had never worked together, had only met today, Wycza and Devers on the plane and Carlow in Parker's apartment. It was hard for them to know how to deal with one another, in what areas each was reliable, in what areas they would be stepping on sore corns. Carlow and Wycza, looking at one another in the faint illumination of a nearby streetlight, tried silently to come to an opinion about Devers, and at the same time to gauge one another. Wycza finally dropped his eyes and nodded slightly, with a small shrug, as if to say, "What the hell, let him have his try, we can cover if we have to." Carlow pursed his lips and faced front before answering, moves that clearly said to Wycza, "It's your decision, then, I'm only the driver, and if it bounces back on us later, I'm not the one that did it." Aloud, Carlow said to Devers, "If you think so."

"It's worth a try," Devers said. Twisting around, he said to Wycza, "Judge it for yourself. If they're still gonna cause trouble, you jump right in." So that Devers, too, was being cautious with a new partnership, and not taking all the responsibility on his own shoulders.

Wycza nodded. Devers would shoot one of them in the shoulder, and then Wycza would shoot all three of them in the head. "Fine," he said.

The back room never occurred to stockbroker Andrew Leffler when the robbers broke into his house in the middle of the night. He woke up when the ceiling light flashed on, and sat up astonished to see two men in black clothing, with black hoods over their faces, standing in the bedroom doorway, pointing pistols at him. In those first seconds of wakefulness, he thought of them as merely burglars, come to steal anything of value he might have in the house.

Automatically his right hand fumbled to the night table for his glasses. In the other bed Maureen had also awakened, and he heard the sharp intake of breath that said she, too, had seen the men and the guns. But she didn't scream, and that reminder of Maureen's stability and presence of mind helped diminish his own rising panic, brought on by the fumbling his startled fingers were doing with his glasses. Not being able to see properly only made things worse.

"Take it easy," one of the men said, "and nobody gets hurt."

Finally getting his glasses on, fitting each wing over his ears, he changed his opinion all at once, and decided these two were kidnappers. *Let it be me they want,* he thought, *and not Maureen.*

With his glasses on, he could see them more clearly. They were both thin men, seeming even narrower because of the black clothing. They held their guns steadily, and they had separated, moving so they now flanked the doorway. But also, Leffler noticed, so that neither was in a direct line with the windows.

One of them said, "Get up. Both of you. You can put on robes and slippers, that's all. You won't need anything else, it's nice and warm out."

Leffler thought, *Both of us?* "Just take me," he said. "I'm all you want."

"Don't waste time," the man said. His voice was strangely altered and dehumanized by the black hood. "If we have to carry you out," he said, "we'll make you regret it."

Her voice shaky but her manner amazingly firm, Maureen said, "We'd better do what they say, Art." And she was the first one to throw back the covers and get out of bed.

Leffler hurried to stay with her. It enraged him that these men were seeing his wife in her nightgown, even though the thick cotton showed nothing, and the gown was so voluminous that even the shape of her figure could only be guessed at. But his sense of personal intrusion, of property violation, began with Maureen in her nightgown. His own voice shaking more with outrage than with fear, he said abruptly, "You two will pay for this, you know."

They didn't bother to answer, and somehow that was worse than any possible cutting reply. Hearing his brave but ludicrous cliché echoing over and over in his mind, Leffler became embarrassed, and found himself hurrying into his robe and slippers, as though to get this humiliating experience over with as rapidly as possible.

When they were both ready, one of the gunmen said, "We'll turn this light off now, but we'll have a flashlight on you, and we can see pretty good in the dark, so don't get cute. You just walk on through to the front of the house, open the door, and go on outside."

Argue with them? Try to talk them out of their plan, whatever it was? Leffler hesitated, but he knew no argument would do any good, that he would only finish by embarrassing himself again, so he took his wife's arm, and the two of them walked together down the hall toward the living room.

For the first few steps they had light-spill from the bedroom for illumination. Then that was turned off, and a small uncertain flashlight beam took its place; mostly it was aimed at their backs and threw great misshapen shadows of them out ahead, lighting little but the walls and furniture to either side. They were moving through their own home, along a route they could have walked blindfolded, but somehow this method was worse than being blindfolded; the constantly altering shadows, the flickering flat distorting light, changed the familiar terrain into unknown territory, and when they entered the living room Leffler struck his knee painfully against the corner of the piano stool.

Maureen's hand grasped his forearm. "Are you all right?"

"I'm fine," he said, and though it hurt like fury, he managed to walk without a limp and to restrain himself from bending down to rub it. He would not display weakness in front of these men. Nor, under the circumstances, in front of Maureen. Patting her hand on his forearm, he whispered, "I'm sorry, dear."

"Don't be silly." She squeezed his forearm, and he felt her smiling at him. "This is just an adventure, that's all," she said.

An adventure. *I am fifty-seven,* he told her in his mind, *and you are fifty-four. We have no need for adventure.*

But he didn't say anything aloud. And her calm bravery carried him through the house and out the door, the two gunmen following silently in their wake.

And still he hadn't thought of the back room.

Nick Rifkin lived upstairs over the bar. The bar was called Nick's Place, and the whole building was in Nick Rifkin's name, but he didn't actually own any of it. As he explained to his friends sometimes, "I just kinda hold it for some guys."

Nick was fifty-two years old now, a cheerful heavy-set guy who enjoyed playing bartender, living in a kind of semi-retirement. A reliable soldier with the local organization since he was in his teens, he had stood still for a vehicular homicide rap one time that had really belonged to a very important local guy; he'd served five years and three months, and when he'd gotten out his reward had been Nick's Place. Downstairs the bar, upstairs the apartment and the unofficial loan operation. He got slices in both places, did very well, had some fun, and enjoyed life.

The loan operation was quiet and simple, and most of the borrowers were people from the straight world: businessmen in a bind, operators who needed some quick short-term cash, people whose square-world credit rating was maybe bad, or credit all used up, or something like that. They could borrow big amounts from Nick, amazingly big amounts, and it didn't matter much to Nick or the people behind him if the debts were ever paid off. All you had to keep current with was the interest: two percent a month, every month. Miss a month and some guys come to visit and talk. Miss two months and the same guys come back, but not to talk.

With loans going out and interest coming in, there was always quite a bit of cash moving through Nick's Place, but there wasn't much to worry about. Nick subscribed to the Vigilant Protective Service, and the local police patrol car knew to keep a special eye on Nick's Place; and anyway, who would be dumb enough to go after money that belonged to men like Ernie Dulare and Adolf Lozini?

Somebody. The bedroom light went on and Nick opened his eyes and two guys were standing there with hoods and guns. "Holy Jesus," Nick said, and struggled to sit up. His wife Angela's heavy arm was across his chest, pinning him to the bed, but he finally managed to shove the arm away and hunch up to a sitting position, blinking in the glare of the overhead light.

"Get up, Nick," one of the hooded men said. "Get up and open the closet."

"You're out of your minds," Nick said. Squinting, rubbing his eyes, trying to wake up enough to think, he said, "You got to be crazy. You know whose money that is?"

"Ours. Come on, Nick, we're in a hurry."

Angela groaned, bubbled, snored, and rolled heavily over onto her other side. One thing you could say for Angela: when she was asleep, she was asleep. Nick, with one tiny corner of his mind grateful that she wasn't awake to yap and complain and carry on, slowly kicked his legs out from under the covers and over the side of the bed. "Christ on a crutch," he complained. "What the hell time is it?"

"Move it, Nick."

The floor was cold. The air-conditioner hummed in the window, making cold air move like invisible fog along the floor. Nick, sitting there in white T-shirt and blue boxer shorts, frowned at the one who was doing the talking, trying to see his face through the hood, trying to recognize the voice that was calling him by first name. He said, "Do I know you?" And then, in the process of asking the question, he suddenly came fully awake and realized he didn't want to know the answer to it. If a guy has a hood and a gun, then neither one of you wants you to see his face.

Besides, Vigilant had to be on the way. These guys must have busted in here, so that meant Vigilant would be coming, and so would the cops. So all Nick had to do in the meantime was obey orders and be ready to drop to the floor.

Right. He got to his feet, saying, "Forget it. I don't want to know if I know you."

"That's smart. Open the closet, Nick."

"Yeah, yeah." He wished he had his slippers. "And the safe," he said.

"That's right," the gunman said.

These people knew a lot. They knew the money was in a safe, and they knew the safe was in the bedroom closet. Thinking about that, wondering how much else they knew and what was letting them be so calm about heisting mob money, Nick opened the closet door and went down on one creaking knee to slowly work the combination dial on the safe. While behind him the two guys stood waiting, guns in their hands. And Angela snored. And Nick wondered how long it would take the Vigilant people to get here.

When the buzzer and light went off in the Vigilant ready room, showing that a break-in had just occurred at Nick's Place, Fred Ducasse switched it off and went back to the magazine article he was reading on the latest concepts of crowd control, in a trade journal called *The Police Chief*.

The problem was, there was only so much you could do with

a pinochle deck. So long as Philly Webb had been here they could use the deck for its original purpose—pinochle—and play three-handed, Ducasse and Handy McKay and Webb. But Webb had left half an hour ago to drive for Wiss and Elkins, who were running the job with the stockbroker, Leffler, and that had been the end of it for cards. Ducasse and Handy had tried gin rummy, war, blackjack, ah hell and casino, and not a one of them was worth a damn with a pinochle deck.

So they'd finally hunted around for something to read instead, and in an inner office with a cluttered desk and paneled walls they'd found a shelf full of magazines, all of them specialized law-enforcement or security-agency trade journals. With nothing else to do, and time hanging heavy on their hands, Ducasse was reading about crowd control and Handy was reading about closed-circuit-television security systems.

About five minutes after the Nick's Place buzzer had sounded, the phone all at once rang. Ducasse and Handy looked at one another, and Ducasse said, "Parker?"

"Maybe not. We better put our boy to work."

The guard they'd kept out was tied and blindfolded in a chair by a desk with a phone on it. Handy went over there and rested his hand on the guard's shoulder. "Time for you to go to work," he said.

The guard licked his lips, but didn't say anything. Handy could feel the muscles tensed in the man's shoulder. Rapping the shoulder with his knuckles, gently but firmly, he said, "Remember what we talked about. You bring trouble here, you'll get unhappy."

"I remember." The guard's voice sounded rusty, like someone locked in solitary for a week.

"Clear your throat."

"I'm all right."

The phone had rung three times by now; that was enough. "Here we go," Handy said. He picked up the receiver and held it to the guard's head, holding it at a slight angle so the guard could feel it against his skin yet Handy would be able to hear what the caller had to say.

There was a very slight hesitation, and then the guard said, "Vigilant."

"Hello, is this Harry?"

"Uh— No, it's Gene."

"Whadaya say, Gene? This is Fred Callochio, downtown. Anything shaking?"

"Not here. Not for a couple hours."

"Nice and quiet, huh? That's good."

"How about you?"

"Nothing much. You know, Monday night."

"Right. Same here."

"So I'll see you, Gene."

"Right, Fred. So long."

Handy, crouched close to the blindfolded guard so he could hear the conversation, waited for the click of the other man hanging up, then cradled the receiver and said, "What was that all about?"

"He's a cop," the guard said. "A desk sergeant downtown, Police Headquarters."

Ducasse had come over. He said, "Is that normal, him calling you?"

It wasn't; they could both see it in the guard's hesitation. Finally he said, "Not every night. Sometimes he calls."

Ducasse and Handy looked at one another. Handy said, "They know something's happening. They're looking around for where it is."

Ducasse offered a pale grin. "Let's hope they don't find it."

"They won't," Handy said. He squeezed the guard's shoulder in a congratulatory way. "You did very nice," he said.

The guard had nothing to say.

Handy and Ducasse were walking back across the room toward their magazines when the alarm went off again. They both looked at it, startled, and then Ducasse checked the number on the light with the chart on the console in front of it. Then, switching the alarm off, he turned with a grin to Handy and said, "The stockbroker."

When Andrew Leffler realized the gangsters were taking him to the brokerage, he knew there was no longer anything to worry about. They had brought along his key ring from the dresser, apparently intending simply to unlock the front door and walk in, not realizing that no one at all could enter the place at night, not even Leffler himself using a key, without setting off an alarm at the protective agency. Within minutes the police and the private protective agency's guards would be swarming all over the place here, and surely these men were too professional to put up a dangerous kind of resistance. So it would all be over very, very soon.

When they had left their house, they had been put in the back seat of an automobile waiting in the driveway, with a third gunman at the wheel. Leffler and his wife had been ordered to get down on the floor of the car and huddle there during the entire trip; probably to keep them from seeing the faces of their captors, who took their hoods off for the drive through the city streets.

To the office. The men put their hoods back on, hustled the Lefflers in their robes and slippers across the dark empty sidewalk to the storefront office, and one of them put his key in the lock and opened the door. Leffler almost smiled when he saw that.

And still he hadn't thought of the back room. This was the Tyler office of Rubidow, Kancher & Co., a New York brokerage firm, and he was the man in charge here; he took it for granted these men were after negotiable securities, bearer bonds and paper of that sort, and that he had been brought along to open the vault, with Maureen's presence to assure his cooperation. But as to the back room, he almost never thought about that himself, and so few other people were even aware of its existence that there was never any conversation about it and no reason to anticipate its mention by anyone. In fact, probably because of his own slightly uneasy conscience toward it, Leffler generally made a conscious effort *not* to be overly aware of the back room.

It had begun, a dozen years ago, with his next-to-youngest boy, Jim. All of his five children were doing well now, grown and married and scattered across the United States, none of them a cause for worry or upset, but that hadn't always been true. Jim had gone through a troubled adolescence, involving drugs and theft and other things the Lefflers had never wanted to know too much about, and if it hadn't been for a man named Adolf Lozini, there wasn't any question but that Jim Leffler would be in prison today, or at the very best an ex-con out on parole, his record smeared and his future prospects ruined.

An attorney named Jack Walters had been the one to suggest, during that bad time, that Adolf Lozini might be able to help somehow. Leffler hadn't wanted to put himself in debt to a man who was a known criminal, a syndicate gangster, but what was the alternative? He couldn't permit Jim to go to prison, not if there was any chance at all to save him.

There had been that chance. And all in all the price Lozini had demanded had not been a hard one to pay; in the course of his dealings with legitimate businessmen over the years, Leffler had more than once been asked to skirt much closer than that to the edge of the law. Because all Lozini had wanted was the back room.

Most people who own stock do not keep the certificates physically in their own possession. Their broker holds the paper for them, both for safety—he will either have a vault on his own premises or will lease vault space from a nearby bank—and for convenience when the inevitable moment comes to sell the stock again. Rubidow, Kancher & Co. being a large firm with a large and aggressive local office in Tyler, the brokerage did have its own vault, a double-roomed structure at the rear of the company's offices on the first floor of the Nolan Building on London Avenue. The vault shared a wall with the bank next door but had its own security system, installed and maintained by Vigilant. The larger front room of the vault was used for storage of most stocks and bonds, as well as company records. The small inner section, called the back room, was reserved for seldom-used papers, for the more delicate private transactions, for U.S. Treasury bonds and other highly negotiable securities, and for Adolf Lozini.

Lozini kept money there. So did several of Lozini's associates, men named Buenadella and Schroder and Dulare, Simms and Shevelly and Faran. And Jack Walters, too, the attorney who had originally brought Leffler and Lozini together.

For these men, the back room of Rubidow, Kancher's vault had a great advantage over either a foreign bank account or an American safety deposit box. Unlike the foreign account, there was never any problem about transporting the funds to or from the back room, nor was there that slightly uneasy feeling of being, after all, at the mercy of European banks and European governments which could at any time alter their politics, change their laws, redefine their banking practices.

As to a local safety deposit box, that was reasonably secure so long as a man was alive; though even so, it was possible for a district attorney with sufficient cause to get a court order and have such a box opened. But if a man should die, that's when the true flaw in the safety deposit box would reveal itself; as a portion of the dead man's estate, the box was required by law to be opened in the physical presence of the executor of the estate and a representative of the bank and an official from the Internal Revenue Service.

In the back room at Rubidow, Kancher, such problems didn't exist. Adolf Lozini and his partners could add or subtract funds at any time, and if one of them should die, the others would take care of things. For Leffler, there was no risk, nor even any inconvenience.

At least, there never had been. But tonight, once Leffler and his wife were inside the office with the two hooded gunmen— the third man had stayed outside with the car—one of the men immediately said, "Okay, Mr. Leffler, let's go take a look at the back room."

It wasn't until later that Leffler thought how impossible it was for these people to know that familiar in-office term; at the moment he only felt the shocked realization that it must be the Treasury bonds they were after. And his immediate response was to try to save the bonds by lying: "I can't do that. There's a time lock on the door."

"You get one try at being stupid," the gunman said, "and that was it. There's no time lock on the vault. You do your back-room business at night."

Leffler stared. *Lozini,* he thought, but couldn't believe it. A streetlight outside the plate-glass window filled the front office with a deceptively dark pink glow; in that light, Leffler tried to read the featureless hoods and the stances of the bodies. How much did these two know?

Everything. One of them said, "That's right, Mr. Leffler, it's the mob's money we want."

It's caught up with me, Leffler thought, sagging at once into despair, and he moved along uncomplainingly when one of them took him by the elbow and steered him deeper into the office, away from the pink sheen of the streetlight and toward the darkness of the vault.

Nick Rifkin wished his wife wouldn't snore like that. It was humiliating to him, in front of these bastards. He stood beside the bed, barefoot, feeling chilly, and watched one of them fill a leather bag with the money from the safe while the other one stood back by the dresser and kept an eye and a gun on Nick. And Angela, undisturbed by light, by conversation, by anything at all, just lay there on her back with her mouth open and snooooored. Christ, she was loud.

Finally he couldn't take it any more. To the one by the dresser, he said, "You mind if I turn her over?"

"You should turn her off," the guy said. "Go ahead."

"Thanks," Nick said, but he kept the sarcasm muted. Turning, he put one knee on the bed, leaned over, and poked Angela on the shoulder and the upper arm until she snorted and cleared her throat and complainingly rolled over onto her side. And became silent.

Nick straightened up again, to see the other one coming out of the closet, carrying the closed and full leather bag. Nick looked at the bag, sorry to see all that money go. No matter what happened, no matter who else got blamed for this, some of the shit was bound to fall on his own head and he knew it. "You guys are really making me a mess," he said.

The one by the dresser said, "I'll give you inside information. You won't even be noticed in the rush."

Nick gave him a sharp look. For the first time it occurred to him that maybe something more than a simple heist was taking place here. He'd heard rumbles the end of last week, some kind of trouble, a guy that was being looked for—could this be connected?

Uh uh; that was something else he didn't want to know. "I'll take your word for it," he said.

The one with the bag said, "You're such a smart individual, Nick. You're really okay."

"Don't bother to give me a reference," Nick told him.

The other one said, "I'll give you something better, Nick. A little suggestion."

Nick watched him, waiting for it.

"Pretty soon," the guy said, "you'll want to make a phone call, tell somebody about this."

"More than likely."

"Call Dutch Buenadella," the guy said.

Nick frowned. "Why?"

"He'll be interested, Nick."

The one with the bag said, "Nick, you have to come for a walk with us now."

Nick said, "Why don't I just sit down here and count to a million?"

The one by the dresser said, "Humor us, Nick. Do it our way."

They'd given him advice about who he should call, so they mustn't be planning on killing him, or injuring him very badly. Something like a knock on the head he could live with. "Okay," he said. "It's your act, why should I horn in?"

As they were leaving the bedroom the snoring started again. Nick shook his head but didn't say anything, and walked on downstairs, the guy with the money ahead of him, the other one bringing up the rear.

Downstairs they strolled through the bar, and it occurred to Nick to wonder why he wasn't hearing from the Vigilant people.

So they must have cut the wires, these two.

They opened the front door, and Nick stood to one side for them to go out, saying, "Come back soon."

"Come on outside with us, Nick. Wave us goodbye."

"Listen, fellas," Nick said, "I don't have any shoes."

"Just for a minute. Come on." And the guy took his arm and walked him outside.

It was warmer out there than indoors. Nevertheless Nick felt stupid to be standing around on the sidewalk barefoot, wearing nothing but T-shirt and shorts. The nearest streetlight was half a block away, and there wasn't any moon tonight, but still he felt exposed and open, as though hundreds of people were watching him.

Not hundreds. Just three: the two thieves, and their driver in the Pontiac waiting at the curb.

The guy with the money hurried directly to the Pontiac, sliding into the back seat, pushing the leather bag ahead of himself. The other one pulled the bar door shut and tested the door to be sure it was locked. "Goodnight, Nick," he said, and Nick watched him cross the sidewalk and slide in front next to the driver. The car pulled immediately away, and Nick turned back to the bar door.

It was really locked. He rattled the knob, but that wouldn't do any good. "Shit," he said to himself, and walked around to the side of the house, where the bright yellow light marked his bedroom window. "Hey, Angela!" he yelled. Then he found some pebbles and threw them up at the window. Then he yelled some more.

Finally he had to go around front and find a big stone and throw it through the window in the front door and let himself in that way.

They took all the cash; no stocks, no negotiable bearer bonds, nothing but the hidden cash. Leffler watched it all disappearing into two blue plastic laundry bags, and after the first shock he simply waited it out. Lozini and the others couldn't blame him; after all, he wasn't a bodyguard or a murderer. He wasn't a criminal at all, merely a stockbroker, he couldn't be expected to defend their money against people like this.

The vault lights were on, since they couldn't be seen from the street: bright fluorescents reflecting hazily from the brushed-chrome fixtures. The two men in their dark clothing and black hoods had a silence and swiftness and coldness to them that seemed invincible; no one could defend that money against these two.

How miserable Leffler felt. Maureen stood next to him, her hands closed around his arm just above the elbow, giving him strength with her presence and her touch, and he knew this whole thing was his fault. Endangering her, getting himself in this horrible position. Somehow, a dozen years ago, there must have been some other way to deal with the problem, to help Jim without entangling himself with such people as Adolf Lozini and these two gunmen.

And now they had the money. Carrying the laundry bags, they moved to the vault entrance, and one of them said, "We'll leave the lights on. Or do you want them off?"

The switch was outside. "On," Leffler said. "Please, on."

"Right." The man hesitated, then said, "You'll be okay. Somebody'll get you out in the morning."

The compassion in the man's voice enraged Leffler more than anything else that had happened. "You're the ones who won't be all right," he said, and his voice was trembling with his fury.

The man shrugged; he and his partner stepped outside, and the heavy vault door was pushed shut. "Thank God," Maureen said.

"I'm through," Leffler said. His throat kept closing when he tried to talk, his words came out half-strangled. "I don't care, Maureen, I don't care what happens. I'm finished with Lozini. No more."

"It's all right, dear," she said, and put her arms around him, cradling his head against her gray-and-black rough-feeling hair. "It's all right now," she promised.

And like a fool, like a child, like some helpless ninny, he found himself weeping.

Ben Pelzer stopped next to his car, the key in his hand. While Jerry Trask and Frank Slade kept an eye up and down the street, he stooped slightly, holding the suitcase full of Frank Schroder's money as he slipped the key into the lock in the door.

Out of the corner of his eye he saw the movement, and looked up with a sudden presentiment. Two men were getting out of the next car back, and even before he saw the guns in their hands he knew it was a hijack.

Trask and Slade were the defenders. Pelzer had a pistol under his jacket but he never even thought of reaching for it. He turned away instead, his movements fast and jerky as a silent film, leaving the key in the car door as he headed diagonally across the sidewalk, behind Jerry Trask, away from the two guys from the other car.

Trask and Slade had seen them at the same time, and both reached for guns. Stan Devers shot Trask in the shoulder and Trask turned half around and fell to his knees on the pavement. Slade was bringing a pistol out and Dan Wycza waited two seconds after Devers' shot before putting a bullet in Slade's forehead.

Mike Carlow was starting the engine of the Ambassador, hunching slightly over the wheel, watching the play outside, ready to drop along the seat out of sight if one of those other people actually managed to get a gun out.

It wasn't going to happen. Trask, on his knees, in profile to Devers and Wycza, went on doggedly tugging at the gun under his jacket. "Asshole," Devers said, and shot him in the ear.

Ben Pelzer kept running, zigzagging away down the sidewalk, toting the suitcase. If he'd dropped it, he might have been able to get away. Wycza and Devers fired at the same time, and Pelzer splayed out, then somersaulted onto the sidewalk. The suitcase skidded away until it brought up against a fire hydrant.

Wycza and Devers got back into the Ambassador, and Carlow drove down the block and stopped next to the hydrant. "I'll get it," Devers said, acknowledging that he'd been wrong. He got out, picked up the suitcase, put it in back with Wycza, and slid in next to Carlow again.

Forty-seven

Parker sat and listened to them tell each other about their scores. They were all up, all of them happy and excited because they'd made out tonight. "It was so *easy*": they all said that, at one time or another.

Wiss and Elkins were the first ones back, bringing with them the biggest score of the night: one hundred forty-six thousand, four hundred eighty-seven dollars, the money from the vault at the stock brokerage. "They were really putting it away for a rainy day," Elkins said.

Philly Webb, who had driven Wiss and Elkins here, had immediately gone away again to get Handy McKay and Fred Ducasse from the Vigilant office. Before he got back, Carlow and Wycza and Devers came in, with a scuffed suitcase from the dope dealer containing eighty thousand, eight hundred and twelve dollars. "We should have a night like this once a year," Wycza said.

Devers was so pleased he was almost drunk with it. "What the hell," he said. "Why not once a month?"

Dalesia and Hurley and Mackey arrived next, with the smallest take of the night: seven thousand, six hundred twenty-five, from the loan-shark operation. That was less than Faran had suggested would be there, but by then nobody much cared. Besides, Mackey was full of funny stories about Nick, the guy who ran the place, and about his wife, who slept through the whole robbery. "He'll wake her up tomorrow morning," Mackey said, "and he'll say, 'Sweetheart, we got knocked over last night,' and she'll say, 'Schmuck, leave the drinking to the customers.' "

Parker didn't do any of the talking. He watched and listened, letting them work out their pleasure and their nervous excitement; it wasn't even three o'clock yet, plenty of time left to get his own work done.

Webb came back with Handy and Ducasse, and then everybody was here. The money was brought back out and recounted, and all the totals added up to two hundred seventy-six thousand, two hundred eighty-seven dollars. The money was stacked up on the dining table, and Mackey said, "Son of a blue bitch, boys, that's a quarter million dollars."

"Pencil and paper," Hurley said. "I want to know what my piece is."

It turned out to be an even twenty-five thousand, one hundred seventeen dollars apiece. Nobody could believe a big number like that would come out even when divided by eleven, so three of them did the division, but it kept working out. Twenty-five thousand, one hundred seventeen dollars a man.

Elkins nodded, smiling. "That's a nice night's work," he said.

Parker said, "Now we do another night's work."

They all looked at him, and he could see that in the pleasure with their success, they'd forgotten about him and what was supposed to happen next. It brought them down off their highs, one at a time. He waited it out, waited till the smiles left the faces, waited till the eyes got the flat look back again, waited till they were ready to go back to work.

"Right," he said.

Forty-eight

Calesian could feel it slipping away. He'd had it in his hands, he'd held it just long enough to know what it really was, and now it was slipping away.

That bastard Parker. They'd get him, of course, they'd finish him off, either tonight or tomorrow or sometime later this week, but it was going to be too late for Calesian. The power that had skidded through Buenadella's hands and into Calesian's was gone again, running out like sand through the bottom of a sack. And not a damn thing he could do about it.

Buenadella's house was a goddam fortress by now. There had to be at least forty armed men in here, plus Dutch himself and Ernie Dulare. Also a guy named Quittner that had been sent over by Frank Schroder. Quittner was a cold bastard, tall and skinny and pallid and silent as death. He wasn't a part of anybody's action, wasn't a regular at all. He belonged to Frank Schroder, the way a horse belongs to a mounted policeman. Most of the time Quittner didn't even seem to exist; just every once in a while Frank Schroder wanted a representative somewhere, on something he considered very important, and here came Quittner, empowered to act on his own, to make Schroder's decisions for him, and then to fade out of the picture again.

So now the power lay between Quittner and Ernie Dulare. And when the crisis was over and Quittner disappeared once more, that would leave Dulare the man in control.

It was strange about power. Al Lozini had held it in his hands a long, long time, unquestioned and unchallenged, but

Dutch Buenadella could bleed it out of him slowly over three years without Lozini ever even feeling it: getting the money, getting the right men, inching the reins into his own hands.

If the guns hadn't come out, the shift in control would have been seamless and simple and straight, as automatic as the movement of a teeter-totter. But once Parker and Green had come to town and the balance had gone, once violence had become the only way to make things right, Buenadella had lost the rhythm, had ceased to function, and it became inevitable that the reins would fall from his grasp again.

But not back to Lozini. Once a man was drained of his power, he seemed to lose the assurance that had won it for him in the first place. Lozini with his mastery intact would never have gone after Calesian himself with a gun, just as Calesian would never have dared to shoot a Lozini who was still in charge; so in a way it was the knowledge of his powerlessness that had killed Lozini more than anything else.

Something like that was also happening to Buenadella. For a while Calesian had seen himself as the silent partner, the power behind the throne, with Dutch Buenadella nominally in charge. But then Parker had brought in an army from some goddam place, he'd attacked in a way that hurt too many people and that neither Buenadella nor Calesian could deal with on their own, and Buenadella's loss of control became apparent to the wrong men: to Frank Schroder and Ernie Dulare.

So that's where the power was now, in the hands of Ernie Dulare and of Frank Schroder's man Quittner, sitting together at the desk in Buenadella's den, making their phone calls, making their decisions without consulting Buenadella, picking up the reins in every way. Tomorrow, when Quittner stepped out once more, Ernie Dulare would be the man holding Al Lozini's power in his hands, with Schroder as his ally and Buenadella as his satellite.

And Calesian? Dulare had made it plain when he got here tonight, in a few harsh cutting remarks, that he felt this mess was more Calesian's fault than anybody else's. He'd made his peace with Buenadella, and he'd apparently chosen to turn Calesian into the goat, the one whose bad judgment had brought this trouble down on everybody's head.

Which just wasn't fair. It was Buenadella who had started the power play in the first place, and it was Buenadella who had taken Parker and Green's money, and it was Buenadella who had ordered Mike Abadandi to go kill them. But all of that was being forgotten now. The only things being remembered were that Calesian had killed Al Lozini and that Calesian had fired on Parker and Green after Buenadella had worked out an agreement with them. Nobody was making a big point of blaming Calesian, nobody was arguing with him and giving him a chance to defend himself, but the feeling was obvious in the air. Calesian was out. Not yet, but soon; Farrell would be elected mayor, and would appoint his own police commissioner, and it was only natural to expect the new commissioner to do some reshuffling of assignments. Calesian would lose his slot with the Organized Crime Squad, would be shifted to Public Relations or the Red Squad or some other meaningless backwater, and that would be the end of him. His last state would be worse than his first; less power than before, after having for just one day tasted more power than he'd ever dreamed of.

Was there a way back? Not yet, not that he could see, but still he couldn't just give up. He had to hang around, watching and waiting, hoping for some break somewhere; sitting in Buenadella's den, obscure and ignored in a corner, he watched Dulare and Quittner over at the desk, like two military commanders in a field headquarters setting up for a major battle. Watched and listened and hoped for some new hole to open, some other route back to the trough of power.

Dulare was on the phone now, talking to Farrell. Until a day or so ago direct communication between Farrell and anybody at all on this side of the fence would have been unthinkable; but now they were in a crisis situation, and security was going by the boards. Besides, with the election tomorrow it was too late for anybody to get political mileage out of Farrell's connections; and after the man was elected, what was anybody going to do about it?

Dulare was saying, "George, you just sit tight. You've got good security around you there, and . . . I know they did. That's why your security's so much better now. You stay there, stay out of it, stay above it. Do your early morning voting booth number, then fade away again and let it all happen. We'll take care of things on the outside . . . They also serve, George, who only stand and wait . . . I know it. If I'd been in this earlier it wouldn't have happened . . . That's right, George, that's just what's going to happen . . . I definitely will, I'll let you know first thing . . . That's right. Goodbye, George."

Dulare hung up, made a face, said to Quittner, "The man's a bigger asshole than Wain ever was."

"He'll do," Quittner said. He had a soft voice, with no strength in it; he was frequently hard to hear. "He's just frightened, that's all."

Dulare grunted, and looked at the sheet of paper he'd been doodling on. "I keep thinking," he said, "there must be other places for them to hit. The Riviera. Nick Rifkin's Place. Your man Pelzer."

"They know a lot," Quittner said. "They know more than I do. Nick Rifkin, I knew nothing about."

"A little loan operation." Dulare shrugged, turning that conversation aside. "The question is, what else can they hit?"

"What else is there for them to know about?"

"It's that goddam Faran," Dulare said. "He's a hail-fellow-well-met, let's get together have a couple drinks. You sit with him, you trade stories, pretty soon he knows everything you do."

"He's too expensive," Quittner said.

"Frank's got a lot of friends," Dulare said. "A lot of buddies. They'll all want to forget it, let him go, not make a big deal."

"He's too expensive." Quittner had a cold, soft, unemphatic way of repeating himself that was much more impressive than a lot of shouting or a whole array of different arguments.

Dulare shrugged. "Let's see if we get him back alive," he said. "Then we can talk it over."

There was a silence. Calesian watched Quittner turning it over in his mind, watched him decide not to repeat his comment again but to let it go for now, and knew that Quittner was determined that Frank Faran should die. There seemed to Calesian no question but that Frank Faran was soon going to be dead.

What did Quittner want? While he and Dulare went on

talking about other potential places for Parker to hit, Calesian studied Quittner, trying to understand the man. Would he be taking over when Frank Schroder died or retired? Schroder was in his sixties now, so that was a possibility, and Quittner had the look of someone patient enough to wait things out. But did he want any more? It was hard to see Quittner, for instance, in Al Lozini's role; the man in charge had to have the potential for some sort of human contact with the people under him, and Quittner seemed just too cold and withdrawn, he seemed to live too completely inside himself. It was impossible to think of Quittner hosting one of those gourmet dinners that Al Lozini used to do once or twice a week.

All at once Calesian felt an almost physical pain of nostalgia for the way things used to be. Way back, four or five years ago, back when Lozini was still completely in charge, before Dutch had made his move, before anything had happened. How easy and good that all seemed now.

No. With a sensation like an iris being slowly forced shut, Calesian put away that weakness. He had been thinking about Quittner, wondering what kind of man he was, wondering if there was any way that Quittner could be useful in Calesian's rehabilitation. There had to be some way to keep from being bounced out of things by all this—was Quittner the way?

Dulare was on the phone again, talking to Artie Pulsone over at Three Brothers Trucking. They had twelve radio-equipped delivery trucks over there, and Dulare had arranged for them all to be out on patrol, driving around the city, looking for trouble. They were in steady touch with Artie at the office, and Artie would occasionally check in by phone with Dulare.

Quittner had gotten to his feet and was over by the French doors, looking out at the floodlit shrubbery and lawn. Being casual, not knowing what he would say but only that he had to start with some sort of try, Calesian stood up and strolled over next to him. "One thing's for sure," he said, also looking out toward the lawn. "He won't get in here, anyway."

"He'll come for his friend," Quittner said.

Calesian looked sharply at him, surprised by the calm assurance of the man. How could he be so positive what Parker would do? "I think he'll call," Calesian said. "Sometime tomorrow. The way he worked it with Al Lozini."

"He'll come for his friend."

Despite the situation he was in, Calesian felt irritation and couldn't help showing it. "What makes you so sure?"

Quittner glanced at Calesian. His eyes were pale blue, they almost looked blind. Without expression, he said, "You shouldn't have sent him that finger. He wasn't the right man for that."

It wasn't smart to try defending himself, but Calesian couldn't hold back. "That's easier to see now," he said. "At the time, it seemed the right thing to do."

"He wasn't the right man for that. He never was."

Quittner turned his head again, looking out at the lawn. Calesian tried to find something else to say in his own defense, but was distracted by the sound of the den door opening. It was Buenadella.

He looked terrible. It was amazing how much he'd changed, just overnight. Inside his big frame he looked shriveled and stooped. His face was fixed in downward curving lines, like the unhappy side of a comedy-tragedy mask. He had sent his family out of the city and he should have gone with them, but he'd insisted on sticking around. Not that he could do any good; he'd become an old woman, fretful and frightened.

Dulare was just hanging up the phone. Looking up, he said, "How's it going, Dutch?"

"Any news? Did they find him?" A faint whining note had come into Buenadella's voice; it was the worst of the new characteristics, weak and grating.

"Nothing yet," Dulare said. "How's life upstairs?"

"The doctor says Green was awake for a while."

"No shit," Dulare said.

Quittner turned away from the window, his attention caught. Calesian kept watching Quittner.

"Just for a few minutes," Buenadella said.

Quittner, walking over to the desk, said, "Did anybody talk to him?"

"He wasn't awake that way, to have a conversation. It's just his eyes were open for a little while."

"If he really wakes up," Quittner said to Dulare, "we want to talk to him."

Calesian, having stayed over by the French doors, touched his palm to one of the glass panes. It was warm, warmer than the air in the room, so it must still be hot outside, even though the glare of floodlights made the greenery out there look cool.

Buenadella said, petulantly, "I don't see why we don't kill him. That's the only reason Parker's coming here, isn't it? Kill him, leave him on a street downtown, the way Parker left Shevelly."

Dulare, speaking with controlled impatience, said, "He's a playing card. So long as we have him, Parker can still be ready to deal."

"What if he tries to break in here?"

"Good," Dulare said. "I'd love it."

Calesian turned and looked out the window again. Buenadella was saying something else, that whine still sounding in his voice, but Calesian didn't listen. He was trying to think of how to square himself with Quittner.

Did somebody move there? Out toward the end of the lawn, amid the individual clumps of bushes.

No. It was just nerves. Calesian squeezed his eyes shut and looked out again at the glare of light. Nothing. He would let Quittner know just how much clout he had in the police force, how many men owed him favors. Then the lights went out.

Forty-nine

Wiss carried the bomb, one he'd made in an empty soft-drink bottle out of materials from his safe-cracking bag. Elkins did the driving, and when they reached the electric company substation he merely slowed down, looping up onto the sidewalk while Wiss leaned out of the car window and tossed the bottle underhand. It arched up over the fence as Elkins accelerated away, landing in the middle of the high-voltage relay equipment, and exploding on contact. It wasn't a very big explosion, nor very loud, but it cut off all electric service in that section of the city. Driving along in a world suddenly without streetlights or traffic lights, with utter darkness on all sides of them, Wiss and Elkins headed back again toward the center of the city; they had one more job to do tonight.

When the lights went out, the darkness was more complete than city dwellers ever know. High thin stars defined the moonless sky, but the earth was black wool, across which men stumbled, blinking, moving their arms out in front of them like ant feelers. The defenders in the Buenadella house stared out windows at nothingness, clutching guns, squinting, trying to see with their ears but hearing nothing more than their own breathing and faint creaking noises from the man at the next window. "Shut up!" they whispered at one another. "I think I hear something." A couple of them, seeing light flecks before their eyes, fired aimlessly into the dark, the muzzle flashes a quick red light that they didn't know to look away from, making them more blind than ever.

The two men inside the TV repair truck across the street, surveillance specialists from the state CID, didn't know at first there was anything wrong. They had their own electric power inside the truck, and the camera through which they looked at the world outside was equipped with infrared. But then, just as they were realizing something had happened, the rear doors of the truck opened, a flashlight shone in at them, and a voice said, "Don't reach for any guns."

They might have reached for guns anyway, despite the fact that they couldn't see past the hard brightness of the flashlight, if they hadn't simultaneously heard the sound of shooting flare up over at the Buenadella house, reminding them that they were after all only technicians. Bewildered, but understanding instinctively that this wasn't a mess they wanted to involve themselves in, they both raised their hands.

Tom Hurley held the flashlight, while Ed Mackey with his hood over his face climbed into the truck, disarmed the two men, and tied them together back to back with their belts and shoelaces. Hurley said, "Make sure that camera isn't working."

Mackey looked at the camera, then hit it three times with a gun butt. "It isn't working," he said, and he and Hurley left the truck and went over to the house.

Stan Devers had gone up a telephone pole half a block away shortly before the lights went out. He was equipped with insulated gloves and a pair of heavy wire cutters, and while there was still light to see by, he made sure he had the group of lines leading to the area of the Buenadella house. When the lights went out he worked by feel, scissoring through the lines, hearing the musical notes when they snapped. Finished, he dropped the wire cutters into the oceanic darkness below him, and went slowly backward down the pole, feeling for the metal rails. He had no sense of height in this blackness, and it soon seemed to him it was taking too long to get down the pole. Leg down, hand down, leg down, hand down; surely he should have reached the ground by now. A stupid panic tried to rise up in his chest, and he felt the idiotic urge to just jump out from the pole into the black, drop the rest of the distance, however long it was, get this damn thing over with. And still he kept inching and inching and inching his way down the rough wood surface; and when his foot did finally thud against the ground, it came as a surprise.

The three drivers, Mike Carlow and Philly Webb and Nick Dalesia, had been waiting in three cars parked a block away. When the darkness hit, they drove forward, using parking lights only. Ahead of them they saw the spot of light where Mackey and Hurley were dealing with the men in the TV repair truck. They drove on by that, and made the turn onto Buenadella's property; as they turned, they switched on their headlights, high beams, four bright lights per car.

Men upstairs in the front windows had seen the faint outline of automobiles coming, defined by the yellow glow of parking lights, the dim red luster of taillights. They'd readied themselves to fire, but the sudden blinding glare of headlights left them with no targets to shoot at.

The three cars ignored the circular driveway. Spreading out across the lawn, evading the crooked sundial, they came to a stop about twenty feet from the house, in a widely separated row, all pointed directly at the front door. In all the surrounding blackness, the façade of the Buenadella house showed up like a painted bas-relief on a velvet wall.

The three drivers got out of their cars and moved quickly around behind them. They had pistols in their hands, and they used the cars as shields as they scanned the front windows of the house. Anyone intending to shoot out the headlights would have to show himself in a window; at the first sign of any movement in one of those windows, all three drivers would open fire. The headlights would stay on.

At the rear of the house, Parker and Handy McKay and Dan Wycza and Fred Ducasse had waited for the darkness, crouching in the shrubbery at the far end of the lawn. In the lighted windows inside the house they could see men moving back and forth, in conversation together or watching, and each of them chose an indoor target. Parker, on one knee with his gun hand supported on the other knee, sighted on the figure in the French doors in Buenadella's den. That was Calesian there, and it was right to kill him this way, with their roles reversed.

When the lights went out, Parker squeezed off two shots. He heard the other three around him firing, and when they stopped, there was a ragged response of gunfire from the house. "Wait it out," he said, speaking into the darkness.

Dan Wycza's voice sounded from his left, saying, "I wonder did I get mine."

That was all any of them said until they saw the sudden blare of headlights from the other side of the house. The house was silhouetted by the lights; it was like an eclipse of the moon.

Parker got to his feet. "All right," he said, and he and the three others walked forward across the lawn to the house.

Fifty

When the lights went out, Buenadella knew he was a dead man. A small wailing cry came out of his mouth and he wasn't even aware of it; his eyes were wide open, staring into the darkness, trying to see the thing that was coming to run him down.

He heard the shooting, and the sound of broken glass, and he heard somebody say, "Uhh." Who was that? Calesian?

Ernie Dulare was cursing: quietly, methodically, in a cold rage, like a man counting to ten. Quittner, his voice soft but his words fast, said, "Stay down. They're shooting through the windows."

"Oh, God." Buenadella felt trapped. He couldn't be indoors now, he had to be outside. The darkness made the walls and ceiling close in on him, press against him. Moving with unconscious familiarity across the room, he headed toward the French doors, ignoring what Quittner had said about the men outside shooting through the windows. Behind him he could hear Dulare punching vainly at the telephone. "Hello. Hello," Dulare said, angrily, then he was heard slamming the receiver down. "They've cut the line."

Of course. Buenadella had already known that. He neared the French doors, and someone grasped his arm. Someone breathing noisily through his mouth, as though he had severe sinus trouble.

Buenadella could be no more afraid. He accepted this with the calm of paralysis, saying, "Yes? Yes?"

"Dutch." It was Calesian, his voice sounding clogged. "Dutch. It's—" The hand tugged at his arm; Calesian wanted him closer, apparently wanted to whisper to him.

Buenadella leaned forward, dazzled by the darkness, having no idea what any of this was about. He felt Calesian's warm breath on his cheek, and turned his head, and blood gushed warmly from Calesian's mouth. It smelled acrid and stinking; Buenadella recoiled from it, his mind filled with confused images of vomiting and slaughterhouses, and his sudden movement destroyed Calesian's balance. Calesian fell against Buenadella's side, nearly knocking him over. Buenadella braced himself, flailing backward with one arm for a wall or the desk or anything, and Calesian slid down Buenadella's body and fell away onto the floor.

Dulare was saying something. Buenadella knew he should be listening, but all his attention was centered on the fact that some soft part of Calesian was still pressed against his ankle and foot.

A hand—again—on his arm; this one rougher, more urgent, shaking him. Dulare's loud voice: "Dutch? Goddammit, man, is that you?"

"What? What?"

"Listen to me, for Christ's sake."

"Calesian," Buenadella said. He was feeling around with his free hand for Dulare's position. "He's shot. Don't, don't step on him, he's down by—"

"Screw Calesian. Do you have an emergency generator in this house, or don't you?"

"Generator?"

"Electric generator, goddammit."

Quittner was over by the door somehow, had apparently opened it; the sound of firing was louder from that direction now. Quittner said, as softly as ever, "Something's happening up front."

Buenadella tried to concentrate on the question. "Generator. No, we never needed one."

"We do now," Dulare said. "Do you have a flashlight in here?"

"Uh—no. In the kitchen there's one, in a drawer there."

"Well, if we can't see," Dulare said, "neither can they."

Quittner said, "There's light up front."

Dulare said, "There is? Come on, Dutch."

"Calesian," Buenadella said helplessly. "He's on my foot."

"Oh, for—" There were kicking sounds, sliding sounds, and the pressure left Buenadella's foot. Dulare's hand felt for him, grasped his upper arm. "Come *on*," he said.

Buenadella went with him. In the hall there was a faint light, they could see the doorway leading to the dining room. Dulare said, "What the hell is that?"

Quittner said, "We'd better go see."

The three men moved cautiously down the hall, and just as they got to the dining-room doorway a man came through from the other direction: Rigno, one of Dulare's men. "Mr. Dulare," he said. "Is that you?" He sounded tense, and a little out of breath.

"What's going on up there?"

"They got cars," Rigno said. "They spread them out on the lawn, facing the house, with their headlights on. We stick an arm out the window, they shoot it off."

Dulare, his frown evident in his voice, said, "What the hell is that for?"

Quittner said, "Because they're coming from the back."

Dulare, sounding unconvinced, said, "You mean a diversion?"

"No," Quittner said. "The only light source is in front. They'll come in from the back. We'll be between them and the light, so they'll be able to see us, but we won't be able to see them."

"Son of a bitch," Dulare said. "We've got to put out those fucking headlights."

"Mr. Dulare," Rigno said, out of breath and apologetic, "you couldn't stick a mouse out one of them windows without it getting its head shot off."

"Come on," Dulare said. He and Quittner and Rigno hurried away together, toward the front of the house.

Buenadella had come this far only because Dulare had dragged him along. Now Dulare had been distracted by a more urgent problem, and Buenadella was left on his own. For half a minute or so he simply stood where he was, looking at the darkness, listening to the sounds around him: sporadic gunfire, men running, men calling to one another.

Gradually it came in on him what was happening here. This was his home, the home of a legitimate businessman. It was full of armed men, and shooting, and the bitter stink of death. Calesian's blood was on his shirt and the side of his neck, caking there, itching, still smelling sick. His family had been driven from the house, he himself was being destroyed.

By two men. Parker and Green. Parker, and Green.

He looked up toward the ceiling, up where Green was. They should have killed him right away, yesterday afternoon. All of this business; he should be dead now.

Buenadella turned and shambled toward the stairs. There were silences around him, then little flurries of sound: shooting or voices. Then silence again. He ignored it all, made his way to the second floor, and moved down the corridor toward the guest room, where Green was lying. His big frame had always before this given an impression of controlled strength, but now his movements were loose and shuffling, as though his brain were no longer fully in contact with his body.

He reached the closed door of the guest room. This was a dark area of the house, far from front windows. He touched his palms to the door for a moment, feeling the coolness of it, then slowly turned the knob and pushed the door open.

All he could see was the rectangle of the window. He stepped in, then a figure moved in front of that lighter rectangle, and he stopped, suddenly bone-cold with fear.

A voice spoke at him from across the room: "Who is it?"

He wasn't going to say anything, would pretend there was no one here; then he recognized the speaker. Dr. Beiny. Sagging with relief, leaning his shoulder against the doorpost, Buenadella said, "It's me, Doctor."

The doctor, his fright showing through an attempt at waspishness, said, "I shouldn't be here. This isn't fair, Mr. Buenadella, I'm not a party to this, I shouldn't be here at all."

"You can go," Buenadella told him. "You can get out of here any time you want."

"How can I leave, with all this shooting?"

Buenadella moved into the room from the doorway. "Go on

now," he said. He felt a sudden savage pleasure, a need to hurt someone. "Just explain to everybody you're a noncombatant," he said. "Tell them you're a medic."

"Mr. Buenadella, I can't—"

"Get out of here!"

"There isn't any way for me to—"

Buenadella closed in on him, following the sound of the voice. He reached out, his clutching fingers closed on a face, a working mouth. He slid his hand down, grasped the throat, squeezed. "I said get out of here," he said. In the doctor's presence, he was feeling stronger and stronger; his own weakness seemed to have dissolved in the presence of this other man's greater weakness. "Get out or I'll kill you myself."

"You're—you're—" The doctor's hands clutched at the hand holding his throat. "My God, you're strangling me!"

Buenadella gave him one shake, and released him. Speaking in the darkness, permitting any expression at all to cross his face because no expression could be seen, smiling broadly with his lips curling back from his teeth, he said, "Now. Get out now."

The doctor didn't argue. He scurried by, bumping into Buenadella on the way, stumbling into some piece of furniture, patting the wall, then making it out into the hallway. Buenadella followed, cautious but still somewhat familiar in this house, and found the door he'd opened; he closed it, felt for a key, found none. No matter.

He turned the other way, moved slowly across the room, hands out in front of himself at waist height, patting the air. Finally he found what he was looking for: the metal strip at the foot of the bed. As he moved along that to the left, there was another sound of a gunshot, seeming much closer than any of the others. He paused, frowning, listening, but heard nothing more.

He rounded the foot of the bed, stopped there, fumbled in his pockets for matches. Finding some, he lit a match and saw Green lying in bed, his head propped up on two pillows, his eyes open, looking directly at Buenadella.

"Uh!" Buenadella dropped the match and it went out. He could still feel the eyes looking at him.

Was Green capable of movement? Was he creeping this way

along the bed right now, was his bony hand reaching out from the darkness? Breathing faster and faster, Buenadella tore another match from the pack, nearly dropped all the matches, managed to light the second one, and Green was there exactly as before.

Too exactly. Buenadella moved to the left, but the eyes didn't shift.

Was he dead? Buenadella watched, and slowly the eyes blinked. When they opened again, Buenadella could see that they were looking at nothing.

"You'll never see anything again," Buenadella told him, and the bedroom door opened.

He turned his head, and wasn't surprised that it was Parker, standing in the doorway, a gun in his hand. Buenadella threw the match away from himself and took two fast steps backward, trying to hide himself in the darkness of the room. He left himself framed by the rectangle of window behind him, but he didn't know that.

"Goodbye, Buenadella," Parker said, and Buenadella thrust up his splayed-out hands to stop the bullet.

Fifty-one

Approaching the rear of the house, Parker moved with wary caution. He knew Handy and Dan Wycza and Fred Ducasse were on his flanks, but he could neither see nor hear them. The house was dead ahead, but invisible; the closer he got to it, the less help he received from the car headlights around on the other side.

The glow from the headlights didn't reach all the way through the house; there were too many rooms, too many walls, between there and here. There was no definition of the windows along the rear wall, though occasionally still an upstairs window became pinpointed for an instant by the red flash of someone firing a gun at shadows. Parker was moving toward his memory of the French doors, though he was deflected at times by shrubbery. Still, it was the French doors he wanted; Calesian and Buenadella and Dulare had all been inside there, with another man.

A sudden flurry of shots came from the right, five or six shots, and the sound of breaking glass. Parker moved forward through the grass, forcing himself not to hurry. The house was very close now. He reached out, took two more steps, and touched wood. The frame of something. His hand moved to the left, touched siding, moved to the right, found a small pane of glass. More glass—the French doors.

They opened inward. He pressed slightly, and the door eased open without a sound. Cool air-conditioned air came out through the opening. Standing next to the frame, not to outline himself against the sky in the doorway, Parker listened to the interior of the room.

Nothing. A door was apparently open on the other side, and through it came sounds of movement, shouting, hurrying, gunfire; but from the room itself no sound at all.

Parker went down on hands and knees. His pistol was in his right hand, and now he held a small pencil flash in his left. He moved into the room, keeping low, patting his left hand out ahead of him onto the floor as he went. Once clear of the doorway he angled to the left, still on hands and knees.

His probing left hand touched something: cloth, a trouser leg. He crawled up the length of the body, aware now of the odor of blood, and when he reached the face he clicked the flashlight on and off, giving himself light for a milli-second. He studied the afterglow in his mind, and recognized the face: Calesian. So it had been a good shot.

And the rest of them had left the room. Moving without thought, leaving this entrance unguarded.

It wouldn't be for long. Dulare would think of it in time, and send some people back here. Parker got to his feet, crossed the room toward the space the sounds came from, and found the doorway. He stepped through and noise came from the left. Looking that way, he saw a faint blue-whiteness: headlight glow. And two bulky shapes came trotting around the corner, belated guards for the French doors.

The shapes stopped. Parker could make them out against the pallid light, but for them he was shielded by total darkness. One of them said, huskily, "Jesus Christ, it's dark back here. Where is this fucking den?"

"Wait a minute. I've got a match."

Parker shot them both, before they could light a match and alter his night vision. Then he turned the other way, moving along a black hallway. In a house this size there had to be a rear staircase, and if Grofield was still alive, it was upstairs that Parker would find him.

A doorway. From the floor on the other side, this was the kitchen. He took a step, halted, listened. Breathing? In a quiet but confident voice, Parker said, "Where are you?"

"Huh? Over here, by the window."

Parker moved diagonally away from the voice till he saw the rectangle of window, and the darker shape within it. The shape said, "You think there's any of them around this side?"

"Yes," Parker said, and shot him, then turned to the wall, felt his way along past appliances, found a swinging door with another room beyond it, ignored that, came to a wall turning, another door. This one opened inward toward the kitchen, and beyond it narrow stairs led up to the left.

He was halfway up when a frightened, heavily breathing man started down, muttering to himself. Parker waited, and felt the bulky leather bag before he touched the man. He had put his flashlight away, and now his free hand skittered up the man's sleeve to his throat.

"Aaa!"

Parker pressed the pistol against him. Quietly he said, "Where's Green? Where's the prisoner?"

"I— Dear God. I don't have anything to do with this, I'm a doctor."

Parker pressed him harder against the side wall hemming in the staircase. "You work on fingers?"

The man shuddered all over, like a horse. His throat worked beneath Parker's fingers, but he didn't say anything.

"Where's Green? Fast!"

"Upstairs! Second door on the left. You've got to understand the position I was in, I didn't have any—"

Parker held the pistol back three or four inches and fired. He let the body tumble down the stairs, and went on up.

Blackness up here. No way to define the space, but it was probably some sort of hallway. Parker moved along the left wall past an open doorway and then to a door that was closed. He opened it, and saw a room lighted by a match in Buenadella's hand. Grofield lay under blankets on a bed, either dead or unconscious.

Buenadella saw him in the doorway and threw the match away, hiding himself in the darkness. But then he stepped backward till he was between Parker and the window, making a silhouette that was as good as sunshine.

"Goodbye, Buenadella," Parker said.

Fifty-two

The power substation went out at three twenty-two. An emergency relay system had been set up in Tyler five years before, after a summer of blackouts caused by power overloads, that would bring power in from other parts of the national grid if this substation were to go out. But the emergency system used the same distribution equipment from the same substation, and that equipment was now out of operation. It would take nearly six hours to rig up a temporary alternate distribution structure and return electric power to the west side of Tyler.

When the electricity went off, the Police and Fire Departments in the affected area went immediately into a standard emergency procedure; stand-by men were called in, extra telephone answerers were assigned, more patrol cars were readied to be put on the street, and selected radio-equipped fire engines went out to patrol the area. Two shopping streets were within the affected zone, so the principal concentration of police and fire attention remained there. Residential sections remained mostly unpatrolled, except in response to direct telephone complaints.

When the shooting started at the Buenadella house, the neighbors within a block radius were startled out of sleep. Nine families were awakened, and for all of them it was a terrifying and bewildering experience, with thoughts of invasion and revolution running through their heads. First there was the gunfire, and very quickly after that the discovery that the electricity wasn't working. And when they tried to call the police, as practically all of them did, the phones weren't working either. One man took his family and a shotgun out to the half-forgotten fallout shelter he'd installed behind the house way back in 1953; feeling an exultant sense of vindication, he bundled everybody inside, switched on the emergency generator, checked the load of his shotgun, and prepared to shoot any neighbor who tried to get in. Two other men armed themselves with rifles and stationed themselves by their front doors. Most other families sat around flashlights or kerosene lamps or the blue light of gas stoves and talked together in frightened undertones; nobody seemed to know what was the right thing to do. It was twenty-five minutes before one man finally got himself dressed and went out to his car and drove away from the neighborhood to find the police or a working phone or at least some explanation of what was going on; and by then the shooting had mostly died down.

At the Buenadella house, Handy McKay and Dan Wycza and Fred Ducasse moved room by room through the first floor, clearing Dulare's men as they went, making sure that nobody alive was behind them. Parker stayed upstairs in the doorway of Grofield's room, waiting and listening. Mike Carlow and Philly Webb were out front, using their cars as shields and peppering anybody who showed in a front window. Two of the headlights had been shot out, but that left ten still shining. Nick Dalesia had joined Stan Devers on the right side of the house; in the dim light-spill from the front they made sure nobody came out any of the side windows, to get around behind the people inside. Ed Mackey and Tom Hurley were doing the same thing on the left.

Dulare's people were bewildered and leaderless. Half of them were dead or badly wounded, and the rest had no idea what they were supposed to be doing. Dulare and Quittner kept trying to organize a defense, but in the darkness and confusion there was no way to maintain any kind of general communication. The defenders were like steers in a pen, being shot down by men sitting around them on the fence rails.

Six men up on the second floor clustered in the blackness of the central hallway and whispered together, trying to decide what to do. A couple of them were in favor of going down the front stairs and joining the fight, but the rest would have nothing to do with it. One suggested they try jumping out windows onto the lawn, but another one said, "There's guys out on the sides of the house. They'll blow your head off, you stick it out there."

"For Christ's sake, how many of them are there?"

"I think there's a hundred."

They talked about it some more. They were the full complement of Dulare's men up here now, and they didn't like being stuck on the second floor. A couple of them suggested they simply go down the back stairs and out the kitchen door and get the hell away from here, but the others decided that wouldn't work either; any man who ran away would sooner or later have to answer to Ernie Dulare. One said, "So we go down the back stairs and get these bastards from behind. Do the same thing to them they're doing to us."

Parker, standing in Grofield's doorway, listened to the entire conversation. If they'd decided to run away, he would have let them go, but in the end they chose to go down to the kitchen and try attacking the invaders from behind, so that was that. Parker took the flashlight from his pocket as he followed them to the stairs, waited until he was sure they were all in the narrow walled staircase, then stood in the doorway at the top, switched the light on, and began firing into them.

Downstairs, in the main parlor off the front staircase, Dulare and Quittner sat on the floor away from the windows, and in the reflected headlight glare tried to put together some kind of sensible defense. Dulare's man Rigno was out roaming around the house, calling in the rest of the remaining men, gathering them all here in this room. Quittner was saying, "They don't have much time. They know they have to hit and run, before the police get here."

Dulare grunted. "They *are* hitting, goddammit," he said. "I picked the wrong side in this fight."

"No," Quittner said. "You had to side with Buenadella. So does Frank, that's why I'm here. No matter how much destruction this man Parker causes here tonight, he's still only a transient, he'll come and go. The organization has to stay together."

"We're goddam falling apart right now," Dulare said.

Across the main front hall, Fred Ducasse slowly entered the formal dining room. Everything was clear ahead of him, but he didn't know about the man lying on the floor to his right, over by the archway to the front hall. For just a second Ducasse was framed against a window behind him and to his left; a bullet hit him in the right side of the head, knocking him into a hutch filled with pewter and memorial plates.

More men crawled into the front parlor, staying below the level of the windows. Rigno was in last, and reported to Dulare: "That's all there is. I shouted upstairs, but there's nobody up there."

Dulare did a fast head-count, and there were seventeen men in the room, counting Quittner and himself. "We've got to sit tight," he told them. "We'll get cops here pretty soon, these people will have to take off. All we do for now is sit here and wait them out."

That's when Handy McKay rolled the bomb through the doorway.

Fifty-three

Frank Elkins parked across the road from the hospital and switched the headlights off. Then he and Ralph Wiss waited a minute to get used to the darkness.

Across the way, the hospital showed the only lights in the neighborhood. It was equipped with standby electric-generating equipment sufficient for operating rooms, medical machinery, refrigeration equipment, and some internal lighting, but not enough to illuminate the parking lots or other outside areas, so from here it was merely a pattern of lighted windows hanging in black space.

Wiss said, "It looks like a Halloween pumpkin."

Elkins squinted. "I don't see any face."

"No, a pumpkin done like a building. You know? Instead of a face."

Elkins frowned in the darkness, uncomprehending. "A pumpkin done like a building?"

"Forget it," Wiss said. "Come on, let's go."

They got out of the car—the interior light was an oasis of warm yellow while the doors were open—and walked across the road and up the driveway to the hospital building. The Emergency entrance sign was off, but they could make out the blacktop lane leading around to the side. They walked around that way, and saw the glow of low-wattage bulbs in the vicinity of the glass doors leading into Emergency. In the yellow-brown light two ambulances were parked near the doors, facing out.

Avoiding the light, Wiss and Elkins skirted the Emergency

entrance and made their way toward the rear of the building. Light-spill from windows over their heads gave a faint yellow sheen, enough for them to see what they were doing.

Inside a fenced enclosure was the hospital's motor pool: four more ambulances, a mobile operating unit, and two other specialty vehicles. Wiss touched the simple padlock closing the gate and it opened for him. He stood by the gate and waited while Elkins selected the ambulance he wanted, crossed the wires under the dash, and drove the vehicle out without switching on its lights. Wiss locked the gate again, got into the ambulance with Elkins, and they rode together out to the street. Elkins stopped next to their car, and Wiss said, "I'll follow you. I don't know the way."

"Right."

Wiss changed over to the car, Elkins switched on his headlights, and the two vehicles drove away.

Fifty-four

Parker held the flashlight while Handy worked on the wall safe in Buenadella's den.

The whole thing had taken less than half an hour. Fred Ducasse was dead. Tom Hurley had been shot in the arm, not badly, and had been taken away by Nick Dalesia; they wouldn't be coming back. Dan Wycza and Ed Mackey and Stan Devers were upstairs strapping Grofield onto a mattress for the trip down and out of the house. Philly Webb and Mike Carlow were away getting other cars, to replace the ones that had been shot up a bit on the lawn.

Just as Handy popped the safe, Devers walked in, preceded by his own flashlight. "The ambulance just pulled in," he said.

"Good."

Handy was pulling wads of cash out of the safe. "Looks good," he said.

"Here." Parker gave him the flashlight. "I'll be right back."

Parker and Devers walked to the front of the house and outside. The cars were still on the lawn but their headlights had been switched off, so the only light out here now came from the ambulance. It had just come to a stop in front of the door. Frank Elkins got out, grinning, and said, "Looks like you handled things without me."

Devers said, "We went through like a cold wind."

Elkins had left the engine running and the lights on. Coming around to the near side, he gestured at the ambulance and said, "Isn't she pretty?"

"Fine," Parker said. It was a Cadillac, a long low vehicle of the kind used by private ambulance services; he had told them specifically he didn't want the big boxy kind used by official agencies. This one would look more natural on the highway. It was painted white, and the hospital's name was on the doors in blue lettering. Parker said, "I'll have to do something about that name."

Elkins said, "How long to get him where he's going?"

"Twelve, fourteen hours."

"Shit, you can do that run. You'll be out of this state by morning."

Devers said, "Let me see if I can find some paint. They had lawn furniture here, they might have some of that white spray enamel." He went back into the house.

Elkins said, "It was interesting, Parker. Ralph's waiting for me. See you around."

"Right."

Elkins walked out the driveway to where Wiss was waiting in their car. Parker opened the rear door of the ambulance, saw that it was heavily equipped inside, and looked up as Ed Mackey and Dan Wycza came out, carrying Grofield between them. They had taken a mattress from a single bed, strapped two long boards underneath it and Grofield on top of it, and carried him down the stairs that way. Parker helped transfer Grofield to the bed inside the ambulance and strap him in, and while he was doing that Carlow and Webb came back with fresh cars. Mackey and Wycza got in with Carlow and drove away, and Webb said, "Anybody else gonna want a lift?"

"Devers and McKay."

"They better hurry. I'm beginning to get nervous."

Webb was right. Half an hour was long enough; law could come by here at any time. Parker turned toward the house, and Devers and Handy came out together. Devers was wearing some sort of white jacket, and had found a spray can of white paint. He went to work removing the hospital name from the near door while Handy gave Parker a small light blue suitcase. "I found this in a closet and put the money in it."

"You count it?"

"Just over fifty-eight thousand."

Parker looked around. Darkness everywhere except for the flashlights and headlights right here. "Not enough," he said.

Handy said, "What did they owe you?"

"Seventy-three." Parker looked at the house. The explosion in the living room had blown out the windows. He shrugged and said, "I'll settle."

Handy laughed. "You'll settle? I think you can say you collected."

Philly Webb said, "Listen, you want a ride? I'm anxious to get out of here."

"Right," Handy said. "I'm with you."

Devers was coming around the back of the ambulance, meaning to remove the wording on the rear door. Webb said to him, "You coming?"

Devers looked at Parker. "Why don't I ride with you?"

Parker didn't see the point. "What for?"

"You like my white coat? If there's any trouble, you're the dumb driver and I'm the bright young intern." Devers grinned. "I feel like going for a ride," he said. "I never went anywhere in an ambulance."

"Then come along," Parker said.

Fifty-five

Vibration.

Grofield opened his eyes, and what he saw made no sense to him. A low curved ceiling, chrome bars. Vibration under his back. He tried to lift his head, but it was too heavy; every part of him was heavy, he could barely move at all. Slowly he turned his head to the left, and there was a window there, no more than four inches away. Daytime. Countryside rushing by. *I'm in a train,* he thought, and tried to remember where he was going. Then the vehicle he was in passed a slow-moving car, and he realized he was on a highway, in a camper or a trailer or some damn thing with a bed.

He let his head roll back the way it had been before. Low padded ceiling. Chrome bars. A faint recurrent clinking sound.

A goddam ambulance!

Now what? he thought, and faded out of consciousness again.

When he came back, the quality of the light had changed; it must be afternoon. The vibration was the same. This time, he remembered the previous waking, and then began to remember things from the other direction: who he was, and that he owned a summer theater. He was broke, as usual, the theater in its normal desperation. He had gone with Parker to a place named . . .

Why couldn't he think of the name?

He almost drifted away again, trying to remember the name of the city, when all at once he remembered being shot.

Buenadella, the French doors, the man out there on the lawn. "The son of a bitch didn't kill me," he whispered. He was in awe of that.

"Hello?"

A voice. Grofield looked around, turning his head in small increments, and a cheerful blond fellow in a white jacket loomed over him. "Be damned if you aren't awake," he said.

"A distinct surprise to both of us," Grofield whispered. He tried to make sounds with his throat, but the equipment there seemed too weak for the job. He whispered, "You a doctor?"

The guy laughed. He was really in high spirits; but on the other hand, he hadn't been shot. He said, "You like the coat? Gives me that official look."

"I was shot once before," Grofield whispered. "When I woke up, a beautiful girl was climbing in the window."

"Aw," the guy said. "You're disappointed."

"Just so I wake up. The girl's name was Elly."

"Right. I'm Stan Devers. Your friend Parker is driving this thing."

Grofield tried to turn his head; it wouldn't go. Parker was driving the ambulance? He whispered, "What the hell happened?"

"Well," Stan Devers said, "that's a long story."